Damon Undone

The Deverells
Book Five

D1519901

Jayne Fresina

A TWISTED E PUBLISHING BOOK

Damon Undone
The Deverells, Book Five
Copyright © 2017 by Jayne Fresina

Cover design by K Designs
All cover art and logo copyright © 2017, Twisted
E-Publishing, LLC

ISBN-13: 978-1547069149
ISBN-10: 1547069147

"We're not going to get along, you and I, are we?"

"Good god, I hope not."

Thus begins the acquaintance of Damon Deverell and a young woman he finds under his feet one evening, at a ball to which he isn't invited. She reminds him instantly of someone he knew before, but that would be impossible, of course, because *she*—the girl from his past—was entirely a construct of his own imagination. Wherever this disturbingly real woman came from, he's determined to maintain a cautious distance. But when he's hired to keep an eye on her, Damon's resolve to keep it "merely business" is soon threatened by some fresh-baked muffins, a pair of ankles he wishes he'd never seen, and a certain bold, independent American woman who boasts of a "very efficient right hook".

Miss Epiphany "Pip" Piper has been sent into exile abroad, where her father hopes she'll learn to cool off her hot temper, acquire some elegant manners, and, hopefully, find a titled husband. Mr. Prospero "Smokey" Piper, of Louisiana and various other parts unknown and best unmentioned, claims to be the first ambitious and wealthy American businessman to think of this idea, but just like his very first boyhood attempt at building a whiskey still behind the family outhouse, this plan doesn't exactly turn out the way he expects either.

And although explosions are inevitable, it's not his grandmother's drawers in danger this time.

When these two stubborn young people— Damon the "merciless shark" of a lawyer, who likes his world in order, and the utterly disorderly Miss Piper, a "despicable girl of whom nothing could be made" find themselves thrown together by mischievous fate, it's not just a battle of the sexes or even a comedy of errors...

It's a chemical reaction that will change both their worlds forever.

"This is not a romance."
- Pip Piper, 1850

Prologue
1836

"Trust nobody. Remember, there is no soul on earth who has your best interests at heart more than you."

Remembering his father's stern advice, Damon Deverell, at just ten years of age, proudly kept his small chin up and his lips pressed tight, speaking to nobody, as the mail coach trundled slowly along the bumpy coast road, carrying him off to boarding school for the first time.

With a wide, dry-eyed gaze, he peered out through the grimy window and quickly sought the little island that jutted up from the sea. There, clawing its way out of that rock, stood his father's house— the stark silhouette of a hunch-backed ogre, against the pink yolk of sunrise. Once the coach turned, the boy knew he wouldn't be able to see the familiar turrets any longer, so he stared now until his eyes were sore, taking it in and storing it within the young, but very orderly, vaults of his memory

Somber-faced, he sat quietly, bouncing in the seat, his booted feet swinging, legs too short to touch the floor of the coach. In his lap he held a stack of school books and a package tied with string. Pushed into his hands at the last minute by Mrs. Blewett, his father's cook, he knew it contained an entire seed cake. It was her way of wishing him well on his journey, without making a fuss, without words or soppy gestures of which his father would be scornful. Nobody ever wanted his father's contempt or disapproval, for he was the greatest, wisest, strongest man in the world, the undisputed ruler of that little kingdom on the rock.

Soon the bend in the road would come and the castle over the causeway would disappear. His breath misting the glass, Damon pressed his face closer to the window, watching.

There she was, standing on the edge of the cliff, her small, thin shape lit by the awakening sun, her long hair blowing slowly in the breeze off the sea— so slowly, the gently curled locks seemed to be reaching into the air, like tentacles, lamenting this goodbye, begging him not to leave. She raised her hand as if it were heavy, and waved.

He knew, in his heart, this was the last time he'd ever see her. They'd both have to get used to the idea.

Together they'd enjoyed many escapades along these cliffs and beaches, but this adventure was one he must undertake alone, leaving her behind, even if she was the best, most loyal first mate a bloodthirsty pirate captain ever had.

He had to give her up. Damon didn't have time for those games anymore.

His father said he was a clever lad and that great things would come his way if he worked hard at school. Other folk told him he was the most like his father of all the Deverell "cubs".

Although he might be nothing more yet than a "thwarted stump"— as his sixteen-year-old brother called him— one day he would grow tall enough that his feet would not only touch the floor of this carriage, but he'd be able to stretch his legs right across to the other seat, the way he'd seen his father do. People would have to curve their necks back to look up at him.

So what use would that little girl be to him then? Boys weren't little forever, and grown-ups didn't have make-believe friends. Had no one told her that?

Still she waved, not ready to lose her friend yet. And now she ran, barefoot in the long, reedy grass, stumbling and tripping, trying to catch up with the mail coach.

Daft 'apeth, as Mrs. Blewett would say.

Damon turned sharply away from the window, remembering how proud his father was that he never cried.

He wouldn't look back at her again, he decided.

The small boy rubbed his chest where it felt hollow and achy. The new shirt and waistcoat itched under his smart, blue cutaway, the sleeves of which were too long for his arms, coming to a halt just short of his fingertips. His father said he must grow into it. His father talked a vast deal about what must be for his fourth son, as if there was never any doubt.

Here came the bend now, and after that the coach horses would pick up speed. Damon gritted his teeth, his jaw hurting, his throat tight, as he felt the thunder of hooves sweeping him away from *her*, away from childhood games and into manhood, which was not only a black tunnel of intrepid mystery, but also a place of stern expectations to be fulfilled. Anxiety thumped hard through his small body as his legs swung from side to side.

He took a deep breath and, rather than fall prey to the warm, sympathetic smile of the elderly lady seated opposite, he closed his eyes tight.

Mrs. Blewett's cake did not survive the journey. It was crushed to crumbs beneath his sweaty, determined grip. But that resolute little boy endured. And he did grow into his coat. Indeed, within a year he'd outgrown it, setting a remarkable pace for achievement in everything he did. The other coat, with its pockets still full of all the usual schoolboy treasures, such as conkers, marbles and bits of useful string, was set aside for one of his younger brothers. Only one item was transferred to the new coat, where, folded neatly, it was tucked inside a notebook.

It remained with him ever after, a solitary keepsake of a long lost childhood.

Part I
Nonesuch and Master Grumbles

Chapter One

May 1850
London

An evening out in society for Miss Epiphany Clodovea Piper— known to her friends as "Pip"— was seldom anything to be excited about. If left to her own preferences, she would stay by the fire, fling her corset into the farthest corner, light a cigar, drink a glass of bourbon and read something entirely unsuitable— the sort of behavior that, so she'd been warned, would lead to hysteria of her feminine parts, not to mention a "wandering womb".

At this point she really wouldn't blame her womb for running off to join the circus. She'd pack it a basket of chicken. Would it send her letters, she wondered, like those her sister used to write whenever she "ran away from home" as a child.

Dear P;

The food here is poor, but the company a vast improvement. I bet you are all sorry I left, so next time you will be sweeter to me when I have a pimple. Do send my music box, my new muff and some of Delphine's taffy to Billy-Joe Bullard's tree-house...You may tell pa that I shall be gone quite some time and he is not to look for me as he will never guess where I am...

But, for now, none of Pip's body parts had worked up enough sisterly vexation against her to go exploring on their own. Not even as far as the nearest neighbor's tree-house.

And quiet evenings in with her own

entertainment were out of the question. At the age of one and twenty, with a strong constitution and most of her wits, Pip was supposed to be in want of a husband, and there were several folk determined to find her one, whether she liked it or not.

"You may not be the prettiest or most congenial of creatures, especially compared to your sisters," her Aunt Du Bois often remarked, cheerfully pragmatic as ever, "but you have the plain essentials, Epiphany. You are not fundamentally lacking. There is no reason why you can't find a man, especially with your dowry. Much that is unfortunate can be overlooked in a bride with adequate birthing hips and a good dowry."

To which she would reply with equal joviality, "And to think, I feared the age of romance had died with the great poets Byron and Shelley."

Sadly the sarcasm went over her aunt's head. "You don't need a poet, *ma cher*," she assured Pip. "You need a man of action, not one who wastes his time, and yours, sitting in the bath, pondering his shriveled fingertips, drinking all the best Bordeaux and thinking up flowery words that rhyme. And when he is not in the bath, he is flirting shamelessly with your friends, setting light to the drapes when he leaves a candle untended, falling into the magnolia bushes, and staining your Chinese silk dressing robe, which he has lain about in all day and has no right to wear."

"That seems...curiously specific."

"Bombastic fools with a fondness for frills on their shirts and the sound of their own voice. No, no! What you need is a practical fellow— one who can do his duty as necessary, but never meddles in the household accounts and, most importantly, is outdoors as much as possible. Men have a tendency to track mud about the house when they come indoors, so it is useful to find some excuse to keep them out. Most enjoy the fresh air and exercise. It is beneficial for their health and their mood, and it puts them to sleep sooner."

"I suppose if confined inside too long they gnaw upon the furnishings."

"But don't you worry, *ma cher*," said her aunt, not listening as usual. "We shall find someone for you. There is many a mossy stone yet unturned. You'd be surprised what one can find lurking beneath."

No, she really wouldn't. She'd met a lot of toads already.

Although Pip could do nothing but admire her aunt's enthusiasm, which remained remarkably undaunted in the face of several setbacks, she hoped, eventually, to be left in peace. Once she was sunk into eccentric decrepitude, which was not many years ahead— she worked artfully toward it now— nobody, not even her father and sisters, would surely want her exhibited about the place, except perhaps as a cautionary tale. In the meantime, to keep everybody happy, she went through the motions. Like a bowel, she thought wryly.

Tonight, here she was, yet again, about to enter the fray.

As they converged with other guests to ascend a wide flight of marble stairs, her aunt whispered on the apex of a tense breath, "Lord Boxall would be an excellent catch for you, and his godmother promised to manage the introduction this evening." The lady's excitement cooled only somewhat when, in the riotous melee, a tipsy gentleman almost knocked her off her feet and a chattering young girl's elbow struck her in the forehead.

"*Mais*! Look at this crowd! I did not expect so many. Come see, *cher*!" Rubbing her wounded forehead with one hand, she gestured with the other for her niece to stand closer. Rising on tip-toe to gain a better view over the heads of the swelling crowd, she exclaimed, "Look about you. Lord Boxall is a tall young man, *vayan*, with good hair."

"Well, that's not too broad a description," Pip muttered. "At least we can be sure he has a head, since there is hair attached to it."

"He is fluent in Latin, enjoys the harp and has just returned home from a year abroad. His godmother thinks it is time he married. His first name is Bertie, and he is the son of a Marquess. What else could you possibly need to know? Marriages are often brokered successfully on far less information."

Her aunt was, of course, well versed in the art of marriage and husbands, having disposed of several herself. Not all of them her own. Queenie Piper Du Bois had spent twenty years touring Europe on her deceased first husband's fortune, picking up a few other lonely, elderly noblemen along the way and brightening the last few years of their dotage, whether they made the arrangement official or not. Her last marriage— to a young man for once— had lasted only five months before Remy Du Bois, a charming, restless rake, left her a widow again. This appeared to have put her off marriage at last. Perhaps it had much to do with the fact that when he died she discovered that her "beloved Remy" had spent more money than he ever earned, living entirely on promissory notes. The shock of learning that everything he owned was begged for, borrowed or stolen, had resulted in a broad streak of silver through Queenie's dark hair. At least, she blamed that vivid, rather handsome lightning flare on her last husband's antics. But she faced this tragedy as she did any other, by blotting away her tears, tightening her corset another inch, and with that formidable Piper spirit, continuing onward, head high and bright eyes shrewdly on the lookout for another opportunity. Just not another husband for herself.

"I was sore bereft when *ma cher* Remy passed on," she liked to say with a dramatic hand to her brow. "I shall never find another dear fellow like him. I am now resolved to eternal widowhood."

For the time being she had settled in England, referring to it as her adopted home, and she already thought of herself as an expert on London society and manners, even going so far as to speak, at times, with a frighteningly inept semblance of an English accent. Nobody had yet told her how bizarre it sounded. Her English acquaintances were either too horrified or too polite to mention it, and her American nieces, accustomed to her eccentricities, merely found it amusing. Pip, especially, enjoyed the awkward, confused glances caused by their aunt's Louisiana British patois.

"I understand Lord Boxall is, like you, a little unconventional," the lady added. "I doubt you will find *this* one disappointing. I'm sure he'll suit you *en plin*!" This confident assertion of a perfect match, based on nothing more than a random friend's vague recommendation, appeared to be the final word as far as Aunt Du Bois was concerned. She turned away to gossip avidly with another lady and paid her charges no more attention for now.

The crush of well-dressed folk on the staircase became very hot and discontented. For some reason the forward flow had trickled to a complete stop and now the unruly horde was stuck in place, only able to bulge sideways or, with some pushing and shoving, reverse the way they had come in. Pip would gladly have done the latter, if it were not for the sisters flanking her— a formation that was probably deliberate.

She sighed heavily. "Since I know nothing of Latin or harps, I don't hold out much hope for this fledgling romance with young Bertie Boxall of the fine face and good hair."

"If you make no effort to be pleasant to the gentleman," her elder sister lectured wearily, "then you have nobody to blame but yourself."

"Why do you assume I will not be pleasant, Serenity? I am one of the pleasantest people I know. Dogs love me, and they are excellent judges of character."

"Dogs only love you because they have no idea what you're saying, and you feed them scraps from your plate at dinner. With people you are stubborn, combative and argumentative, and you are more likely to stick a fork in a man's hand as let him taste your dinner."

"It is called the love of hearty debate, sister. And it was not a fork. How many times must I tell you all? I rapped him on the knuckles with a berry spoon, because I did not care much for his straying hand. I am certain there would be questions raised if *I* were to try and molest somebody's raspberries at the dinner table."

Her sister glared and flipped open her fan. "You also have a sense of humor that, since it amuses nobody but yourself and is of a puerile nature, ought to be kept silent in company."

"So when you say I should be pleasant, you mean stupid. I must agree with everything that's said and have no opinion of my own. And God forbid I laugh."

"Certainly the way *you* laugh, sister. It is not ladylike. Especially not here."

"Then please do tell me how I am supposed to laugh in this society?"

"Sparingly and lightly. A keen, interested smile is far more agreeable. More flattering to the facial features. One should always appear interested in the conversation, no matter how dreary the subject. You saw how I smiled indulgently throughout Major Broughton's treatise on cricket yesterday, even though I had the toothache."

"I did indeed, and I admire your fortitude, Serenity. When it comes to the conversation of Major Broughton I should as soon plug my ears with olives. But that could be said of most conversations I've had to listen to of late."

Her sister looked at her as if she thought Pip might actually have olives secreted about her person for that very purpose. "Then if you can think of nothing *appropriate* to say in the company of Lord Boxall I suggest you remain silent and pretend you have a sore throat. You cannot do any more harm with your lips shut than you can with them open."

"So I should stand mutely, while I am judged as if I could be the last remaining ham hock on a questionable butcher's stall?"

"With that scowl on your face you'd be lucky to get anybody to look at you at all. Medusa had a more welcoming countenance."

"Good. I would rather have a head full of snakes than dance with any of these nincompoops, and there are quite a few of them I should like to cast into stone. Not that anybody would tell the difference."

"Lower your voice! Remember how fortunate we are that Aunt Du Bois managed to secure invitations for us." Serenity's fan worked rapidly as she tried to cool her increasingly pink face and trembled against the temptation to raise her own voice in an unladylike fit of pique. "There are many titled gentlemen present." She stilled her fan and whispered behind it, "That one over there is a viscount, I believe. Or will be, one day."

Pip looked and saw exactly what she expected: a rather wet looking fellow with a stoop, droopy, indolent eyes, a mottled nose and oddly arranged hair that could be hiding a bald spot or, as she preferred suggesting to her sister, a small door for the purposes of winding his brain with a key. A service for which he was clearly overdue.

A grey-haired lady with a very dour expression and one stiff finger that she flourished like the prodding point of an umbrella, followed closely behind him, chattering shrilly so that he could not get a word in.

"That must be his lady wife steering him up the stairs, reminding him which direction to walk. No doubt she also reminds him how to wipe his nose and put on his shoes."

"I happen to know it's his great aunt. Clearly you can see she is much older. Besides, I heard he is not married."

"Ah! Hence your interest. Make haste then and seize the sad, endangered creature, sister," she exclaimed. "Save us all several hours of dire humiliation tonight by catching him now, and then we can go home. I suppose you are fortunate that he yet has some teeth in his head. He doesn't look as if he could put up much of a fight and a strong gust of wind would surely damage him beyond repair. Better put your fan away, Serenity, lest any of his noble parts should accidentally drift off in the violence of your passion. You'll need all his pieces intact."

"Oh, hush! For pity's sake. People might hear. For somebody who does not like to be judged on her appearance you are mightily quick to judge others."

She sighed. "I suppose you are right, sister. I am duly chastened." But without her sister to tease it wouldn't be nearly as much fun.

Serenity gave her another hard appraisal. "Stop tapping your fingers on your fan. Your tapping fingers are always a sign of mischief afoot." Her eyes became two dark thorns, ready to prick at anything they saw out of place. "You had better not think to embarrass me into leaving early this evening. We will stay until it is fashionable to leave and if you try so much as a silly voice or an odd laugh— or that drunken lurching thing you like to do when dancing— I shall never speak to you again."

"Do not taunt me with such a promise."

"One of these days you will pay heed to me. I am never granted the respect I am due as the eldest and I—" She caught her breath. "Oh, mercy at last! I see people moving forward. It is almost our time to go up and be announced."

"Let joy be unconfined."

Serenity shot her one last frown and turned her head away.

After a short, thoughtful pause, Pip prodded her in the shoulder. "But to what *drunken lurching thing* do you refer, sister?" She'd always assumed it was other people who got in her way to ruin the formation. For once this was not something she did purposefully to irritate anybody.

Snap! Serenity's fan was off again, fluttering wildly, despite the danger to all those fragile aristocrats, raised in the rarefied, undisturbed air of hothouses. "I swear, sister, you pluck at my last nerve." She grandly swiveled away completely, as if even looking at Pip would further test the elasticity of that infamously much-tortured nerve.

Now it was the turn of their younger sister to attempt entreaty in her own, gentler fashion. "I know you only say all that to tease, Pip. But do try to maintain an even temper tonight. You must promise to smile and be agreeable. It keeps everybody so much happier. Besides," she smiled hopefully, "you might even fall in love. Such things do happen."

"My dear little Merrythought, I will do my very best to please you." Glancing around, one hand to her neck, she winced. "Although I already feel the assembled rabble sucking the air out of me. The challenge of holding my tongue will doubtless suffocate me, and I'm not yet ready to die." With a sly peek under her eyelashes to enjoy her elder sister's reaction— demonstrated just as effectively by those rigid shoulder blades and the reddening of her ears as it would be by her face— she added, "I have far too much life yet to explore and considerable wickedness of which to partake. In point of fact, I do not intend ever to depart this life. Even as my parts wither and fall like leaves from the trees, I shall live on interminably, scaring folk in dark corners, free to say and do exactly as I please with nobody to censor me. Because, as our sister says, one must respect the elderly. Of which she is one, of course."

While the target of her teasing caused an even wilder breeze with her fan, the younger sister looked worried and whispered, "Oh, don't torment Serenity. You wouldn't want her to get so over-heated that she develops a rash."

"I may be blamed for a great many things, Merry. But I refuse to be held responsible for the balance of our sister's delicate and capricious complexion."

"Just try not to cause any damage tonight, Pip. To yourself or anybody. Or anything. Especially not to Lord Boxall. We wouldn't want another scandal."

Pip smiled at that sweet, anxious face and squeezed the small, white-gloved hand that rested in hers. "Fret not, Merry. I have not forgotten that you lent me your best lace shawl tonight." Releasing her sister's fingers, she patted the borrowed garment where it draped over her shoulder. "It will not be out of my sight all evening. I vow to defend your shawl against any would-be thieves, from wind, rain, fire and spilled punch. Indeed, this shawl is likely to keep me out of trouble, I shall be so busy guarding its virtue and decorum that, for once, nobody need worry about mine."

Her sisters exchanged glances, neither looking at all mollified, and then they continued up the steps behind their Aunt Du Bois, leaving Pip to follow.

Well, she thought glumly, her smile melting away

now that it no longer had an audience, her sisters would not be the only souls surprised if she survived an event unscathed. But she bolstered her spirits with the reminder that all she need do was get through this ordeal for another year and then she could go home. This was not a permanent exile and, once it was over, Pip would have proven three things to her father: that she had learned to hold her temper, that she had matured into a responsible young woman— despite the ever irresistible urge to tease her sister— and that no matter how far afield he sent her, she was never going to find a husband. He might as well settle his mind to the idea of letting her work for the family business and take her place at last as his "right-hand man". Not every woman was meant for marriage and children. Some could be useful in other ways.

Pip had decided, long ago, that she had far more to offer the world than birthing hips. One day she would stop her father lamenting his lack of male heirs and make him see that he had a daughter who could, given the chance, be every bit as useful as a son. More so, in fact.

Alas tonight, before she even entered the ballroom, proceedings had already started off on the wrong foot. Or rather, under it.

The infamous Miss Epiphany Piper's forward progress came to an immediate halt, accompanied by a loud and dreadful ripping sound.

As her aunt would say, *Merde*!

Chapter Two

"I cannot think why you bother me here, man. This business can be dealt with on the morrow. Step aside."

"Lord Roper, I have attempted this conversation with you thrice and you are always caught up with something else to do. Would you prefer we drop the case? Since you avoid discussion of the matter, I wondered if you had changed your mind. That you had come, perhaps, to realize you were mistaken."

"Certainly not!" Maroon-faced, the blustering gentleman rocked on his heels and blew out a heavy gust of port fumes. "That scoundrel will be brought to justice. I am intent upon it."

"Then you still charge that your servant, John Wilson, is responsible for damage to your property, theft of items from your house and the poaching of pheasant from your land?"

"My *former* servant, Wilson. Yes. Now get out of my way. This is neither the time nor the place."

"I must inform you, your lordship, that John Wilson maintains his innocence and claims you have a motive here other than the pursuit of justice. He has, in fact, related to me— and to my clerk— a full account of all that took place. *All* that took place between the two of you."

The significance of that word "all" hung heavily in the air between the two men, for they both understood its meaning, although only one of them would admit to it.

"Balderdash! The man is a villain— and an audacious one to commit such slander." Lord Roper tilted to one side at a dangerous angle, requiring his thin, fretful-looking wife to bear more of his weight than she ever carried on her own two feet. "Did I not hire you to work for me, young man?" he slurred. "Is it not your purpose to convince the magistrate of that swine Wilson's guilt, rather than come to me with tales of his supposed innocence? To attack me, in a public place, with *his* scandalous falsehoods?"

"I had no choice but to meet you here, since you continually ignore my visits and messages."

"Do you imagine that I— a peer of the realm— can be summoned at your bidding like some snot-nosed little errand lad? You forget with whom you are dealing...*boy*." Clearly, Lord Roper had forgotten the name of his solicitor, or perhaps he had never paid heed to it. Why would he? "Do you imagine," he continued, "that a gentleman of my standing can be hounded in such a disgraceful way, even at a ball? I was led to believe that your firm is one of the best in London, and I was told that you, despite your youth, have the reputation of a ruthless shark. But now it seems I must tell you your job."

"I know my job, Lord Roper."

"Then do it. You'll take your fee readily enough, to be sure."

The reply was calm, steady. Nobody would suspect the rising temper beneath. Nobody, unless they knew him very well, would see the restlessness bubbling just below the surface as this young man gave a quick tug to the knot of his neck cloth. "I merely wanted you to be apprised of Wilson's claims. So that you have a chance to be prepared, should you still wish to proceed and have the case heard in court."

"*Still wish to proceed?* Why should I care what some thieving servant has to say? Why should anybody? You damnable lawyers! Looking to get more money out of me, I daresay. Are none of you to be trusted?"

"You may not care what he has to say in his defense, Lord Roper. But it will be heard. In court. In front of others. It will, undoubtedly, appear in the newspapers. From there it will reach the eyes and ears of a great many. A word, once it is printed, is often believed, whether there is truth in it or not."

Roper's eyes bulged, and his cheeks puffed. Finally, he sputtered, "Very well! What is the blackguard saying about me then? Don't look at my wife; this is naught to do with her. She understands nothing. She knows nothing. I insist you tell me what the villain has said."

"John Wilson claims that you know where the missing items are and that the damage to your property is the result of your own negligence and temper. As for the brace of pheasant, he claims there never was any on your land. He contends that this action brought against him is meant to alleviate you of the need to pay wages long overdue. Wilson drew my attention to the fact that, over the course of five years, you have brought the same case against six other former servants of your household too—alleging destruction of property, robbery, the taking of livestock, etcetera. Even, at times, the *same* livestock."

Outrage bubbled out of his lordship's small, tight mouth. "What the devil are you suggesting?"

He thought it was clear enough, but apparently not. So he explained carefully in his low, measured voice, "That you are either extremely unlucky in your choice of servant, and manage always to hire from the criminal class, or that you are forgetful in the payment of wages and in the handling of your own possessions when you make gifts of certain pieces of property."

The gentleman's color deepened further, in such contrast to his white hair that his head began to look like a slab of bacon. His pale wisp of a wife was surely about to crumple under his swaying weight.

"You believe his word over mine? I am the accuser in this case, am I not? And he is merely a servant! I see you common upstarts band together, is that it?"

"It matters not whom I believe, your lordship. I was hired by you and so *you* I came here to counsel." The "upstart" shot another quick look at the quietly suffering Lady Roper. "If you continue with this case, your...habits and companions, *private* matters, may be discussed."

Finally, he thought he was making a dent in the thick head of his client. From the expression on Lord Roper's face, the vociferous fool began to see that he might be better off letting this particular former lover slip away into the sunset, along with his secrets and the gifts given to him over the course of the affair. Unlike his other servants, Wilson was unafraid to speak up, comfortable in his own skin, and bold enough not to be intimidated by the presence of a magistrate.

Lady Roper might not suspect where all the family treasures had truly gone over the years, but she would be the only soul still left in the dark if John Wilson told the court everything that had occurred between himself and his master. It would be the sort of scandal loved by the newspapers and readily devoured by the public. The former footman was not only bold and a born performer, he was also desperate and enraged, and even though exposing the truth of his association with Roper was a great risk to himself, he was likely to do it, just for his moment of infamy in the broadsheets and to know he would not go down alone.

Of course, Roper's former footman could be discredited, for he, like most men, had his own set of addictions, troubles and enemies. And he was not particularly clever. The magistrate would favor Roper in the case since they undoubtedly belonged to the same club and held the same view of servants. Defeat would not, however, prevent Wilson from saying his piece. Loudly. In court. Damaging one who did not deserve it— Lady Roper.

Yes, it would surprise a great many people to know, but this upstart young man, this notoriously hardnosed, coldblooded lawyer, had developed a shameful soft spot for that lady. He had no explanation for it, but there it was.

If Messrs. Stempenham and Pitt discovered that their most dedicated young employee had gone there tonight to talk his client out of a case, they would, to put it mildly, not be pleased. But in his opinion, Roper's wife had suffered enough during her twenty years of marriage. This upstart lawyer may not be known for charitable deeds himself— even his own father called him a merciless bull shark— but he could still recognize, somewhat reluctantly, the good in others when he saw it.

Lady Roper, so easily dismissed by her husband as a cipher who knew and understood nothing, was a virtuous, honorable woman, one of the few who tried to help the many poor, cold and hungry of that town. She did so without looking for reward or praise, or even notice. Throughout her husband's excessive gambling, drinking and adultery, she simply got on with her life, quietly and selflessly working to improve the lot of others.

"We make the best we can of the cards we are dealt, do we not, young man?" she had said softly to her husband's lawyer only the day before, after he had waited in vain to catch Lord Roper at home. "To survive in this world we do what we must, not always what we would like to do. Then we find ourselves running in circles, getting nowhere." In response to this rather cryptic comment, he had managed the closest facsimile he could to a smile.

But as he was about to leave her house on that occasion, Lady Roper, not discouraged by his chilly manner, had asked whether he had children and, hearing that he was not married, urged him to find a wife quickly.

"Such handsome children you will make," she had said, beaming and patting his hand with her own powdery soft fingers. "They will put a smile on your face. They will wipe away that frown. Babies make the world a better place. I always regret that I never had any of my own. Perhaps you will bring yours to visit me one day before I am too old. I should like the merry company."

This busy young lawyer could not remember ever having his hand patted in that comforting manner. His father's cook, the most maternal figure in his life, had shown her care and concern through food— there was no illness or insult one of Mrs. Blewett's puddings couldn't cure— but there was not much softness about her. In fact, most of the time she pretended she didn't even like him and that she only fed him because she was obliged by the terms of her employment. Once, many years ago, after he'd had a fight with one of his brothers, the cook had tried to ruffle his hair as she passed the kitchen table, but he, thinking she meant to cuff him 'round the ear, had ducked out of the way quickly. It was all very awkward. To his intense relief, Mrs. Blewett never tried again.

No other lady within his memory, which was vast and detailed, had ever looked at this young man in a motherly way, or spoken to him as if he deserved and needed kindness. They always assumed he had everything he wanted. Even he assumed it.

After all, bull sharks took what they wanted, whenever they wanted it. And nobody petted a shark.

Therefore, he was completely flummoxed when Lady Roper, so casually and warmly had touched his hand, patted it and then — of all the odd things to do— squeezed it gently, as if in sympathy. "There must be a young lady waiting for you somewhere."

"For her sake," he'd replied grimly, "I hope she's not waiting."

He preferred mature ladies who were, preferably, already attached elsewhere and would not impede too long upon his own time. Wouldn't want any woman nurturing ideas about a future with him. And babies? He'd never seen the point. There didn't appear to be a shortage in the world; more of a surfeit in London to be sure— urchins running about shoeless, begging to be fed.

Still, the shock of Lady Roper's concern for his happiness, and the unexpected contact of her hand upon his, had left an odd, not displeasing sensation. It lingered long after he returned to his office.

He wondered how much the lady knew of her husband's indiscretions. Certainly he did not want to be the instrument by which she found them all out.

For a full half hour or more yesterday, he had sat at his desk, studying his hands and toying with his pens. His office was always extremely tidy, everything in its place. He kept his quill pens in an important order— the most recently used put to the furthest end of the line, set there to dry and be mended, while the pen left unused for the longest time was, by then, closest and most convenient to his hand. The ink pot was directly above it, kept filled, the lid wiped clean each time it was closed at the end of the day. Wax wafers on the left, candle on the right, along with the pen-knife for cutting nibs and a pounce pot for blotting. It was the order in which he had kept his materials for the past few years. If anybody attempted to move anything, they were barked at so severely that they never went within three feet of his desk again.

Yesterday, after Lady Roper's astonishing gesture of kindness, he had moved his pens around without thinking, getting them out of order, restlessly arranging and rearranging, while dust beams twinkled and danced in the wedge of spring sunlight through his window.

The lady, he had finally decided, did not deserve to be ridiculed and subjected to the humiliation of scandal. If he could help her escape that fate, he would do so. Nobody need know why he did it. There would be no risk to his merciless, uncompromising reputation. Even the lady herself had no idea of his intention to help her.

So he had followed the Ropers that evening, hoping to have this case dissolved, to make her husband see the stupidity of his accusations. Alas, just as he felt Lord Roper weakening toward the side of prudence, their conversation was interrupted.

He tried to ignore it as long as he could, but the wretched woman behind him was insistent as a fly buzzing around his head.

Chapter Three

"Pardon me, sir."

No response.

He stood upon the left corner of that borrowed shawl, which must have fallen from her shoulder and dragged to the floor without her notice. Standing one step below and with his back to Pip, in deep conversation with the people behind, the man who held her shawl hostage was apparently unaware of the struggle he caused.

Only when she tapped his shoulder with her closed fan did he slowly look back, scowling.

"Pardon me," she repeated.

"Why? What have you done?"

Pleasanter, less aggravated faces could be found before feeding time at the zoological gardens in Regent's Park, she mused. He reminded her at once of Master Grumbles, an Irish wolfhound her father once owned. That gentle giant of a dog had followed her everywhere with a misleadingly depressed expression, as if the onerous responsibility of looking after her was almost more than it could bear, despite the fact that they always had a great deal of fun together and nobody had ever told the dog it *must* be her companion.

"Sir, your foot." Pointing the end of her fan downward, she gestured to the item that kept her prisoner. "If you don't mind."

"My foot?" he snapped impatiently, his mind clearly on other matters he deemed more important. Perhaps he was thinking of a bone he'd buried and trying to remember where. "What? What about it?"

"It's on my shawl."

His irritable gaze finally shifted to the marble steps as he swiveled partially around. "For pity's sake! Why the devil do women need all these blessed... *attachments?*" he growled at the lace shawl, holding it up to peruse the large, dirty hole he'd rendered there. "Something this flimsy has no practical service whatsoever and merely gets in the way."

As she too assessed the damage, her heart sank. Merrythought had only lent her the shawl because it was the general consensus, as they exited the carriage, that Pip's gown showed a grievous amount of shoulder and bosom— something nobody had noticed before they left the house because she was late coming down, dragging her feet. Pip seldom studied herself in a mirror, so little interested in what she wore that she was most likely reading a book, writing a letter, or playing solitaire while being hoisted, laced and primped into her clothes by her aunt's dutiful, but not terribly sensible maid.

The wolfhound growled onward under his breath, "Too many frills and furbelows dangling off you. As if all the hoops and petticoats aren't enough to keep us at bay. I believe the soldiers at Agincourt wore less armor."

Before he got any more dirt upon her sister's shawl, she snatched it from his over-sized paw and draped it over her arm. "I quite agree. I'd be more content in my drawers alone, but I suspect this society would be outraged by the sight. Believe me, I've considered it more than once, even if it was only to liven up the proceedings."

About to dismiss her by turning away again, instead he pivoted fully around, his gaze sharpened, those cool, gun-metal grey eyes inspecting her thoroughly. She stood before him, pinned to the spot, feeling as if invisible, commanding fingers gripped her face and held it to the light. "What's *wrong* with you?" he demanded.

Where does one start, she thought wryly. But, of course, she must keep up appearances, for her sisters' sake. "I cannot imagine what you mean," she replied with all necessary hauteur. "There's nothing wrong with *me*. At least I'm in marginally appropriate dress for a ball." He, on the other hand, was not. Surrounded by gentlemen in crisply groomed evening attire, he stood out in his top boots, riding breeches and tweed coat.

His thick hair was damp and tousled enough to suggest a very recent ride through the rain, in great haste and hatless. The state of his boots and breeches— for he wore no spatterdashes— also revealed the muddiness of the streets through which he had traveled. Apparently he cared little for the impression he made in the grand entrance hall of Lord Courtenay's town house and had as much concern for his appearance as Pip had for her own. The mud specks across his face— which she first mistook for freckles— told her that he, unlike most gentlemen on the staircase, had not consulted any of the mirrored panels on the wall. The skewed sideways knot of his neck cloth, smudged with the same grimy prints as the fingers of his gloves, hinted at the frequent tugging of an angry, frustrated hand. Everything about him suggested disdain for convention and so much impatient haste that it seemed as if he moved at speed, even while he stood still before her. And she must be moving with him, for her heart raced and all the other people on the staircase became mere blurs of color.

Most young men she met struck her immediately as uninteresting, their minds sluggish and as little predisposed to anything beyond their own uncomplicated, immediate pleasure as plump cats on a sunny veranda. But this man's face was guarded and clever, his eyes lit with the restless, hungry, throbbing gleam of a hungry, bustling internal life. It drew her in; made her curious and challenged at first sight. Made her want to wipe away the remaining mud spatters for him, even at the risk of being bitten.

He squinted hard at her. "There *is* something wrong with you." Moving up to join her on the same step, the man persisted, "You speak... strangely."

"Do I?"

"Yes, there is something the matter with you."

"I can't think what you mean."

And then his eyes flared, "You're a bloody American."

She drew a quick breath, standing as tall as she could— which, in her mind, was six foot at least, and in reality was a little over five feet and two scant inches. Allegedly. She was certain the measuring stick lied. "Yes," she said proudly, "I am American."

"Why didn't you say so then?"

Eyebrows raised, she replied, "I beg your pardon. I didn't think that was what you meant by there being something *the matter* with me. Something *wrong* with me."

He huffed, apparently amused in an arrogant way. "Didn't you indeed?" Shaking his head, he added, "Americans at the Courtenay's spring ball. Whatever is the world coming to? Still, I suppose it's a comic novelty for the luridly curious. Last year I heard they had acrobats and a fortune teller. Lady Courtenay once rode in on a unicorn, so they say." He flicked a finger across his nose, disposing of several dried mud flecks, as he exhaled a curt sigh. "It must be exhausting coming up with a diversion nobody has yet thought of. But Americans? I didn't realize old Courtenay had such a riotous sense of humor."

Pip smiled brightly in a manner that would have fooled nobody who knew her. "Just you wait. In a year or two we'll be all the fashion and everyone will want one. Even you."

"I wouldn't make a wager of it." His eyes narrowed, fingers paused in the process of fidgeting with the knot of his neck cloth again. "What are you doing here in any case?"

Now that was an odd question, she mused. "Why does one usually attend a ball?" But when answered by his silence and another thorough perusal that could only be described as darkly suspicious and slightly indecent, she added, "I'm a spy, of course. Why else would I be here amongst you miserable people? Certainly not likely to have any fun, am I? Somehow your countrymen manage to take the pleasure out of everything with all your stifling, petty rules of etiquette. You wouldn't know a good party if it ran up and slapped you. I have already been warned that I must not, under any circumstances, laugh out loud in this society."

"A spy?" he muttered. "I might have guessed."

"Our government sent me to understand the workings of that." With her fan she pointed up at his mouth, almost touching it, "English Stiff Upper Lip."

He did not flinch away from her fan, but looked at it and then at her again. "And what have you discovered?"

"That it keeps you all in a state of pompous and frigid inflexibility, so confined by your traditions, unwelcoming to foreigners and outraged by anything different or new, that you dare not move forward."

"I can see you have your advantages as a spy, being so... short of stature. Indeed I barely knew you were there." With airy nonchalance, hands behind his back, he added, "Until you began to make noise."

She laughed. "Oh, I may be short, but I have ways of bringing men down to my size. I wouldn't underestimate me, if I were you, sir."

Once again he had begun to turn away, but then stopped. "And how, precisely, do *you* imagine you'd bring *me* to my knees?"

Every gemstone and crystal bead surrounding them flickered and dazzled like sunlight caught on the ocean tide, but he rose up out of those glistening waves— Poseidon in a wrathful mood— and cast his menacing shadow over her.

She could almost taste the air of prerogative that rolled off his shoulders.

Walk away, Pip, her inner voice of reason urged. *Don't say anything more. Don't cause a scene. Think of your sisters.*

But the dreary expectation of another stagnant, lackluster evening ahead kept her lingering on the staircase, flirting with handsome menace and— as her father would have pointed out, if he were there— spoiling for an argument.

Besides, she was heartily sick of being dragged out into this society, just so she could be lectured at and looked down upon, yet again. A curiosity, an exhibit, as this young man had suggested.

Thus, the voice of caution, silenced by a firm hand across its lips, was dragged out of harm's way.

"Be warned, sir, that I have a very efficient right hook and a rotten temper. Being American I am not afraid to use either."

"Praemonitus praemunitus."

"I beg your pardon?"

"Latin. Forewarned is forearmed."

She dismissed that with a flip of her fan. Ancient languages were, in her opinion, best left in ancient times. "May I remind you that we won the war?"

"All that trouble of a revolution and here you are, back again."

"Why are Englishmen so dreadfully smug? Anyone would think you actually have something to be smug about, but I've seen no evidence of it."

"I believe you're the one doing all the boasting, madam, not me."

"Even before you opened your mouth, the arrogance was all over your face."

"Stop looking at it then. Nobody's forcing you, are they?"

Pip realized she'd been staring into his eyes and even when she blinked to free herself, it didn't help. Instantly her gaze was drawn back again, helpless to resist the fascination.

A teasing light, devious, even wicked, and yet at the same time almost playful, simmered and sparked in the rich layers of his regard. Looking into those magnetic eyes made her very hot and flushed, which was not like her at all.

On the other hand, he seemed equally sunk and

unable to pull himself out.

"Mulier est hominis confusio," he muttered.

Something like alarm quickened within her heart. If she was not very much mistaken that too was Latin. *Uh oh.* She eyed his unconventional attire again, and that wavy head of hair, which, although it was in some disarray, refusing to be tamed by the fingers he scraped through it, still managed to be wildly beautiful. Like the mane of a Friesian horse.

"You wouldn't by any chance," she caught her breath, "be Bertie Boxall?"

"Why would you want to know?" he demanded, eyes narrowed.

"Because I'm supposed to be an amiable mute in his company."

He drew back and for a moment she thought he might laugh. Instead he cleared his throat, shoved impatient fingers through that good hair yet again — did he do that to draw attention to one of his best features, she wondered?—and looked around briefly, before fixing her once more in his stern gaze. "An amiable mute? Wouldn't that be nice. Probably too late to begin now."

"So you are Bertie Boxall? I mean...Lord Boxall?"

"Little late for that formality too, isn't it?"

Merde! Should she curtsey? No. Why should she? "Your godmother told my aunt that we could be introduced tonight," she blurted. "Should we wish to be."

"You don't sound very keen."

"Well, I wasn't. I mean...I'm not." What in damnation *did* she mean? She flipped open her fan and smartly hit herself on the chin with it.

"I don't suppose I was to be warned about you

skulking in wait, was I? Typical."

"It was not my idea," she protested. "I'd rather be at home. But when one is not fundamentally lacking one has no choice, according to my aunt. And I never skulk. Skulking is the last thing I would do. It is something that suggests a person is sorry for their very existence and I have no regrets about mine. None whatsoever. Even if other folk do."

There was an awkward pause while he looked her up and down and she fluttered her fan so hard her wrist ached.

Finally she snapped it shut again and exclaimed, "Pray, don't think for one moment that I am looking for a man. Or that I am, in any manner, in need of one."

"Well, I certainly don't require a woman. I have everything I need in my life. But of course, sometimes it's for the best to get it over with and halt the incessant nagging. I suppose one has to put oneself out occasionally for the good of others. So if you need a charitable favor..." He shrugged in a lackluster fashion. "If you're desperate, I'm sure we can come to some marital arrangement. Just try not to get under my feet."

Although often irritated by the arrogance of the male species, she was seldom amused by it too. He couldn't possibly be real. This must be a practical joke of some sort.

She studied his face for a clue, but his countenance gave nothing away now. He had suddenly assumed a mask of cool detachment to cover all the intriguing layers she'd seen there in the beginning. Like the majority of Englishmen she'd met, he seemed to have acquired that expression from a manual entitled "The

Art of Boring Yourself to Sleep While Standing."
Such a tome surely resided on bedside tables across
the country, and there was probably an entire Chapter
devoted to the avoidance of outward displays of
emotion.

Pip hastened to assure the fellow that he was in
no danger of her requiring such a doubtful "favor"
from him. "I'm not the sort of female who feels that
her existence, her entire purpose in life and all her
hopes for happiness, revolve around a man."

Despite that deliberately bland expression, when
his gaze wandered to the base of her throat and
slowly back up the side of her neck, it left a
considerable number of goose-pimples in its wake.
How he did it, she had no idea. If only she had a
berry spoon at hand with which to rap his knuckles.

"Indeed," she choked out on a thin breath, "the
very opposite is true. I find men to be wholly
disadvantageous— obstructive to my contentment,
destructive to my equanimity and, ultimately,
adversaries to my success in life."

He folded his arms. "So many big words to say
so little of consequence."

"So little of consequence?" she repeated flatly.
"Very well, I'll make it simpler for you, Lord Boxall.
This woman no marry."

But as she turned away he caught hold of her
arm. "A woman shares in her husband's triumphs,
naturally. What need does she have for her own?"

Now he was really getting her dander up.
"Marriage, *sir,* is an inconvenience put in our way to
stop us from reaching our full potential. A woman of
a certain age must have a husband, so I am told, to
keep her out of trouble and away from sin. In other

words, to prevent her from having any enjoyment in life."

"Sounds reasonable to me."

"I'm sure it does. To a man with the reasoning capacity of a walnut."

"You think marriage is any more convenient for a man?" He released her arm, and Pip wondered why she had not shouted at him to do so before that. "The management and training of a wife is an onerous, mostly thankless task. A sensible fellow shouldn't take up the burden unless he's prepared, understanding how his own pleasures will be curbed, his patience tried, his time commandeered for wasteful pursuits, and his finances depleted."

She stared. "I cannot decide whether you are the most awful man I've ever met or the most comical clown."

"Or a walnut."

Again she studied his face, trying to ascertain whether he was teasing her.

"Have they decided on our wedding date yet?" he asked, while restraining what appeared to be a yawn.

"Who?" she exclaimed crossly.

"Your aunt and my godmother, of course. The architects of this most heinous plan to end all joy in our lives."

"I don't think even my aunt would get that far ahead of herself as to plan a date."

"Excellent, because I'd rather it not interfere with Ascot and then, of course—" He rubbed his chin, pondering the air above her head. "—There is Glorious Goodwood, followed by the grouse season."

"I can assure you I won't interfere with any pleasure of yours. You can attend every horse race and hunting season you care to. I have no plans to be *managed* and *trained*."

"But this introduction is the first step toward the fate ultimately awaiting us." He waved a long finger in her face. "Awful as it might be, some things cannot be avoided, young lady."

"Oh yes they can. Surely you don't care to be pushed into this either. I very much doubt anybody has control of you."

"Of course not." He gave a curt laugh. "I'm a man."

"You say that as if it's a qualification, rather than a shortcoming."

"I have no shortcomings."

She studied him thoughtfully. "Despite that remarkable, seed-ox confidence, there must be something amiss for your godmother to be pushing you at somebody like me. I would have thought you'd have a hundred prospects from which to choose. Safe, properly raised, dainty, English roses, who will never argue or even speak unless spoken to. They will play the harp for you until their fingers bleed, whereas I should just as soon crack you over the head with it the first time we quarrel."

Had he just moved closer? Perhaps it was merely the pushing crowd that made him sway in her direction. "It's inevitable that we'll quarrel?" he asked.

"I doubt you and I would ever do anything else."

"Oh, I can think of a few things—"

"You're a dreadfully smug, officious Englishman, and I'm a willful, independent-minded American. Oil and water have a more convivial relationship. Two brick walls have nothing to do, except stand against each other."

His gaze had returned to her face, where it settled with a slightly quizzical squint. "Shouldn't you stop talking?" he muttered gruffly. "And be— what was it you said— amiable? I'm not sure we have the same definition of that word."

"Shouldn't you apologize for ruining my shawl?" It was no good, she couldn't stop her tongue. His brazen, arrogant gaze lured it out of her, as music from a conjuror's pipe drew a serpent from its basket. "I thought English gentlemen were supposed to be chivalrous at the very least. Don't you pride yourself on it?"

With a deep sigh, he reached inside his coat and brought out a worn leather wallet. "This should more than cover the cost, so you can stop squawking about it. In fact, I'm being generous. You carelessly let that bit of flotsam drag along the carpet. And you needn't expect an excess of pin money when we're married, so you'd better start looking after your garments with greater care."

"I don't need your money!"

"What are you whining on about then?"

"A genuine 'sorry' would cost you nothing. This lace was made by nuns. In a convent."

"Really? I don't know much about nuns, but I daresay they need something to pass the time between prayers and self-flagellation."

"My point being that this is extremely rare craftsmanship, labored over for months, perhaps years. Probably irreplaceable. What am I to tell my sister when she sees this?"

"I would imagine the hole speaks for itself. Like the one in your face."

She ought to be offended, outraged and all those

other good words. He ought to be slapped. But Pip could give as good as she got, she loved a good debate and there was nobody to stop her enjoying this one. "Don't you look where you're putting your big feet?"

"They're not generally in the vicinity of delicate lace. At least..." the wicked hint of something like a smile briefly lifted one corner of his mouth, "nothing that's seen the inside of a nunnery."

Yes, she could well imagine.

His godmother's description had done him an injustice. Unconventional, yes, that much was true. And handsome— *vayan* as her aunt said. But that barely touched the surface. How was such a man to be described?

Her thoughts momentarily wandered off, along with other parts, until she corralled them back into proper territory. "Might I suggest you stamp about with greater caution in future?"

"I'll stamp where I please." Again the quirk of his lips, evocative of sly amusement. "The beauty of not having an interfering wife. Yet."

"Not that you'd feel any obligation to listen to her anyway."

"Well, she is meant to be mute and amiable, so I'm told. I'm not holding out much hope."

Clearly, getting a proper apology from the rude fellow was out of the question.

Her next statement was, perhaps obvious, but she felt it needed to be said. Just to clarify. For the both of them.

"We're not going to get along, you and I, are we?"

"Good God, I hope not."

* * * *

A dancing coil of her hair had become dislodged above her right ear. With every word she sputtered, that curl bounced indignantly, like an exclamation mark of sorts, but she seemed unaware of it. Or perhaps she didn't care.

He kept looking at it, resisting the near overwhelming urge to put it back in its place.Made his palms itch and his jaw grind.

He gave the knot of his neck cloth a terse tug and cleared his throat. But the urge to touch her and see if she was real remained undiluted.

She was a curious, apparently fearless creature, with far too much to say for herself. Leaping to conclusions about his identity— with only a little encouragement from him.

He ought to walk away and leave her there, but he couldn't seem to do it. She had sprung up behind him without warning and now gave him her full attention, not looking slyly for anybody else in the room or sneakily checking her reflection in the mirrored wall panels. It was almost as if she existed solely for him and, if he left, she would disappear in a puff of smoke. She seemed to be all alone and nobody else was looking at her. Perhaps, he mused, she really wasn't there.

But from what part of his usually sensible, highly intelligent, no-nonsense brain would he construct such a creature?

Warily he took stock of the image before him.

Her lips were very full; her eyes an extraordinary color— dark purple, luxuriant, like the fine cloth once reserved only for royalty. In this candlelight her skin was honey brown and yet seemed to hold within it a silvery glow. The translucent, shimmering quality of her complexion reminded him of the seedpods of Lunaria Annua — or 'honesty' as the plant was more commonly known. What would Americans call it? He had no idea. It was one of the few plants he could name as he'd always been drawn to it and, as a boy, had put some on his mother's grave every spring. It was his mother who had called it 'honesty', although he had only learned that from his father. His mother died when he was barely two, so he had no memory of her. Pity.

Oh, Christ. Why these rambling thoughts about flowers, seedpods, and his dead mother? He was usually much too busy and sensible to ruminate over childhood memories, or regret the lack of any.

That stray, dancing curl had somehow become entwined around her teardrop earring— amethyst, like her eyes.

Before he thought about what he did, he had reached toward her with one finger and flicked the curl free. It was soft, smooth, light as a whisper.Almost a kiss.

Where the devil *had* she come from? And he didn't mean the country of her origin. He wouldn't be at all surprised to find that she had been put in his way to cause trouble. In that moment a simple, chance collision seemed the most implausible reason of all.

As his father would say, women were always up to something.

Mulier est hominis confusio. Woman is the ruin of man.

The last time he saw his imaginary partner in crime — the little girl he'd once called "Nonesuch"—

she was standing on the cliffs, waving goodbye as he rode off in the mail coach for boarding school at the age of ten. He thought he'd left her behind forever, along with boyhood. She wasn't happy about it then, didn't like to be dismissed and sent back to whatever creative part of his imagination she'd come from. He should have known she wouldn't go quietly.

Well, now, apparently, she was back for vengeance.

Chapter Four

Preparing to make her grand exit once again, Pip found herself stuck, almost pulled off balance. This time his foot was on the hem of her gown and she felt the stitches straining where bodice met skirt.

Looking arrogantly down at her, arms folded again, he said, "Since there is nobody here to introduce us properly, shouldn't you tell me *your* name?"

With a proud angling of her shoulders and a flourish of that torn shawl, she announced, "My name, sir, is Epiphany Piper. Let that be a warning to you."

"Hmm. No doubt your reputation precedes you and I ought to know the name."

"You suspect correctly, Lord Boxall." She tried to free her skirt by tugging gently on it, but she was stuck fast. "Perhaps you could take your great, muddy paw off my gown, before that too is destroyed."

"But you can't go, because you belong to me."

She could scarce believe her ears, although they were usually most reliable. "I beg your pardon?"

"I thought we just decided to give it a try. Now that you've warned me."

"Are you quite mad?"

"But it's been decreed by your aunt and my godmother. Clearly you haven't met my godmother, or you'd know she's not to be gainsaid."

"Lord Boxall, I wouldn't *give it a try* with you if your queen herself decreed it."

"Why not?"

Again she had cause to doubt the veracity of her

hearing. She squared her shoulders and faced him boldly. "Because you are arrogant, insufferably rude—"

"You don't find me at all attractive?" He looked mystified.

"I— no, I don't. I mean to say, I'm sure that you are." She flapped her fan wildly. "In a common way. But I don't. Find you. That."

He looked at her for another long minute, stormy eyes scanning her person as if they read a lurid pamphlet all about her antics, printed on her clothing. Usually, once a man discovered the extent of her awfulness, he made some hasty excuse to go back to the unchallenging comfort of his port and dice. But this one was not going anywhere. Neither was he letting her escape. He must enjoy a good fight too. Probably never lost one.

He had a raw, heated masculinity, forceful and unapologetic. Just like his large feet. Lace shawls, she mused, were not the only things such a man could ruin without remorse. She ought, perhaps, be somewhat afraid. But none of the sensations currently careening through her could be mistaken for fear. Even the ones she couldn't name.

Then, finally, his lips parted and he exhaled a low, reluctant grumble, "Just as well I'm not Bertie Boxall then, isn't it?"

She stared, a cold rush of blood apparently leaving invisibly through the soles of her feet. "You're not...he?" Her fan closed with a snap and she gripped it tightly, until she felt that rapid beat of her heart finally slow to a calmer trot. "So you lied." And why should that surprise her? He was a man, wasn't he?

"You came up with the idea. I didn't disabuse

you of it."

Of course he would not act contrite about that either. "I suppose you amused yourself with my misconception."

"Immensely." He smirked.

"I might have known." She sighed, shaking her head. "You didn't look the sort to have much familiarity with harps."

He had made a fool of her.

And she had made a bigger one of herself by leaping to conclusions? Chagrinned, she must admit that it had not taken much luring for her to make a wrong turn and think what she wanted about him.

Pip felt her pulse falter uncertainly. Her fingers were digging hard into her closed fan and for once in her life she didn't have another word to say.

"Damon Deverell," he announced suddenly.

Having waited a moment and found nothing more forthcoming, she regained command of her tongue, her wits and her pulse. "Is that your real name? Or a condition of the English digestive system that prohibits a smile and good manners?" She imagined her sister chiding, *hardly the sort of thing one talks about...*

But he, still not scared away, merely inclined his head a half inch toward her and said, "It's a warning in return for the one you gave me."

"Duly noted." *Deverell.* Where had she heard that name before? For some reason she could hear her father pronouncing the name in his mellow voice, his tongue lingering over the ls and rolling the r.

She saw him glance at the dance card she wore on a string around her wrist.

"I'd write you in," she said pertly, "but I haven't

one free space to spare."

"I can't dance anyway," he replied.

"Feet too big, I suppose."

"I'm not invited to the ball. In fact, I'm likely to be escorted out by four or five burly footmen very soon."

Ah, that explained the lack of evening clothes. A young man who turned up at events to which he was not invited could only be trouble. She was amused, though, that he had to tell her the footmen would be burly and several in number, just to be sure she wouldn't think him capable of being thrown out on his ear by one slight fellow.

"What are *you* doing here then, if you didn't come to dance?" she asked, intrigued even further.

"Business."

"What gentleman brings business to a ball?"

"I'm not a gentleman. I'm a lawyer."

"Ah. That explains so much." She laughed. "As my father would say, *can't teach a pig to sing*."

"Your father has something against the law?"

"Just against those who take advantage of other folk's misery."

"I don't apologize for making a living."

"You don't apologize for anything, do you?"

"Why incriminate myself?"

"You must be a great pest. Do people avoid you in the street?"

"Not if I see them first."

"So you chase them down in places like this."

But looking over her head, he had caught sight of someone in the crowd and his expression changed, hardened again. Following the path of that fiercely direct gaze, she found a tall, slender blonde woman at the end of it. Very handsome and very much aware of the fact, pretending that her pale blue eyes did not see the young man who watched her. When the woman nodded stiffly in response to something her companion said, her diamond earrings glittered like a winter's sun on a frosty window pane, blades of cool light cutting across her slender neck.

In that moment the surly young lawyer seemed to have forgotten Pip's presence, and she was not a girl who stood around waiting to be remembered. Of course his attention would be stolen by a woman like that one over there, she thought glumly. He might be English and peculiar, but he was, above all else, a man.

However, his foot still imprisoned her skirt hem and when he felt her trying to get away again, he grumbled, "A minute, Miss Piper. I'm not done with you yet."

She thought abruptly of a cat toying with a mouse. And she no more enjoyed being toyed with than she did being made a fool, or forgotten about.

"Where are you staying in London, madam? Tell me. I insist."

No, *if you please...;* no, *if you would be so good as to...* "Why? Do you mean to visit? I shan't be at home to callers so you'll have a wasted journey."

"How do you know you won't be at home? You don't know when I might call."

He questioned her as if they were in court, she mused. "For you I'll make a point of being out. I don't forgive men who've deceived me for their own amusement. Besides, Englishmen are tremendously boring."

He scowled. "Just answer the damned question."

His tone was loud enough now for other people nearby to hear.

Pip felt the blonde woman's gaze reaching over the distance and scraping razor-edged tentacles over her flesh. And she knew he was aware of it too. A little smirk of bitter victory twitched at one corner of his mouth— proof that Master Grumbles played a game with her to get the Ice Queen's attention.

Raising her voice to match his, she exclaimed, "Will you move your damned foot off my gown, sir, or do I have to take it off?" He'd cursed out loud so why shouldn't she? He was a very bad influence, it seemed. Not that she needed any, as her father would say.

"Take which off?" he muttered. "Your gown or my foot?"

"Either."

"I wait keenly to see which you choose, madam. I suppose you have a gun under your garter. I've heard about you lawless revolutionaries, shooting each other's hats off for entertainment."

She smiled with her best attempt at demure sweetness, leaned slightly toward him and dropped an unsteady curtsey. Without taking her gaze from his face, she assured him softly, "I don't have a gun about my person this evening. Alas. But next time I shall, and you can be sure I won't aim it at your foot or your head, despite the tempting enormity of both. For your arrogance and the trick you just played upon me, I'll aim midway between them. Might be a much smaller target, but I do like to show-off my sharp-shooter skills."

His foot was finally withdrawn from the skirt of her ball gown.

"Why thank you, sir," she exclaimed, fluttering her lashes. Leaning closer still, she flipped open her fan and whispered behind it, "I wish you the best of fortune then, Master Damon Deverell. May you not fall down any mine shafts as you stumble through life with those uncaring big feet."

"Hmm?"

"I said, may you not fall—"

As he bowed toward her and she rose up from an awkward curtsey, his breath blew against the side of her cheek and it felt as intimate and improper as a public kiss. She completely forgot what she was saying.

Fan snapped shut again and with the damaged shawl folded over her arm, she hurried up the steps after her disappearing sisters. When she reached the top and looked back, curiosity getting the better of her pride, he remained where she'd left him. Staring up at her, appalled and no longer smug. Perhaps even slightly confused.

He was only lucky she *didn't* have a gun in her hand after the liberty he'd taken. To let him know this, she angled her fingers like a pistol and pointed at him, one eye closed, pretending to aim and fire.

To her surprise, he stumbled backward, dramatically clutching his chest as if he felt the blast. Not where she would have shot him though. His heart would have been an even smaller target, perhaps, than where she intended to pierce him with her imaginary bullet.

She laughed.

By pretending to be Lord Boxall, he had played her for a fool— that was true—but she hadn't enjoyed a debate quite so much in years. No harm done really. He was lucky she had a thick skin and absolutely no romantic expectations.

Deverell. Where had she heard that name? Why did it echo through her mind in her father's voice?

She stood still and closed her eyes.

"Over the side of the boat he went, and into the dark river. I fired at the fellow as he dove in...thought I clipped him, but I couldn't know for sure. The cheatin' scoundrel would have to swim fast to outpace the alligators lurking in the water, so if I didn't get him, I reckon they did."

It was a story her father had told many times.

"That young man took a fortune off me at the card tables on that riverboat. Others too. Nobody knew where he came from— hell, some folk said— but he was a damn clever villain. Never seen silver eyes like his on any other man. Seemed like they could read me and every thought before I had it, every move before I made it. True Deverell he called himself, but I doubt that was his real name. There was a rumor," and here he would laugh as hard as he could, *"that he was really a wolf that taught itself to walk upright, then stole a suit of clothes."*

Deverell.

What a strange coincidence, not only that she should meet a man with that same last name, but that he should also have the same untamed presence. Not to mention the eyes of a beautiful, but wild creature. A beast that could eat her whole or nibble her slowly all over, depending upon his hunger that day.

And she wasn't sure which terrible possibility thrilled her more.

Much to her chagrin, she realized now that the feeling she'd mistaken for alarm when she first thought he was Lord Boxall had, in fact, been excitement. Terrible and dangerous excitement that could not possibly do anybody any good. Especially not when she had plans for her future and was supposed to be behaving herself.

Perhaps there was harm done, after all. She shouldn't forgive him that readily for making a fool of her, deceiving her so wickedly. He was clearly the sort of scoundrel who got away with his behavior and she could, reluctantly, see how.

"Who was that?" her aunt wanted to know.

She exhaled a heaving sigh. "*Not* Bertie Boxall." But the "Unfortunately" she kept to herself.

* * * *

For such a small person she took up a great deal of room, he thought, watching as other folk gave her a wide berth. He should have done the same, of course, and steered his course well clear. Too late.

When he said there was something "wrong" with her, he ought to have said "different". Only now did he realize his mistake, which was odd since he was usually very circumspect with his words, but she had taken him by surprise, forced a reaction out of him before he was prepared. In any case, it was all downhill from that remark.

She was a singular creature. Energy bounced off her in the softly bristling glow of candlelight, so that one could almost hear it humming across her skin. For just a few moments she had lifted his spirits. Now that she was gone he felt slightly... deflated.

Their encounter brought to mind a story his father once told him, of how he met his current wife, Olivia.

"I found her under my feet."

His father liked to make bizarre claims just to

raise eyebrows.

I once fought a dragon.

My mother was a mermaid.

When I was a young man, I out swam an alligator.

And when it came to Olivia— *I found her under my feet and knew immediately, in some strange way, that I would have her one day. Not then, of course, because she was too young and innocent still and I had yet to corrupt her. But my name was already carved inside that woman and I felt it there, as if I could rub my finger over it and trace the words.*

Damon Deverell stared after the disappearing figure and suffered a stark premonition, a jolt worse than the slap of his father's hand against the back of his head for being pert or disrespectful. He knew, in that moment, that however the American came to be under his feet, she would— against her will and his— become a significant part of his life. He felt his name in her, the same way his father once felt his own marked inside a woman.

"Englishmen are tremendously boring," she'd said.

Boring, indeed! She might think she knew Englishmen, but she didn't know him.

For some reason, of all her insults, that one struck hardest.

In the corner of his eye, he saw a man in evening suit conferring with a liveried servant and pointing his way. Rather than wait for an escort out, he turned and made his own way down the steps, his stride easy and unhurried.

He heard someone mutter, "Who the devil is that?"

Another faceless voice answered, "That *is* the devil. Or the devil's son, at least."

"Looks like he bloody-well owns the place."

"No doubt he could. If he wanted."

Damon smirked as he strode onward.

"There is nothing those Deverell boys can't have, once they decide it's theirs."

Yes, he'd heard that many times.

The sons of True Deverell had been raised to view London as their own town, *their* hunting ground, *their* territory. Although their father was not welcomed among the upper classes, he had — like a wolf among sheep— terrified their exalted ranks, stirred up enough havoc to scatter the flock and made his mark among them, indelible as a bloodstain.

People in this society did not like outsiders.

Is that why Damon felt an immediate connection with that young woman? She didn't fit in there any better than he did.

How in the world did Miss Piper, of the astonishing violet eyes and "very efficient right hook", come to be there, under *his* feet, masquerading as his once-imaginary friend— that naughty tomboy "Nonesuch", disturbingly, and rather lusciously, all grown up. Not that he could be interested, of course. He had enough to manage with his current lover, Lady Elizabeth Stanbury, and sometimes he didn't even know how he'd come to be embroiled in *that* affair.

Well, yes he did— a mixture of ennui and restiveness after a self-imposed three-year fast. He just liked to pretend he didn't know how it had happened, as if it was nothing, really, to do with him. As if he had not pursued her for the pleasure of the challenge and the profound satisfaction of claiming a woman who thought herself so superior to a Deverell.

As Damon stepped into the street, he saw a face

he recognized— a fellow with whom he once shared a Latin tutor at university. He stopped to offer a word of warning. "Ah, Boxall, you're late! There is the most rabidly eager young chit looking for you in there. Apparently she's been promised an introduction by your godmother."

"Oh, lord, not another one." The indolent young man rolled his eyes and slouched against the railings. "What's she look like?"

"Well...I'd rather not say." He made his face grim. "But appearances aren't everything, are they? Look on the bright side. She's exceedingly keen and so, I believe, is her chaperone. To be rid of her." With one hand he patted the other fellow's shoulder in a comforting fashion and followed it up with the final crushing statement familiar to all young men. "I'm sure she has a *lovely* personality."

It was all he need say. Boxall turned on his heel and stumbled back the way he'd travelled, possibly to the nearest tavern.

Really, Damon mused, he was becoming quite the doer of good deeds. He just wasn't sure for whom he did this one.

Chapter Five

Boston, Massachusetts
One year earlier, May 1849

"Spirited? *Spirited?*" Mrs. H. Thaxton-Choate, who was every bit as sharp-edged, thorny and unromantic as her name, sat ramrod straight, only her right eyebrow showing any sign of flexibility, and even that in one point and one angle alone. "Your daughter is just plain wild, Mr. Piper. She's entirely unsuited for the sophisticated ballrooms of New England. I cannot say for certain where she belongs, but I can assure you it was a mistake to bring her north."

And Mr. Prospero "Smokey" Piper, who was just as extraordinary, unconventional and unforgettable as *his* name, hitched to the edge of his seat. "Come now, my Pip's a unique young lady, and I don't deny it. She's an original. When they made her they broke the mold."

"With good reason."

"She can't be that hopeless, Ma'am. Can't *you* teach her what's right— a fine, tight-stitched, dignified lady like yourself? Don't look like much could squeeze by you and not have some of that high class varnish smeared off on it. Surely those fancy manners are like horse sweat and hound dog; a man can't be rid of the stink once he's rubbed up against plenty of it."

Her eyes took on the hollow stare of a cadaver. One that suddenly awoke to find itself abandoned in a morgue reserved for undesirables and the unclaimed. "It seems there has been some misunderstanding, Mr.

Piper. I chaperone young ladies in society and make introductions that can lead to marriage. Advantageous, mutually beneficial marriage. I don't herd wildebeest across the prairie."

"Perhaps it's costing you a little more to put her out and about, because she ain't a natural beauty. Is that it? Well, I've no objection to sweetening the pie if necessary, ma'am. I want the best for my daughters, and I'm willing to pay. What's your price? Don't be afraid to name it."

Her voice became very tight, squeezed out from some withered, desolate place inside her narrow frame. "I'm afraid no amount of money can help your daughter find a suitable husband here. Not now that she's shown her unladylike temper in public." Finally, and with supreme reluctance, her dead gaze drifted left to observe the subject of their discourse.

Epiphany quickly switched her full attention to the antics of a particularly lively wasp, which she'd observed for some time in her peripheral vision. It must have come into the parlor along with the vase of sickly sweet lilacs that perched on the console table behind the stern frills of Mrs. Thaxton-Choate's day cap. Yes, even that woman's frills were stern. To Pip's amusement, the adventurous wasp periodically enjoyed a thorough examination of those neatly pressed, white linen ruffles, between dancing in and out of the lilacs, or hovering over that prim shoulder, where it must have located the remnants of breakfast marmalade, left there by an impatient brush of the lady's hand.

Pip had promised her father to let him do the talking, and she always kept her promises. Or tried. On this occasion, she managed by the skin of her grinding teeth, until Mrs. Thaxton-Choate added, "And I fear Miss Epiphany's little display of unseemly fervor yesterday evening will severely curtail her sisters' options too."

That was the final straw. Pip bounced to her feet in another example of that very same unseemly fervor.

"Punish me, if you please. I never wanted to be a part of this cattle auction. Everybody here is so busy pretending to be something they're not, that there is no integrity, no sincerity, no kindness! It's all shallow, stupid, self-absorbed and meaningless, and I'd rather be anywhere else. But my sisters did nothing to deserve your recriminations. They should not suffer."

"A pretty speech indeed, Miss Epiphany," came the sharp reply, bony hands knitted primly together in her lap. "So charitable and self-sacrificing. Sadly, your behavior last night did not reflect the same worthy values. Your dear sisters are stained by association, and you should have thought of that. In fact, you should have *thought*— of anything— before you acted in such a shameful manner."

"Madam, I defended myself and my family. And I would do it again, if necessary. I refuse to stand quietly by while some oily tick insults us."

Pip suddenly felt her father's hand around her elbow, tugging her back down onto the settee beside him. His voice remained calm, smooth and slow as a swinging hammock on a warm summer evening. "If this is about that skinny young feller's black eye, Pip said she's sorry. Now, surely, we can settle that business."

No response, just that corpse glare and a further stiffening of her rigor mortis.

"Tell you what, ma'am," he added in a conspiratory tone, leaning forward, "we'll let him take a swing at Pip in return and then he'll feel better about it, eh?" No sooner had the last word left his mouth than his lips curved in one of his most charming smiles. Epiphany's father had quite a repertoire of these smiles, all cheekily effective at chiseling their way into hearts and pockets.

None, however, chipped any stone off that proud edifice known as Mrs. H. Thaxton-Choate. "That *skinny young feller*," she repeated crisply, "happens to be a Delaware Moffat."

"Well, fancy that." That slightly crooked smile his daughter loved so much widened further as he sat back in his chair. "And we're the Louisiana Pipers."

"Are you suggesting that Mr. Ernest Moffat should be allowed to punch your daughter in return for his black eye?"

"I've seen the slight feller. He won't do any damage. Pip can take care of herself, but he can give it a try if he feels inclined to let off some steam."

The woman's eyes gleamed with vitriol. "Mr. Piper, I see it's a challenge for you to take this matter seriously. As it is, apparently, for your daughter too. But you must understand, there is an order to be kept here among society's elite, a pyramid of reverence to which we must adhere at all times. The Moffat family is highly regarded, and your daughter—"

"Their money came from gunpowder, didn't it? Ain't that much different to how I got my start as a boy. Lot of explosions came along with that too, in the still, behind the outhouse. One blast took out my grandmother's last tooth and blew her best patchwork drawers clear across the creek." He winked. "But our family's gunpowder comes in a bottle."

"I daresay it's taken just as many men to hell."

He laughed. "Quite frankly, ma'am, if I had to choose either way to die, I'd sooner go with Ol' Smokey Piper's Best Bourbon, wouldn't you?"

"I never touch the demon drink."

He kept his smile, muttering through his teeth, "I might have guessed."

"I beg your pardon, Mr. Piper?"

"It's a pity you don't try a sip, ma'am. A little bit o' the demon serves a purpose, I reckon. After all, there wouldn't be no angels without demons, would there?"

"And how do you reach that conclusion?"

"Life is all about balance, ain't it?"

"It's all about what's right and proper, Mr. Piper."

"You mean to say, what's right in *your* opinion."

The eyebrow peaked again and the wasp, which had just landed upon her shoulder, took off vertically as if it felt the vibrations of her anger. "In this case, my opinion is the only one that matters. I cannot provide further introductions for your daughter. Nothing can be made of the girl. Her despicable behavior is giving me and my service a bad name."

Pip looked at her father and sighed. "I told you, pa. It doesn't matter that I apologized, even though Ernest Moffat is a lazy, no good, lug-legged loafer. He being an *alleged* eligible bachelor, I'm supposed to let him treat me like a fresh-killed skunk carcass on a hot day and not say a word about it. Least of all, give him what he deserved. Heaven forbid."

Mrs. Thaxton-Choate, a near omnipresent force in New York, Boston *and* Philadelphia— according to her curt, white calling cards— blinked just once, and it was almost possible to hear the tiny blue veins in her eyelids crackling under the weary strain. "Mr. Piper, I fear your daughter's schooling did her a disservice. Of all the books she's read, it seems she overlooked *The Art of Good Behavior.* I heartily recommend you find her a copy."

Epiphany replied before her father could. "Has Mr. Moffat read *True Politeness; A handbook for gentlemen?* No. I daresay it has too many words of four syllables and too few illustrations. He's a barely sentient creature, who wears too much Macassar oil in his hair, can do nothing for himself and carries a letter of credit written on his father's account. Excuse me if I fail to swoon in his presence, but I've seen tadpoles I'd deem more *eligible.*"

"That's quite enough, Miss Epiphany. Your further views of young Mr. Moffat are not necessary."

Her father chuckled drowsily. "Yes, I'd say you made your opinion clear enough when you flattened the feller with a hard right, Pip. You left a lasting impression."

The despicable girl of whom nothing could be made, turned to Mrs. Thaxton-Choate again and said, "Everything about this place is as artificial and counterfeit as that sofa you're sitting on. And you're welcome to it, for I don't want to live in a world where nothing is genuine, where you're all just poor copies of what you wish you were."

The woman's face remained unmoved, apart from a slight curve to her lips, the hint of a condescending, even pitying smirk. "*This,* young lady, is an antique, Louis XIV settee. From France. But I wouldn't expect you to recognize such an object, of course."

"Ma'am, aside from the fact that your *antique* has hardly an ounce of wear on it, the scroll work along the back is overdone for the period and the shape of the leg is all wrong. A true chair of that era would have straight, baluster-turned legs and certainly not ball-and-claw feet. In fact, the wood work is all far too overwhelming for the piece." She paused. "But far be it from me, an uncultured— oh, what was it the Moffat boy called me?— *Southern Bumpkin Swamp Crawler* to tell you any of that."

Her words fell heavily, parting the thick, lilac air of pretention like Moses before the Red Sea.

Distant footsteps busily crossed a parquet floor somewhere in the house and, beyond the heavily netted windows, horses' hooves trotted by at a brisk, steady clip. No other sound pierced the stillness, until Mrs. Thaxton-Choate gave a startled yelp when that lively wasp finally flew into her line of sight, aiming directly for her nose.

Since she refused any assistance from Mr. Piper, they left the room soon after, abandoning her to lone battle with the excited wasp. The last vision Pip enjoyed of that lady was of her cap ruffles flapping with an unusual lack of discipline as she ran around the reproduction sofa and yelled hysterically for her maid.

"So what do I do with you now, young lady?" her father muttered as they came out into the sunlight. "I brought you up north to attend that female seminary for a modern schoolin', like you wanted. I thought your outspoken, independent ways would be more accepted here. But now you've gone and made yourself as unwelcome in these marble mansions on the avenue as you were among the delicate Southern Belles sippin' lemonade on the veranda back home."

"Exactly." She sighed, hugging his arm. "I'm about as welcome in these fancy parlors as a wasp in a bouquet of lilacs. I can't stay here now, can I?" After finishing at the seminary, she'd spent just one month out in Boston society among all the arrogant "swells" like Ernest Moffat, and that was more than enough to sorely try Pip's endurance. But she was deeply sorry if she'd spoiled anything for her sisters. "Surely the venerable Choate can be persuaded to keep Serenity and Merrythought under her wing," she added thoughtfully. "Once the embarrassment of my presence is gone, and things have calmed down, they'll have plenty of beaus in no time."

As far as Epiphany there was no reason for *her* to remain in the north that summer. It was time she went to work for the family business. But she must edge her way gradually around to that.

Holding his arm even tighter, she slowed her pace and beamed up at her father. "How handsome you look today, pa. If I'm not mistaken you found a barber before collecting me from Aunt Abellard's this morning."

"Indeed I did, Pip."

"And that is a delightful, warm, powdery scent. What is it, pa?"

"It's a new concoction— called *Jockey Club*, so they tell me. Although it don't smell like horses, so I'm guessing it's a sort of jockey club where they dress up fancy to ride, but nobody truly has any contact with the beasts themselves."

She chuckled. "That is the most delightfully succinct castigation of these folks that I have ever heard."

He shook his head. "But you must stop being so sharp-tongued, young lady. Everybody has their imperfections. Even you."

"Oh, I freely admit to *my* faults. It's insufferable people who think themselves above fault and free of sin that I cannot abide. Their affectations and artifice make me itch."

"Hmm. And that temper of yours isn't mellowing with age. Your Aunt Abellard said you told a certain high society matron that she shouldn't get her head wet for fear of shrinking her brain."

"No. Well, yes...but it wasn't *exactly* like that. On the one and only evening I had the misfortune to meet her, she told me, quite unsolicited I might add, that my eyes are too close together, my lips are unrefined, my brows lack elegance, my nose is too blunt, my skin is too dark and my hair is too wild."

"I see, but—"

"I'm too short, too plump, too opinionated. My ears stick out too far. My face is too round. I have no fashion, no manners and no sense of propriety."

He squinted. "She told you all that in one evening?"

"In one two-minute introduction. However, I hear that to be noticed by her at all is considered remarkable and once her barbs have been shot, one is supposed to curtsey politely before scurrying off to alter everything that displeased her." She sighed. "I chose another option."

Her father shook his head again.

"I simply returned the favor. I advised the lady that, if she went out in the rain, all that boot-black she used on the grey in her hair would run like molasses in July. And then I added the part about her brain shrinking too, because by then I was madder than a wet cat." She sighed heavily. "I must confess, pa, there was a large, strawberry gateaux behind her, which distracted me. The anticipation of that delight meant that my tongue wandered off on its own. You know how I am in the presence of good cake. I quite forget myself."

Her father's lips freed a slight groan. "Yes, indeed. I've often wondered why some young man hasn't figured that out yet for himself."

"But she gave me her unwanted opinion of my appearance, so why should I not do the same for her?"

"Sometimes a little pretense and forbearance is necessary to get along in this world. It's a sign of maturity, you know Pip, to learn how to put on a smile, hold that temper, and not retaliate. There are times when it does no harm to save your breath and someone else's feelings."

"Why should I take trouble for her feelings? She had no concern for mine."

"You're only nineteen—"

"I'm twenty, pa!"

"Well, she's your elder. You should be respectful and not talk back, regardless of what she has to say."

"So as long as a person's old it doesn't matter what comes out of their mouth? Good lord, I can't wait until I'm forty!" She looked around, her jaw clenched. "The world had better watch out."

"We all know you have opinions; don't mean the rest of the world wants to hear every one of 'em Not everything you're thinking inside has to show on the outside. That's the difference between being five and surviving to twenty-five."

"Nobody told *her* that, clearly, and she's well beyond twenty-five."

"Her behavior and survival ain't my business, young lady. Yours is." His gaze pierced her with a glare that was, like his smiles, effective at breaking down defensive walls, but far less subtly or pleasantly. Whenever he felt it necessary to use such an expression on his middle daughter she knew his patience was at its limit and she was in danger of making him raise his voice above that lazy afternoon timbre. "If you let folk know what you're thinking all the time you can never surprise 'em, never out play 'em. You must learn to keep thoughts and plans closer to your chest, Pip. Otherwise they'll know all your sore spots and how to poke 'em. If you'd walked away from that woman with a smile on your face, she wouldn't have the slightest idea what was on your mind and that would have been the winning hand. Would have shown her that she can't get to you. Same with young Moffat."

Although Pip knew he was right, it took some swallowing of her pride— which everybody agreed was an obnoxious part of her— to reply, "Yes, pa, of course." Needing her father in a good mood, she sought another subject. "Is this a new waistcoat, pa?" She placed her free hand upon her father's chest and patted the embroidered silk. "It's very fine material."

Swiftly diverted from their previous conversation, he puffed out his chest. "You don't think it's too...colorful?"

"Certainly not, pa," she exclaimed. "How could you ever be too colorful?"

"Well, there is a youngish widow I'm thinking to

court, and I don't want her to see me as brash and gaudy."

She laughed, relieved to see his eyes lighten again. "Any woman courted by you should think herself extremely fortunate and could not possibly find any fault. You are the most dapper gentleman I know." Pip always enjoyed the admiring glances thrown their way as she walked along any street with him, for even though she knew those looks were not meant for her, she could still bask in their warmth, taking pride in her father as if she had put his parts together and polished him herself.

He was just starting to grow a little silver at the temples, which only added an air of distinguished authority to his mellow, amiable charm.

"I don't think any man I meet could ever live up to your example, pa," she said proudly. "It's most unfair for them, but no other gentleman holds a candle to you."

He gave her a quick, narrow-eyed look. "Is that so?"

"Of course, pa. You've spoiled me."

"I probably have," he grumbled, but his eyes glittered with amusement as his lips softened in another smile, and a moment later he was preoccupied tipping his hat to a pretty, blushing young lady who passed on the pavement. "I suppose you're a good girl at heart, Pip," he allowed reluctantly, setting his hat back on his head. "Perhaps it's not so bad that you know how to defend yourself. Who knows what's brewing around the corner for any of us in this world, with things the way they are? All this change and nothing certain."

After a few more steps, Pip cleared her throat

and said jauntily, "I thought I might come home with you now and get to work at Smokey Pipers, where I—"

"But I seem to remember you and I struck a bargain, young lady."

"Did we?"

"I agreed to let you come up here and get that education you wanted, but in return you promised me that at the end of these three years you would—"

"Oh, pa! Just look at the beautiful, brilliant pink of those saucer magnolias," she exclaimed. "Is it not exuberant and cheering to the very soul?! When one walks out in nature, one can forget the awfulness of people. Does that glorious sight not put spring in your heart?"

"Never mind spring in my heart. It's your head and what's put in there that I worry about. You promised me that as long as I let you study at that seminary you would seriously set your mind to the idea of getting wed and providing me with mischievous, curly-haired grandchildren."

She exhaled a deep groan. "I thought you'd given up on that idea by now."

"Yes, I expect you did, but at my age three years ain't that long to wait. Not nearly as long as it is for you. And I ain't yet losing my memory."

"Nor are you ready to be a grandfather, surely! You're much too young."

"Then I'll be a *young* grandfather, won't I?" he replied smoothly. "I'll be young enough to teach my grandsons all they need to know, because I can't leave them in your hands. Lord knows what you'd teach 'em."

"But what is the point of all that education if it

must be entirely wasted? I'd rather come home now and help you with the business." As they strolled under the trees, she closed her eyes to enjoy the tickle of filtered sunshine on her face. "Because you will hand it down to me one day, won't you?"

"Will I?" He laughed. "Not if you can't learn to hold that temper. In business you can't let your competitors know how and where to prick you with their thorns. And you have to be civil, sometimes even to folks you don't like. With your hot-head I don't know if you would be the right choice for Smokey Pipers, indeed I don't."

She opened her eyes and looked at him as he began to hum a jolly, carefree tune, his expression giving nothing away. Frustrated, she couldn't tell whether he was teasing her. That, she supposed, was what he meant by being able to keep his true thoughts and intentions inside.

Her father couldn't hide everything from her though. Once, some years ago, she'd walked into a room unnoticed, just in time to hear her father declare out loud to a group of gentlemen that the biggest regret of his life was that he had no sons, only daughters. A wounded young Pip had set her mind, there and then, to the idea of becoming a businesswoman with no time to spare for a husband and children. She had vowed to herself that her sex wouldn't stop her from doing all the things a son could have done for him. And more.

But she had a challenge on her hands. Occasionally Pip's antics made her father laugh, but there were times when her behavior did not please him as much, especially when his mind was too heavily burdened with some trouble he would not share with her. On the other hand, her sisters were always smiled at benignly, no matter what difficulty he was in. When they entered a room, he lightened his voice and changed the subject, but he didn't necessarily bother to do so when Pip walked in. Sometimes she was glad of that, other times she wondered whether he simply hadn't noticed her there.

Of course, it was entirely her fault. Her sisters never caused him any consternation, but did exactly as they were told and what was expected. They were decorative, engaging when called upon to be so, and not at all prone to "unseemly fervor".

Pip felt like an angry parakeet— one that everybody was annoyed at, but nobody wanted to let out of its cage to set it free. Trapped there, she pecked at her own feet out of boredom, occasionally squawking insults at anybody who stuck a finger through her bars.

She tugged on her father's arm, and he paused his humming.

"Serenity may be the eldest, pa, but she has no interest in business. She yearns to be a devoted wife, mother and hostess, all things I'm sure at which she will excel."

"Hmm." One thumb hooked in the pocket of his waistcoat, he pretended to consider. "What about Merrythought? Might leave her in charge of the business. She has a good head on her shoulders. When she uses it."

"Merry is the sweetest girl that ever lived, but you know, as I do, that she is much too kind-hearted and would let everybody take advantage of her. What Old Smokey Piper's Bourbon needs at the helm is somebody relentless, bloodthirsty and cutthroat." She tried on a bright grin. "Somebody who takes after her darling, incorrigible, progressive-minded father."

A low chuckle rolled out of him. "Flatter me all you want, I ain't givin' up on finding you a husband, Pip. One way or another. We Pipers never give up. Not in our nature. There's always another way to conquer the mountain, girl. If someone like that Choate woman gets in our way, we go around them and over them, and we don't pay them no more mind. We're adventurers and speculators by nature. So if *New* England don't know what to make of you, perhaps Old England will. I ought to send you to my sister Queenie, your Aunt Du Bois, and see what she can do for us."

Mr. Prospero "Smokey" Piper, of Louisiana and various other parts unknown and best unmentioned— a man who believed that when one ran out of opportunities one simply made more— was the first ambitious and wealthy American businessman to think of this idea, not that any history book or self-professed "expert" will tell you that, because...well, just like that first attempt at building a still behind his family's outhouse as a young boy, this plan didn't exactly turn out the way he expected either.

And although explosions were inevitable, it was not his grandmother's drawers in danger this time.

Chapter Six

The Offices of Stempenham and Pitt
London, 1850

Tobias Stempenham was a tall, spare fellow, whose piercing, heavily lidded eyes and bony, sharply sloped nose contributed to the appearance of a hungry hawk. The older he got, the more gaunt and starving his look, as evidenced when one compared the living man with the thirty-year-old image in the oil painting behind his desk.

Sometimes, when Damon looked at that portrait and then the man who sat before it, he felt an overwhelming sense of doom, for this could one day be him. Time pulled him inexorably toward that end, and there seemed scant chance of changing his fate. His path had been set long ago.

Wisps of sandy and grey hair, now blown haphazardly about the man's head, were all that remained of the lush mane he sported in that grand portrait, and his body was now at least six inches narrower all around. The bones in those once fleshy, spoiled hands— resting on a book in the portrait— were gnarled and distorted now, the fingers often hooked into claws that could barely hold a pen. Only the intense stare in his ever-vigilant eyes remained the same, its affect quite unfaded over the years. If anything, it was fiercer now, less tempered with youthful enthusiasm, the softer padding worn away there too. And when Tobias turned his gaze upon a person they had better be prepared with either unflinching truth, or a very, very good lie.

"Roper," he barked at Damon that morning. "Explain."

"His lordship decided to withdraw the lawsuit, sir."

"And his fee."

"Yes." Damon stood his ground before Tobias Stempenham as few men could or would. It was one of the reasons why he was first employed by the firm. As the old man had snapped, when his partner protested the hiring of such a strongly opinionated young man, "*There is a limit to the amount of fawning and arse-kissing I can take. This one will make a blessed change.*"

Today Damon knew he was fortunate the old man liked him. Or as much as Tobias ever liked anybody.

"He tells me you ruddy talked him out of it."

"I merely told him his options, sir. I prefer that a client understand all the possible outcomes."

"Humph. I suppose I ought to sack you for costing us."

This was threatened once every few months, and Damon's reply was always the same. "It'll cost you more to lose me."

The old man knew this was true, of course. Damon was their most promising young lawyer, and Stempenham and Pitt did not want him working for any other firm in London. His energy and reputation helped keep them busy with clients. Men admired his tenacity and courage, while women admired...whatever it was they saw beneath his hard exterior and detached manner. That was still a matter for debate. Damon didn't know what women saw in him either and was just as bemused as anybody.

"Lucky for you, Deverell, we have just been commissioned for another case. A curious matter, but one that pays even better, and you're good for the unusual cases." Tobias rasped out a quick chuckle, his lips cracking open in the shadow of that beaked nose. "A Mr. Prospero Piper, an American businessman—yes, I see your surprise, but apparently our successful reputation is known even so far abroad—wants an eye put on his daughters while they're in London, to keep them out of harm's way. Letter arrived yesterday. You can see to it. You're the only one with enough vigor to chase three young girls around Town, picking up after 'em and undoing any damage before it gets in the broadsheets. Or back to their father across the Atlantic."

Damon was seldom shocked. Today he was, for a moment, too unsettled to reply. *Piper.* He should have known she'd cross his path again, sooner or later.

"What's with the gormless face? Up late last night, Deverell? I've told you before, a man cannot burn the candle at both ends for long. It'll catch up with you."

"I confess, I am confused by this request," he muttered. "It seems an odd task for us."

"There's been some legal issue at home. A weak-chinned boy with a moneyed father took offence to something one of the girls did and won't shut up about it. So they've been sent here to stay with an aunt, out of the way. But Mr. Prospero Piper wants to be sure there's no more bother while they're here. Should there be any ruckus, he wants it dealt with at once. Nipped in the bud, as they say, the damage mended. And fellow is paying handsomely for the effort, so you needn't look so peevish."

Damon shook his head. "I've never heard of a solicitor hired on retainer to keep a woman out of trouble."

"They do things differently in America, I daresay. Since he's so generous, and must not have anything better upon which to spend his money, who are we to complain? Can't fault him for having the foresight. Women and daughters can be a wretched nuisance, and I should know with six of 'em at home myself." He paused, sniffed. "Which reminds me— don't suppose you're in the market yet for a bride, eh?"

"No. Sir." He paused and then added, "Unless you'd like to give me a substantial raise with which I might be better able to keep a wife."

Of course, they both knew he didn't mean it. Damon Deverell was not the marrying kind and asking for a large raise from Tobias Stempenham was akin to whistling in the wind.

"With your stinking rich father?" the old man croaked. "What do you need with my money?"

"I prefer to make my own fortune, sir, than rely on his. Besides, my father has enough offspring to strain his finances."

"At least your father had all sons. No daughters to drain his coffers."

"He has one daughter, sir."

"Only one?" Tobias sniffed miserably and bent over his desk. "Lucky wretch. And here I am with half a dozen I cannot be rid of."

"You have my deepest sympathy, sir."

"You're sure I can't tempt you with one o' my girls? They're not much to look at, but they can keep a clean house and cook a plain dinner."

"Once I have a house to keep clean, sir, I'll give your kind offer all due consideration. At present I have only cramped lodgings with space for myself and a few bold mice. And I usually eat my dinner here, at my desk."

"Aye. Well, always worth a try." The old man groaned deeply. "Got to be rid of 'em one day, before they eat me out of house and bloody home. Six thoroughbred horses would be cheaper to keep and handsomer to look at."

Damon hid a smile and reminded his employer, "But about the Piper girl, sir. Are you certain this is—"

"If you ask me, that American chap has the right idea for managing his daughters. Send 'em far away and pay someone else to watch over 'em. An ounce of prevention is worth a pound of cure. Who knows," he shrugged, "it might become a regular practice, with females getting so out of hand these days. Women's *suffrage*." He huddled deeper into the arch of his shoulders as if he felt a sudden blast of cold air around his ears. "Demanding the vote and whatnot. Stopping addle-pated wenches from getting themselves arrested might become our bread and butter."

But Damon was thinking about a certain pair of extraordinary eyes, quarrelsome lips, and tempting shoulders. Softly rounded, smooth, sun-kissed skin, and a rich, warm voice with a laugh never far away. "Isn't there anyone else who might suit this task better? I do have other cases—"

"Aye, but you don't have Roper's case anymore, do you?" The old man leered, scratching the end of his nose with one crooked finger. "You can take this one instead, since you've arranged yourself some spare time."

Ah. So this was to be his punishment for turning the other fee away. Damon was annoyed. Surely putting him onto this strange case was akin to using the best soldier to stand behind and beat a damned drum. But often he was the errand boy, the messenger, the fixer. Especially when it was a task nobody else wanted.

"What's the matter now?" Tobias roared. "You look like a ferret just ran up your breeches."

"It's...I met one of them."

"Oh? And?"

"Short, chatty, willful brunette with lavender eyes, a great many opinions about Englishmen, and, so she tells me herself, a splendid right hook. We took an instant dislike to each other, so I may not be the ideal man for the job."

Tobias gave a gruff chuckle. "You're always the man for the job, Deverell. You get it done. And this is good money for naught, if you ask me," he said, nudging papers across his desk with those rheumatic knuckles.

"Naught?" Damon grumbled. "You just said women can be a wretched nuisance."

"Not for you, surely." Tobias feigned surprise, leaning back in his chair. "The merciless Master Damon Deverell doesn't quake in his boots for a woman. Now don't you let us down. Take a firm hand to the wayward wench. You've got a reputation for being an utter bloody bastard to maintain."

* * * *

Two days after the Courtenay's ball, Damon, in

his best "utter bloody bastard" mode, was at the door of a smart house in Belgravia. He estimated it to be one of those rented for around fifteen hundred pounds a year, perhaps more. Clearly, as his employer had stated, Mr. Prospero Piper liked to throw his money around and had plenty to throw. Why shouldn't he catch some of it?

His previous reservations about this job had fallen away. Damon was always up for a challenge and he liked clearing up messes, but there had been very few cases of the interesting sort falling into his lap of late, and life had begun to feel rather narrow. Ready for some fresh air and fireworks, therefore, he stood at the door in Belgravia, warm spring sun in his eyes, newspaper tucked under one arm, and felt just a slight tremor of excitement. But he was careful not to let it show on his face; had that reputation to maintain.

The door finally opened, a footman appearing before him in solemn, resigned weariness.

"Are the ladies of the house at home?"

The footman blinked slowly, as if invisible strings tugged his eyelids downward. "And whom might I say is calling?"

"Deverell. Damon Deverell. If Miss Piper pretends not to remember me, tell her it's the one with the big feet. The one she shot at."

That got the footman's interest and woke him from the somber gloom of despondency. "I see. Kindly...wait here. Sir."

Thus he was left on the step, the door closed again while the footman's steps echoed away down the corridor. A few minutes later, the door reopened in a hurry and a woman in a silk robe, with a feathered turban on her head snapped at him to leave his card. He sensed at once that she would have sent the footman back to get the card had she not wanted to appraise him with her own eyes. The informality of her costume told him that her curiosity was greater than her propriety. Her eyes were bright, very intense, scouring his person with practiced speed as he handed her his calling card.

"She shot at you?" Her countenance and tone showed no surprise or horror, merely a slight impatience and more than a little morbid curiosity. "Where? I don't see any holes in you."

"Just a jest, madam. I was unharmed. As you see."

She considered briefly and then said, "Come pass by tomorrow, young man, when I've looked you up."

But she was not fast enough to stop Damon's hand on the door, holding it open. "Madam, I think you misunderstand. This is not a social call. I'm not here as a prospective suitor. I came here on business for Mr. Prospero Piper."

She glared at his hand and then at him.

"Apparently his daughters might need an ally in London," he added, turning the folded newspaper to show her the cartoon featured there. "And it seems to have fallen to my lot."

* * * *

Pip was the last to enter the room and had just come in from a morning walk in the park. As it happened, and although she tried to occupy her mind with anything else, she'd been thinking about Damon Deverell ever since the ball, so when she saw him standing in her aunt's drawing room with his back to the fireplace, she exhaled a small, wheezy, high-pitched "Oh, no", and prepared to walk out again, sensing she was in trouble. Exactly how or why, and whose fault it was, she didn't yet know. But it was definitely trouble.

"Epiphany," her aunt called out, "come sit, *ma cher*. This is Mr. Deverell, a lawyer."

He looked at her, bowed his head and put both hands behind his back.

Apparently he was not about to confess that they'd met before. She certainly wouldn't either. In truth, Pip still couldn't decide whether she forgave him for tricking her so easily, making her such a prize fool, and leaving her wishing she was five feet eight inches with golden hair and a willow-wand waist. Something she had never before wanted or cared about— fortunately, considering her penchant for cake.

The air in the room felt oddly thick and hot. Aunt Du Bois was, strangely enough, still in her dressing robe and turban, an outfit she wore in the mornings before the proper number of coffee cups had been downed, the drapes opened and her mood readied to tackle the day's challenges. The fact that she had not bothered to change into anything more appropriate suggested that their aunt considered their visitor a "nobody", yet his purpose there must be fairly urgent for she had gathered her nieces together on the sofa and hadn't even waited for a maid to light the fire.

"What do we want with a lawyer?" Pip exclaimed, not moving another step, one hand still on the door handle. "Is this about that idiot Moffat again? What now, for pity's sake!"

"Your father has hired the firm of Stempenham

and Pitt to watch over you. This young man is—"

"*Watch over me*? I'm not a child."

"And I am not a nursemaid, Miss Piper," he said in a low, measured voice. "I have been tasked with advising you, while you remain in London. Your father seems to think certain issues might arise and that, if we were already hired to stand at your side, any difficulties, misinterpretations and misunderstandings might be avoided. In advance."

She laughed, finally closing the door and crossing to a chair by the window. "You mean you're supposed to stop me from burning my fingers on a hot frying pan? Because I am far too stupid to save myself."

He replied evenly, "I can't stop you from burning your fingers, Miss Piper, but I can stop it from costing your father his fortune."

"Well, you've been sent on a fool's errand. We don't need you. I can just stay indoors if I'm that much of a problem. Gladly."

"Epiphany!" her aunt exclaimed, "your father knows what he's about. I have no great fondness for lawyers myself, not since they took all my beloved Remy's possessions away after he died and I was sore bereft," hand to brow, "but I can see we must suffer this gentleman's advice, if it is what your father wants. A necessary evil, perhaps."

Since leaving the room in a temper would only make everybody's concern seem appropriate, Pip sat primly, chin lifted and hands in her lap. It took supreme effort, but she managed, with nothing more than a short, tense sigh.

The man by the fire watched her with eyes the color of very hot smoke. "Your father's wealth will no doubt make you all subject to some unwelcome attention here. His anxiety, therefore, is understandable. If you have any concerns or questions, ladies, I ask that you bring them to me. And that," he winced at Pip, as if she gave him a sudden bout of indigestion, "is all I ask. I have no intent to intrude. I shan't be an *obstruction*. Or prevent you from having any enjoyment in your life."

"I suppose our father has already paid you, so you're keen to look useful," she said. "Or as useful as a man can look."

"You won't even know I exist. Like any good servant."

But with his lack of humility he could hardly enter a room unnoticed and merge with the woodwork, she mused. "Well, if our father wants to waste his money, I can't stop him and neither will you, of course. Might as well get what you can out of us."

"Just doing my job, Miss Piper. No need to punch *me* in the eye." She was certain she saw his lips fight a sudden twitch of amusement— one that apparently took him by surprise and confusion, for he colored slightly and almost dropped the newspaper he held.

"People do love their gossip, on both sides of the Atlantic, it seems, Mr. Deverell."

He crossed the floor in a few long strides and placed in her lap the newspaper, neatly folded to show an artist's rendition of herself, in a ball gown, raising her fist to a terrified young gentleman as onlookers gasped in shock. The description beneath the sketch explained the titilating scene.

"*Miss E. Piper brandishes her mutinous fist before*

injuring Mr. Moffat the younger."

She was horrified. How quickly that story had followed them to England. Had it flown with pigeons?

"According to the article, young women in America are becoming more and more difficult to keep in their place. Something to do, perhaps, the author suggests, with a Women's Rights Convention held in Seneca Falls, New York, only a year before Miss E. Piper landed the infamous punch that knocked poor little Moffat off his feet." He paused, his lip quirked again before he was able to resume with a grave expression. "The author concludes that, hopefully, this feminine discontent will not find its way across the Atlantic, even though the pugnacious Miss Piper has."

All Pip could find to say was, "It doesn't look anything like me."

He tilted his head, examining the picture upside down. "They have made you considerably taller and heftier. Probably to make Moffat look more tragically pathetic, the hapless wounded party."

"He doesn't look anything like that either."

"It might be a challenge, Miss Piper, to capture the parties or the moment accurately, but it won't stop them speculating in ink."

"Well, it's not fair. They don't have my side of the story."

"Quite. So perhaps there is some purpose to my existence after all."

She thrust the paper back at him. "I'm sure I don't care what people say. Let them talk."

"Oh, they will, no doubt." Rather than take the

paper from her, he backed away. "We don't hear of many young ladies starting a fist fight in London ballrooms, but I understand they do things differently in America."

She said nothing, tightening her lips peevishly. Looking into his eyes had the same unsettling affect as before, and she ought to know better this time, so she carefully looked away.

"May I enquire," he said resignedly, "what brought about the swinging of your fist on that occasion? Merely for my own edification."

"If you must know, he called me a southern bumpkin swamp crawler. Not the worst thing I've ever been called, but I found his face particularly nauseating. It didn't help when he referred to my father as a jumped-up, opportunist half-breed, and suggested that my sisters and I would fare better at a quadroon ball, where we might find wealthy men to make us their concubines."

Ah. That shook his jaded expression.

Pip heard her sisters gasp and caught the demure semi-faint with which their aunt attempted to make everybody think she'd never heard such words and suggestions uttered in her presence.

But Deverell's gaze was fixed, slightly horrified, upon Pip.

"It's called placage," she continued, enjoying the mayhem as her aunt's second attempt, with wilder gesticulations, knocked over a potted plant. "Perhaps you are not familiar with it, Mr. Deverell. It is an arrangement without a binding legal marriage, but gives the man— her *protector*— all the rights of a husband."

He cleared his throat. "I believe I understand

how it works."

"So I took slight offense at the young man." Pip smoothed down her skirts and sighed. "Perhaps my physical reaction could have been more restrained. But we Pipers never do anything by halves."

Her aunt had picked up the toppled plant, but still held a torn leaf in her hand. "Will you stay for breakfast, Mr. Deverell?" she inquired hastily. "We were just about to—"

"No," came the curt response. "As I said, this was business. Not a social call." He gave a brief bow to the room in general and said, "I am at your service, ladies, unfortunately for us both. Good day." With that he swept out, closing the drawing room door just short of a slam.

"Well, I declare, that young man could make use of a few etiquette lessons," their aunt muttered, fanning herself with the ragged leaf. "Despite some severely bosom-palpitating good looks, he has a distinct lack of finesse."

To which Pip replied, "If you ask me, bosoms palpitate far too easily, and I'm sure Damon Deverell has made a fool of many young women who ought to know better." She glanced out of the window to see him leave the house with his commanding stride. "I don't suppose a man like that needs finesse and manners to get his wicked way with anybody."

Suddenly cognizant of the others looking at her curiously, not entirely sure of what she'd just said out loud, and needing something to do, she got up and tossed the newspaper into the fire, stabbing it afterward with the poker and considerable relish.

Chapter Seven

"Well, I must wonder at your father, hiring that *drigay*."

All three girls looked up as their aunt, still in her evening gown, came into Serenity's bedroom a few nights later.

"I just received a great deal of information about that young lawyer and his family of reprobates from my good friend Lucille Winstanley."

Pip, sprawled across her sister's bed with a history book, looked down at the page again, feigning complete disinterest.But she could not close her ears.

"His father opened a Gentlemen's gaming hall in Mayfair, some thirty years ago, and has made a fortune from it. But he's *divorced*! Lord knows how many children there are— from both sides of the blanket. He treated his wife terribly, ruined her reputation and then abandoned her. Nobody knows where he came from, but as a young man he was a rake of the highest order, and his sons, by all accounts, follow in his footsteps. As for the daughter, she is just as bad— seduced the Marquess of Redver's son, who also happened to be the fiancé of my friend Lucille's daughter Louisa. It was a terrible scandal, and poor Louisa never recovered from it. Then, after the Deverell girl had ruined that boy, she dropped him for another man! But not before involving him in the shooting of an aristocrat in the country."

"Sounds painful," Pip remarked drily. "There are few worse places to be shot at than in the country."

"Furthermore, the eldest *lejitimm* Deverell boy killed a woman. Murdered her some years ago.

Strangled her, beat her and left her for the wild animals to pick at. He escaped justice because his father paid off the magistrate, but everybody knows it to be true. The youngest boy was sent down from Cambridge for bare-knuckle brawling. That's the Deverells for you."

"Murder and bare-knuckle brawling?" Serenity exclaimed, setting her hairbrush aside and exhaling a self-satisfied snuffle. "Surely Pip would fit right in. I thought I sensed a spark when that lawyer came to visit. He did say he didn't think anybody could do her beauty justice in a sketch. It would be just like Miss Contrary, naturally, to take a fancy to a man like that."

"That is not what he said," Pip exclaimed. "It was a comment about the event itself being a challenge to draw accurately, not my appearance."

"I thought Mr. Deverell was delicious in a menacing, heart-stopping way," little Merrythought chimed in from her perch at the end of the bed. "He looked almost exactly how I imagined Sir Francis Varney in *Feast of Blood*."

Really, Pip mused, they ought to curb Merrythought's reading of lurid novels and penny dreadfuls. They were making her altogether too overheated and susceptible to darkly handsome rogues.

"Now, girls!" their aunt cried, clearly frustrated that nobody was taking her seriously. "You didn't come all this way to lower your standards and become embroiled in further notoriety. Your father entrusted me to keep you away from dangerous men and find the right sort of husbands for you here. That means ancient lineage, tradition, nobility and class. What you girls need is a touch of fine European noble blood.

You're here to undo damage," she shot a sideways glare at Pip, "not make it worse. My brother wants titled husbands for his daughters, something to show off back home, not some nothing you could get over there, some little upstart *batar* who works in a law office. And he is one— our friend Damon Deverell. A *batar* — a bantling boy, a packsaddle brat, a bastard. His mother," she added dramatically, as if all those words were not sufficient to make them understand, "was never married to his father."

Pip finally closed her book. "You may rest at ease, aunt. I believe we're safe from Damon Deverell's attentions. He didn't look any happier about being hired for us, than we are about having his services foisted upon us." She poked Merrythought with her toe. "And I would never let my dear little sister fall prey to the wicked transgressions of a filthy lawyer. I'd tie her up in the attic first."

"Nevertheless, they do say he's a merciless fellow and never loses a case, so it's just as well your father has procured his services to be on our side." Aunt Du Bois walked across the room with her quick step and proceeded to braid Serenity's hair, even though the girl had begun to do it for herself. Apparently she was not braiding it to the proper specifications. "But there is no need to mingle socially with that young man. He should be no more to any of us than a servant, as he said himself."

Pip chuckled. "I'm quite certain he was being sarcastic, aunt."

"But it's true. He's nothing to us but a hired man."

"And not a very polite one," Serenity added. "Distinctly common."

"He *was* considerably brusque and not at all friendly," Merrythought joined in eagerly. "Like that porter who dropped my trunk on his toe at Southampton. I wondered, in fact, if somebody had dropped something on Mr. Deverell's foot."

Pip was thinking again about the old story their father liked to tell, of a mysterious fellow called True Deverell, narrowly missing a bullet by leaping into the Mississippi and out-swimming alligators in the dark. A wolf in man's clothing. Listening to her aunt and sisters, she realized no one else had recalled the tale, or if they did, they had not yet made a connection to the name. Perhaps it was just as well. Master Grumbles did not have much good on his side as it was.

She sat up, hugging her knees, watching their aunt's quick fingers twisting through her sister's hair. "But if the senior Mr. Deverell is a successful man of business now, despite his humble beginnings, we have no right to look down upon him. Surely we must remember that our own father overcame similar struggles."

"Your father has always been a gentleman," her aunt replied sharply. "He abides by the law—"

"When it suits." As her father liked to say himself, nobody ever got rich without breaking a few rules.

"— and he attends church on Sundays. Furthermore, he does not throw his seed about indiscriminately and unapologetically, defiling more young maidens than he has hot dinners."

All three sisters smothered their chuckles at that last sentence, particularly at their aunt's accompanying gestures. One could take Queenie Du Bois out of

Hog's Flank, Louisiana, dress her up and give her airs and graces, but one could not quite take the Hog's Flank out of Queenie. Especially when there were no guests present to impress.

"But our father has never forgotten his impoverished beginnings," Pip insisted. "I doubt he would begrudge any other man their success in life."

"Perhaps not. My point is that he would *not* approve the sons of such a man as suitors for his own daughters. One can admire the beauty and skill of the fox without rewarding it by opening the henhouse door."

Yes, they all knew what their father wanted for them, of course. Prospero Piper had high hopes of finding titled sons-in-law of whom he could boast, adding legitimacy to his own social standing across the Atlantic. The idea of outdoing the likes of Mrs. H. Thaxton-Choate, stepping over her and flicking mud in her eye was, no doubt, where he came by his scheme.

"You'll see, Pip," he'd assured her, "What you need is a chance to shine where there's less competition. You'll be a novelty, a little fresh air in those stuffy English parlors."

He was right about his daughters being a "novelty" abroad, but that was not such a good thing as he'd anticipated.

In England, the ancient rule of primogeniture existed to keep fortunes in the hands of eldest sons only, preventing large estates being broken up piecemeal. The idea of daughters being their father's heirs and having equal shares in his fortune, therefore, was unheard of among the aristocracy here. As a result, wherever they went, the Piper girls were looked at with mistrust by the women, and lurid curiosity by the men. Aunt Du Bois used every artful wile to get them invitations into society, but they were not welcomed in a friendly way, and Pip could only imagine how everybody was impatient for them to leave so that they could become the topic of conversation.

"If you must enjoy a dalliance of that nature," said her aunt suddenly, breaking into her reverie, "you can wait until your duty's done."

"A dalliance?" Had she missed part of the conversation?

"Once you have a proper, suitable husband and have provided him with a son and heir, then you might, discretely, arrange such a man on the side. A *lagniappe*. There is always some benefit in a little something extra. Since a husband often takes a mistress, a wife may have a lover." She paused, touching the back of her own hair, pursing her lips at her reflection in the mirror above Serenity's head, "I can see the appeal of that young man, Deverell. He is not, by any means, a trial to look upon. Not at all. Yes, I can see how he might take the chill off the long, damp English winter nights."

Pip hid her smile behind her book and thought she ought to warn Damon Deverell against coming to their door again. He might find himself lassoed by their aunt's silk stockings, despite his utter unsuitability for *them*. So much for the demure swooning Queenie employed when she felt the need.

"At least you, *ma cher*," the lady continued, her hands resting now on Serenity's shoulders, "had success at the Courtenay's ball. I believe that Mortmain fellow is quite smitten with you."

The elder sister colored up and turned her gaze away from the mirror. "Perhaps."

"Mortmain?" Pip exclaimed. "The fellow that smells of fusty closet and camphor oil? Good lord, he almost put me to sleep on my feet. What a mumbler! I don't think I understood more than three words out of him all evening. The rest was merely noise, like the rumble of a distant train that never reaches the station, because it keeps running out of coal and steam."

"There's nothing wrong with a quiet-spoken gentleman," Aunt Du Bois replied swiftly. "The British are, on the whole, much more reserved. Mortmain may be a clumsy dancer and lack a few social skills, but I'm told he rarely ventures down to London — only occasionally to visit his great aunt— and prefers his home in Yorkshire, where he enjoys many outdoor pursuits. If Serenity has caught his eye and keeps it, she could do far worse. He is, after all, the son of a viscount."

Serenity smiled, attempting to look bashful, but succeeding only in resembling the cat that stole the cream.

"I felt sorry for him," Merrythought ventured tentatively. "He seemed so very shy and awkward. I just wanted to tell him it didn't matter if he got the steps wrong."

"You marry him, Serenity," their aunt continued excitedly, focused on her eldest, most beautiful niece, "and as soon as his father drops dead, you'll be a Viscountess. It's just what Prospero wants for you girls." She patted the girl's shoulder. "Imagine! The Viscountess Mortmain. And, as I said before, if you don't like the fellow so much, after the first son is born, you can make your own life too. That's how they do it here."

"So divorce is scandalous," Pip remarked coolly from the bed behind them, "while adultery is acceptable, even expected?"

"Divorce cannot be kept out of the public eye."

"I see. It's all about appearances, of course. Doesn't matter what goes on behind closed doors, or how unhappy she might be, a woman has no choice but to put up with it."

Her aunt waved a dismissive hand. "Marriage is protection. A *saj fem* learns how to cut a place for herself within those constraints. It can be a very comfortable arrangement."

Serenity barely blinked an eye at this conversation. Having always thought herself bound for some sort of greatness, it had never been more apparent than now that she was prepared to make any personal sacrifice to achieve that goal.

"He has to ask her first," Pip pointed out, bringing the other ladies sharply back to earth. "Since it takes him so long to get one clear word out, you might be in for a long wait."

Serenity got up and turned down the oil lamp. "At least *I* make the effort. I am grateful for the opportunities that arise, and I make the most of them. I don't sit about pouting or causing trouble so that angry young lawyers have to be hired, no doubt at great expense."

"I do not pout. Pouting is something I would never do. It suggests weakness of spirit and lack of spine." She said nothing about the angry young lawyer.

Once their aunt had gone out again, the girls

lingered in Serenity's room as they usually did to discuss the day's events and anything they wouldn't want their aunt to hear. Sometimes, if she was in a pleasant mood, the eldest sister would take this time to pass down petticoats, garters or chemises that had worn out their first flush of newness. But tonight Serenity was in no mood to be generous and, instead, looked for some way to jab back at her sister.

Tying a ribbon around the end of her long braid she said, "If that lawyer fellow— Deverell— didn't impress you, why defend his father's background? What does it matter to you what anybody says about that family? Unless, of course, you *have* taken a shine to him."

"I simply maintain that we should be honest, remember our own background and not look down our noses. Why disparage a man who has made his own success, much as our father did?"

"Because our father wants better for us. He wants to be sure folk never look down on us again. There will be no need for us to dwell upon hardships, or acknowledge certain branches in the family tree. Not once we write over our history with a new one."

"I suppose I will be one such unsightly branch swiftly pruned out of your history, as soon as you're a countess."

"*Vis*countess. And yes, of course, once I'm married, I shan't own to you being my sister, unless you learn to behave yourself in public and stop irritating everybody with your opinions. What do you expect?"

"Oh, sister!" Merrythought cried, "You won't really disown us, surely."

"Not you, dear. Just Pip, because she just can't

behave herself. She is an embarrassment."

Pip leapt off the bed and tossed a pillow at her sister. "Well, I could never marry a man if it meant disowning my family, forgetting my history or rewriting it. I don't pretend to be something I'm not. I never could."

"Which is why you will end your days a stubborn old maid, invited nowhere and liked by nobody because you're so disagreeable."

"It's called having principles, sister. I know what I am, and I won't change to suit anybody else. They can take me or leave me. It's their issue, not mine."

Merrythought yawned sleepily as she leaned by the door. "I bet, if you ever met a man and fell in love, you would change, Pip. Then you wouldn't be so annoyed all the time. Aunt Du Bois says you have too much frustrated energy. It's something to do with the moon and tides."

"And wandering wombs, no doubt." She chuckled.

"But you might fall in love one day," her little sister persisted. "It could happen to anyone. Even you. Aunt Du Bois says the stubborn ones always fall hardest in love."

"Love?" Serenity gave a little snort. "Nobody said love has anything to do with marriage. That's another misconception you both labor under. If Pip understood that, she wouldn't make a such a fuss out of finding a suitable husband."

Poor Merrythought was alarmed. "But if it's not about love, what is it about?"

"Survival," Serenity replied firmly, throwing the pillow onto her bed and thumping it hard. "This is a world that would just as soon trample women like us into the mud and leave us for dead, as it would lend us a hand to climb out of the mire."

"You make it sound like a battleground, sister. Like war."

"It is. The sooner you both realize that the better. Marriage is really no different to being fitted for a new winter coat to keep you warm when the frost sets in. Or finding a good, strong horse to get you across that muddy battlefield, to where the ground is firm and dry. To where the sun shines and things grow. Nothing can grow in mud."

"That's not true," Pip pointed out. "Things do grow in mud. There is a saying: the lotus flower blooms most beautifully from the deepest and thickest mud."

Serenity stuck out her tongue. "You always think you know better, don't you? Nobody can tell you anything. Now you're an expert gardener too."

"No. But I have some familiarity with mud."

"And it's time you stopped fighting in it with little boys who pull your hair. You're much too old and it long since ceased to be amusing. If you stopped rolling around in the mud like a piglet, we wouldn't have been sent here in the first place. This is your fault, remember? I didn't want to come here, but thanks to you and your temper I had no choice. Now at least I'm making the best of it and don't spend my time whining. Go to bed and leave me in peace."

So the other two went to their own rooms, but Pip sat up for a long time, mulling over Serenity's words.

Her sister, sadly, was right; this exile was *her* fault. This was a situation she had caused, and she had no right to complain now if they were to be watched over and guided by the stern hand of Master Grumbles, or if Serenity married the most awful dry stick on earth.

She couldn't stop her sister from making such a mistake, could she? Certainly Pip never welcomed interference in her own life, so it would be hypocritical to push her nose into that of her sister. Besides, they might be family, joined by blood— whether Serenity wanted to admit it or not— but all three Piper girls were very different in nature. They all wanted something different from life. Who was she to judge her sister's choices?

As she had reminded herself at the Courtenay's ball, she need only get through this, show herself to be improved, and then, thankfully, go home— once the dust had settled over that Moffat business.

Perhaps, she thought despondently, there would arise another opportunity to impress Bertie Boxall. If she pretended to make an effort, would it stop everybody poking and prodding at her? Her father had told her that she must learn to keep her thoughts and plans to herself, so it might be a good idea to brush up on her Latin and non-existent harp skills. Let everybody believe her chastened and reformed. Didn't have to marry him, did she? But if she gave the appearance of trying, nobody could say it was her fault then when she went home without a husband.

Alas, Pip could rouse little enthusiasm for the idea of being an "amiable mute" in the company of Lord Boxall. The extraordinary Master Grumbles lurked in her mind, his long-suffering face following her about, his big, muddy paws lumbering through doorways after her. Even though they were mutually decided that they would never get along, he still trailed behind her, never far from her thoughts.

Now it was his job to follow her.

And Pip, who generally had opinions about everything, had no idea how she felt about that.

Chapter Eight

"Do sit still, Pip! I can't get your nose at all if you keep fidgeting! Now your face looks like a sundial with too many shadows! The Dangerous Mr. Deverell was right when he said your beauty could not be captured."

"For pity's sake he said nothing of the sort. How many times must I hear this misrepresentation of what that damn lawyer had to say? It's not as if he said much at all, but for some reason you've all chosen that one sentence and utterly twisted it around."

"Don't say *damn*!" Serenity muttered, barely moving her own lips.

"Sometimes it's the only word that will suffice." She winced. "Oh, now I have an itch." One shoulder to the window frame, she rubbed herself up and down, while both sisters exclaimed in frustration at her inability to be still. "You cannot expect me not to itch," she complained. "It is inhumane. I have no command over my itching. Believe me, I wish I did."

"You probably caught fleas from that wretched mutt you were playing with in the street yesterday. I told you to leave it alone."

Pip was sorely tempted to reply that befriending a stray mutt with fleas was probably safer than encouraging the likes of painfully dull Edwyn Mortmain, but she bit her tongue. Part of her hoped that if she said nothing at all about that man, Serenity might eventually grow bored with him— as she once would of a toy in which Pip showed no interest.

Her father would be pleased, she mused, to see

how his troubling middle daughter finally learned how to hide her thoughts from the enemy. Well, most of the time.

"Pip has no more ability to sit still and be elegant, even for five minutes, than she does to hold her tongue for that long," exclaimed Serenity, who posed beside her on the window seat, fingers plucking at the frothy petals of a peony. "I declare a child of three is less of a fidget." This too, of course, was meant to goad her into an argument. On rainy days, when they were shut indoors with no visitors, the need to poke at each other was worse than ever.

But instead of rise to the bait, Pip carefully agreed with this assessment. "It is true I cannot sit with no occupation for this long. I cannot help but think there are so many other things I ought to be doing."

The rattle of rain against the window and the soft tick of the mantle clock only made it worse for her, a spiteful reminder of time passing and all the things she wanted to achieve with her life. After all, one never knew how much time one had. Their own mother had died young and although the Pipers were a healthy lot— even robustly so— they were prone to suffering tragic accidents. Perhaps due to that same restless, adventurous nature that would not let her sit still.

Family history warned her that there was no telling when one might be run over in the street by rampaging bulls, sucked into quicksand, drowned in a flood, struck by lightning, carried off by a tornado and never found again except for a shoe, be set light to by an errant spark, or blown up in the privy by an explosive combination of heat and gases.

Life was unpredictable and calamitous.

Yet here she was, obliged to be still and have her unsightly features set down for the future amusement of great nieces and nephews. All the excitement, it seemed, was happening to other people elsewhere.

But just as she lamented the tedium of her life in eternally damp exile, the drawing room door flew open and their aunt dashed in, flustered and flapping her silk clad arms as if they were wings.

"Lord Boxall has sent you a present, Epiphany, *ma cher!* Could it be his apology for missing the ball last Tuesday? There is hope for you then, after all!"

Pip took the package warily, opened it and read the note inside.

Despite the wisdom of your warning, madam, I fell.

At once she remembered her caution to Deverell: *May you not fall down any mine shafts as you stumble through life with those uncaring big feet.*

The replacement shawl was very beautiful, with embroidered peacock feathers against a stunning azure background. Miracle of miracles; the arrogant bastard did have a conscience after all. And some taste in shawls. For only the second time in her life— both because of him— she was rendered temporarily speechless.

"You must send a reply, Epiphany. The messenger boy is below, waiting to take your thanks to Lord Boxall. Now, let me see." Tapping a finger to her lips, Aunt Du Bois paced before the fire. "We must proceed with care. You should tell him that—"

"I know what to do," Pip exclaimed, feeling flushed herself, remembering again the soft brush of his breath against her cheek. He might as well have licked her face. "Contrary to popular belief I do have some experience in these matters. I am not completely feral. Excuse me!"

She left her aunt and sisters standing in some bewilderment, while she hurried down to the kitchen and found the messenger boy seated by the fire. At once he leapt to his feet and gave a quick little bow. "Is there a reply, madam?" he chirped.

"Yes, there is. Tell the man who sent you here that it is nobody's fault but his own if he falls and I am not the woman who will pick him up again. I am far too busy. I forgive him for the deceit last Tuesday— he is fortunate I have a dark sense of humor— but he needn't think I am in any way charmed. I'll leave that to the other ladies, of which, I am sure, there are plenty." She paused, smoothed a hand over her bodice, caught her breath, and added hastily, "And thank him for the gift. It is *quite lovely*, as you British say. My sister is exceedingly grateful. Can you remember all that or should I write it down?"

The boy grinned. "I'll remember. I'm good at memberin'."

She gave him a coin, and he tipped his cap and turned for the servant's entrance. Pip whistled. He stopped and looked back.

"And tell him...I still don't care for lawyers, whether he's on my side or not, and the next time I have cause to shoot at him it will be with more than my fingers." She took a freshly baked bun from the table and tossed it to the boy. "That's for coming out in the rain."

His grin even broader, the messenger boy caught it and ran off, yelling, "Thanks, missus."

There, she thought with a satisfied nod, fingers drumming against her waist, *that ought to be the end of it*.

Abruptly remembering her sister's warning about those tapping fingers, she stilled them at once.

Later that day, she handed the shawl to her little sister. "Here, Merry, you must have this. It is much too fine for me, and since I ruined yours so dreadfully..."

"Oh, but Lord Boxall meant it for you, sister!"

"Then if it is mine, I may do with it as I please, may I not? I insist you have it. Leave it in my hands any longer and who knows what fate shall befall it! Surely such a lovely garment deserves better." Somehow she didn't feel safe keeping it. If she wore it around her shoulders it would make her think of the Dangerous Mr. Damon Deverell even more than she did now. Merry was, of course, precluded from such inconvenient ponderings and fears, having no idea that the shawl didn't come from Lord Boxall at all.

Aunt Du Bois, meanwhile, had already taken matters into her own hands, not trusting her niece to send an appropriate reply, and had granted a dinner invitation to Boxall and his godmother. "We should seize this opportunity at once. His lordship must be interested in Epiphany after all."

"He hasn't met her yet," Serenity quipped.

The Boxalls came to dinner the following evening, and the sallow-faced young man was happy to take credit for the gift of a shawl. Only a brief glimmer of surprise showed through the inebriated, confused fog when Pip mentioned it. He seemed just as startled when he first set eyes on her— as if he'd expected something quite different. Definitely something worse. Possibly with scales, cloven hooves and a horn growing from her forehead.

"How clever of you to know the colors of that shawl would suit me so well, when we had never even met," she exclaimed, beaming so hard it hurt her face.

"Oh...I...have a talent for these things...picking out the perfect gift...whatnot."

"Such a shame you missed Lord Courtenay's ball."

He scowled. "Yes, it was rather. Ran into a friend outside who...told me how crowded it was. Put me off going in." Then he laughed abruptly, spilling wine from his glass. "I'll get vengeance on Deverell for that."

"Deverell?" she asked softly, as if it barely mattered and she was merely being polite.

"Oh, just an old university acquaintance. Not really my sort of people. You don't know him." Then he looked wary, sheepish. "Do you?"

"I don't believe so." She smiled. "Should I?"

He signaled sloppily for more wine. "I would advise you to steer clear of him. Fellow's an out and out cad, like the rest of 'em."

"The rest?"

"Deverells, of course. Villains, murderers, thieves, seducers. You must have heard the name."

"I believe my aunt mentioned something."

"Humph." He sniffed, watching as the butler refilled his glass. "I hope she gave you warning. Although, at least, you ought to be safe from Damon," he muttered. "He always preferred married women, and I doubt that's changed. Less chance of being trapped, he used to say." He made a dismissive gesture with his hand, loosely flapping it through the air. "There was a saying at Cambridge, that Damon

Deverell changes women whenever he needs a new shirt or hat, because they would always buy those things for him. Dressing him up as if he were a pet. Can't imagine what they see in the fellow and I doubt they could say either." He leaned closer to whisper in Pip's ear. "I once heard a woman— whom I later concluded to be severely addled— call him wickedly remorseless and utterly despicable, only days before I walked into his lodgings and found her in his bed."

She thought of the stunning blonde lady at the ball and how Deverell's attention had been seized the moment he saw her. How his expression hardened. A spark of recognition had passed between them, passionate and angry. Thus, for those few moments he had forgotten Pip entirely.

No surprise really.

He was rude and obnoxious, but she was still amused by him. Other women probably felt the same and some, no doubt, succumbed.

In truth she couldn't make Deverell out, no matter how much time she reluctantly spent thinking about him. She suspected that very few people would know him well, even if they thought they did. At the ball, he had cleverly let her believe what she wanted, and then observed with cool bemusement while she got herself tied up in knots over it. Perhaps he did the same to other people. That was what her father meant by keeping one's cards close to one's chest, of course. Damon Deverell had it down to a fine art.

The day after dinner with Lord Boxall another gift arrived for Pip.

This time it was a toy bow with a set of rubber tipped arrows,

For Miss Piper; to practice her aim, for the next time we meet.

"Well, that's an odd present to send to a lady with whom one has dined," her aunt exclaimed. "Still he is British. Perhaps it's some quaint custom. Ah yes, of course, cupid's arrow!"

Pip could only laugh. Clearly the bow and arrows were in response to her comment to the messenger about Deverell being shot at properly the next time she had cause. He dared suggest she needed better aim. Ha! Cocky bastard. Literally.

He was thick-skinned and hard-headed. Just like her. Just like Master Grumbles who had followed her about despite the great inconvenience.

Well, at least they had made a tentative peace of sorts. He had replaced the torn shawl for her sister, showing himself to be not entirely without remorse. And she had forgiven him for making a fool of her.

But they were, neither of them, at risk of a dangerous flirtation. Damon Deverell preferred married ladies and she was very far from the sort who would pine for him intolerably, buy him new shirts, be able to think of nothing else whether he was with her or not, and feel her heart plummet each time he looked admiringly at another woman. Pip had always pitied girls whose lives revolved around the ridiculous fairy-tale of romance. It was never going to happen to her, and she'd decided that years ago.

So she sent no message in response to the bow and arrows. Wouldn't want to encourage him. She did, however, amuse herself greatly by practicing in the small garden, using Merrythought's discarded sketches for targets.

And when Serenity complained primly one day that all the arrows went into her face, Pip insisted it was simply unavoidable.

"I can't help it if your forehead takes up the most space on the paper."

At which, Serenity replied, "To provide *you* with a weapon, Lord Boxall is either a fool, extremely cavalier with his own safety, or the bravest man alive."

Pip smiled at that, for Master Grumbles was clearly all three of those.

Chapter Nine

"Trust you to stumble over one of those Piper sisters," Ransom muttered. "I'd warn you to stay away, but I know exactly what good that will do."

"I'm not pursuing her," he assured his brother. "It's nothing like that."

"Hmm. What is it like then?"

"It's business, not pleasure. I'm supposed to advise the Miss Pipers on matters of the law and keep them out of harm's way while they're here."

"Aha! The fearsome name of Stempenham and Pitt on their side is meant to scare off any potential advantage takers too, no doubt."

"Something like that perhaps."

Ransom smirked. "I hear they're a fascinating lot. Curiosity has been known to undo a Deverell before. And we can't have you picking up bad habits from wayward colonials."

"That's sweet coming from a man whose bad habits are legendary."

"Of course, you do lead a life of strict piety these days, don't you?"

"Hardly piety, brother. I suffer my share of sins."

"But no female in your bed for three years? Can't be healthy."

"Since university I've been too busy."

"Don't work too hard." Ransom grinned slowly. "A man has to make room for a little fornication here and there." He paused, eyeing his brother curiously. "Father still reminding you of how William Pitt the Younger became Prime Minister at the age of only twenty-four, I suppose?" he teased.

"Hmm." And they both knew his father did not merely intend to give a history lesson.

Last Christmas, during Damon's short visit home to Cornwall, his father had said, "It's time you ran for a seat in the House of Commons."

But Damon didn't particularly care for politics. He saw the corruption, the jobbery and bribery, and he did not want to be a part of it. Sadly, his father had always kept these plans for him and when his father had plans they were never easily tossed aside or changed.

So he had simply nodded and agreed that he would give it "serious consideration" that coming year.

"Mind yourself and keep your hands clean," his father had advised. As if that was how most politicians succeeded. A laughable concept. "This is the time for men like you, son. This country has been ruled by the propertied nobs for too long. There is social mobility now. Revolution will come about in England not through war, but through laws and government. The working classes are finally getting a voice. Can you not feel the bite of change in the air? Of rebellion?"

"Yes, sir," he'd replied.

His father had looked taken aback. "Yes, sir? That's all you have to say? No argument today?"

All he could say to that was, "It's Christmas."

It was true that of all the Deverell boys, Damon was the one who dared quarrel, face to face and out loud, with their father. On the other hand, Ransom, the son most often in trouble, merely stopped talking to his father when he was angry and then the two men communicated by throwing things. Damon was the son who argued with words.

On that occasion, last Christmas, he had looked at the few silver threads running through the black hair at his father's temple, watched him holding his newest child with a smile the size of an ocean on his face, and decided to let him have the "Yes, sir".

He'd always known it was his job to make their father proud. All hopes rested on him. It was too late to go back now and say he didn't want that burden. He was certainly too proud to say he couldn't manage it.

But a quiet discontent had brewed inside him for some time. He needed a little rebellion of his own, and shortly after that Christmas he'd met Lady Elizabeth Stanbury. Immediately he'd decided to end his fast. So much for keeping his hands clean.

Until recently, Elizabeth had led him on a spirited chase, but Damon, with single-minded purpose, had won his way into her bed. Of course, Deverells always got what they wanted— as the saying went. And although she still pretended he was too lowly for her, still liked to act as if he had seduced her and she could do nothing about it, when he saw her at the Courtenay's town house, he had recognized that look in her eye— the sharp spear of jealousy as she saw him in lively debate with the American. It had certainly made his mistress particularly lusty in bed the following evening.

So, unbeknownst to his elder brother, Damon had as much "fornication" in his life as he wanted— in fact it was getting more savage and demanding by the day— and he could have no interest in Miss Piper.

A troubled, argumentative, young woman, put

out into the marriage mart by her relatives— whether she liked it or not— was the very last thing he needed in his life. Lady Elizabeth Stanbury, on the other hand, was safely married, in need of entertainment, and not in the least desirous of a romantic suitor. That was the beauty of older women: they didn't waste time, but knew what they wanted, appreciated what he gave them, and didn't get all mopey-eyed if he forgot their birthday or some other anniversary, such as the day they first met. They didn't want protestations of undying love. Married women wanted the same thing he wanted and nothing more. Besides, he had worked for so many weeks to make Lady Elizabeth succumb, he ought to be content now. Other men would certainly envy him, as he told himself every time she did something that made him grind his teeth.

Miss Piper, as he'd said to his brother, was merely business, not pleasure.

But Ransom was in a teasing mood. "Father would say she's bound to become a distraction, and you know he has big plans for you. Can't let anything get in the way of his ambitions for the golden boy."

"Very amusing."

"He wants to keep you out of trouble, away from scandal. I don't want him coming up here and cursing at me for encouraging you in some ill-advised romance with a flighty American, who is, it might be said, *a fugitive from justice*." He grinned. "Sounds like a tragedy poised to happen and I get the blame for everything as it is. Perhaps I ought to confer with father, before I help you with this wayward American woman."

Damon knew his brother enjoyed wielding this

sort of pompous, older brother authority over him. Eventually, like anything with which Ransom tried to amuse himself, it wore itself out; one merely had to be patient. So he replied steadily. "I told you, it's simply business. I've been hired to do a job and that's all. I need some information, and I know you can get it for me."

As the manager of Deverell's Gentlemen's club, Ransom knew everything that went on in that town. It was this ability to collect other people's secrets, particularly those of a darker nature, that made him an extremely useful ally — or the worst of enemies, depending upon your point of view.

"You want me to find out who took the gossip about your American hussy to the newspaper."

"There has to be somebody with an axe to grind."

"And this is...business?"

Damon reached over his brother's desk to straighten a glass paperweight and a pile of papers that had bothered him since he entered the room. "Absolutely."

"Why go to all this trouble?" Ransom grumbled, clearly suffering that day from a lack of sleep and an excess of drink the night before. "It's just a story in the newspaper. The devil knows there's been worse printed about us. A damn sight worse."

"That doesn't mean it's right. Sooner or later somebody has to stand up and put a stop to it."

"Father would say, why bother? He never explains or feels the need to defend himself."

"Well, that's our father." And sometimes Damon thought it might have been nice if their father did stand up and defend himself. Supposedly he was writing his memoirs to explain a lot of things, but since nobody had seen them yet their existence was in dispute. "Miss Piper's father feels differently, it seems. He's hired Stempenham and Pitt to put right any misunderstandings. So that's what I mean to do."

Ransom glowered at him darkly. "Yes. You always were one for lining up the edges, straightening things, putting them in neat order. Even as a child. Used to bloody annoy the hell out of me. Like sharing a bedchamber with a damnable monk."

When Damon's mother had died, True Deverell took him and his elder, full-blood brother Justify, to live with the rest of the family at Roscarrock Castle, on a small rocky island off the Cornish coast. From then on, all True's children lived, played and fought under the same roof, until they were sent away to various boarding schools, or, in the case of the daughter, sent off to spend time with her mother. At Roscarrock, a Camelot-like castle sometimes shrouded in a magical fog that might have been summoned by Merlin himself, they had a mostly happy existence with very little discipline— at least, none that was obvious to the outsider. But somehow their father kept them in a line, albeit one that was loosely configured, the boundaries reliant on his mood that day. He usually gave them their head, until, for whatever reason, he suddenly remembered that they were his responsibility and felt the need to rein them in. Since the reining in was neither pleasant, and as unpredictable as an English summer, the boys soon learned to keep their worst behavior out of his sight. Just in case.

Three of the boys— Ransom, Justify and Damon— had shared a bedchamber. While Justify and Damon, accustomed to life in a small cottage with their mother, kept their side of the room shipshape, Ransom's side was a tumble of confused mess: broken cricket bats, discarded riding boots, sticky jam pots stolen from the kitchen, stained shirts and pages torn from books, scribbled on with dirty words and naughty sketches just to shock one of his many unfortunate nannies. A thousand times he was told to make his side of the room neat, and a thousand times he left it just as it was, sometimes adding to the wreckage, pounding through it in a new pair of boots, breaking and crushing whatever he stepped on in his temper. It was clear to the perceptive, watchful Damon that Ransom merely bided his time until he was of age to leave the house and live where he chose. He blamed the divorce entirely on their father and was the only defender of his mother, Lady Charlotte. Yet, underneath all the shouting, Ransom still yearned for his father's attention and approval.

All True's sons fought for his notice in their own way, and every Deverell "cub" had a raw confidence, the ability to ignore the outraged slights of society with as much aplomb as they broke its rules in the first place— a talent they had learned, or inherited, from their notorious father. But although his brothers careened through life like a handful of scattered jacks, never knowing or much caring where they might land, Damon had one thing they lacked— an instinctive caution.

Six years younger than Ransom, as a child Damon had looked up to the other boy, thought him daring and bold, wished he could be more like that himself and less anxious about life, less of a worrier in general. In fact, he had occasionally pushed himself into perilous situations in some attempt to earn his brother's respect, terrified out of his wits but always determined. No doubt the admiration he felt for Ransom was only deepened by the fact that his elder half-brother thought *him* an annoying gnat to be swatted away impatiently. Eventually Damon had given up and given in to his guarded side, abandoning those ill-fated attempts to be as reckless as Ransom, and instead being content to please their father.

At last, now they were older, the brothers had formed a tentative alliance of mutual tolerance for each other's differences and reluctant recognition for their similarities. It was an attachment still growing, slowly and guardedly. Damon had high hopes of one day receiving a hug from his brother instead of a hand shake. Small steps. Not that he would know quite what to do with such a gesture, if he ever received it. Like that hand pat from Lady Roper, it would utterly upset the routine of his day.

Still it wouldn't be unwelcome.

Looking at his ill-tempered brother today, Damon felt as if he had worked harder for this man's friendship and acceptance, than he had for admittance to Lady Elizabeth Stanbury's bed.

"Will you help me or not?"

Ransom sighed and rolled his eyes to the plaster cupids that grinned stupidly down from the ceiling. "I just don't know whether I should. What do I get in return?"

"Remember all those times you sent me off on missions for you when we were young?" Damon persevered. "When we played the Knights of Camelot. Of course, I wasn't always allowed to participate, but once in a great while you humored me— when you had use for a small, *thwarted stump* of a boy who would do anything to be included. And I was just foolish enough to oblige. Surely you owe me one favor." At least one.

But Ransom could be aggressively unhelpful when suffering one of these bleak moods.

"Christ, haven't thought of that in years." Head pressed back against his chair, Ransom studied his brother again for a long moment. "Being father's favorite, you always got away with things. You were always forgiven. So, yes, that made you a useful brat from time to time." He leaned forward again to clip the end of a cigar and light it, using a candle from his desk. "Now you're the dull lawyer who spends all his evenings bent over papers, working late and wasting candles. No more reckless games for you, eh? No more angry schoolmasters' broken curricles, or even angrier schoolmaster's seduced wives. That's all forgotten for you. These days you might as well live in a bloody cloister. Father really believes you're the angel of the bunch, his ace in the pack, now that you've reformed your naughty schoolboy ways. But then, sometimes a man sees only what he wants to see."

Of course, his brother knew nothing about Lady Elizabeth Stanbury. Or did he? Sometimes one should not ask "how" when it came to information Ransom procured, for the only thing at doubt was the "when".

Damon said carefully, "I simply decided there are enough madmen in the asylum known as our family. Somebody has to keep the lamps and fires lit without burning the place down."

There was silence again while his brother leaned back, eyes closed. Damon thought he'd fallen asleep there and then, until those dark, haunted and weary eyes opened again, just halfway.

"And there's something else you need from me," Ransom muttered. "I can feel it as you hover before me like the grim bloody reaper. What is it? What else do you expect me to do for you?"

"That woman you were seeing recently, the one who writes for the ladies' magazine. Is she still enamored of you, or did she come to her senses yet and kick you out of her boudoir?"

"Dottie?" Ransom grinned. "She remains very much enamored. Why?"

Watching the glowing tip of his brother's cigar, Damon moved a crystal ashtray closer to where the ash was likely to fall. "Perhaps you might put an idea into her head about a piece on the American visitors. Something light and sweet. Something that shows them for what they really are— three young ladies, far from home, experiencing a different world. Surely that would be an interesting story. Cheerful, colorful."

"I don't know why you're bothering," his brother said again, yawning widely, stretching both arms over his head, careless about the ash from his cigar. "Calling in all your favors from me, seems like a lot of trouble for one little wench."

I don't know why you're bothering, was something Ransom often said, while plowing through his life in the same way as he once stomped carelessly through the wreckage of his bedchamber, airily "not bothered" by the destruction. Probably waiting for somebody to dare tell him he was being an ass, so that he could laugh in their face and show how "not bothered" he was by that too.

"Will you assist me in this endeavor or not?" Damon rubbed his forehead to relieve the frown he felt pressing on it.

Abruptly Ransom laughed. "Come on, little brother. I know there is a woman somewhere, isn't there? Not the American perhaps, but somebody. It's not possible for you to be celibate for so long, I'm sure. For some reason you're keeping her a deadly secret, that even my sources struggle to uncover, so I can only conclude she's married and has great cause to stay that way. Not still that Latin tutor, surely. Tell me and then I'll do what you want."

"If you're going to question me about my affairs, perhaps I ought to ask you about yours. I know Dottie isn't the only one at the present time. What about the French tart from the music hall stage? Belle something? Of course, there are many more. I don't suppose you can tell them apart or remember all their names. Why bother to learn them, when they'll be in and out within a few weeks at most? Or, perhaps I should say, you will be."

"No need to get yourself into an apoplexy, dear boy. It is my duty, as the eldest, to look out for you in matters of the heart."

"Don't do as I do, do as I say, eh? Just like father. I don't see how I can be expected to win a seat in the House of Commons when I have the rest of you dragging the family from one scandal to another." By then he had raised his voice to a roar without even meaning to do it. Nobody ever pricked a temper out of him the way Ransom could. "Why is it all on *my* back?"

"Tsk, tsk, I see the vein bulging in the side of

your neck. Calm yourself before it ruptures."

Damon swung around and strode for the door, but his brother's voice stopped him.

"Alright! Alright! Don't go off in a huff, little brother. Keep your lover a secret if that makes you happy. I will check my sources for you and find out what I can about the naughty Miss Piper and her enemies on this side of the Atlantic. And I will put the thought of a story in dear Dottie's ear." Ransom chuckled low, flicking his ash into the proper receptacle at last, much to Damon's relief. "I wouldn't want you to say I never do anything to help. Just don't blame me when it all goes awry and Miss Piper leaves you with a black eye too."

He replied through gritted teeth. "How kind of you to help."

"As I said before, I could advise you on the art of juggling females, but you think you know better. So have at it. Just make sure to tell father I tried to talk you out of it. I'm sure I'll take the brunt of his wrath anyway." Ransom's eyes turned even darker as he drew on his cigar and blew out a ghostly cloud of grey. "By the way," he added suddenly, as if he'd just remembered, "I can tell you that Miss Piper is just twenty-one, likes to take long, improper walks all on her own and has a sweet-tooth." He winked. "Their cook likes to tell stories to the chimney sweep who flirts with one of my maids. Anything else you want to know about her, just ask, little brother." He laughed. "Did you think you were the only red-blooded male who might be interested in a little novelty piece?"

Damon felt his blood cool. It wouldn't be the first time his brother looked to steal a woman from under his nose. But then he shook the thought off. This was merely business, not pleasure. His brother would not goad him into acting as if it was anything more. So he smiled. "I hope you're ready to duck a few punches. I'd start getting more sleep, if I were you."

Chapter Ten

Lady Roper sent him a message, thanking him for intervening in her husband's "ill-wrought" lawsuit, and inviting him to tea. Damon, never comfortable with displays of gratitude, which seemed to him a waste of everybody's time— of course they were thankful to be got out of a sticky situation and he was only doing his job— so he would usually decline. But this time he accepted. Why not? The old lady was plainly left alone a great deal by her husband and needed company. Why should he not spare a quarter of an hour?

"Whispers in certain neighborhoods, Master Deverell, inform me that you are a young man who can get things done," the lady said to him as she poured the tea that day. "And now I see it is true for the bold way you dealt with his lordship. He does not generally listen to anybody, and I had begun to wonder if an excess of wax should be syringed from his ears. It would have to be done while he was knocked unconscious, of course." She looked away from him with what was almost a dreamy expression— and just a hint of gleeful malice.

Damon set his hat on the seat beside him. "I was merely doing my job, Lady Roper."

Her eyes refocused on him. "But that's just it. You weren't doing the job, were you? You were talking yourself out of one. And you did so as a kindness. To me."

He shrugged uneasily. "As you said to me before, Lady Roper, we all do the best we can with the cards we are dealt. I am no saint, but if I see a cruelty or an injustice I try to right it."

"Yes, indeed." With an unsteady hand she passed him a cup and saucer, the china rattling together and making his teeth hurt. "I am flattered you remember anything I said, but then, I suppose, as a lawyer you have need of a very good memory." She beamed. "And a very determined spirit."

"I suppose so."

"We have great need for young men like you in this world, Master Deverell."

He winced and sipped his tea. "Do you?"

"There is, I think," she tilted her head, eyes twinkling, "a little naughty charm in you. An allure that could take you far. Although you try to keep it well hidden, young sir, behind a gruff exterior. I suppose you don't know yet how to use that gift properly. Fortunately for the ladies!"

"*Charm*?" His teacup rattled even more precariously.

"Oh, I do not mean the pretty charm of a music box waltz, or a country field of buttercups. I mean the charm of dark and sinister magic. A natural, primordial ability to captivate and then persuade. A great power and dangerous in the wrong hands." She slid a large slice of cake onto his plate. "Of course, if used for good, it could have enormous benefit to those less fortunate."

He squinted. "Could it?"

"And since you are here, I wondered if I might impose upon you..."

Thus it began. Lady Roper, he soon discovered, was not nearly as faded and frail as appearances suggested. In fact, she had a very strong mind and an equally strong hand, steering him skillfully into helping her causes. Of which there were many.

His simple acceptance of tea in her parlor was the first step to becoming involved in her quiet efforts to clean up the filthy streets of London, provide better services to the poor and improve access to medicine and education. Once she had him trapped on her sofa, tea cup in one hand and sponge cake in the other, she spoke quickly and firmly of all the things he could do to assist her. Damon saw her eyes darting constantly to the clock and guessed she tried to fit it all in before her husband returned and she must resume her usual act of the fragile, empty-minded old lady.

He felt powerless to resist and actually wondered whether she'd put something stronger in his tea.

"The moment we met," she told him, "I recognized that persuasive, merciless charisma. Some men have to try too hard, they have to be forceful and raise their voice and shake their fist." She shuddered. "They perspire and get very red in the face. Most unbecoming. But you do none of that. Getting what you want comes quite naturally to you. Makes you a very useful person to have on one's side."

The duration of his visit expanded from an anticipated quarter of an hour, to two full hours. And Damon began to realize that she had, from that first pat upon his hand, deliberately drawn him into a web of sorts. Because of that gesture he had undone her husband's lawsuit on her behalf, and now he was further under her thrall.

"Madam," he replied sternly, "I believe *you* can give lessons on ruthless charm."

Before he left Lady Roper's parlor that first day, he had promised to help her with her missions in the poor communities of London. But Damon had secured a few small favors from her in return.

* * * *

Social invitations soon began arriving at the rented house in Belgravia. A few elderly, very well respected ladies came calling, and then the little silver dish in the hall, usually empty, was suddenly filled with cards left behind.

The editor of a popular ladies' magazine wanted to publish a story about the Miss Pipers, highlighting their youthful delight in the fashions of London, their eagerness to enjoy the Season and, in fact, revealing how they were not so very different to other young ladies of the age."I don't understand the sudden interest," their aunt exclaimed, "but we mustn't look this gift horse in the mouth. However it came about, we'll seize our opportunities!"

The weather improved. At the house, velvet winter drapes were taken down and replaced with summer linen, and paper fans filled the cold fireplaces with color. Rugs were taken out for a beating and moved around when they were put back, so that sunlight would fade the pattern evenly over time. A symphony of birdsong greeted the opening of windows every morning and the clouds no longer seemed so oppressive, even on days when the sun still struggled to shine through.

Pip was glad to get out more often for walks in the fresh air, although the unpredictability of a sudden British "drizzle" still caught her out frequently.

In general, life was less grim. She might even have begun to like her temporary home a little.

* * * *

He saw Miss Piper across the street one day as he was on his way into the offices of Stempenham and Pitt. She was with her aunt and sisters, who all carried hat boxes. Nonesuch trailed behind the others, empty handed until she stopped to purchase a newspaper from a boy by the park railings. Her aunt looked over one shoulder and shouted at her not to dally, but she still paused to share a word with the boy, before she tucked the newspaper under one arm and walked on. Apparently she liked to keep abreast of current affairs and didn't care about print getting on her clothes.

Whether she saw Damon or not, he couldn't tell.

Every day, after that, he saw her stop and get the newspaper from that same boy across the street from his office. Most of the time she was alone, which, in itself was unusual for a young, unmarried woman, and caused several disapproving glances from folk she passed on the pavement. But she didn't seem to care. Of course, she could defend herself if need be with that efficient right hook, he thought with a wry smirk.

Damon made certain to be early at his desk each morning so he wouldn't miss this sighting of Nonesuch. It became a new part of his routine, along with freshly baked muffins provided by Lady Roper, who had taken to sending him a basket for his breakfast, apparently intent on feeding him up as if for a harvest sacrifice. What was it about him, he wondered vaguely, that made women want to give him food— particularly cake? Did they think he needed sweetening up? Whatever the lady's reason, and he had no doubt there was some ulterior motive, Damon enjoyed the muffins as he drank his morning coffee and watched the street come to life outside his window.

He could not be fully content, however, until he'd seen Miss Piper appear around the corner to fetch her newspaper. Then he knew all was well with the world and everything in its place.

It was a puzzle as to why she walked so far from Belgravia to get the newspaper every morning, when there were surely many other boys on her route from whom she might have made her purchase. She must like the boy by the park. Or perhaps she enjoyed the exercise and the fresh air.

And why the devil was he trying to make sense of anything she did? As long as she had no violent encounters in the street and didn't try to pick anybody's pocket, it was none of his concern.

One morning, as she strode around the corner in a jaunty yellow ensemble, the previously innocent looking clouds overhead suddenly cracked apart to douse the street in a hearty spring rain shower.

Nonesuch was unprepared and, within seconds, soaked to her skin.

Damon knew he could have sat there and pretended not to see, but watching her try to find shelter under a wet, crumpled newspaper was too much. He could do nothing else, but put down his pen, run outside and bring her into the building.

The clerk looked over his spectacles as Damon led her through the front door.

"Rainin' out, I see," the fellow remarked drily.

Once inside his own office, Damon shut the door and set his desk chair— the only seat in the room— by the fire for her.

"Miss Piper, don't you possess an umbrella?" He looked, in some distress, at the rainwater pooling around her feet and onto his well-swept, wooden floor boards.

"I do, but when I set out this morning the sun was shining."

He shook his head. "One must always be prepared for the weather here."

"Thank you for that. It is something that would not have occurred to me, as I stood in the street steadily being drowned." But she looked around his office with eager eyes and, having removed her wet bonnet, seemed to forget the rain and her dampness immediately. Rather than sit, she took a quick tour of the room. "This is a very small office."

"I prefer to call it," he looked her up and down, "bijou."

"I thought you were more important than this."

"No. I am quite unimportant. As you see." Truth was he didn't want a bigger office. He liked this one, tucked out of the way, contained and tidy. It always took people by surprise, and he liked to do that, catch them when they were startled. Because it was such a small space, clients often marched in with a long stride, expecting this to be merely an antechamber and looking for a door into a larger room beyond. When the one and only door was soundly shut behind them and they found themselves sequestered in that small, tight square— a space in which there was no hiding— they immediately forgot all the lies they had composed to tell him. But to her, all he said was, "They mostly keep me busy here with the cases nobody else cares to handle."

"Like keeping me out of trouble?"

"Precisely."

Her gaze had drifted over the basket of muffins from Lady Roper. "I suppose... you are young still," she said, "and everybody must start somewhere, even with the most unpleasant of tasks."

"Indeed."

"But take heart, one day you might have an office with more than one sorry candle and a desk in it. You might even have carpet and a stuffed animal head of some description on the wall."

"A man must have something at which to aspire."

Once again she looked at the muffins and then away to survey the view through his window. "I thought I saw you coming in here last week, but I didn't know for sure if it was you. Of course, from across a street all men look the same and there is nothing particularly special about you."

"Miss Piper, you really shouldn't be walking about in London unescorted. But I'm certain you know that. You're simply remarkably obstinate and resistant to rule."

"I prefer to call it," she spun around to give him a brisk up and down assessment of her own, "self-sufficient."

He sighed and gestured to the chair. "You may as well sit. The rain could last a while." He didn't like her wandering about, moving things, dripping all over the place.

"Am I not in your way?"

Yes. Exceedingly. "I invited you in, didn't I?"

"I suppose you wanted to amuse yourself by making sport of me again."

"Miss Piper," he assured her somberly, "this is a place of business, not sport. Please do sit." The room was too small for two people to walk around comfortably, while avoiding contact with each other *and* the chair. And neither of them seemed very good at standing still.

But she ignored his request. Instead, sweeping restlessly around the room again, she said suddenly, "Why did you pretend that shawl was from Lord Boxall?"

"How else might I have got it into your hands? I sincerely doubt your aunt would approve a gift from me."

"How do you know that?" Her eyes narrowed.

"I'm a Deverell. I know of few guardians who would welcome such a suitor for their maiden charge."

"But you're not a suitor."

"A gift would make me one in the eyes of this society. A proper young lady should never accept a gift from a man unless he is an acknowledged, approved suitor." He paused. "And I know that Prospero Piper wants titles and land for his daughters."

"You're very well informed."

He gave a little smile. "I have to be."

She walked by the window, her fingertips trailing along the ledge. "What else do you know about us then?"

Rather than answer that, he picked up Lady Roper's basket and held it out to her. "Would you care for a muffin, Miss Piper?"

"Well, I—" She clasped her hands together. "I shouldn't really."

"They're very good. Freshly baked. Still warm."

Naturally, she could not resist. He had barely got the word "warm" out and she was advancing with an eager gleam in her eyes. Finally she sat, but he was still not safe from her inquisitive nature. Spying the one and only ornament in the room, she pointed to it with her muffin. "Who's that? Your sweetheart?"

He looked over at the little oval silhouette above the mantle. "That's my mother... Emma Gibson."

"It's a very pretty profile." She eyed him thoughtfully. "She must be very proud of you."

His reply was a curt, "She's dead."

She licked her lips. "Oh...I'm sorry."

"I was two and have no memory of her. Just the silhouette." He'd often thought that must be why he took such effort now to remember everything and file it away in his mind. Every detail. He didn't want to lose anything like that again.

After a short pause she said, "My mother died also, just a year after Merrythought was born. I was four. Serenity likes to say it's a good thing our mother passed away when she did, so she didn't have to see how badly I turned out."

She had said nothing about his mother not having the last name of Deverell. It was breezed over with the same apparent ease with which she shrugged off her sister's callous remark. Now she ate her muffin and continued to admire the little silhouette until the unpredictable rain halted. Then she retied her bonnet ribbons, thanked him for the shelter, and was on her way again.

Standing in the door of his office, basket in one hand, Damon watched her leave and felt again that deflated sensation. As if he was a toy she'd picked up to play with briefly, before dropping him again.

"Who's that then?" the clerk wanted to know.

"A very difficult client."

"Oh, aye? What's she done then?"

"I'm not entirely sure," he muttered.

"Guilty or innocent?"

"Unabashedly guilty I would say."

"But you don't know her crime?"

Damon thought about it for a moment. "I have a feeling it's a crime as yet unknown to me. I... have no name for it." When he glanced over at the clerk, he caught the other man quickly looking down at his desk, his shoulders trembling slightly. "Something amuses you, Tom?"

"Naught amuses me," the clerk exclaimed, as if the very notion of it were scandalous.

"Good," he snapped, straightening his neck cloth with a sharp jerk of the hand. "See to it that nothing does. This is an office of work, not frivolity."

* * * *

The next morning he paid the newsboy to slip a note inside the paper for her. It took him almost a full hour to decide what it should say. Another unusual occurrence and an utter waste of his time, probably.

I have a surfeit of muffins again, should you care to partake.

There could be no harm in asking, he reasoned. Muffins were hardly the first step to a passionate affair. But he waited on tenterhooks that morning until he saw her, cheerfully marching along the street to get her paper.

She stopped, as usual, to chat with the boy by the railings. Early sunlight kissed her bonnet tenderly as she bent her head and opened her reticule.

Damon quickly looked down and rearranged his

pens.

Muffins. What a stupid, blithering idea that was! He felt his face grow warm. Damn it! He'd dropped a pen to the floor.

By the time he was upright again, rubbing a banged head and opening his eyes, she was crossing the street and on her way toward him, whistling a blithely merry tune, much to the evident outrage of anybody she passed.

A quick check of his office assured him of everything being tidy and in its place. But he leapt up to give his mother's silhouette a hasty polish on his shirt sleeve before slipping it back on its nail above the mantle.

* * * *

"I hear you have muffins."

What else was there to say? It seemed foolish to waste time on chit chat and niceties. He wasn't the sort with whom one shared thoughts on the weather.

He was rubbing the back of his head. Showing off that lovely head of hair again, she thought. "Yes. I am in possession of muffins again," he muttered hoarsely. "Do come in."

Nobody else had yet entered the offices of Stempenham and Pitt. Not even the clerk was at his little crooked desk yet in the front room. The shelves and desks, overflowing with scrolls of paper and thick, dusty books, sat poised in wait for their day to begin, while soft sunlight reached tentatively, shyly through the windows.

Deverell led her into his office again, grabbed a grey cutaway from the back of his chair and hastily shrugged those broad shoulders into it.

"Forgive the mess," he said.

His was the tidiest office she'd ever seen. Inside her father's one could hardly put one foot before the other without tripping over a pile of paper. But she replied, "I shall try."

Today, he had a pot of coffee on an iron trivet, warming by the fire. From this he poured them both a cup and she was somewhat amused, having never been served coffee by anybody but a footman before.

"Do you bake your own muffins?" she asked mischievously.

"No. A lady friend provides them."

"Oh." That took some of the pleasure out of it.

Until he added, "An *old* lady friend. Not intimate."

"Well, I'm sure there's no need to explain to me."

He gave her a dark look. "Isn't there?"

Pip shrugged. "You can have all the lady friends you like. I'm only here for the muffins."

"Are you?"

"Your note said you had a surfeit, and I wouldn't want you to have to eat them all. It's the least I could do to relieve you of a few. Besides, I know how you've been helping us, so I ought to be cordial and polite." She paused, eyed him dubiously, and then added, "This is nothing romantic. It's only cake."

He pushed the basket of muffins into her hands in such a surly fashion that she thought she'd said something to offend him. "Why don't you sit down?" he grumbled.

"There's only one chair," she pointed out.

"How many do you need?"

So, despite the ungraciousness of the offer, she perched on the hard chair behind his desk, while he paced before the little window, periodically glancing out of it in a furtive manner.

"I suppose," she ventured, "if people see us alone together like this they might talk."

He stopped pacing and put both hands behind his back. "Your father is a client. You've a right to be here. Nothing odd about it. Not that anybody would dare push their nose into my business. Eat, Miss Piper."

After a while, she said, "Is this where you question witnesses? Would you badger and bully me into a state of confusion and wild contradiction, until I confessed to all my evil deeds?"

He stared hard at her.

"My aunt says Deverells are extremely wicked and that, being a lawyer, you would only do nice things for people if they paid you."

"I cannot argue with that assessment."

"You don't defend yourself?"

"Why would I? I am the very worst of men. Your aunt is right."

She watched him for a moment, while he resumed his back and forth patrol at the window. "Grinding one's teeth is a terrible habit," she warned. "I knew a man once who—"

"Eat your muffin, Miss Piper."

"Shouldn't we have some conversation to pass the time?" she asked politely.

He shot her a scowl. "What about?"

"Well, let me see...books?"

"I read for work, not for pleasure."

"Theatre?"

"I don't have the time to waste."

"Music?"

"Lot of racket mostly."

Pip laughed. Enjoying her muffin, she studied the dark walls of his office again, as she did the day before. She found it fascinating. All those neat stacks of paper, locked boxes guarding dark secrets, and the scratches and marks on the old paneling. No decoration except for the small silhouette of his mother. Nothing else to soften the fact that this is where truth was weighed and fates held in the balance before they went before the magistrate. "It's not a very cheerful room," she concluded out loud.

"It's not meant to be."

How many clients had entered that room in the past, she wondered. Hopeful men, distressed men, angry men. And women too, of course, some coming to plead for his help, clutching their hands in prayer and holding them to heaving bosoms. She'd read enough stories to know that women always had bosoms that heaved when they had to beseech a man for his mercy. Pip's bosom didn't heave anywhere for anybody. Serenity had said it was because she didn't lace her corset tight enough.

"What are you thinking about now?" he demanded, staring out of the window, his back to her.

She chuckled dourly. "I very much doubt you would want to know. You might blush."

"I don't blush."

Hastily she sought another subject. "You're very young to be a lawyer, are you not? Does it not take years of study?"

"For me it didn't."

"You must be very clever and studious."

"If a man wants something he should work hard for it. And not be distracted."

She nodded. Yes, he plainly was not a man who stood for much nonsense. Which made their first encounter and the way he'd teased her, quite inexplicable. "So what does the Dangerous Mr. Damon Deverell do in his time away from work, if he does not read or attend the theatre? I suppose you like cricket. All Englishmen love their cricket. We could talk about that."

He turned to look at her, arms folded across his chest. "What do you know about cricket?"

"You'd be surprised. I was recently treated to a lecture by a gentleman who extolled its virtues for a full three hours over tea and crumpets. I know all about bouncers, gogglies and silly-midwickets."

"The term is googly, not goggly."

"Are you sure?"

"Absolutely."

"Ah." She nodded. "Your turn to choose a subject then."

But instead he stood there, staring at her until the silence became heavy and charged, like the air before a storm.

"Is that how you intimidate defendants in court?" she chirped, determined to keep the mood light and teasing. "I daresay I would find all my darkest secrets wrenched out of me by such a look. I would talk myself into a hanging."

"Silence makes you uncomfortable?" He came over to put some pens back in a line after she'd moved them about as she spoke.

"I'd much rather know what a person is thinking, than have them hide it from me with stony silence. Although I have been told that I should learn to be a little less transparent myself. Chatter less and conceal more." She briskly brushed crumbs from her skirt into her cupped hand. "I'm not sure I shall ever manage it and, as you see, when there is a silence I feel compelled to fill it. I suppose it's because I tend to think I've done something wrong if the other person is too quiet. My sister thinks I have too many opinions, but once we're in the grave it'll be too late to express them. While we're alive we ought to make noise, in case somebody mistakes us for a corpse and buries us, don't you think?"

"Nobody, madam, could mistake you for a corpse."

She walked by him to toss the crumbs through his window, the rusty latch giving her a fight until he came to help with a stern, quick pull. "Will you take one of your muffins to that newsboy? He looks hungry, poor thing."

"They're my muffins, and I'll do with them as I please."

There was little conversation after that. Pip drank her coffee and then was ushered out again. Having gone to the trouble of inviting her back, he now seemed in haste for her to be gone. She stopped in the door, resisting his efforts to push her out.

"I think you're the oddest man I've ever met."

"You haven't met the rest of my family."

"I've been advised to stay away from Deverells."

A slight smile turned up one corner of his lips. "Not doing a very good job of it, are you?"

"I am too easily tempted by cake," she replied ruefully.

He huffed, but it was almost a laugh. "Come tomorrow." And he hastily averted his gaze. "If you like."

"If I like?" She put her hands on her waist. "You can't admit you might like me to come?"

"We will never get along, remember?" His gaze returned to her face. "It's been decided. And this is not romantic."

"True." The sun had moved around since she entered his office and now it stung her in the eye as she looked up at him. She squinted. "I daresay one might share delicious muffins with one's sworn enemy. As long as you don't poison them."

"Sworn enemy?" He quirked an eyebrow. "Has it sunk that far?"

"We Pipers don't do anything by halves."

Oh, even closer to a laugh this time, but it was curbed quickly. He adjusted his neck cloth. "Come if you like. It's up to you. I'm sure I don't care, and I'd just as soon have the peace and quiet. I'm boring that way. You know us Englishmen and our stiff upper lips."

He was not only the oddest man she'd ever met; he was also the most frustrating.

"Grinding one's teeth is a terrible habit," he reminded her smugly, before closing the door in her face.

* * * *

She came every morning for almost a week, always very early so that he was alone.

Every day she said the same thing. "What shall we talk about today?"

Usually he didn't answer, because she already had a subject in mind and needed no encouragement to rattle on. History, science, the state of the roads, the bond she'd formed with a stray dog... Damon never knew what it would be.

Finally, on the fifth day, he answered, "Must we talk at all?" Sometimes talking tired him out; he did so much of it every day, persuading people in court and out of it. Words could be exhausting.

"I'm trying to be sociable," she said, pert, sitting with her hands in her lap, like a little girl at her lessons.

"I'd rather not."

"What would you *rather* do then?"

Damon swung around on his heel and paced the other way, his pulse quickening. Only an artless innocent would ask that question of him, he mused. He had no right to invite her here like this, clandestine, illicit— call it what you will— he knew what he was doing and no good could come of it. Not for her. He was not looking for a wife and marriage. Tempting as she was, he couldn't have her, not under the terms he wanted. "Eat your muffin, Miss Piper," he snapped.

Suddenly he heard the legs of his chair scrape across the stone floor. "If I eat another crumb, I'll burst out of my stays."

He smirked at his reflection in the window. "Can't have that, can we?"

"Doesn't your lady friend wonder who eats her muffins with you?"

"No."

"If you don't like conversation, what do you do with your lady friends then?"

Before he knew what was happening she was behind him, tapping him on the shoulder with one finger. She'd taken her gloves off to eat.

He turned to face her.

And had a second thought.

Perhaps she was not so innocent after all when she asked her questions. A sultry gleam lurked under her lashes, heightened color suffused her face in the warmth of the sun through the window, and she had just dampened her lips, which made them look even fuller. The damnable woman was clever, witty. She must have come there knowing what might happen.

When he gripped her by the arms she made no protest, although her lips parted a little and a small gasp exited her mouth. It was not a sound of shock or fear, but excitement. Anticipation wrought of curiosity and a certain adventurous spirit. She lifted her face, her gaze locked to his.

Damon's heart raced as it had not done in a very long time. It almost took his breath away. He forgot, for just a moment, where he was, and imagined himself back on a Cornish cliff side with his childhood partner in mischief. The only difference being that they were both grown up today and other games were afoot.

Oh, and she was real. Flesh and blood. Warm and soft. Sweetly scented, mouthwatering in a way of which she could have no understanding.

He lowered his lips to her forehead and closed his eyes, inhaling her perfume. Lavender. Just the faintest trace of it in her hair. Slowly his lips moved to her temple and then back down to her nose, planting the lightest of kisses upon the tip.

"You want to know what I do with my lady friends," he murmured.

"Yes," she gasped out. "Clearly you don't have much conversation." And then she, impatient, rose on tip toe to press her mouth somewhat clumsily to his.

Pulling her closer, he moved out of the light of the window and deepened the kiss, tasting her thoroughly, restlessly. He needed more. Much more. Her bare fingers ventured to his cheek and then his hair, exploring, stroking. Something— a raw sensation he'd never before felt— flooded through him so fiercely that he feared he might fall. Needed the wall to hold them both up.

Damon took her hand and felt that smooth skin, his thumb sweeping over her palm. A hard, driving rhythm pounded through his head and all the way down to the soles of his feet.

Deverells always got what they wanted. So why shouldn't he have her? In that moment all other considerations vanished, snuffed out like a candle in a draft too strong, too forceful to withstand.

He kissed her again, savagely this time, greedily, his blood hot, his head dizzy. He clutched her body to his, her thumping heart to his, fitting her against him so that she would be left in no doubt of his desire for her. He felt her lips parting, yielding. Damon let his hand slide down to haul her closer still, his fingers spread around the alluring curve of her bottom. Her gasp shattered against his tongue, and he delved deeper, plundering and claiming.

But suddenly she stepped out of his grasp, tugged her hand from his, reached for her discarded gloves and tried to pull them on. "Don't get any ideas, Deverell," she exclaimed on a taut rush of breath. "It was just a kiss and I was curious. I don't want a man, as I told you before. I haven't the time or the patience and there are a great many things I want to achieve with my life. Just because I'm a woman it doesn't mean I can't."

"Make up your mind. You started this, madam."

"Indeed I did not. You lured me with muffins." She fumbled over her gloves so badly that she dropped one. "This is not a romance. Kindly don't mistake it for one."

He pushed himself away from the wall, regrouped, licked his lips where he could still taste her, and somewhat breathless himself, said, "Let me help."

"No. Thank you. I can manage. I never need *help*, for pity's sake. *Help* is the last thing I would ever ask for."

After watching her for a minute, as she puzzled over the number of fingers on her hand and tried to match them with the corresponding holes in her glove, Damon stepped up and gave his assistance. He expected another protest, but none came. Instead she seemed to feel the need to explain her behavior.

"It's been a very dull few months," she muttered, her expression glum.

"I'm sure it's hard to be so far from your home."

Her lashes swept upward, her eyes pinned to his face. "Yes."

Damon looked down again, fixing the tiny buttons at her wrist. "Don't worry about me getting ideas above my station. I know what I was hired to do. This is only business." He cleared his throat. "From now on."

Not another word passed between them that day, but he did succeed in slyly measuring her pulse with the pad of his thumb and finding it raised to a hectic pace in concert with his own heart's beat.

When she was gone, dashing away across the street, Damon stood in his office with the gentle flood of morning sunlight warming his face, and stared at the wall paneling where he had held her as he drank that kiss from her soft, quarrelsome lips. Suddenly he could see every scratch and knick, where other folk had leaned and bumped against it over the years. Where clients nervously squirmed against the paneling as he questioned them.

But although he had many questions for the redoubtable Miss Piper, he found himself quite at a loss to ask any, since he had, inexplicably, given her his seat. Every time she came into the room he let her have the one and only chair, while he paced stupidly like a naughty boy brought before the headmaster. He couldn't, for the life of him, understand why he did it.

Then she had the audacity to suggest she didn't start that kiss.

Damon made up his mind that he would not let her in again. Next time she came to his door, he would tell her he had a client and that she should go back to Belgravia. Because that kiss could only lead him down a troubled path away from a peaceful life. And clearly, just as she found it impossible to resist fresh baked muffins, he was finding it just as challenging to resist her chattering lips. She had more treacherous curves than the cliff road that led to his father's island. And too many bends in the road tended to make him sick to his stomach, so it was something of a surprise to him that he'd embarked upon this particular journey so keenly. Well, no more. He'd have to put a stop to it before he ventured around one curve too many.

However, that evening he had another visitor. Working late by the light of a candle at his desk, he was startled by the shrill sound of a woman's voice demanding to know which was his office, followed by Tom's protest as she evidently pushed the clerk aside.

Damon put down his pen and sighed softly. He might have known it couldn't last.

"I know what she's been up to," were the first words out of her aunt's mouth as she pushed her way into his office. "She thinks she can hide it from me, but I'm no stranger to the tricks young girls use. She's been coming here, without my consent, and you've encouraged it. Now something's happened between you. I don't know what, for she won't say, but I know men like you, young sir, and I won't have it."

"Thank you, Tom," he said softly to the clerk who, looking extremely bruised and fearful, slid out and closed the door behind him.

"You have no thought of marriage, do you?" she exclaimed. "Well?"

"I'm not the marrying kind." He'd never seen evidence of marriage making anybody happy. Although his father seemed content now with Olivia, it was early days yet and True Deverell's past history did not suggest he would go easily into the winter of his years with only one woman at his side. Most marriages, however they appeared on the surface, did not bear up under close scrutiny.

"As I thought, and even if you did have such an idea in mind it would pass before the ink was dry on the license. Just as soon as you'd had your way with her you'd be off, leaving my niece damaged goods. Come near that girl again and I'll take those proud seed-bags off you, slowly, with a nutcracker."

"Forgive me, madam, but I'm quite sure you have no right to tell me what I can and cannot do."

"Try to go against me, sir, and you'll find out

what I can do and how painfully I can do it. No doubt you're after the money, is that it? I won't let you feed that girl your poetry, young man."

"I've never fed a woman poetry in my life."

"No, but you're feeding her somethin', I guess."

He picked up the basket from his desk and held it toward her. "Muffin, madam?"

She flared her nostrils and pointed at his ink pot. "You, young sir, will write a note to my niece and I shall dictate it."

"Madam, I really don't—"

"Unless you would like me to cause trouble for a certain married lady friend of yours, young Master Deverell. Ah, yes, that surprises you, doesn't it?"

It more than surprised him. Damon was alarmed, so much so that it must have shown on his face.

"I'm a lady who has seen it all and travelled the world, young sir. And like you, so I hear, I am not averse to fighting dirty when needed. Now, you've got one plaything already, so you set my niece aside, and then you and I needn't have any further harsh words between us. You do the job for which you were paid by her father— manage the gossip and keep her out of trouble, not in it. Or I can let her father know what's been going on and you can lose a valuable client."

He gave no argument. Damon wrote the note, as she wanted, and put it into her hand. It was for the best, he thought. He had, already, decided to end Miss Piper's morning visits and at least this way he didn't have to say it to her face and risk weakening. Oddly enough, a man who had squared off, undaunted, against some of the most vicious delinquents and cunning rogues from London's underbelly, Damon suffered a considerably painful qualm at the thought of turning that small, amusing creature away from his door.

"From now on, young man," her aunt exclaimed, snatching the letter from his hand, "you stick to what you do best."

He couldn't resist a wry comment. "That's what I was trying to do, madam."

"I suppose you think that's funny."

Hastily straightening his lips, he replied, "Certainly not, madam. This is an office of work, not frivolity. Ask my clerk."

From then on he gave Lady Roper's muffins to the newsboy across the street and decided his fascination with Nonesuch was over. Thank goodness, because it was all getting out of hand and he did rather want his chair, and his tidy office back. Not to mention keeping his nuts uncracked.

* * * *

The sealed message was waiting by her breakfast plate the next day. According to the butler it was delivered in the early hours of the morning.

Madam; please do not put your reputation in danger by coming here alone again. Listen to those who would advise you wisely. Our meetings, from now on, should only be in the company of your aunt and to discuss the matters for which I was hired.

Sincerely,

D. Deverell, Esq.

Well, that was decidedly more formal than his usual notes. One might even call it polite. A polite dismissal.

Pip said nothing to anybody and put the letter away in her own writing box. In truth she'd felt foolish after leaving his office that day. What had overcome her so suddenly that made her curiosity bubble over? Although she would like to deny it began with her, she had put her lips to his. Then, of course, he took the control out of her hands and she felt something like panic as the reins slipped from her fingers. There was a moment when she thought she couldn't stop it. But then she did. It took her breath away, left waves of heat pounding through her body.

Worse, even than his improper caress of her derriere, was the calm way he then replaced her gloves for her, his own hands so steady, while she made such a mess of trying.

Such a man could do anything and not be troubled by it, show no remorse.

Yet, he had replaced her sister's shawl with something even more beautiful.

Pip found that she could not shut him away into any of the boxes she usually reserved for men. He refused to fit into any. Left her confused, unsettled.

Later that day, her aunt commented on the fact that she was unusually quiet.

"Am I?" She smiled brightly. "I cannot think why."

Her aunt leaned over and whispered, "Sometimes the more necessary the choice, the harder it is to make. We ladies must have all the willpower when it comes to men. It is for our own good."

Nothing else was said, but it seemed evident that Aunt Du Bois had somehow found out and put a stop to her mornings with Deverell. It was, no doubt, inevitable that somebody would have found out eventually. And really, how far could it have gone?

She would have needed to let out her clothes if he continued plying her with those delicious muffins.

Chapter Eleven

Damon would not have gone to the races at Ascot in June that year, had he not been invited by his half-sister, Raven, whose husband had a horse running in the Royal Hunt Cup.

I hear you're all work and no play these days, Raven's letter to him had said, *but that makes you in danger of becoming far too dull. I shall collect you promptly at eight.*

She never left any room for debate, never asked, merely told. Ransom liked to say that his sister had emerged from their mother's womb already ordering the midwife about and causing their father to wear his boots out from pacing. She hadn't stopped since. Being the only girl in the family, Damon suspected she had learned early on to be assertive. Certainly none of the Deverell boys would have fussed over her or treated her with kid gloves, even if she'd let them.

As it happened, he was glad of a day out in his sister's company, which was always enjoyable and easy. Since Raven's marriage had taken her away into Oxfordshire for most of the year, and her husband was not a terribly sociable creature, she did not often come up to Town. Damon had missed seeing her about, teasing her and laughing together at the snobbery of the people around them.

But as soon as he stepped up into her carriage that day, she wanted to know, "What on earth is the matter with you now?"

"Hmm?"

"You don't look very happy, brother. You look tired, beaten and worn as one of my old dolls. I might expect that from Ransom— the wild company and sleepless hours he keeps— but not you."

Damon was puzzled. Why would he not look happy? He was enjoying an affair with a passionate and inventive mistress who made no demands upon him outside her hotel suite bedroom; he was in good health and his career proceeded well enough. He had succeeded in managing a number of good works— pro bono— on Lady Roper's behalf, and often paid secret afternoon visits to her drawing room, where she exhibited an astounding ability to beat him at chess, despite her claim of never properly understanding the rules and her childlike "surprise" with each victory. The weather was excellent and he had been looking forward to his sister's company. But apparently none of this showed on his countenance.

"You need a dose of salts, young man," Raven teased. "That's what Mrs. Blewett would say, if she saw you today. *You need a dose of salts and one of my jam puddings.* You always were her favorite, of course, and she'd make you anything you desired whenever you came home from school or were sick."

Damon scowled across the carriage. "Mary Blewett merely likes to feed people. And when I was a boy I liked to eat. Supply and demand is our only connection."

"It's how she shows you her affection, as you well know. But then you like to pretend you don't know how everybody is charmed by you, whether they want to be or not."

"*Charmed?*" There it was again. Lady Roper's words continued to haunt him. What the devil was he doing that made people think he had charm? He drew a nervous hand back through his hair, fingers scraping at his scalp. "There is nothing charming about me."

She laughed. "There shouldn't be. You can be so very insufferable and, of course, we all know you have no heart. But there is something about your darkness that is, in itself, strangely endearing. Or perhaps enthralling is a better word. I suppose the more horrid you are, the more we want to save your soul. The more you need us."

"You make no sense, Raven. Marriage has pickled your brain."

"On the contrary. It has made me see things with greater clarity, because the world has stopped rushing by and I can look at people in a way I never did before. And I see before me a very clever young man who, today, for some reason, is sad. A young man who once thought he had everything, but, today, feels as if he has nothing and he can't understand it."

He thought of the way Lady Roper had patted his hand and how everything after that moment had suddenly seemed different. Changed. As if a candle blew out and forced his eyes to adjust in the dark.

"So why are you gloomy today, brother?"

"I can assure you I'm perfectly content," he replied.

"Stempenham and Pitt treat you well?"

"Well enough."

"I'm surprised they haven't made you partner yet. I read of your successes all the time."

He winced at her enthusiasm. "It's only been three years since I joined them."

"But you're a prodigy. Everybody says so."

"Really?" he muttered scornfully. At Stempenham and Pitt they mostly called him an "upstart" or a "young whippersnapper". The fact that he was a Deverell meant that he was eyed with a certain amount of distrust still, despite his many successes for the firm. His was a hard, uphill climb, which made it all the more frustrating when people like Ransom assumed he had everything handed to him as their father's favorite.

He said none of this to Raven, of course. There was no point, for when she had an idea in her head she galloped off with it, heedless of any cautionary shouts.

"Soon there will be room to move up. Surely the principals are old men now and ought to retire," she said.

"Hmm. If you say so." *But extremely unlikely.* Tobias Stempenham came into work every day merely to escape the ceaseless nagging of his wife and the shrieking demands of his six daughters. Another example of why a man should avoid marriage.

"No interesting clients of late?" she asked.

"Nothing you'd find very exciting." Swiftly he changed the subject. "How's married life?"

She looked smug, sinking back into her seat. "Perfect in every way."

Ugh. He couldn't bear it when folk talked glowingly of matrimony. It was either a fib, stupidity or deliberate blindness to save face. He had no patience for any of that. "Of course it has only been a few years," he pointed out briskly.

Raven laughed. "Don't worry. I'm not going to recommend that *you* try it."

"Good."

Plenty of time for the joyous lovebirds to grow tired, he thought. Soon they would feel crowded in their cage and start pecking at each other, for that was what usually occurred. Raven was hardly the sort of woman for whom the bounds of marriage could stay comfortable for long. Soon they must chafe. Damon often wondered, in common with many, whether the Earl of Southerton knew exactly what he'd taken on when he married Raven Deverell. Everybody said the man was eccentric, which might explain his fascination with a wife who could only make his formerly peaceful life messy and noisy in the extreme.

But she was looking damnably pleased with herself. Was she expecting again? He certainly would not ask.

Within half an hour of arriving at the racecourse he saw Elizabeth and her husband, standing with a large group near the royal enclosure. He had known she would be there, of course, for most of society was in attendance. She was probably surprised to see him, however. Damon had not told his lover that he'd been invited there. Elizabeth, like most of her class, always claimed to be shocked and appalled by the way the Deverell family managed to go wherever they wanted, take whatever they wanted, and nobody seemed capable of stopping them.

Her eyes met his, and he felt the usual shiver of anticipation for the next time she would rake her sharp fingernails down his back. She did not look away demurely, but glared hard, as if she hated him, before she turned her head.

He wanted to laugh out loud. Elizabeth did love to remind them both of his "inferiority" and how fortunate he was that she came down from her lofty heights to roll around in his bed, what a great favor she did for him. For him, the grubby little lawyer who also happened to be a Deverell.

But however she wanted to play the game,

whatever made her feel better about fucking him, he didn't particularly care. Women always needed a fantasy in their head. Men just got on with it for the raw pleasure, they didn't dwell upon the whys and wherefores.

Yet another reason why marriage —a permanent commitment— was such a bad idea for both parties.

"I didn't know you were acquainted with the Stanburys," his sister remarked, her tone edged with a distinct chill as she said the name.

Damon realized she must have seen the look pass between him and Elizabeth. There was not much Raven missed. He'd have to be more careful. He still didn't know whether Miss Piper's aunt had merely thrown a lucky guess at him; whether she, like Ransom, knew there was an affair but didn't know with whom, or if she truly knew of his involvement with Elizabeth Stanbury.

"Lord Stanbury is a client," he muttered. "He hired me to manage a land dispute and some other legal matters of his estate last year."

When he looked at Raven, her face was grim. "George Stanbury once used a very dear friend of mine extremely ill. He is a cruel, selfish, arrogant... *arse*."

He managed a half smile. "It's business, Raven. It's not necessary that I like my clients. As long as they pay me, that's all that matters."

"Working for such a snake would make my skin crawl!"

"Snakes have as much right to fair representation in law as any other creature."

"Ugh. You would defend the serpent in Eden."

"Why not? There are always more sides to a story

than just one. Trust nobody."

"I do not know how you can be so mercenary and heartless."

"Which is why I am the lawyer and you're not."

"And, perhaps, the reason why you are so unhappy."

"For pity's sake, I am the happiest damned soul I know. I can't help it if my face doesn't suit your idea of mindless, carefree euphoria."

Sudden loud laughter. Something familiar about it. A warm recognition.

He turned his head and saw, a short distance along the railing, Miss Epiphany Piper, with her sisters and— much to his annoyance— Bertie Boxall. None of them had seen Damon.

She wore lilac and carried a white parasol. He stared.

Nobody else laughed the way she did. Genuinely, richly, lustily. Unapologetic. No attempt made to stifle it.

Today she wore short gloves that matched her gown. He remembered the softness of her bare hand crushed in his fingers, the rapid pulse in her wrist; the taste of her lips yielding under his— but not too much, still ready to argue, wanting everything her way and on her terms. Which made her difficult, and yet even more delicious. More alluring. Was it the challenge that drew him in? Whatever it was, it was fierce, hot and without mercy. It was quite different to what he'd felt when he first saw Elizabeth and decided he wanted her. But surely it came from the same place, didn't it?

His chest began to hurt, as if he'd been running and was out of breath.

"Who's that?" his sister demanded, linking her arm in his to keep him at her side.

"Who? Where?"

At that very moment the one he referred to in his mind as Nonesuch looked over and caught his eye. She quickly glanced down, but a few seconds later stole another peep from under her lashes. "Do you know them?" Raven demanded. "And don't try to lie. I can tell from your face— and hers— that you are acquainted. I am intrigued, brother."

He cleared his throat. "They're Americans. Exiled here because of some...some scandal at home." In his four and twenty years he'd never been tongue tied over a woman and he'd be damned if he let it happen now. Over that little menace whose aunt wanted to crack his nuts.

"You've met them?"

Damn. He'd almost steered his sister into the railing. Why on earth was he acting this way? *Concentrate on your feet. Yes. Better.* "Their father is a client." He felt confused. Hot. Irritable. He hoped that would be an end to his sister's curiosity. But he might have known it would not be.

"She keeps looking this way. Of course, you are intolerably handsome. I suppose she can't help herself." Raven shook her head. "That charm again! That devilish charm about which you profess to have no control or even knowledge."

He exhaled a tight groan. "I can assure you she does not think me charming. All Englishmen bore her apparently." *So what the devil was she doing with Boxall, possibly the most tedious of all men he knew?*

No sign of her aunt, he noticed.

"The last time I met an American, I bit him,"

Raven said proudly. "Cornelius Vanderbilt was his name, I remember."

"I have no doubt he remembers your name fondly too. I am surprised he hasn't put it in a lawsuit."

"How like a lawyer to think that. You would scout for his business and put your own sister in the dock, mercenary brat!"

After a while he shot another quick, sideways glance along the railing. Ah, Nonesuch talked to Bertie and her attention was on the horses.

Still no sign of the fearsome aunt.

Now that he knew it was safe, Damon risked another, longer glance, taking her in slyly and rather greedily. He hadn't seen her since that day in his office and the unexpected kiss, but of course he still did his part to make certain any gossip about her was stifled, or at least partially discredited. With Ransom's help he'd traced that story about Ernest Moffat's blackened eye back to the Winstanleys, who apparently had a cousin in Boston. Miss Piper's aunt would be shocked to learn that her niece's problem had followed them across the ocean and into London drawing rooms through the mean-spirited loose tongue of a woman she apparently thought her friend— Lucille Winstanley. Women were treacherous toward each other in sly ways that men never employed, he mused. Two-faced was a term that barely scratched the surface.

Trust nobody. Miss Piper's aunt should have been taught that lesson.

His gaze wandered across the grass again to the lilac hem of a particular gown. He'd often caught himself musing on the curves hidden under those skirts. The warm, soft treasure he wanted to trail his fingers over. To possess. To conquer.

Christ, the sun was hot today.

It was odd that another woman's figure should steal her way into his mind, even now that he had Elizabeth to slake his lusts and keep those necessary parts in good working order. And he had wanted Elizabeth for a long time, worn her down determinedly until she succumbed. She was all he needed. All he had time and space for in his life. Other men would envy—

Why was Nonesuch laughing? That idiot Boxall could not possibly have anything clever enough to say that would amuse her.

Of course, Boxall would know she had a rich dowry purse. Young women with their sort of wealth, as Ransom had said to him, were unheard of. She might think she could escape marriage, but other people would put a stop to that and if she was not careful she could become prey to the worst sort of fortune-hunter. He supposed that was one of the reasons why Prospero Piper had hired a law firm.

Look at the fool, leaning all over her. Probably drunk again. Miss Piper swung her parasol casually, but Damon suspected she would use it as a weapon if the fool moved any closer. Nonesuch would.

"Is that not Bertie Boxall?" Raven exclaimed suddenly. "We ought to acknowledge him, at least. You were university friends, were you not?"

Damon knew very well that his sister was far more curious about the American girls than she was worried about snubbing Boxall, whom she had always called "a grievous, drunken oaf who cannot get out of his own way."

"Ah. I just remembered!" He tried to dig in his heels. "Something I have...a man over there I have to see."

But there was no stopping Raven, or getting out of *her* way, as she tugged him along toward the little group beside the railing.

* * * *

"Lady Southerton! You look very well. And Deverell. I thought that was you."

Pip steeled herself to look over with nothing more than casual interest as Lord Boxall greeted the approaching couple. The woman had bright green eyes, sparkling with undisguised mischief, and lush black hair that bounced, in long, shining ringlets, over her shoulder. She walked with a confident stride, smiling, holding Damon's arm tightly as if she thought he might run off. The handsome family resemblance was unmistakable, even before Bertie advised out of the side of his mouth, "This is Damon Deverell and his sister, the Countess of Southerton."

A countess in the family? Her aunt's friend had left out *that* tidbit when she sought to slander the Deverells, she mused. Surely her aunt would have been impressed by that and less hasty in her condemnation of the "*drigay*".

Before Bertie could introduce Pip and her sisters, Damon Deverell who looked to be in a very bad mood, and seemed to want to get it over with as quickly as possible, exclaimed, "The Miss Pipers and I are acquainted. Their father is a client of ours."

His eyes were very dark, his jaw arrogantly squared, as he looked from Bertie to Pip. And she, her contrary nature amused, replied, "Yes. Mr.

Deverell has been appointed our nursemaid while we're in London. So watch out, Bertie, you might be subjected to some very stern questions while you're in my company. And I might even be spanked."

"Indeed," Deverell muttered, "you ought to be."

Bertie sputtered indignantly, "Well really, I'm quite sure—"

"I know Lord Boxall and the impetus that drives him already." He looked at her. "I'd have a great many more questions for you, Miss Piper."

"You think I have wicked intentions toward Lord Boxall," she exclaimed mischievously. "Do you think I might damage him irreparably?"

"Very probably."

There followed an uneasy silence, because nobody knew whether Deverell spoke in jest and his face wasn't about to give them any clues. He looked rather belligerent today, Pip thought, as if he might have got out of bed on the wrong side. Or out of the wrong bed.

Finally his sister, the Countess of Southerton asked how they liked England. Pip left her elder sister to give the polite response, since she was too preoccupied trying to make out what was happening on Damon Deverell's face. Something must have occurred to put him in an even worse mood than he was the first time they met.

Finally, because he was glaring at her, unblinking and rigidly annoyed, she was obliged to ask softly, "Are you quite well, Mr. Deverell?"

He brushed his free hand across his face and she wondered if he tried to push his expression into a better shape. "*Quite*, madam. And you?"

"Bursting with rude health. As always."

Now his gaze slipped to Bertie Boxall. "So you met his lordship, after all."

"Indeed. My aunt invited him to dine after he sent me an *exquisite* shawl," she replied. "Lord Boxall certainly knows the way to a girl's heart with such a beautiful gift."

"Your heart?" he shot from the corner of his mouth. "Is that what he's after?"

Nobody else listened to the two of them. His sister loudly entertained the others with a story about her husband's horse, which was running in the next race, and she happened to be every bit as fascinating to look at as Damon. But Pip watched him instead, taking it all in, to be sure that her memory of his features had not missed anything out. She felt oddly refreshed by the sight of him, like a thirsty plant that had been kept too long in the sun and everybody forgot to water.

"Are you betting on your brother-in-law's horse?" she inquired softly, taking a few casual steps away from the others.

He followed her. "No. I don't gamble. Not anymore." Still that intense stare, as if she'd torn something of *his*.

"But does your family's fortune not have its roots in—"

"What does that have to do with me? I'll make my own fortune."

Clearly she'd hit a soft spot. "That's admirable," she assured him. "I cannot mock you for that intention."

He fidgeted with his neck-cloth. "I suppose you've heard all about us."

"From whom?"

"Your suitor." He glowered over at Bertie. "No doubt he has many good tales to tell you. I hear your aunt is acquainted with the Winstanleys. They must have shared many a scandalous morsel about my family too."

"Are the stories not true then?"

"Depends which bit of gossip you require verifying."

She grinned. "About your preference for married ladies."

Although she only meant to tease playfully, he was evidently in too grim of a mood to play along today. "What does it matter to you?" Hands behind his back now, he jerked a quick nod toward Boxall and growled under his breath, "Thought you weren't looking for a husband. Don't they all bore you?"

"What does it matter to you?" she replied, smartly tossing his own words back at him.

"Of course, women are notorious for changing their minds on a whim."

She felt the heat rising under her lace collar. "I had better not stand here talking to you any longer. You're a bad influence."

"I am?" His deep, low voice sank into her like warm fudge sauce into a soufflé.

"And I am supposed to listen to those who would advise me sensibly, aren't I? As you said in your note."

"I *am* here to counsel you."

"But you have a very odd way of doing it. So I ought to stay well away," she tapped the handle of her parasol against his chest, "from you."

He caught the handle and held it. "I still have a job to do."

"But I have been on my very best behavior and not raised a single fist, or stabbed anybody with a hatpin, despite the temptations."

"Part of my job, Miss Piper, is to keep you away from danger. Especially fortune-hunters."

Frowning, she tugged her parasol from his grip and took several more, swift steps away from the others, pretending to take greater interest in the horses. She did not expect him to follow again, but suddenly he was behind her. The air changed, thickened with the heaviness that came before a storm. Pip had no need to look over her shoulder to confirm his presence there.

"My father sent me all this way to be among dull, tedious Englishmen so that this sort of thing wouldn't happen," she added in a rushed whisper.

"What sort of thing?"

"I'm sure he thought you'd all be too dignified, stiff-lipped and gentlemanly to scrap with me, and that if I found nobody willing to argue, I'd finally learn to hold my tongue. Sending me here was the closest he could get to shutting me in a padded cell. I'm convinced of it."

"So what you're saying is that I am *not* dull and tedious, after all."

Rather than answer that, Pip decided to plunge in, regardless of what she probably should or should not say. "I see Lady Elizabeth Stanbury over there." Bertie Boxall had identified that slender, elegant, blonde woman for her.

"So?" he snapped. "What of it?"

"You know her, do you not?"

"Her husband is a client. Why?"

"She is very beautiful."

"Is she?"

She looked at him over her shoulder. "Don't you think so?"

He gave no reply, but fussed with his cravat yet again, as if it might be too tight around his neck.

With an impatient gasp, she turned fully around, handed him her parasol, and reached up to loosen the knot of that troublesome cravat for him, as she would often do for her father. "Mr. Deverell, you ought to know that I don't care about gossip. I don't listen to it, although I can't prevent my ears from hearing it, of course. You know what gossiping tongues have done to me and my sisters. According to some stories, the cause of Ernest Moffat's blackened eye was a lover's tiff and I was not only his paramour, but his father's too. That I was his father's concubine, his placee, a kept woman." She patted the finished, improved knot and took her parasol back from him. "So yes, I know how one simple fact can be twisted and expanded until it bears little resemblance to the truth. Gossip is nothing to me, no more than horse manure in the street— an inconvenience to walk around."

His eyes warmed a little, but he seemed uncertain today, not his usual confident self at all.

"Where's your delightful aunt?" he said suddenly. "Not here today, overseeing her nieces to be sure they don't meet any young men like me?"

"She was under the weather this morning. Lord Boxall and his godmother were happy to bring us."

"I bet they were."

"I thought you didn't gamble?"

He half turned away and shook his head dolefully. "He's in debt up to his scrawny neck. That's why his godmother is pushing him. That why he's

170

here with you."

"And to think, I imagined he was besotted with me. How lucky I am to have you, my aunt *and* my sister, to remind me of the grim, ugly truth, just in case I should be swept away with the romance and imagine a man might want me for more than my dowry."

"Just warning you. It's my job. Men can be unscrupulous."

She laughed. "Is that not the wolf warning the sheep?"

"I see the amiable mute part still isn't working."

"Mercy! I had forgotten what fun it is to argue with you."

His eyes glittered, his gaze stroking roughly over her face. "Likewise."

She laughed a little breathlessly. "What shall we disagree about next?"

"Boxall," came the immediate reply. "He's no good for you. He'll spend all your money and then run off with a chambermaid."

"Oh lord," Pip rolled her eyes. "He's harmless enough. I'm in no danger there."

He scowled, tugging on the cuffs of his cutaway. "Interesting how your aunt approves of a drunken wastrel like Boxall, but threatens me with nutcrackers."

"It's all about the title. But she assures me that once I'm married I can take someone like you as my lover. A little something on the side." It came out of her before she could prevent it. Like so many things. In the surprise and excitement of seeing him again, she couldn't stop herself chattering. Or her fingers tapping against her closed parasol.

Why did he not give one of his sharp replies? Appalled, she suddenly realized he might have taken her remark as an actual suggestion.

"I didn't mean—"

"I hope not." It was a taut interruption, squeezed out between gritted teeth.

"Rather hypocritical of you, isn't it?"

This time, nothing. Had she finally rendered *him* speechless? After a full two minutes of awkward silence, he returned to the others, muttered something to his sister and dragged her off in another direction.

"I thought you hadn't met Deverell," Bertie exclaimed, coming to stand stiffly beside her.

"As he said, he was hired by our father. It's not as if I know him... socially. I'm just a client in his eyes."

"Well, I didn't care for the way those eyes looked at you."

"Yes. He's not terribly polite."

"*Polite?*" Bertie scowled. "Manners have naught to do with that man."

She smiled, turning away to watch the race.

He did look at her in a very wicked way, she thought. It was enough to make her perspire under her lace collar. If her bosom ever began heaving in his presence, she'd know she was seriously in trouble.

* * * *

"Why on earth were you so discourteous to Miss Piper?" Raven exclaimed.

"I was merely being myself."

"Determined to prove me wrong about the charm? Good lord, there was no need to be so utterly miserable. What are you afraid of?"

"I'm not afraid of anything." He squared his shoulders. "We've both decided already that we don't like each other, that's all."

"Yes. So I saw. " After a pause, Raven added, "I thought the eldest Miss Piper was very pretty. I'm sure, if they are on the hunt for husbands, they'll do well. Something a little exotic and interesting is always welcome."

Damon shrugged. He thought Nonesuch was the most wretchedly beautiful woman he'd ever seen, but he would, under no circumstances, tell his sister that. He would keep it to himself, along with all the other things he'd begun to think about her. At night. In his bed. When he was with Elizabeth and should have been thinking about her instead.

Had his ears deceived him, or had Nonesuch just suggested she might take him for a lover once she was married? It was just sinking in. The audacity of such a suggestion made by a woman to *him*. Of course, she was American; she might not realize that it was up to him to seduce her, and that such a decision was not hers to make. She should be coy, reluctant, play the game. Not make such a brazen announcement as if it was all entirely up to her and he was just a plaything to be picked up and set down on her whim.

And where, exactly, would that lurid gossip about her being the elder Moffat's mistress come from? She should be more decorous and not talk of "placages"— arrangements of that nature between men and women. Ladies might know of such things, but they did not talk about them in public. Her tongue had no doubt got her in trouble before. All it took was one prying busybody to overhear half a conversation and build the rest of it with supposition and spite.

Once I'm married I can take someone like you as my lover. A little something on the side.

Such a thing for a young woman to suggest! What was the world coming to? Suddenly he was prudish.

But that wasn't what bothered him the most.

He didn't like the way the American woman made him feel. It was unpredictable, uncontrollable. Damon knew where he was with Elizabeth Stanbury, who was far more suitable for his adult life. Nonesuch belonged in the grubby-faced, playful boyhood he'd left behind.

But something restless broiled within. Everything that had previously made him content was suddenly constricting, somehow false. As if he wore another man's coat and boots and tried to make them fit.

And what troubled him the most about Miss Epiphany Piper was not her bold manner, or her quarrelsome tongue, or even the possibility of her aunt's wrath— it was simply that he did not like sharing her time and attentions with those of another man, whether it be Boxall or any other entitled brat. For the first time in his life he felt possessive over a damn woman.

He would never share her with another man. He couldn't be her *little something on the side.*

He wanted more.

Somehow he had to conquer this needy, impish creature of discontent growing inside of him. Somehow.

Chapter Twelve

The proposal came at the end of June. She knew he'd been pushed into it by his godmother, and probably by her own aunt too. They were all going to be disappointed.

"I'm sorry, Bertie, I cannot think of marriage at this time. I hope we can remain friends. But I have far too much to do with my life." Pip had prepared her response, just in case this moment ever came, no matter who asked her.

"You led me to believe...you were fond of me."

This is what happened, she thought glumly, when a person was obliged to hide their true feelings and not say what was in their head. When one was forced to be nice, patient and obliging, no matter what. She had followed her father's advice and look where it got her. Nice, apparently, didn't always pay.

"We have known each other little more than a month, Bertie. Been in company together no more than five or six times—"

"Eleven!"

"Oh," she faltered. "Eleven? I must confess I wasn't really counting."

His face was very long and pale. Too much wine the night before— or that morning. Had he needed something to strengthen his courage before he launched into this proposal?

"You cannot seriously think to marry me after so short an acquaintance," she added, bemused, even a little sorry for him. Did he think he had monopolized her time so that she thought of nothing else? Or nobody else.

If only her life was that simple.

He pouted. "It's not rare to form an attachment in a few weeks. Marriage shouldn't trouble either of us too much."

She got up from the chair, feeling penned in by the boy who knelt before her. "I'm afraid it would, most certainly, trouble me. Where would we live, for instance?"

"We'll have a place in Mayfair, of course, for the season, and a little place in the country for the rest of the year. Nothing fancy. Just forty rooms or so."

Something with room for his godmother, she supposed. All of it purchased with her money.

She frowned, hands on her waist, fingers tapping. "You're prepared to overlook the gossip and my great infamy?"

"Yes. I am." He beamed. "Besides, you're not so strange now. People are becoming accustomed to—"

"You're not afraid I might punch *you* in the eye or commit some other bodily harm against you?"

"Why would you, my dearest, when I shall give you no cause?"

She very much doubted that.

Of course, he was on his best behavior now because he wanted her dowry and, ultimately, the one third portion of her father's fortune. She didn't need Damon Deverell to advise her of that.

"I'm sorry, Bertie. It's out of the question."

"Why?" he demanded, smile gone instantly, replaced by an unbecoming pout.

"Because in another year, I shall be going home to work for my father's business. Eventually I want to become his right-hand man. So you see, I can't be a wife. I simply won't have the time for a husband and a family of my own. It wouldn't be fair to any man I married, for work would take my attention away from him."

He stared, confused. "You don't want—? But all young women want to be married."

"Not this one, I'm afraid. I wish I did. It would be easier." She smiled. "But as I said, I hope we can still maintain a friendship." She needed him to keep her aunt from dragging any other possible suitors to her for an introduction. "I know, Bertie, that you are not particularly in haste to marry— me or anybody— and that your godmother put you up to this, because of my dowry. Is that not so?"

The young man made a grunt of agreement and flopped backward into a chair. She was amused at how easily he admitted his mercenary intentions.

Pip poured him a brandy and took it to where he sat. "Well, then. If we maintain our 'courtship' it should keep them quiet and content, for a while at least— both my aunt and your godmother."

He took the glass, looking a little less sulky. "I suppose so. An engagement would do the same, however."

"But that would encourage them to order wedding clothes and start making arrangements. We don't want it to get out of hand. It wouldn't be kind to them."

Downing the brandy, he made no reply.

"Keep things the way they are and that should be enough. Just... don't call me dearest," she added, flinching.

"What shall I call you then? Not still Miss Piper, surely."

"You may call me 'Pip'. It's what my friends call

me." She saw nothing amiss with that familiarity, and it was certainly more palatable than "dearest".

* * * *

The Winstanley's town house was in the process of being shut up for the summer, dust sheets already shrouding the furniture in some rooms and trunks cluttering the hall, packed ready for the requisite summer in the country, away from the ripe stench of overheated London gutters.

Lady Lucille Winstanley, dressed in travelling garments, received Damon in the morning room, looking somewhat flustered and impatient. He knew she would not have agreed to see him at all, if it were not for the fact that he'd helped her once dispatch a blackmailing lover, and a shop-lifting charge involving a card of lace that she claimed to have taken outside merely to see in the light. Both issues Damon had managed without bringing either to her husband's knowledge and keeping them out of the newspapers.

She could not, therefore, turn him away from her door. But it did not mean that she need be civil. He was still a Deverell, a bastard's bastard— as the lady had once referred to him when she didn't know she was overheard— and a lowly solicitor.

"What can have brought you here today, young man," she exclaimed, standing by the sunlit window, one eye on the list in her hand and the other supervising the loading of trunks onto the carriage in the street. "As you see, I am busy." She opened the window to shout terse instructions to the coachman and two footmen who sweated in the sun and, of course, couldn't be permitted to remove their liveried coats. "There are two more larger ones in the hall.

Make haste and stop dragging your feet. You cannot stack them that way or they will be unsafe. Don't toss his lordship's new gun box about like that! Where is his valet? Paul! Take the gun box and you load it. No! Let him...*you*, yes you do it. Oh, for heaven's sake!"

"I am also constrained for time, your ladyship. I won't keep you long, but there is a matter of some urgency that I must clarify with you."

"Go on then," she snapped, still preoccupied with the chaotic scene through her window.

"It was brought to my attention that someone in your household has been — how can I put it— *spreading the muck*—"

That got her attention. Her head snapped around, and she fixed him in a startled gaze.

Damon hid his smirk, carefully looking down. How he loved using deliberately earthy terms when dealing with these high and mighty characters.

"— spreading the muck about those young American ladies staying with Mrs. Du Bois."

She folded the list in her hand. "I cannot think why this would be brought to me. Servants will talk and there is—"

"Servants aren't the only ones who talk. *Friends* talk too. And you are very good friends with Mrs. Du Bois, so she has been led to believe. It would be most unfortunate if the lady should learn where those rumors found a footing in London, would it not? She strikes me as a lady who stands for no nonsense, and she is very protective of her nieces."

"What are you trying to accuse me of, young man?" Head up, eyes flaring, she put up her best shield.

"*You*, your ladyship? I would not dream of

accusing you. Surely you are above reproach. I merely wanted to apprise you of the fact that somebody in your household is responsible for causing a certain young lady and her family a great deal of embarrassment." Damon strode up to her, hands behind his back. "I believe the worst of it is over now, but it was still an unfortunate business. A great shame that somebody should have been so spiteful toward a young lady who did them no harm."

"Perhaps that young lady should learn not to make an exhibit of herself then and hold her temper." "And others should hold their tongue? Especially those of greater maturity. After all, does not everybody make an occasional mistake that they might not care to have bandied about, to follow them wherever they go? What is the saying? Nothing is more dangerous than a friend without discretion; even a prudent enemy is preferable."

Two hot spots of color blossomed on her cheeks in the sun's glare. She reached around and shut the window.

"Lady Winstanley, I don't care for snakes in the grass and I believe, in Louisiana, they eat them. In a stew."

She leaned away from him until her head almost hit the glass. Her eyes widened.

"I wouldn't like to be on Mrs. Du Bois' bad side. I have seen her in a rage, and she's quite a fighter. So if I were you, I'd take care of the rumors I listened to about those women. I might even make an effort to put it about that they are very pleasant, virtuous, modest young ladies, and if anybody tried to whisper otherwise in my ear, being a *friend* of Mrs. Du Bois, I would take issue with it. I would put them in their place, set them right. Because it would be most unwise to make an enemy of your friend. And their friends." All this he said very evenly, quietly, his tone conversational. "Don't you think, your ladyship?"

She worked her mouth, her eyes watering. He suspected she'd bitten her tongue.

"It would be the decent thing to do," he added. "After all, one needs one's friends in this world. They are few and far between. And when one has a very good friend— regardless of where they came from— one never knows who *their* friends might be, or what powers they might have at their disposal."

Finally she cleared her throat. "Yes. I see. I shall look into it at once, and take steps if I find that anybody here has been—"

"Shoveling the horse-shit?" He shifted back a step and nodded solemnly. "I'm sure Mrs. Du Bois would be grateful, as would Mr. Prospero Piper and any friends of his."

"I see," she said again.

"Well, I shall leave you to proceed with your journey, Lady Winstanley. May you have a pleasant, *quiet* summer in the country." He gave a quick bow and walked out.

Lady Lucille Winstanley was one woman who would be in no danger of thinking him *charming*, he mused.

* * * *

He tried to put Miss Piper— her shoulders, her eyes, her lips, her hands and her curves— out of his mind by sating himself in bed with his lover.

It didn't work.

Lady Elizabeth might have appreciated the

sudden burst of savage enthusiasm in her bed, but Damon felt only dissatisfaction and failure. And he didn't approve of failure.

He began to feel a sense of relief whenever Elizabeth had some obligation that kept her at her husband's side for a few days and when summer came she, along with the rest of "Society", fled to the country. Damon, enjoying the peace, threw himself into his work again, living a life that his brother mocked as "austere".

Lady Roper, who also remained in Town, probably to escape her husband's company, often called upon him for assistance dealing with crooked landlords, leaking roofs and over-flowing gutters. He refused his fee. These tasks didn't take up much of his time, and he liked the sense of accomplishment they brought to him. But the lady still insisted upon sending baskets of baked goods to his office and sometimes a bottle or two of very good wine.

Through a short note from Miss Piper's aunt, sent to Tobias Stempenham, he learned that they too were leaving London, but there was no mention of where they were going. A few times he rode by the house they had rented in Belgravia, but there was no sign of life within and soon the windows were boarded up, suggesting that even the servants were gone. There was nobody left to ask where they went. If Ransom had any further information about them, he didn't volunteer it, and Damon wouldn't ask. He knew better than to prod Ransom's curiosity any further on that subject and risk more taunting. He had felt the danger of getting too attached to her, too possessive.

But toward the end of that summer a new rumor

surfaced quietly. One of the Miss Pipers was engaged to be married, and Lord Boxall was the gentleman hinted at in the matter. Damon hesitated to believe it of her. She was too clever, too determined to get her own way, to fall into that trap with Boxall. On the other hand, her aunt was also a force with which to be reckoned. Had Nonesuch finally put her pirate sword aside, allowed her resolve to be broken down, and accepted a man for his title?

"Those American girls are very bold, so I hear," Lady Roper said to him one day as they played chess in her parlor.

Startled, he looked up from the board. "American girls?"

"Yes. Those young girls you asked me and my dear friends to help put out into Society."

"Ah. Yes. They are quite bold. Confident. I am advised they do things differently in America."

She nodded. "They have their attractions, of course. Some men like that wild streak. Alicia Renwick is acquiring one of them for her appalling godson, Bertie, poor thing."

Which subject of that sentence, he mused, was the "poor thing".

"They are rich, of course." The lady sighed. "That brings the worms out of the woodwork, and Bertie spent through his fortune the moment he came into it."

"I'm quite sure those women can handle the worms," he said, managing a tight smile. "They're rather independent-minded."

But even as he attempted to remain cheerful, this conversation with Lady Roper seemed to suggest that the worst had occurred.

The weather changed and autumn swept in, blowing dead leaves across his path, sending fog to meet him in the early morning as he rode to the offices of Stempenham and Pitt. A chill set in, and it seemed to reach right inside to his bones. Shadows followed him wherever he went, echoes of Miss Piper's laughter, faint traces of her scent on the neck cloth she'd once retied for him— he left it unlaundered— and the bloody cheerful newsboy by the park railings, who was always eager to ask whether he'd seen her lately.

Then Elizabeth Stanbury returned to town. Traveling ahead of her husband and apparently eager to see her lover, she came to Damon's lodgings early one morning, waking him from his bed. Her iciness had thawed somewhat, her summer in the country being less enjoyable than she expected and making her— so she said— miss his company.

When he saw bruises on her wrists, she treated them lightly, but made no effort to deny they were her husband's doing.

"You should leave him," Damon told her, hastily pulling a shirt over his head, wondering why she surprised him with this visit after those summer months of no communication whatsoever. It had been his plan to end their affair as soon as he saw her again, but she caught him by surprise that day and, for once, there was a fragile vulnerability about her.

She'd never been to his lodgings before, and she looked terribly out of place in those tidy, but plain, sparse surroundings.

"Leave Lord Stanbury?" She'd laughed, and it was like ice cracking on a pond, a sharp, jagged sound that raised every hair on his body, and made him fear

184

somebody might need rescuing. "And do what? Live in a place like this?"

Of course, Elizabeth refused to entertain the notion of separation from her husband. She was trapped in her unhappy marriage, as much as poor Lady Roper was in hers. To leave George Stanbury would mean leaving life, as she knew it, behind. It was unthinkable and so she put up with the hardships in order to enjoy the luxuries of financial comfort. Mercenary, but how could he fault her for that? He was not romantic either and understood the way the world turned.

"At least I have you, do I not?" she said to Damon, her blue eyes cool and brave as she drew a fingernail slowly down his unshaven cheek. "My one, simple pleasure. You cannot deny me that."

She came to him, and only him, with those bruises on her pale skin and the autumn chill clinging to her hair. There was no one else in whom she could confide, no one else to give her comfort. Or so she said. If he shut his door to her and he later learned that something dreadful had happened, he would never forgive himself.

Damon had many faults, but he could not turn his back on a woman in trouble. It was a failing he had only recently come to see in himself, although it must always have been there.

Elizabeth needed him, and she had no one else, it seemed.

"How I have missed you," she purred against his neck, "and...this."

There was nothing he could say in return, but she didn't notice his silence.

As she had said to him before, it wasn't his

conversation that she needed, in any case. Unlike a certain other woman of his acquaintance, Elizabeth was not much of a talker.

It was their last time and over in a moment. Later he told her it could not continue. He would help her— find some way for her to separate from Stanbury. He could advise her, protect her. Eventually, perhaps, he could help her stand on her own two feet.

She looked at him with an expression he did not recognize.

Months later he would remember that strange look on her face and only then would he realize that she came to him that day— to his humble lodgings— for one reason only. It had made her seem more vulnerable than usual, when she was not surrounded by the luxury of her hotel suite. But when it was done she wanted no more "help" from him. He had served his purpose.

By the time he understood all this, of course, it was too late.

Part II
Mulier Est Hominis Confusio

"It's merely business."

- Damon Deverell 1850

Jayne Fresina

Chapter Thirteen

December 1850
Somewhere on the Yorkshire moors

Fat fists of bitter cold, spiteful wind pummeled the sides of the carriage and rocked it violently from side to side, while other unseen, rioting hands pelted snow at the small window. Mother Nature and her minions shuddered and howled around him in a savage, primeval rage, as if some terrible, ancient injustice had been committed against her. Surely the world was ending and they would all soon be sucked into a void of despair. It was chaos, madness to be out traveling in such a storm.

Good. Perfect.

Tonight he relished the savage weather. It suited his vile mood. Suited him, in fact, in every way. Perhaps, he thought with dark humor, he'd finally found something that understood him. Somewhere he belonged. He'd become one with the tempest and traverse the countryside wrecking havoc. Why the hell not? Who could bloody well stop him?

With arms folded and chin buried beneath the high collar of his greatcoat, one booted foot propped up on the opposite seat of the swaying carriage, Damon Deverell stormily assessed his past, his present and his future, with the same ruthless, angry intensity in which he did most things.

It could never be an easy task, he thought grimly, for any son to bear upon his shoulders the weight of a father's greatest expectations. But when that father is True Deverell— a charismatic figure who, against all odds, raised himself from nothing and made his own fortune— the need to impress him, and the improbability of ever doing so, could become a weight of such unwieldy proportions that a young man's spirit is crushed beneath it.

And Damon, now almost five and twenty, had struggled restlessly under this encumbrance for many years.

Alas, although driven to succeed with the same powerful, natural urge that causes a dog to chase a rabbit, and often resented by his brothers for what they saw as favoritism, he suspected he still remained largely a disappointment to the one man whose approbation he'd ever wanted. His father's criticism came often; his praise rarely.

It had never stopped Damon trying or hoping, of course. Even when he told himself that he did neither. Looking back now, he saw how hard he had fought, how almost everything he did was done in some attempt to gratify his father.

Until now.

Six days ago, for the first time in his life, he had openly defied the man. Oh, he'd threatened to do so before, but for once his temper was stretched to the limit and in that moment of awakening— when he opened his eyes to what his life had become—he acted on that threat.

Years before, his father had said to him, "While I expect all my cubs to make the most of an education and the advantages I did not have, I anticipate the most from you. I see you going far, my boy. Farther than all of them."

So why was he singled out by True Deverell as the son with the greatest prospects? According to his father it was because he would never be led astray by his heart. Nothing would ever render a crack in his ruthless strength and uncompromising determination. His father recognized all that, even in Damon's youngest days.

"You're a fortress, boy. A merciless bull shark." Only his father could speak of those characteristics as if they were favorable. "We'll see you in parliament one day."

That was one of True Deverell's greatest ambitions for his fourth son, of course. Just one of them.

And what did Damon want? As a boy he would have joined the navy, given the chance. But his father steered him away from that idea and Damon, yearning— above all else— to please the man around whom his world revolved, let himself be steered. Apparently his "ruthless strength" was nothing when it came up against his father's will. But, as a certain young lady once said to him, two walls have nothing to do, except stand against each other.

Damon often felt his father's restless frustration and wondered why that usually perceptive man did not feel his in return. Perhaps True Deverell mistook it for something else, after all he had assumed his son had control of life. He'd assumed a great deal.

"You're not nearly as jolly good fun as your brothers," a woman said to him once, her tone accusatory.

"No," he'd replied somberly. "I don't have my siblings' capacity for rampant, carefree disorderliness. But then, somebody has to keep their wits about them."

Those who had known his father as a young man saw a remarkable resemblance in Damon. But was that, he wondered now, a result of nature, or of having molded himself into the instrument through which True Deverell might fulfill his own ambitions?

Damon matriculated at Cambridge university when he was just sixteen, graduated at nineteen, and then spent only two and a half years studying at Gray's Inn before being called to the bar. His meteoric rise, so he'd been told, was unprecedented. All this made him what his sister called a "prodigy". But really he thought it was boredom and restlessness that drove him to accomplish so much, so quickly. He could never get enough, never get quite what he wanted. He blazed through books like a wildfire through a dry forest, wrote faster than anybody he knew, absorbed information like a sponge, and remembered, down to the tiniest detail, every little thing he'd eaten at dinner on the eighteenth of February in the year 1840.

As a child, people had thought him odd. Then he learned to hide his unique skills and tuck them down inside. Perhaps that was why he created an imaginary friend, he mused. His friend, Nonesuch, didn't think him strange or annoying. She didn't mind his foibles and the way he had to keep everything in order. She held his hand without fear, without running away and exclaiming that she felt it throbbing with something dangerous.

The adult Damon took pride on being very much in control. While his siblings had a penchant for chaos and calamity, if Damon bumped into anything it was usually a calculated move to incapacitate his prey— like that bull shark with which he'd been compared.

Working in a law office he'd witnessed the turmoil and destruction that willful abandon and the pursuit of expensive pleasure brought to other men's lives, so he strove to avoid it. He was never generous on a whim, or foolishly extravagant. He hadn't gambled in years, never played games anymore, never let anybody pull the fleece over his eyes. Damon focused on his work and there was no room in his life for anything that he considered superfluous or purely decorative. His father wanted a bull shark, then he'd get one.

This desire to keep order, practicality and functionality was so rare among his siblings that it gave him the appearance of being a killjoy. He didn't mind that.

And sometimes it brought him frustration to a deadly degree. Which he *did* mind.

Damon Deverell was the son upon whom all hopes rested. A brilliant scholar with a steel-trap mind and the tenacity to succeed no matter what tried to stand in his way, he was supposed to get everything right. His father expected it from the son "most like" himself.

But, in the end, nobody knew Damon quite so well as they thought. Perhaps not even he.

Now, quite suddenly, order and business was in ruins around him. It had all begun to go seriously awry.

And why?

A woman, of course. Why else?

Ah yes, *Lady* Elizabeth Stanbury would pay for this when he caught up with her, he thought with dark relish, as the shuddering, lurching carriage bore him onward through the snow in as little comfort as if he were roped to a medieval wrack and left in the hands of the most accomplished inquisitor since

Torquemada. Every ounce of discomfort he'd
suffered on this journey would be added to the bill of
what that female owed him. Then he'd collect with
considerable interest.

No woman ran away from him. Especially not
when she was carrying his child.

Few things, or people, had ever encouraged such
an enraged reaction out of him that he threw aside his
routine. Certainly nothing had ever caused him to
turn his back on his father like this. That alone made
it necessary to find Elizabeth and make this mess tidy
again. If not, he had lost everything.

"You comprehend nothing of women," his father
would mutter gruffly, if he were there tonight, sitting
in the carriage with Damon. "You're four and twenty.
I've got riding boots older than you, boy."

His father did not have boots that old, of course.
True Deverell wore very expensive boots made by the
finest establishment in London and, whenever he
needed a new pair, had them sent post haste to
Cornwall. But nobody argued this point with him.
Apparently it pleased the "old man" to imagine he still
scratched about in faithful boots from his less affluent
days, and correcting their father was a sport only for
the foolhardy— or for Damon, whenever the sparks
ignited by the friction of their very similar
personalities became too many and too hot, melting
his armor, exposing his nerve-endings to the heat.

The quarrel before he left London to follow
Elizabeth north was one example of this abrasive
clash of wills between father and son.

"I thought you were the cub with all the brains,
but now you let this nonsense distract you."

"You've never met Elizabeth." One could hardly

call Elizabeth "nonsense", he mused.

"I've met her type."

"And what might that be?"

To which his father had replied steadily, with no apparent emotion beyond vague surprise that he'd been asked the question, "Self-interested and conniving. She is by no means a rarity or hard to fathom. The world is littered with Elizabeth Stanburys."

"If you know so much about her—"

"A woman discontent in her own marriage turns her eye to you as a plaything to relieve the tedium, and you, rather than simply enjoy the passing pleasure she offers, suddenly decide to complicate matters by becoming *involved*— of all the bloody stupid things to do."

"She is trapped and unhappy. I can make her—"

"What do you care? The state of her marriage is none of your business, and we are all responsible for our own happiness. The worst thing any man can do is get caught up in other folks' melodrama. If you abandon your position and responsibilities at Stempenham and Pitt to pursue this dangerous woman—a wench who has already run from you once and will do so again— you're a fool boy and far weaker than I thought. If you cannot see that she used you, then you may as well tie yourself to her petticoats, stick a thumb in your insolent mouth and have done with it."

"You never had an affair with a dangerous woman, sir?" he'd snapped sarcastically, knowing the answer to that already.

"I certainly never made a blithering idiot of myself by chasing after one. They came to me or they didn't. It was up to them. I had more important things to do. And so should you."

"What about your first wife, sir? Did you not pursue Lady Charlotte Rothsey when she was engaged to another?" Few folk ever dared raise the subject of his father's first wretched marriage, but Damon did.

"I did not chase that harpy. She pursued me like a bitch in heat. Tricked me into marriage by feigning a pregnancy, I might add. So once again I recommend caution, boy. Learn from my mistakes."

Damon could have pointed out that his father would never have been tricked in that way unless he'd bedded Lady Charlotte Rothsey in the first place— and she surely hadn't held a knife to his throat when he did that. Instead he saved his breath and strode to the door.

"If you go after that woman, you will disappoint me, boy! I wash my hands of you!"

Pausing on his way out, he'd replied, "I thought my choices were mine to make, as long as I take responsibility for the outcome and pay the consequences? Is that not what you always *told* me? Sorry, sir, but I cannot stay here and do nothing in this matter, when there is a child involved. A child that is *my* responsibility. I'm a man now, not a boy."

His father's voice followed him down the stairs. "Learn from my missteps! If you must complicate your life with a woman, surely you can find one who doesn't already belong to another man and who actually seeks out your company rather than runs from it. Let her be a woman of whom you can be proud, not one who tramples on your pride. Let her be a woman who makes you strong, not weak. A woman who will bring something good to your future, not merely strife and vexation."

But how was he supposed to give up and not fight for his unborn child? His father had reared a litter of eight children— at least three of whom were illegitimate, Damon included— and would never have relinquished his rights to any one of them for another man to raise.

So he'd spent these last four days in pursuit of Elizabeth. So far he'd found no sign of her. Nobody he came upon had even seen a woman of her description, and nobody recognized the name. But he wouldn't give up. He knew that world into which his son was in danger of being born; knew its cold, dark and dirty side especially, and he couldn't let it happen.

When he first left London in a blind rage, Damon had blamed Ransom for persuading Elizabeth to flee the city— he knew his brother had met with her— but since then he'd had time to cool his temper and reassess the situation. Many, many miles with no company but his own had forced him to consider other potential causes for her flight.

Finally he concluded that Elizabeth left London in haste, not because of anything his brother said— she would never listen to the advice of someone she saw to be her inferior— but because she thought there was no other choice. A woman raised to maintain appearances at all costs, she chose to stay in her apathetic, but dutiful marriage, rather than leave her husband and be thrown onto the rocky seas of scandal. She could not, by law, divorce her husband, of course; only the husband could apply for such an action, but George Stanbury would surely do so at once if she publicly cohabitated with another man.

Although Elizabeth's reputation would be

shattered and her fine society friends would abandon her, Damon saw all that as a brittle, meaningless veneer in any case. *He* could provide for his child. They would be safe with him, so what did any of that matter?

Apparently Elizabeth did not share this view. She did not trust him to look after her. Whatever his father and elder brother suspected, Damon firmly refused to believe that Elizabeth Stanbury had used him as nothing more than a stud horse, to provide her titled husband and his estate with a long-awaited heir. Only Ransom could think him that naive and easily duped by a woman, and only his father could assume a woman's motives so despicable.

To hell with what anybody else thought; the child — his child—was innocent in all this. The only soul that was. He wouldn't abandon his son or daughter to the Stanburys and their world.

As for the mother of that child, she was ten years Damon's senior, beautiful, icy and stand-offish; an expensive luxury item and one of the rare few he allowed himself, for he was prudent with his finances, as he was with his time. But when he met Lady Elizabeth Stanbury he had been feeling more restive and stifled than ever before, needing something upon which to liberate his trapped energies.

Damon had set about her seduction with his typical, single-minded purpose. Yes, he had let her color his cheek with a stinging slap more than a few times, let her call him a "filthy, despicable Deverell bastard" quite often. Because the sex, once she'd assured herself of his unworthiness and her own superiority, was remarkable— rough, raw and exceedingly zealous.

"I might have imagined this tomfoolery from some of the other boys," his father had muttered when he learned about Elizabeth's condition. "But you, Damon, ought to have more sense!"

Back to the subject of his father's expectations, he thought dolefully. Was there ever a heavier mantle laid on any man's shoulders? Sometimes he wished fervently to be the son of whom nothing good was anticipated, or likely— Ransom, for example. What a relief that would be.

Or perhaps not. When Damon left London, his brother was looking decidedly worse for wear, having encountered some thugs in a dark alley. With his usual "I don't know why you bother" attitude, the badly injured man, propped up in his bed, had told Damon it was just the handiwork of somebody who took a disliking to his face. A disadvantage of being a Deverell *and* a man who didn't care who he offended.

But Damon, having troubles of his own pressing on his immediate attention, had no time to worry about his brother who would, inevitably, bounce back with just a few scars that made him all the more handsome and irresistible to the ladies. Damon had to manage his problem first.

Again, he imagined his father sitting opposite in the carriage and reminding him, "William Pitt the Younger was Prime Minister at your age. What are you doing with your life, boy? You were meant to do all the things I couldn't, because I lacked the formal education. I lacked the opportunities, but I made sure you had them all. And what do you do? Throw them back in my face to pursue an affair with a married woman. A married woman now carrying a child that may, or may not, be yours."

Damon strongly resented the accusation that he could be duped into accepting responsibility for another man's child. He had no reason to suspect Elizabeth had any other lover. Why would she need more than him? Besides, she could easily have told him the child was somebody else's, but she had not.

Nor, however, had she been particularly grateful for his offer of help.

She had told him of the pregnancy after sending him an urgent message to meet her at the suite she kept at Mivart's Hotel, which is where their trysts had always taken place— all except for the last one, when she had turned up, unexpectedly, at his lodgings. After she gave him the news, Damon had quickly set about putting his thoughts and plans in order, deciding what must be done, what could not be done, and what everything would cost. But she had eyed him with cool bemusement, and then curtly assured him, "I don't expect anything from you. What could *you* possibly do for me now?"

Startled that she remained so calm, even offhand about her situation, he had replied somberly, "Elizabeth, there is a child to consider."

"Yes. A miracle, I suppose," she said, her tone droll. "After all this time, I thought it was impossible for me."

"I won't abandon you. We'll manage this. Don't be afraid."

"Why would I be afraid? Women bear children all the time. I'll have the best midwife, of course, wet-nurses to take care of it, maids and nannies."

"That's not what I meant, Elizabeth."

"Then what?" She had almost laughed, her eyes gleaming with amusement and something like pity.

"What can you possibly mean?"

"Don't fear your husband. I'll deal with him. I can look after—"

"How old are you?" she'd demanded suddenly, frowning just a little, probably conscious, as ever, of the wrinkles she did everything possible to avoid. "I forget sometimes your youth."

"Twenty-five. Soon." It sounded better, somehow, than twenty-four.

She had brushed his chin lightly with her cold, slender fingers and said, "And you think you can give me what I need."

"I have done, have I not?" he'd snapped, nodding his head toward the bedroom door of the suite.

"As if *that* is everything," was her weary reply, accompanied by another pitying look— one that might have withered a lesser man.

But Damon thought she was being brave, putting on that aristocratic, marble facade, hiding her feelings. He was certain he was the only man who could help her, whatever she thought. The child needed him, even if she assumed that she didn't.

Ransom, swathed in bandages, peering out from beneath swollen eyelids, had said. "Why don't you wait and see? A pregnancy often comes to nothing. There are so many things that might happen. Until the child is carried safely to term and born living—"

"Because he doesn't have the patience to wait and see whether the brat even looks like him," his father yelled. "He can't wait to ruin his bloody life."

Damon resented that remark too. He considered himself one of the most patient, long-suffering men in all England. Probably in the world. Nobody was more patient than him.

When the devil would they get to this blasted inn?

"Might as well walk there on my own two damned feet," he growled at the roof of the carriage.

In reply, more snow spat at the window of his rocking vehicle and another icy draft reached wiry fingers through unseen gaps to scratch and pinch at his face. Huddling deeper into his tall collar did not seem to help much. The wind here was an unstoppable creature that laughed spitefully at any barrier in its way, and then surmounted it with a gleeful wail of victory.

Damon had always considered Bodmin Moor in Cornwall, just a few miles from where he grew up, to be the wildest place he knew; a landscape laden with sinister shadows and treacherous gullies, prone to unpredictable, fast-changing weather. But here, traveling through Yorkshire for the first time in his life, he discovered a form of climate and a terrain even more brutal.

Before it grew dark out, he'd watched the wind-driven snow bare its teeth— like a tormented, blood-thirsty, white tiger— and roar across the bleak, rough edges of the panorama, tearing at any little bit of exposed flesh with pitiless, jagged fangs, and prowling across the rocky hills to lurk in deep drifts that could swallow a man whole. This snow had no wretched "prettiness" about it, none of the peace and tranquility with which that gleaming white cloaked London streets either. Nature here was unrefined, uncivil, and any attempt made to tame it, however determinedly begun, appeared abandoned midway through. Even the occasional cluster of squat stone buildings, scratched, scraped and chiseled into the side of a hill, seemed starkly menacing and unwelcoming, not many generations away from ruin and fit to offer only begrudging shelter against the elements. It was as if any wandering stranger caught out in this storm had only himself to blame and so could expect no warmth or hospitality from the natives.

But Damon neither looked for, nor expected, a welcome. He was, like that fierce, untamable snow, not interested in making friends.

Now an early winter's night had set in and he could no longer observe his surroundings through the carriage window, but that fierce wind still whittled around every crag and corner, warning all creatures not to venture out into the storm. Not if they wanted to keep their sanity.

Tonight Damon didn't particularly care about that. He couldn't really say what was happening in his mind. Usually sure of where he was going, on this occasion he felt lost.

It was no easy thing to turn his back on the man he'd idolized all his life, to step out from that guiding shadow.

Again he heard his father's voice, a scornful sound that would, apparently, follow him wherever he went. "I hope you don't fancy you're in love with her? You don't know what love is. How could you at your age?"

No, he wasn't in love with Elizabeth. But if she imagined passing his child off as the fruit of her husband's loins, she would have a fight on her hands.

Damon Deverell possessed the same territorial nature as the bull shark too. Nobody would ever take what was his and get away with it. Nobody.

Chapter Fourteen

"What in the name o' Beelzebub brought thee owt in this weather, young 'un?" the housekeeper exclaimed, her bulk filling the small, crooked doorway of the vicarage. "Snow's comin', worse than ever and 'ere you be, owt in it. 'Ave thee nowt in thee skull?"

Pip was accustomed to the housekeeper's brusque manner. The old lady had made her feelings about these visits to her master quite plain. "I've come to see Jonathan, of course, Mrs. Trotter. I've come seeking his good advice."

"Bad job for you, but the master en't 'owme." The woman gave a gelatinous sniff and wiped the back of her hand across her round, red nose. "'Appen the master's gone north and won't be back 'til Sunday service. Now be gone back to where you come from and leave 'im be. Nowt but trouble, you are. Don't thee stand there gawpin. Step owt way and let me put wood in 'ole to keep owt the ruddy draft."

The door creaked shut, a stout bolt immediately drawn across with a loud clang, as if Pip might throw herself at it and start pounding with her fists to break it off its hinges.

"Well, really!" she muttered.

There was no other sound from within the cottage, and it was obvious the housekeeper wouldn't relent and let her in, not even to warm her hands and feet a while by the kitchen fire.

The squawk of an angry crow cracked across the low, brittle, colorless sky, shattering the silence. Pip looked over her shoulder to find the bird lurking in the stark, wintering branches of a tree just over the dry-stone wall that separated the vicarage garden from the churchyard. The crow's shiny black feathers stuck out like sharp prickles as it huddled against the wind, twitched its head to one side and let out another screech, reminding her that she was an unwelcome stranger there. As if she needed reminding.

Like her, the bird was all alone. His companions must have hidden from the weather, leaving one sentinel to guard the churchyard. Or else the crow had fought off any other pretender to his proud throne, high in that skeletal tree.

He reminded her of somebody, but she couldn't think who it might be.

The bird opened its beak for another scornful cry and then took off, swooping in a low circle over her head, before perching on a gravestone beyond the wall. It seemed to want to keep an eye on her, yet, at the same time, knew better than to get too close.

"You're lucky I don't have my bow and arrows," she assured him wryly. "You wouldn't be so smug then."

Caw.

Epiphany sighed heavily as the wind plucked at the ruffles of her shoulder and danced with a large feather in her veiled cap. The crow was right and she had stood there long enough in her cold boots.

Alas she had braved the winter weather that day to come all the way from Whitby on the mail coach and now, without even the sustenance of a warm cup of tea, she must turn around at once and go back. Her black velvet paletot was more decorative than functional and further snowfall seemed likely. A little had fallen that morning before she left Whitby and Lord Mortmain had advised her against going out—

was so firmly in opposition to it, that he refused to let her have the family carriage— but Epiphany had great need of her dear friend Jonathan's counsel that day and she couldn't be talked out of the journey.

Now, her effort, and the risk she took of offending the Mortmains by willfully going off on her own, was all for nothing.

"Of course, it is not the first time my sister has run away," she muttered to herself as she marched down the garden path to the gate, "but she's twenty-three now, soon to be married, and far too old for tree-houses."

Since Jonathan Lulworth, the vicar of Thorford, was not in to help with her dilemma today, she would just have to manage this matter herself.

Do not, her sister's note had said, *under any account, worry or send anybody to look for me. I shall return soon. I am not lost, eaten by wolves or kidnapped by bandits. I merely desire to be alone. To contemplate.*

As Pip passed through the gate and out into the lane, a sharp wind whistled around her skirt, speckles of snow gently drifting with it. She looked back at the vicarage but the door remained resolutely closed, the unfriendly housekeeper cosseted away in the warmth of her kitchen, probably muttering under her breath about "barmpot American girls, allus coming and going at will, untended".

She shut the gate hard and looked up at the sky. Yes, the snow was definitely falling again in earnest and with increasing speed. Large flakes caught on her black net veil.

Glancing down again at her mourning garments, Pip suddenly felt, more savagely than ever, the deep pain of loss in her heart. If only Aunt Du Bois was still with them; she would know what to do. In all likelihood, Serenity would never have dared run off like this if their aunt had not succumbed to a virulent fever soon after they arrived in Yorkshire, leaving the three sisters unchaperoned. The liveliness and enthusiasm with which Aunt Du Bois had bustled them all along was much missed, and so, surprisingly enough, was her guidance. Pip might have resisted her aunt's prodding and poking when she suffered them, but now they were gone and she realized there was a benefit to having somebody else in charge occasionally after all, even if one did not always agree with them. Today she truly felt alone and suddenly older. It weighed heavily on her shoulders.

"Oh, Jonathan, my only friend in this grim place! Why did you have to go away too? You might at least have provided me with a comforting word. As well as tea. Now I shall freeze to death and you'll all be sorry." She shouted back at the house, "I hope you send Mrs. Trotter packing." But she didn't really mean that. She wouldn't want the housekeeper to lose her post, just because *she* was too stupid to stay indoors when a snow storm approached.

Her bones already felt frozen. She was not very good in the cold; much better in heat. Perhaps it was something to do with being born during a fire on a riverboat, she mused.

Caw!

Shaking the new flakes from her shoulders, she brushed down her coat and stuck out her tongue at the arrogant crow, which had flown after her and now sat on the wall. If it was waiting for her to drop dead in the snow, it would be disappointed; the bird would not get to pick the juicy flesh from her bones today.

Pipers didn't give up, however hopeless things seemed; it was not in their nature.

Besides, she was not alone; she had Merrythought. But that brought little cheer. Unfortunately her younger sister, at just eighteen, was not capable of giving much sensible advice and Pip did not want to burden her with worry.

As she trudged back along the lane, hoping the mail coach would be along soon to carry her back the way she had come, the snowfall quickened, tumbling around her in big, plump, glistening flakes. Within just a few moments, the wind grew from a mewling kitten to a roaring lion.

She felt that crow still watching her, following her a few yards behind and perching every so often on the dry stone wall or a leafless branch. Those beady eyes peered through the snow. Waiting. It was ominously quiet now. As if the crow knew something she didn't.

Pip walked along the verge, her head down and one hand on her hat, fighting against the wind.

There were only a few cottages and farms within sight of the church. Perched halfway up a steep hill, looking out over the wildly beautiful Yorkshire landscape, the grave-markers of the cemetery formed a huddling cluster against the howling wind. Some of them tilted precariously as if, over time, nature's force had pushed them just hard enough to move the stone. Jonathan had told her that there was once a Norman castle nearby, but very little of it now remained, random chunks of ancient rubble strewn about in the long grass, like grey crumbs dropped by a clumsy giant on his way across the moor.

On a pretty autumn morning, or a mellow, lazy

summer afternoon, this hill was a place of great natural beauty, but today Thorford churchyard was a grim, forbidding spot, making the retention of cheerful hope even more of a challenge. Even for a Piper.

Had the dreariness of this place in winter been the cause of Serenity's desire to go off alone, as she did when she was a girl in a temper? The skies were so very dark lately, the nights coming early and staying late, and after the shock of their aunt's death, the sisters' mood was already somber and drear. It might have been enough to push Serenity out of the house and onto the moor. The girl was not much of a walker, but when she made up her mind about something she did have a certain determined spirit, in common with her sister. There was no arguing with her in one of those moods.

"Are you sure you can put up with Edwyn Mortmain for a husband?" Pip had asked one morning as they helped dress each other for the day.

"My poor dear girl," Serenity had replied with a languid smile over her shoulder, "any husband is something to be put up with to a certain extent."

My poor dear girl. Serenity had taken to calling her that immediately after the engagement was official, as if she was suddenly so exalted that it hurt her neck to look down at Pip, despite the fact that there was only a year and a half between them in age.

"Well, as long as it's what you want."

"One must do one's duty. This is what I'm meant for."

The Mortmains had invited them all up to Yorkshire that summer, to the family estate, Darkest Fathoms, which turned out to be little more than a ruin overlooking Whitby Bay.

"Do you truly see this as your destiny?" Pip had asked her sister. "To be mistress of a damp, mouse-infested old pile of stone, so far from London and all its attractions?" Her sister was a sociable creature, who would surely never survive without some cause to wear her best ball gowns regularly. But Darkest Fathoms was a long way from fashionable society.

"My poor dear girl, you just don't understand the English. The Mortmains have lived in this place for several hundred years. To you it might look like a drafty ruin, but the British love their shabby aristocrats. That's how they know the difference between old money and new. They would consider it ostentatious to have too much that is modern."

"Call me flamboyant and gaudy then, but I don't think our father has worked so hard to have you living in what amounts to little more than a crypt with bats sleeping in the rafters."

"There are no bats among the rafters."

"Well, something scratches up there at night. Our sister, Merry, thinks it's dead and restless Mortmains. She says, in a house like this, it is more than likely the dead walk abroad. Of course, she's read a great deal on the subject."

"You don't understand. You have no appreciation or respect for lineage, tradition and old world elegance."

Rather than debate the matter any further, Pip had left the house then to visit Jonathan Lulworth, with Serenity calling after her, "I do hope you're not traipsing across the moor again to bother that sad little curate."

She gave no reply.

Pip had discovered Jonathan Lulworth the very first Sunday they arrived in Yorkshire, quite literally tripping over him in the graveyard, while she was distracted reading the carving on a stone crypt and he, stooped over, was tugging on some stubborn weeds growing around it. They quickly discovered a shared love of history and antiques. She began visiting the Thorford vicarage whenever possible to enjoy his extensive library. Sometimes she had one of her sisters in tow for the sake of respectability, but often— under the guise of "taking some air on the moors"— she crept away to Thorford quite alone to enjoy conversation, tea and scones in the good vicar's parlor. His housekeeper had tried, with several stern looks and salty comments, to discourage her visits, but Pip brazenly ignored all that, pretending not to understand the thick Yorkshire accent. In the space of one summer she came to depend upon those little escapes and Jonathan's quiet, tranquil and intelligent company, to keep her from going mad in that mausoleum the Mortmains called home.

The young vicar's kindness and gentleness had soon become dear to her, his friendship invaluable. She could listen to him without taking offense when he sought to advise her, without feeling the need to arm herself with a weapon— verbal or physical. Pacing up and down in his parlor, she confided in him all her worries, shared every disagreement with her sisters, every frustration at life, and he always listened without interruption, ready with insight, assurance and comfort when she required it.

"The incredible Mr. Lulworth, whose name we hear so often these days, must have a way with wild animals," Serenity once remarked, apparently greatly diverted by the friendship. "Or perhaps you are in love."

Pip simply put her nose in the air and let her sister tease. At least, with Jonathan, she felt calm. He did not rouse her temper or make it impossible to be composed and prudent in his presence. One could never be annoyed with Jonathan Lulworth and, in his presence, she was never tempted to do, or say, anything that later struck her as harebrained.

But then, only weeks after their arrival in Yorkshire, their aunt, who had suffered a myriad of inexplicable aches and pains since early summer, suddenly took to her bed. She was dead within a week. According to the physician who examined her, the lady had been "riddled with tumors", a ghastly term that Merrythought used with considerable rolling of the 'r', whenever anybody asked about their aunt's demise.

For the time being, with the sisters in mourning for another few months at least, Serenity's wedding to Mortmain must be postponed.

At the death of their aunt, the girls had all managed their sorrow in different ways: Merrythought sobbed into her pillow every night, convinced that she too was "riddled" with something dire; Pip shook her fist at God for taking a lady who still had so much life in her, and Serenity went very quiet, withdrawing into herself as if it was unladylike to show any emotion at all.

Without their aunt's determination, inherent sense for matchmaking, and some useful but mysterious connections in society, they would not be where they were now, of course. That irrepressible lady had managed to get the Piper girls into more

ballrooms than most folk thought they had any right
to enter. Indeed, Epiphany mused wryly, Mrs. H.
Thaxton-Choate of Boston, New York *and*
Philadelphia could learn a thing or two from Queenie
Du Bois of Hog's Flank.

But after all her hard work, their aunt had not
lived long enough to reap the rewards of success. Pip
remembered the carving on that ancient crypt in
Thorford graveyard: *Death is a bell that tolls for all; only
the hour of its striking is unknown.*

Enough thinking about death, she decided firmly.
Shivering, she looked, in vain, for some sign of a
break in the snow. What she needed now was a dose
of that infamously uncrushable Piper optimism. It
had never let her down before and it wouldn't now
either.

The mail coach would be along soon. Surely.

If not the mail coach, then somebody would
come along. She could not be the only living soul out
on the Thorford road that afternoon — or evening as
it must be by now; at least, the rapid dimming of
daylight made it seem so.

The nearest cottage was shuttered, no sign of life.
People out here on the moor were not keen on
outsiders and it was unlikely they'd greet Pip— a
strange-speaking foreigner— cordially at the door, or
offer shelter. No matter, she thought, quickening her
pace and humming in hopes of generating warmth.
The mail coach would definitely appear over the hill
soon.

Very soon.

Her stomach growled fiercely, reminding her that
she had not eaten today at all. She really should have
eaten breakfast before she left Whitby, but sitting at

the long dining table, bookended by mournful Mortmain faces, who watched her every move as if she were a tigress in an exhibit, was never an enticing thought. It was even worse now that Serenity had chosen to run off on some mysterious journey, leaving only a short note for her sisters telling them not to worry.

At first, Pip assumed her sister would only be gone a few hours and that nightfall would surely bring her back. After all, where could she have gone? A ramble on the moors might keep her sister busy for half a day, but Serenity was not the sort to wander far enough to get lost. She always knew where she was going and it was never too far afield from the safe and familiar.

But as it grew dark out yesterday she still had not returned to the house.

"The wench did not mention a desire to go owt," Lord Mortmain had muttered crossly when told of her lingering absence. "Why would she go alone and not take my son? Women don't go wandering orf. It ain't done."

Edwyn Mortmain was also distressed, but mostly because his father was angry. "I wish Miss Piper had said something to me before she left," he murmured, the words dripping out of his small mouth as if they were pennies for a cold-fingered pauper. "She did not ask for the carriage."

"I should think nowt," the old man grumbled. "Can't get the horses owt just for a pleasure jaunt in winter. What could the wench be thinking?"

Of course, nobody wanted to say out loud what they thought Serenity might have been thinking when she wandered off, but it soon became clear that the

Mortmains were more concerned about losing Serenity's dowry than they were about her safety.

Edwyn and his father, the Viscount Mortmain, now watched Pip and her little sister with a discomforting closeness, as if they too might take flight from the house. Only a day had passed since Serenity left, and already this morning Pip had overheard the Mortmains discussing other options.

"If the eldest girl has turned tail and fled from the altar, one of the others will have to do for you," old Lord Mortmain had croaked from his chair, while Pip hovered out of sight behind the dining room door. "Damn it all, we're not giving that purse back! You can take the mouthy one or the naive one instead. I daresay it makes no difference. Better that than bother with suing for breach of promise. I hear their father retained Stempenham and Pitt, and it's best not to come up against them or we could be worse orf than we were before. No, no, you'll take one of the other wenches if the first does not come back. Get courtin' 'em now, afore the father gets wind of this."

Shock had rooted Pip to the spot for a moment, and then she'd backed away on tiptoe, forfeiting breakfast rather than face their questions and cold stares.

Well, Epiphany might be willing to do a vast many things for those she loved, but she was no martyr, and The Honorable Edwyn Mortmain was a wretched bore, a fact that could not, in any way, be alleviated by the prospect of him one day becoming a Viscount. The idea of being "courted" by such a man was insupportable for Pip, and although, a year ago, she might have had no compunction in telling him so outright, she could not do that now. The Mortmains currently kept a roof over her head, and over the head of her little sister. Tact was a painful, uneasy necessity. This was no time to further upset the applecart.

Oh, her stomach really complained now.

Thank goodness Jonathan Lulworth was not here to witness the gaseous contortions of her intestines. They would both have been mortified. Not that he— being a frightfully constipated English gentleman— would have mentioned it, of course.

* * * *

Abruptly the carriage halted. No warning, no slowing of the wheels, just a sharp jolt and a rattling stop.

Cursing, Damon tugged so hard on the sash window that he almost broke it. He leaned out to yell at the coachman, "What the Devil is it now?"

"Somethin' ahead in the road. Horses won't go 'round it."

He swore again, snow melting on his lips. "Well, see what it is, man! Why do we sit here?"

"But it might be a trick. Might be an ambush."

"For pity's sake!" Damon pulled up the collar of his great coat, opened the carriage door and stepped down into snow.

"I wouldn't, if I were you, sir!" The coachman's voice warbled down to him through the screaming wind. "Take care, sir! There's vagabonds on this road, and they do lay in wait for carriages to pass."

"Splendid." He was just in the right temper for a fight. Cracking a few skulls might release some of this frustrated tension he'd suffered for the last six days of travel— most of it on rough, badly-maintained roads.

"Do mind yerself, sir! A man can barely see an inch afront of 'is nose out there, but the 'orses know, sir. They 'ave a sense for these things," the coachman called out to his only passenger above the mournful winds. "T'aint safe, sir!"

But Damon Deverell refused to be vanquished by the weather, or by some desperate highway robber's trap. He was on a mission and he would not be stopped. Squinting against the snow, he trudged forward, searching the road for any obstacle that might have frightened the horses.

At first, in the light of the carriage lanterns, he could see nothing but white. The wind sought its way under his coat and scarf, wailing in his ears so that no other sound could be heard.

One hand inside his coat, resting on the pistol he kept there, Damon took another step forward. It was then that he finally saw something in the road. Right at his feet. He'd almost tumbled over it.

A bundle of rags? A dead animal?

A wind-beaten black feather fluttered helplessly in the wind.

No sign of blood in the snow, however. The dark animal could not have been there too long for the snow had not yet had time to settle over it.

Whatever it was, he'd have to shift it so that his horses could get by.

Suddenly, as he assessed the crumpled creature and his eyes adjusted, Damon realized it was human. A woman.

Dressed entirely in black, she was bent over, fussing with her ankle, apparently unaware of how close she came to being crushed by horses. Of course, in the howling wind she must not have heard the carriage approach.

"Madam! What the devil are you doing?"

She looked up, sheltering her face from the snow with one hand, and he saw now that the wet feather was merely decoration on a small, veiled bonnet. "Oh, sir," she gasped out, breathless, "I think I twisted my ankle."

No sign of a companion. Out here and all alone? She didn't look like a robber, but she might be a decoy. His hand tightened on the pistol under his coat. "You shouldn't be out in this weather, stumbling about like a drunk in the road. It's treacherous and getting dark. And cold."

"You don't say? Next thing you'll tell me is that it's snowing. How glad I am to have you pointing out the obvious. So very helpful and typical of a man." Then she took a step toward him, yelped and crumpled to the ground again. It was a genuine sound of distress and one he could not ignore.

Oh, damn and blast. Now he'd have to help her. As if he had nothing else to do and not enough woman trouble already.

When she looked up at him the second time, he had moved aside to let the carriage lantern lights gild her face.

And thus he recognized her.

With eyes widened and lips parted, she drew a breath that could only be preparation for a protest— he'd been on the wrong side of a woman's temper enough times to recognize that sound— but Damon swiftly stooped and lifted the figure out of the snowy road, carrying her back to his hired carriage before her startled mouth could make any further noise. Or before he could change his mind and remember the danger of touching her.

The coachman, watching him emerge through the screaming snow with this strange, noisy parcel in his arms, called down from his perch, "What you got there then?"

"A woman. And lucky she's not a dead one. Get the door for me, man."

"You don't have to carry me," she cried. "A helpful arm to lean on would have been sufficient."

"But much slower. You've already caused me a delay, woman."

"I can assure you it wasn't deliberate," she exclaimed grandly, chin up, the frozen feather in her hat scraping his cheek. "My ankles are generally very sturdy. As is the rest of me."

He grunted. "You're certainly no light and dainty bundle."

"Well, gracious, why didn't you just leave me where you found me? If I'm to be rescued I'd rather wait for somebody good-looking, polite, obliging and pleasant."

"Don't want much, do you?" he muttered. "Keep still, woman, or I'll drop you."

Holding the carriage door open, the coachman yelled through the beating snow, "Looks to me like a bundle o' trouble."

"Yes. But somebody has to help her, I suppose."

"I thought you were a Deverell," the old man added, chuckling. "Ain't you riskin' your reputation, sir? From what I 'ear, Deverells don't ride about the country rescuing women. They're most often the ones getting women into trouble."

He heard the bundle give a low groan of despair, as she turned her head away to utter a curse, and that partially frozen feather slapped him once again in the face. Deliberately, he was certain.

Jayne Fresina

Chapter Fifteen

He dropped her to the seat opposite his own, where she commenced grumbling under her breath about the indignity of being carried.

"On our way then, man," he shouted to the coachman before he pulled the sash window back into place, shutting out the worst of the wind. A second later the horses resumed their journey and the carriage rocked again, as it did before, like a small rowboat tossed about on a storm-whipped ocean.

She tugged the torn veil and crisp feather on her hat to one side and glowered at him across the carriage. "Deverell," she exhaled gustily, eyes afire with disdain. "We meet again."

Her flare for the dramatic was entertaining. She ought to be an actress, he mused.

"I suppose you don't remember me," she added.

Could she seriously suppose that to be possible? He kept his expression disinterested— a certain way to annoy any female. "Should I?"

"Lord Courtenay's ball last May—"

"Ah, yes. The American. Fanny Flipperwill... or something."

Her brows arched. "Close enough."

But he was only teasing, of course. "Miss Piper. What are you doing in Yorkshire?" He could still hardly believe it was her. "It was, I think...Ascot...the last time I saw you. Was it?" As if he didn't know exactly where and when. Two o'clock in the afternoon and she was wearing lilac. He'd eaten bread and bacon for his breakfast that day, washed down

221

with beer. It had been warm day, slightly above average for the month of June at 19 degrees Celsius with a light south westerly wind. There had been a grass stain on her hem, approximately two inches in length. Three stitches on the middle finger of her left glove were loose. She had smelled of peaches and lily-of-the-valley. He hadn't fallen asleep afterward until twenty minutes past two the following morning, tossing about so badly in his bed that the landlady thought robbers had broken in.

He supposed most people would remember that a horse named Hagley won the Royal Hunt Cup that day, but what most people remembered was boring to him. No challenge in it.

"My elder sister is engaged to marry the Honorable Edwyn Mortmain, and his family live near here," she was saying. "Didn't my aunt send you a note?"

"She did. But there was no mention of any Yorkshire, or any Honorable. I was merely informed that you were leaving London."

Once the rumors had calmed down and the eldest girl was safely guaranteed a good match, he had, it seemed, served his purpose in her aunt's eyes and been swiftly disposed of.

"Not much to entertain *you* here, I should imagine," he added. "In the way of eligible bachelors, I mean."

"I'm not interested in bachelors, eligible or otherwise, as I told you before."

"Humph." He sniffed, folding his arms. "There was a rumor in London this summer about an engagement, but I heard it to be Bertie Boxall who had landed himself a Piper sister. Naturally, I assumed—"

"You know me better than that, even with so short and strange an acquaintance."

Yes, he thought, his grim mood tempered now, soothed by her confidant reply. He *did* know her well enough. He never had quite believed she would do such a foolish thing. But even so, it had smarted when he heard the gossip, when he saw other folk, like Lady Roper, believing in it.

"I was not entirely sure," he muttered. "You young girls have a tendency toward romantic fancies, and you might have been swept away by that handsome idiot. That is why I prefer a mature woman— those who have experienced a little more of the world and do not expect a fairytale."

She was removing her wet gloves and huffing on her fingers. "I'm certain one conversation with you can disabuse any young girl of her fanciful notions. Prince Charming you are not."

"Really? I've been told I have charm."

She chuckled. "Let me guess. The woman who told you that wanted something from you. A favor of some sort. I don't, of course, so I have no cause to lie."

Damon shifted on his seat and unfolded his arms. It was one thing not to want her gratitude for this rescue, quite another for her not to offer any, he decided. So he said, "It was fortunate for you, that I came along when I did tonight. I've been informed that this road is plagued with undesirables."

"I'd be right at home then, wouldn't I?" came the arch reply, before she turned her head to glare at the snow-spattered window and they rode for a while in rocking silence.

After all this time, here she was again. What strange twist of fate would bring them together once more? If the carriage ride was in any way comfortable he might have assumed he'd fallen asleep and begun to dream.

Her lips were decidedly pinker now that warmth returned to her skin, and a shade of summer dusk still lightly kissed her cheeks. The last snowflakes melted from her hair and the feather on her hat turned limp, drooping as it thawed. He could almost imagine he heard the frost crystals crackling and sighing as they transformed into teardrops, dripping to her sleeve and shoulder. When she shivered and rubbed her arms, a very soft scent, little more than a hint of lavender, meandered across the short distance to where he sat. Instantly he was reminded of last spring, that kiss and her sun-warmed forehead against his lips.

He shouldn't think of it, of course. It was too late for that now and he had other problems.

"I suppose you want my coat," he ventured.

Without moving her head, she slid her wary gaze back to him. "But then you would feel the cold, surely. And I have my paletot."

"That thin, fancy piece of nothing? It's not fit for a middling day, let alone a winter's storm. Why do women never think?"

"We leave that to the men, because in the space of time it takes them to mull it over and discuss the matter, we've usually already done what was needed anyway."

"Do you want my blasted coat or not? I don't need you dying of pneumonia in my company and on my watch. Deverells are blamed for everything, as it is."

Her eyes glittered with silent laughter. But the warm kind that made him think of summer rain. "I'll try hard not to die in your custody and make things messy for you, Deverell."

"Too late." For so many things, he thought with a burst of self-pity. "You've already delayed me. I daresay it couldn't be helped. Women never look after themselves and then they complain when men try to do it for them."

"I can assure you, sir, I've looked after myself for a very long time."

"You haven't been alive for a *very long time*."

"We Pipers have the gift of youthful looks. Don't be deceived."

He shook his head. "If I had charge of you, you wouldn't go wandering about alone in this weather."

"We may both celebrate the fact that you don't have charge of me. In case you haven't already guessed, you'd find me dreadfully disobedient and impossible to train and I'd probably resort to impaling you on a roasting spit."

"You could try," he replied coolly, amused, as he was before, by this small creature's fighting bravado.

"But you needn't worry because nobody has charge of me. Nor will they ever." She paused. "You have a very odd look on your face."

"I... was just thinking of someone I once knew." "Oh?"

"A long time ago." *And her name was Nonesuch.*

His bloody heart ached because he had missed her so.

He thought of Mrs. Blewett once asking why his invisible friend was a girl. Although he'd had no answer for that at the time, now he wondered if it was because he already had enough brothers and his one and only half-sister, Raven, never had time for him when they were growing up. In those days she had little time for any of her siblings, other than Ransom, and together they were thick as thieves, possessing a bond that nobody else could intrude upon. Damon supposed he must have been envious of that relationship.

Whatever his reason for creating "Nonesuch", she was an invaluable ally in those early years, a girl brave and fearless, just as prone to scabby knees as he, but who occasionally showed a vulnerable side and needed rescue— just to remind them both that he was in charge. Together they played bloodthirsty pirate games along the Cornish cliffs and the wind-blown sands, before his father sent him away to boarding school and he had to leave Nonesuch behind. The last sight he remembered of his friend was of a shadow waving from the cliff road as the sun rose out of the sea behind her and made the waves froth.

By the time he had returned home at the end of the first Michaelmas term, Nonesuch was gone. Forever, or so he had thought.

"Isn't it odd, Deverell, that we should meet again like this?" Her stunning eyes twinkled with teasing playfulness, even as he saw her shiver again. "I might almost suspect you of following me."

"I can assure you I have problems enough without chasing after another, Miss Piper."

He scowled with as much fierceness as he could conjure. "Now take my coat, damn you."

* * * *

226

Apparently he found something so terrible about the sight of her person that he couldn't look away. The feeling, she realized, was mutual. Always had been.

The offer of his coat was so churlishly given that she decided she would rather catch cold than accept it.

"No, thank you. My own coat is adequate."

But to her surprise he leaned across and swept his coat around her shoulders, not paying any heed to her resistance. The heavy warmth quickly surrounded her limbs and had the unexpected effect of a calming caress. She was forced to remember the last time they met, at Ascot, when she was left feeling bereft because she'd lost her chance at making peace— had been too busy quarrelling and putting up her prickles. And then, in her prize foolishness, had made the stupidest remark ever about keeping him as a lover on the side once she married.

She'd promised herself that if she ever saw Damon Deverell again, it would be different. She would be sensible, mature, not say anything without thinking carefully first. Not be so swept off her feet with excitement to see him again, that she blurted out any ridiculous comment that came to her head.

Oh, but it was not easy.

He sat back on his own seat, the angry stare renewed. "So I know what you are doing running wild in the county of Yorkshire, Miss Piper, but what were you doing in the blessed road? In a snow storm? Alone? Unprepared for the weather *again*. I don't suppose I can expect any sensible excuse. Americans are known for daft, independent, foolhardy tendencies, of course."

She thought of that crow in the tree earlier, trying to chase her off. So that was it! Here was the very man of whom that rude bird had reminded her.

"I had been to visit a friend. I took the mail coach to Thorford today and started back toward Whitby before the snow began in earnest. I must have missed the mail coach on its return."

"This friend you went to visit did not offer you accommodation or some safe transport? Not much of a friend."

"It would have been difficult for him to do either service, since he wasn't in when I got there."

His eyes darkened. "*He?*" The word exploded out of him like sparks from a magician's firecracker. She felt the stinging heat.

"I thought another carriage of some sort would come along," she replied. "This is the London road, after all."

"But this snow has put a stop to most travelers. It might have been hours before anybody came along. Taking such a chance on this bleak day seems a haphazard way to *look after* yourself."

"I had a...much on my mind."

"Such as?"

Pip barely heard the question, too distracted inhaling the masculine scent of his coat—rich spice and cigars. Having the weight of that garment around her shoulders was almost the same as having his dark embrace around her. It felt quite naughty. Yet not at all unpleasant.

Her stomach grumbled quietly beneath her corset.

Tugging the collar of his coat more snugly around her face, she was conscious suddenly of the fact that her ears must be very red and glowing unbecomingly. It shouldn't matter to her, but it did. Vanity, she thought listlessly. Nothing worse than vanity in a woman who had so little of which to be vain.

"Such as?" he repeated, louder. "What could you possibly have on your little mind? I must know, madam. Your father hired me to solve your problems, did he not?"

"Because he thinks I cannot manage my own." But if she ever wanted to prove herself capable of running the family business, she'd have to show that she could. "Will you stop this carriage and let me out? I can find my own way from here, I think. We must be in Whitby by now, for I just saw the light of a gas lamp in a window."

"Certainly not. You'll stay here with me, so I can keep an eye on you. As your father would have wanted."

She stared at him. "I don't want to be any further trouble. Thank you, but you can let me out now."

"I didn't put myself out to rescue you, just so you can wander off in the cold again and fall under other men's carriages. Like any abandoned piece of baggage in the road." Was that a grin threatening his stern mouth? No. Whatever it might have been, it was gone again before it properly formed. "Once we're at the inn I can leave you in a safe place, out of the weather, and know that at least I've stopped you from getting into any worse trouble."

"Oh, I see. How silly of me. You're being one of those painfully obliging, deadly dull Englishmen, who cannot leave me to get on with my own business. I suppose, being a woman, I'm incapable."

"I'm doing my job, madam. It's merely business." He leaned his head back against the leather seat and she realized then, as swaying lantern light touched his face, how tired he looked. Unshaven and frayed at the edges. As if he'd been traveling for days without rest. "Why do women always resort to these ridiculous measures? Traipsing about in several feet of snow in a frivolous, thin coat. To visit some... man."

"Just because you're English *and* a male, you think you know everything and are perfect."

"And just because you're American *and* a female, you refuse to admit that I do and I am."

"You know nothing of emotion, tenderness and sensitivity."

"You know nothing of reason, practicality and rationality."

Perhaps it was the soothing warmth of his coat, but she felt better now, relaxed, and amused by his pomposity. Once more he reminded her of Master Grumbles, that proudly inconvenienced wolfhound. But she hid her smile. "We're not going to get along, you and I, are we?"

"Good God, I hope not."

Just like old times, she mused.

She had been foolish to think they wouldn't argue if they ever met again. It came naturally to them. It was— dare she think it— comfortable? It might even be their way of slowly circling closer. They were both cynics, cautious and yet curious. Like that crow in Thorford churchyard.

When he stretched his legs diagonally across the carriage, Pip remembered how tall he was, how, the first time they met, he took her breath away by standing over her like a great, leaning redwood tree.

The glimmer of cool bemusement in his gaze now multiplied into many more little stars of curiosity, tickling as they swept her from head to toe.

"When we first met I thought you interesting," she admitted. "I might even have liked you." *Oh, why tell him that now?* She had no idea why that came out. Disaster was at hand if she could not restrain her thoughts from escaping.

"How positively alarming."

"But it passed," she assured him hastily.

"Well, that's alright then."

"I wouldn't want you getting the wrong idea. This is not a romance."

"The thought never breezed within a hundred yards of my well-balanced mind."

It was becoming difficult to take a proper breath with his narrowed gaze fixed upon her. She thought of his kiss, how it had taken hold of her, lifted her up, set fire to her insides. And she'd never quite stopped smoldering ever since. Not in all these months.

"So who is this man you went to visit without a care for the weather?" he demanded abruptly. "You think you're in love with him, I suppose."

"Jonathan is—" She blinked. "What makes you think I'm in love with him?"

"Because you immediately began talking of emotions and tenderness. Feelings." He grimaced in a comical fashion. "Obviously, despite your declaration of not wanting any man to spoil your independence, you imagine you're *in love*." He drawled the words, smirking. "Don't look so worried. It's a feminine failing, and I suppose it couldn't be helped. You were bound to succumb eventually, like all your sex."

"When you are in the mood to talk you can be

dreadfully pompous. I think I prefer it when you're being all somber and brooding and sparing with your conversation. There is much to be said for a silent man." And she laughed.

"You're in love," he persisted, his tone taunting. "That's why you braved the storm today to visit him. Passionate feelings lead to irrational deeds." He sat up straighter. "I had better have a word with this fellow you've taken to visiting in snow storms. I must uncover his intentions. Your father would expect it."

"Dear Jonathan is the sweetest and kindest of men. There is no other like him."

"I'm sure there are folk who think there'll never be another like me, but they don't see that as necessarily unfortunate."

"Jonathan Lulworth," she told him primly, "is the vicar of Thorford, a special gentleman, always mindful of where he puts his feet and where he drives his horses. He does not pry into people's pasts or goad them into arguments—" She sneezed violently. "He is always patient and polite."

Deverell choked out a mirthless laugh. "Sounds very dull. The very worst man to handle you."

"Handle me? I don't believe he would be stupid enough to try."

No, Jonathan was always very proper with her and kept his distance. In fact, it was a little frustrating that he was so well behaved and upright. She'd seen him cast odd looks her way sometimes, but she didn't know whether he was afraid *for* her or *of* her.

Pip raised her chin and quickly dragged that limp, wayward feather out of her face again. "Why don't you stop this carriage and let me out, man?"

"Because I don't feel inclined. You're a danger to

yourself, and somebody has to watch over you."

But suddenly her hand, feeling around inside Deverell's coat for a handkerchief, had discovered the cool metal of a pistol. She caught her breath, shocked. He must have forgotten it was there when he gave her his coat.

Aha! His temporary loss of memory had served to nudge her own. Abruptly she recalled her father's story about the cheating rogue who once escaped a riverboat under pistol fire. It was as if her father was right there beside her, whispering that tale in her ear again. *Never seen silver eyes like his on any other man. True Deverell he called himself, but I doubt it was his real name. There was a rumor that he was really a wolf that taught himself to walk upright, then stole a suit of clothes..."*

The cold metal slid under her palm.

"Such an extraordinary coincidence."

"Coincidence?" he said, not sounding very interested.

The carriage bounced and swayed, so she could barely keep her seat. "Your father once cheated mine out of a small fortune at cards. On a Louisiana riverboat. Did you know that?"

He barely even paused in surprise at this information. "Madam, if I had a shilling for every time somebody claimed my father cheated them out of something, whether it be a fortune, a horse, or their virtue, I'd be a richer man than he."

"Your father *is* True Deverell, is he not?"

"Yes." He exhaled the word so that it was almost a groan, and now he was tense again, his eyes suddenly full of creeping shadows so dark they might have belonged to a demon that clawed its way up from Hell. "He's my father. Why?"

"And he was in America once, years ago?"

"So the legend goes."

"My father never forgot, and I bet your father didn't either, since mine aimed a pistol at him just as the wretch dove overboard into the Mississippi river. My father swore he saw True Deverell out-swim an alligator that night. I always thought maybe he'd drunk too much bourbon, but here *you* are... so I guess the scoundrel really did exist and he survived the river with all his parts intact. Enough to procreate at least."

A new look came into his face then, more deeply engaged. She knew at once that he'd heard the story before. Although perhaps he, like Epiphany, had not believed it until now.

She felt steadier suddenly, more in command of the proceedings, but still excited, a rapid heartbeat leaping and bouncing through her.

"So this won't be the first time a Piper has aimed a real gun at a Deverell, will it?" She withdrew his pistol from the coat and pointed it across the carriage. "Now you can order your coachman to stop and let me out. No need for any further debate. I don't require a man to watch over me, and since you're being so damnably pig-headed I must resort to these measures to get free of you." With her sweetest smile, she added, "I've been practicing my aim, as you suggested, and I am, after all, considerably closer to you than my father was when he had his chance with a Deverell. And *I'm* stone cold sober."

Chapter Sixteen

Damon looked at the muzzle of his own pistol and then at the woman pointing it at him. Careless of him to forget the weapon in his coat. She was a dangerous distraction. But he knew that already.

"I'm afraid I can't possibly comply with your wishes," he said evenly. "You'll just have to shoot me." Of course she would threaten extreme measures which were totally unnecessary. That love of drama again, with a hint of violent tendencies. Very like her aunt.

"Don't talk rot, Deverell. Stop the carriage at once."

"Sorry. Can't do it." He spread his arms along the back of the seat. "Like I said, you'll have to shoot me and properly this time. If you really want to get away."

Even at gunpoint Damon found himself in the mood to tease her again. It was rare for him in general, but around her it came naturally, no matter what their situation. He liked the way her brows wriggled with consternation and her lips puckered, as if she wasn't sure whether he meant his words or not, but she was determined to be outraged either way. Her face was so expressive she could never hide her thoughts from him and that made a welcome change.

"What do you mean— if I really want to get away from you?" she demanded.

"Well, you may as well admit, Miss Piper, that this was your plan from the beginning, was it not?" he said. "Your scheme."

"My scheme?"

"To seduce me."

Her eyebrows arched high. "I beg your pardon?"

"Am I supposed to think it's a coincidence that this carriage before which you hurled yourself belongs to me?" he muttered. "Now you hold me at gunpoint and I am powerless to escape."

She frowned. "But I'm the one escaping."

"Go on then."

"You have to tell the coachman to stop the carriage or I can't get out, can I?"

But he ignored that. "I should have known it the first time we met...the shawl...the revealing ball gown, like a baited hook to draw me in....the kiss *foisted* upon me...the improper suggestions bandied about. You mean to make me besotted, so you might then break my heart and toss me aside. Was this all a vendetta because my father once beat yours in a game of cards?"

"That would be an extremely flimsy reason for a vendetta."

"You're a hot-head American and an irrational woman," he shrugged, "and we, neither of us, like to lose. What other reason do you require?"

She laughed then, but kept the pistol surprisingly steady. "I hadn't thought of the name Deverell in years, until you told me who you were at the Courtenay's ball. Until then True Deverell's miraculous escape was nothing more than another of my father's fables, brought out of its box every time he drank too much and wanted to reminisce about his younger days."

Sounded like *his* father, he mused.

"As for vengeance, Deverell," she added. "If I wanted that from any man I wouldn't use seduction as my weapon. I wouldn't know how to begin."

"Wouldn't you?" he murmured, a little hoarse.

She waved the gun about in a rather worrisome fashion. Good thing it wasn't loaded and ready to fire. "Instead, if I was on a quest for revenge for some outrage committed against my family, I would—"

"Give him a black eye?"

"Since I have a gun, I could shoot him in the kneecap."

"Interesting choice."

"For a start." Her eyes twinkled with that lush, unusual color, as her gaze swept up and down his body. "If he begged for mercy, I might take pity before I reached any parts he really needed."

He felt a laugh working its way up his throat. Once again she had lightened his mood when other women usually darkened it. In her presence he felt his stresses and worries drift away, replaced by the urge to play games, carefree as he once was. She claimed not to like him, but she certainly enjoyed herself in his company, waving that gun about, eyes shining with delight at the capital idea of causing him bodily harm.

She was a puzzle. A captivating puzzle box he didn't quite want to solve, because he wanted to go on playing with her, running his hands, and his mind, over her parts. Calculating her potential wickedness and how he might match it, lick for lick, bite for bite. Thrust for thrust. He pictured his fingers around her wrists, his tongue in the little hollow at the base of her throat, slowly working its way downward...

He groaned under his breath and wiped hot fingers across his equally overheated brow.

At that moment the carriage turned sharply and jolted Miss Piper to the side. Damon quickly grabbed the muzzle and took the gun from her. As he sat back again, holding the weapon, she glowered across the carriage, looking attractively disheveled.

Needing to cast his eyes elsewhere before he did something he would later regret, Damon glanced through the window again, composed himself and said evenly, "Looks like we arrived at the inn finally. I'm ravenous. We'll dine together." One dinner couldn't hurt, surely. He had to eat, did he not? So did Nonesuch, if the low rumblings of her stomach were anything to go by.

"Don't you ever *ask* a girl's permission before you make decisions for her?"

"Why should I? Obviously, I have the advantages of maturity, superior wisdom and masculine excellence."

"You really are despicable, aren't you?"

"You'll dine with me because you're hungry, woman. Be practical for once. I know it must be hard for you to make a rational decision and set emotion aside—"

"Are you mad? You would truly dine with a woman who just aimed a gun at you?"

"I'm accustomed to it. In fact, I've had a great deal worse treatment."

"All of it well deserved, no doubt."

He shrugged, putting his gun away inside his cutaway. "Obviously. I'm a Deverell. Angry women come with the territory."

* * * *

Damon ordered a roast chicken dinner for the two of them.

"What about your coachman and the horses?"

she inquired pertly, as if he might be too mean to think of their comfort.

"The coachman will eat well in the kitchens, don't fret. And the horses will be well tended in the stables. They'll get a good night's rest."

"A night?" she exclaimed. "I can't stay here for the entire night. I must get back to Darkest Fathoms. I don't need any more rumors begun about me."

"Darkest Fathoms? What the devil might that be?"

"The Mortmain estate. It stands on the cliffs, overlooking Whitby Bay. A rather grim sentinel and aptly named."

"That is where you and your sisters are staying?"

"Yes." Her expression was apprehensive for a moment.

He poured wine from the jug between them, urging her to drink. After considering for a moment, she took her dented, pewter goblet and drank, wincing slightly. The wine was, indeed, an acquired taste and strong, possibly the innkeeper's own creation. "So tell me more about these... Mortmains."

"Must I? It's a very dreary subject."

"It's my job, remember? I'm supposed to be watching out for you and your sisters. Unless you prefer to sit in silence, which would be most unlike you, madam."

Once she'd taken a few more sips, and benefitted from the warmth of the hearty fire, she began to talk a great amount, the tension dissipating, dripping off her with the melting snow, words spilling out of her as if there was no way to separate them. As if it was a relief to tell somebody. Damon suspected that unless she suddenly fainted or fell asleep, he'd have to be very quick to get a word in. And she was not the fainting sort.

"The Mortmains wanted my father's money— my sister's dowry— for the estate, of course, but really only to keep it running the way it is now. The way it has been for two hundred years, I'm sure. They're not terribly interested in improving or changing anything, and they must be terrible money managers. My father would be appalled. The Mortmains have owned trading ships for centuries and once had a very successful whaling business, so I'm told, but with the market for whale bone and blubber falling off over the past twenty years, they really have little now but their ancient name and the crumbling ruin they call home."

"But your sister is happy with the match?"

"At first she was quite delighted with the idea of one day becoming a Viscountess. I believe she thought mostly of what her stationary would look like when she wrote home to old friends and enemies, rather than what married life to such a dull man would daily entail." She paused, staring off into the distance. "I must say I was rather disappointed in her lack of imagination." She shrugged. "But Serenity has always been dutiful. She does what is expected of her. Of any woman. And, in all honesty, there were not so many prospects here as she'd hoped."

"Are there not?"

"Your countrymen are not really sure what to make of us. Oh, we are entertaining company for the more adventurous of landed gentlemen— those seeking a little excitement. But marriage isn't what they have in mind. For that they want a quiet, meek, unquestioning English rose, whom they won't have to explain to anybody or apologize for. Preferably a rose without thorns."

"Naturally. Why would a wise man want to complicate his life with a woman like you? A self-professed undesirable who threatens to put a bullet in his kneecap at the first opportunity."

She rolled her eyes and then continued. "In addition to all that, I'm not certain our father's business is deemed entirely respectable."

"Why not?"

Hesitating again, she replaced a fallen lock of hair, tucking it back inside its black net, and glanced nervously around the crowded room. "I probably shouldn't tell you any of this. My sister would say it's wrong to talk about oneself so much. Look at all these people! Where were they when I was alone on that road, waiting for somebody to come by? Nowhere to be found then, were they? Thus I was stuck with you. The dangerous young lawyer with whom I am not supposed to mingle socially."

"It is the very limit, isn't it? Where was everybody else? I ask myself that all the time, when you keep turning up under my feet."

"Now they will look at us and wonder what we're doing together. I'm sure they will imagine many wicked things."

They weren't the only ones he thought darkly, watching her lips as she licked her fingers. But he reassured her. "Feel no anxiety on that score. They're strangers to us, as we are to them. In a place like this nobody knows your past and, in a storm like this, nobody much cares. We're all in the same difficulty, all cut down to the same size and reminded of our insignificance by nature's wrath."

"I suppose so." Refreshed mischief twinkled in her eyes as she leaned forward and made the candle putter with her excited breath. "We could pretend to be other people entirely."

"Indeed. We could be an old married couple for all they know."

"Or young lovers on the run, with a fortune in stolen gems."

"Or a pirate captain and his hostage princess."

She arched an eyebrow. "Or a pirate captain and her hostage prince. *I* pulled the gun on *you*."

"It was inevitable sooner or later."

She laughed.

"Tell me about your father," he persisted, refilling her wine goblet to the top.

So she conceded to his curiosity. "He began his working life as an errand lad for a grocery and provisions store. That tends to make the high and mighty turn up their fine aristocratic noses." Miss Piper then told him about the whiskey still, started by her father in his own backyard when he was a boy, and the various other enterprises by which he expanded his fortune since. "Suffice to say he has many a finger in many a pie," she concluded with a smile of fondness for the large chicken leg in her hand. "My father is a resourceful and inventive man and can make money out of most things."

Again, it sounded very like his own father.

Magical as the whisper of friction one felt across one's skin before a lightning storm, she trailed invisible fingertips across his thoughts and tickled them out of their dour mood.

Damon cleared his throat, abruptly ceased drumming his own fingers against the table and refilled his goblet. He ought to be thinking about Elizabeth and his unborn child. That was enough trouble for him.

Yes. Elizabeth. Focus. The child for which he was responsible.

Ransom had confessed to him that Elizabeth left London to stay with her Grosvenor relatives on the Yorkshire coast, near Whitby, so Damon had followed the road north, hoping to catch up with her at this inn— one at which all carriages stopped to change horses after crossing the moors. But she had a few days head start on him, of course. She could already have reached her destination and gone to ground. No matter; he would find her. He had time. No hurry.

See, he *was* patient. His father didn't know him as well as he thought. Nobody did.

"He doesn't have the patience to wait and see whether the brat even looks like him. He can't wait to ruin his bloody life."

In truth, Damon had begun to wish he never met Elizabeth. If only one could go back in time, turn back the clocks. But he had met her, he had stupidly pursued her, and now he must pay the consequences.

What would his child be like?

Had his father, True Deverell, felt like this about his sons? Uncertainty, fear, trying to keep his feet steady and hold his balance while all around him tumbled? He thought of Elizabeth's laugh again and how it sounded like ice cracking. She was breaking the frozen surface beneath him and he must run for the shore, dodging the rapidly stretching splinters and the tipping blocks if ice under his feet.

As he watched his strange dinner companion devouring a leg of roast chicken with no concerns for ladylike propriety, he considered how very different she was to Lady Elizabeth, who would never eat like this, among the "unwashed" populace. Elizabeth would have insisted on a private room and kept her face veiled. In all likelihood she would never have eaten anything prepared in this place, no matter how hungry she was.

"What's the matter with you tonight?" Miss Piper exclaimed. "You seem to go off in your own world." She smiled. Suddenly she reached across the table and he didn't know what she meant to do. Startled, he grabbed her wrist and held it tightly.

Her pulse was so strong, her skin warm now. And gripping onto her he felt as if she steadied him, saved him from the breaking ice, dragged him to firm ground.

"It's only something on your chin," she said. "Caught on your beard! Gracious! Anyone would think I meant to stab you in the throat."

He saw now that she held a napkin. Not a weapon.

It took him a moment to compose himself and slowly release her wrist.

"Well, do you blame me?" he muttered.

Laughing, she wiped his chin with her napkin, and then, as if it were nothing, resumed her own meal.

He stared, tried to catch his breath. The noise in the room grew to a pounding crescendo and then, thankfully, fell away again to a more bearable level of sound. Resisting the temptation to touch his own face where she'd just touched it, he quickly picked up the broken thread of their conversation and neatly retied it.

"So these Mortmains needed money to restock their coffers and repair their house, and along came your sister. And you said she was happy with the match *at first*? Perhaps now she objects to marriage as a business arrangement."

Immediately she squared her shoulders, eyes flashing. "I'm sure Edwyn Mortmain wants her for other reasons too. Serenity is not like me at all. She is very beautiful, as I'm sure you noted. She is very feminine, not at all quarrelsome— except with me, because I tend to bring that out in people— and she would make any man a perfect wife."

She didn't know she was beautiful, he realized.

He watched her lips moving, but the sound was gone. The clucking clatter of their stranded fellows disappeared, to be replaced by the unsteady rasp of his own breath and the hard punching throb of blood through his veins.

Now she gripped the collar of the coat he'd lent her and pulled it up around her face, as if she'd felt a draft. And he was envious of his damned coat.

Because he was beguiled by her.

When had it happened? When she kissed him? When he held her hand and felt her quickened pulse with the pad of his thumb? When he put his coat around her shoulders and brushed her cheek, accidentally, with his hand? When she wiped his chin? Or when he saw her again for the first time in months and felt his pulse skip with happiness like a spring bloody lamb? It seemed their very first encounter had indeed been a premonition of things to come, and he'd been right when he thought he felt his name carved inside her.

Oh, Christ and all the saints.

He couldn't have this. It was merely business. How many times did he have to say it?

Chapter Seventeen

"What *is* the matter now?" she demanded.

He shook his head, regained his path of thought. "But your sister is primarily thinking of the crest on her stationary, as you just said."

"Many marriages are brokered, according to my aunt. Very few are love matches. I might not approve, but I assumed the *practicality* of marriage as a business agreement would appeal to you, Master Grumbles, even if you're not the marrying kind yourself."

Lady Roper's words crept through his mind. *To survive in this world, we do what we must, not always what we would like to do. Then we find ourselves running in circles, getting nowhere.*

He drained his goblet and said, "So everything proceeds smoothly for the Pipers."

"Not quite. Soon after our father sent the dowry money our aunt died suddenly. That has postponed the wedding ceremony." She gestured at her black dress. "Obviously."

"Good lord." So her aunt was no more. Was it wicked that he felt like laughing? Probably only natural, considering he need not now worry about the safety of his "seed-bags". But he did experience a pang of regret that he would have no more opportunity to spar with her. She was an interesting lady.

"Aren't you going to say how sorry you are? That is the polite thing to do."

"Wouldn't be particularly honest. I mean to say, I'm sorry for you. I'm not sorry for me. She made some rather unpleasant suggestions of what she might do to me if I saw you again in private and fed you any more of my...muffins."

"Oh, dear."

"I must reluctantly admire the woman. No man has ever managed to have quite the same terrifying affect upon me. I'm glad I never encountered her in court."

A long moment of silence followed while he straightened the chicken bones on his plate and she stared at the fire. Then, suddenly, in that way she had of blurting things out, she said, "My sister Serenity has decided to go off on a little trip rather than marry Edwyn Mortmain. But it's too late, of course. The Mortmains have the dowry and won't give it back. Indeed, they may already have spent it. That's what troubled me today when I went to visit Jonathan... oh!" Her expression turned chagrinned. "I don't know why I'm telling *you* all this. I was quite decided that I wouldn't."

Lethargically biting into a crust of bread, she looked away from him and sighed in exasperation, sagging in her seat. Clearly she considered herself utterly alone with these troubles. Thought him incapable of empathy, unlike this wondrous Jonathan.

"It's the food's fault," she exclaimed. "Good food, especially if I'm hungry, always makes me talk too much."

"Really? I barely noticed."

"It's not ladylike, is it?" she added.

"But nothing about you is."

Her eyes sparkled with sudden merriment as she looked at him again. "I'm so glad we don't like each other. Makes it all much simpler, don't you think?"

"Does it?"

"Well, there's no dancing about, no self-conscious simpering. I don't have to pretend to be a prim lady, and you don't have to mind your manners. No effort required. We can merely sit here and talk frankly, unburden our worries, and whatever we tell each other it doesn't really matter, because neither of us truly cares about the impression we leave behind. We're just passing the time in bad weather."

What about that kiss? Did it count for nothing? Perhaps it made her feel safer in his company if she kept up the masquerade.

"You must be greatly concerned for your missing sister?" he asked. "Your father should be—"

"Oh, it is not the first time Serenity has gone off like this. She will probably return in a day or two, acting utterly shocked that anybody should have worried about her while she was gone. Even though that's exactly what she wants us to do."

"But she goes alone?"

"Why not? Like me, she can look after herself. Serenity may appear pretty and dainty, and she pays the most scrupulous attention to ladylike manners— while being observed— but, I can assure you, she is just as much a fighter as I am when it comes to survival and getting what she wants. It might sound odd to you, but I would get no thanks from her, if I took a hundred men out on the moor to search for her remains and wrote to father. She'll come back when she's ready."

"It sounds as if you and your sisters are accustomed to an unusual amount of independence, madam."

She smiled a little. "Our mother died when we were young, and our father found the raising of daughters quite a trial. He never remarried and we traveled a great deal, but there were always women— colorful women— in and out of our lives. Nothing was ever permanent and we became used to that. When life changes around you, almost every day, you cannot afford to get comfortable or take anything for granted. You learn to look after yourself, and you haven't much time for fear of the unknown."

He stared at her, his fingers stilled, spread against the tabletop by his plate.

"Now you know why I'm here, Deverell. What about you? I have confessed enough and now it is your turn. Are you chasing one of those clients that try to avoid you?"

When she smiled it lit up her face. He'd heard that saying before, but never understood it until he met her.

"No. Not a client." His words fell heavily. "A woman."

"Oh." Only a little flicker of surprise. "Did she run away from you then?"

He nodded.

"Why?"

"Who knows really why women ever do anything? You're all unreasonable."

"Didn't you ask her?"

"I haven't yet had the opportunity, have I?" he replied between gritted teeth.

"She left without telling you?"

He bowed his head, his throat feeling tight. That would have to suffice for a reply.

It did.

"At least my sister left a note," she chirped. When he remained silent, she softened her tone.

"Well, that must pain you. I hope you find her. It is a terrible thing to leave a matter unresolved and feelings unexpressed. I always say it's much better to get it all out in the open and say what one's feeling, good or bad. Don't leave your happiness to chance, just because you think you have to be a stiff English gentleman and keep your feelings hidden away. I suppose you never told her how much she meant to you." She took a breath, shook her head. "A lady must have some encouragement, you know."

"She's married," he grumbled, reaching for the wine again, pouring it so sharply and lavishly that it splashed into his goblet and spilled over the brim.

Her eyes widened. "Ah."

"So you see it's a little more complicated than one of your girlish, addled, implausible romances."

She licked her lips. "Had you run out of single ladies that might like your company? I thought there was a surfeit in London."

He merely glared at her, gulped his wine and wiped his fingers briskly on a napkin.

She sighed again, but lightly this time as if to say the conversation was all very tiresome. "Forgive me. I daresay I cannot be the most sympathetic ear for your problems. I am, after all, one of those single ladies paraded, against her will, up and down sundry ballrooms and promenades, in the hope of being found acceptable by some so-called eligible bachelor. Like all other young women, I am seen as a commodity with only one worth. And because I am not the prettiest or the daintiest, I am left to suffer the degradations of being looked over by men I would hesitate to touch with a gondolier's pole. Meanwhile, a man of some intelligence, moderate wit, passable looks in a good light, and thoughtful even when he doesn't want to be— when it's an inconvenience and leaves him without the warmth of his own coat— prefers to spend his time entertaining a married woman." She took a breath at last and he thought he saw a wet gleam under her lashes. "So I hope you understand why I cannot take pity on you."

He quickly wiped his lips on the bundled napkin and tossed it to the table where it landed in the puddle of wine. Usually he would have wiped it up. Tonight he left it. The rebellious new Damon, he thought crossly. "We would never get along. It's been decided, remember? And you don't want a husband of any sort."

A light blush suffused her face. "I spoke theoretically. I was thinking of other ladies, who *might* have found you eligible. I didn't mean for me personally."

"Sounded personal."

She glared. "It wasn't. I spoke for all the women you've overlooked. Respectable young women with..." her pert chin stuck high in the air, "less demanding standards than my own and no other plans in mind for their future."

Damon replied drily. "I doubt there are many *respectable* women looking for a Deverell."

"Are there many of you?"

"Some would say an inordinate amount. We multiply like rabbits." Next year there would be another born, he thought darkly— his own child. Babies had no choice in their parents, but he would do his best not to let the child down. It was an awful responsibility, of course.

For the first time in his life he pitied his father.

"You've gone all white and angry, and you're grinding your teeth again." Leaning forward, elbow on the table, she rested her chin in her upturned palm. "I can hear it from this side of the table."

Could she hear his heartbeat too?

"Best talk about your problem again then," Damon snapped. "I bought you supper. You must repay me with this amusing story of mercenary intentions gone awry." He much preferred talking of her problems than his own, just as he found it easier to manage other folk's difficulties instead of face his own.

Groaning, she sat back, eyeing him irritably. He had already seen her check the contents of a small black reticule that hung from her wrist and from her crushed expression he guessed that she did not have enough money currently in her possession to pay for half the meal. She was, therefore, in his debt. And she clearly didn't like that, anymore than she had liked being swept off her own two feet and carried by him. A woman intent on doing things for herself, wanting everything on her terms.

"Now." He cleared his throat in a no-nonsense fashion and leaned both arms on the table, shoving his plate aside. "How long has your sister been gone on her mysterious odyssey?"

Sullen, she peered at him through half lowered eyelashes. "Since yesterday morning."

Damon shook his head. "If she was my sister, causing all this trouble, I'd tan her hide."

"That would be a shock to her. My sister's hide has never been tanned."

"Nor your own, I'm sure," he murmured, curling his hand slowly as he remembered a certain forbidden touch he'd once permitted himself, in one heated, stolen moment. "I suspect your father's discipline was lax in general," he added tightly.

She had glanced at his hand and quickly away again. "Well, I'd have to find her first, and the Mortmains seldom let me out of their sight."

"They did today," he pointed out.

"Reluctantly. The threat of snow kept The Honorable Edwyn indoors for once, nothing apparently to shoot at. My younger sister Merrythought is confined to bed with a cold, and there was nobody else at hand to act as chaperone. However," she wearily assessed the bones on her plate, "I fear my insistence on going out alone today to visit Jonathan— even just a few miles to Thorford— may already have cost me some of the Mortmain forbearance and good will. Doubtless it has left them even more certain that I lack a few wits. But if anyone might have advised me, Jonathan would."

Jonathan. Even the way she said his name...Damon hastily drained his cup and slammed it down to refill it. "But he wasn't there. You found me instead."

"Yes."

"It seems you're in a pickle, Miss Piper."

She looked at him blankly, perhaps not being familiar with the childhood tongue twister about Peter Piper and his peck of pickled peppers

There was a pause while he rubbed his chin and considered the roof beams. Finally he looked at her again. "It seems I must try to help you avoid this scandal. Your father would expect it. And if you won't let him know—"

"Are you still at our service, even now?" A little

hope in her voice warmed his heart. She pretended not to want his help, but she needed it just the same. Finally, perhaps, she realized it.

"Of course," it choked out of his throat, "I am at your service. For as long as you need me, I will be."

"Oh." She looked down, lashes fanning her cheeks, lips wavering uncertainly.

He wanted to sit beside her and put his arms around her. Instead he could only lean forward, arms resting on the table between them once again. This was merely business. "So, we must ascertain where Miss Serenity Piper might have run off to. And with whom."

"She went alone."

"How do you know she didn't go to meet a lover?"

Her eyes widened and she sat up. "My sister would never—"

"There must be a man, mustn't there? Someone about whom you know nothing."

"But why would she keep such a secret from me?"

"Because you can't keep silent, can you? Not if somebody feeds you cake."

She clenched her lips tightly and looked down at her lap. Damon suspected she had already considered the presence of a secret lover— she was not a stupid woman— but perhaps she did not want to think of the possibilities.

He lowered his voice. "What other men have gone missing at the same time as your sister? That's a good place to start."

"There are only two men in the house. Her fiancé Edwyn and his elderly father. And they are both very much there still, creeping about the shadows."

"What about the servants?" Keeping a grave face, he suggested, "Perhaps there is a saucy-eyed groom with a firm hand on her bridle and a way with the riding crop? Or a rough-necked gardener who promises to trim her hedges and prune her forsythia?"

She scowled. At least she didn't pretend to blush as some young women would. "What sort of man would steal a woman away when she was promised to another?"

"The disreputable sort. A scoundrel with no good in mind."

She looked askance. "I suppose you would know."

"Aha! But I don't think we Deverells can be blamed for this one."

"No," she admitted reluctantly.

"Perhaps your sister decided she did not want to marry without love after all." He sniffed and brushed down his sleeves. "Not everybody does, you know."

"What do you know about marriage or love?" she replied, sounding amused. "I'm sure you never sent a billet doux without an invoice attached."

"I've never sent a billet doux. I have better things to do with my time."

Damon had never been romantic, never sent a woman flowers or poems or anything like that. He'd always been realistic, never syrupy. Wouldn't know how to write a love letter if his life depended on it and Elizabeth had frequently declared herself relieved by his lack of sentimentality. And marriage was a fool's game.

"However," he added slyly, "once you're married

and can take a lover on the side, I'll have to become better versed in the art, shan't I?"

She glared across the table.

"You're still holding that post for me, I hope? A man must have something at which to aspire."

"How very amusing, Mr. Deverell. Since I have no plans to marry, I can't have a man on the side, can I? And if I did take a lover, it wouldn't be one who thinks I'm going to cause bodily harm every time I go near him. We wouldn't get very far, would we?"

He laughed. Couldn't hold it back any longer.

More wine. Yes, that would help numb his thoughts. Lord, he was weary of traveling, still felt the rocking, bouncing forward motion.

Meanwhile his dinner companion continued her unbound chatter, for as he sank into sleepiness, she, it seemed, became more wide awake.

"My sister Serenity would never conduct a clandestine love affair," she announced decidedly.

"Very well then." He sighed. "Think what you will. I tried to help."

She looked skeptical.

"But what will *you* do, Miss Piper, if your sister does not return to walk down the aisle?"

"There is no *if* about my sister's return." Wiping her hands quickly on her napkin, she added, "*When* my sister Serenity returns and proceeds with the business of marrying The Honorable Edwyn Mortmain, I shall petition my father to bring me home. With one success he will surely be content. The climate here does not agree with Merrythought's health and she ought to be home. As for me, I've tried for a year, and he cannot ask more of me than that. He understands the difficulty of selling a product that has stood too long upon the shelf."

More laughter sputtered out of him, unpreventable. "Ah, but I know you didn't try very hard to market yourself, don't I?" A new thought suddenly came to him. "I suppose the masquerade with Bertie Boxall in London was meant to keep everybody happy. Make them all think you made an effort, when in reality you had no intention of accepting him or anybody."

Miss Epiphany Piper had been caught out. She glared, the color draining from her face. "How very clever you are, Mr. Deverell. I knew there must be some reason for your head to be so large."

"Madam, you are, without doubt, the most amusing creature I ever met." He laughed again. It was as if a cork had been released to let it all out. She was beautiful, obstinate and frustrating.

And he was damnably in love with her.

No, no. That couldn't be. Was it the wine he'd drunk, clouding his mind? Yes. He was tired, his nerves torn after the quarrel with his father. That pain was still raw. It had left him vulnerable to odd thoughts.

He quickly set down his goblet. Just in case.

The laughter abruptly halted, he snapped, "Where is that damned landlord with the bill? I'm supposed to wait around all night, it seems."

Eyeing him coolly, she said, "What's the matter with you now?"

"Naught."

"Your face is peculiar, Deverell."

"Thank you."

I don't know how to do this. This is not supposed to happen to me. It wasn't in my plan.

I am unmanned.
I am undone.

"I don't like unpredictability," he growled. "Or feeling trapped."

"Trapped?"

"By the weather. This wretched damnable weather."

Head tilted, she studied him thoughtfully for a moment and then declared, "You, Master Damon Deverell, are all tied up in smug little knots. You may not like to feel trapped, but you have done this to yourself. I hope, for your sake, the right woman comes along one day and unbinds you. So you can breathe again and enjoy life— and all its colorful unpredictability— before it's too late."

"When we first met I thought you interesting. I might even have liked you."

"How positively alarming."

"But it passed."

Any man in her life would probably be driven mad trying to keep up with her, trying to out-think her. Any man in her life, of course, ought to be him. But it was too late and he'd got himself into this mess with Elizabeth.

Irritable, he scratched his cheek and felt the bristles he had not taken time to shave since he began his journey. He must look a sight, he thought.

"Well, I'm going to bed, since I can't arrange transport to Darkest Fathoms until morning," she said, getting up, his coat still around her shoulders. Apparently she'd forgotten it didn't belong to her. "Thank you for the delicious chicken dinner. Good evening to you, Master Grumbles."

"Yes. If you say so."

She waited a moment, her head tipped to one side again, and then she gave a gusty sigh of frustration and marched off to find her room.

Damon watched her go. Carefully he made certain no other men watched her likewise. Once she was safely out of his sight, he summoned another jug of wine.

He expected her to leave his thoughts soon too, just as she left his view. But she did not. The untended, unmanageable American woman lingered in the dark corridors of his mind and would not leave.

Was he in love with her? This surging need to touch her, kiss her, hold her in his arms— even to quarrel with her, if that kept her in his company just a while longer— is that what it meant to love?

He sincerely hoped he was merely drunk.

Chapter Eighteen

The landlord showed her to accommodation that was every bit as tiny as he had sadly promised earlier when he told them he had only two rooms left.

"It has no fireplace, as you see," he pointed out, "but the good thing is, no drafts either, and the heat from the tavern below will help warm the boards at your feet."

"Yes. I see."

"The gentleman below has already paid for the rooms and a bit extra, to make sure you had whatever you needed. So if you find yourself in want, pull on that chord there in the corner and one of my girls will come at once to see what you need. There's water in the pitcher there and a pot under the bed. And I put a bit o' bread and cheese there for you, with some of my wife's bakewell tart."

From the landlord's bowing, scraping manner, Deverell must have paid quite a lot "extra".

"That's very nice," she said firmly. "Thank you."

Finally he left her alone and by the light of a single candle inside a lantern, Pip surveyed the tight space. It must have been a cupboard at some point in its history, for one wall was full of warped shelves, the sticky rings left by storage jars still visible. Another wall held a small, square, rusted window, against which snow had spattered and stuck, filtering a meek and sorry winter's moonlight. The "bed" was actually no more than a short couch with a bolster at one end, an old quilt, and a curtain, thoughtfully provided to pull around it, should she need to feel even more enclosed.

Fortunately Pip was not a woman who suffered fear of tight spaces. In her life she had slept in many different places, which, she supposed, made it easier for her to adjust, no matter what the circumstances. In the early years, with every swing of her father's fortunes, they had changed residence— from a half burned-out riverboat, to an abandoned railroad carriage, to a white-painted Baton Rouge church, left without spire or congregation after a lightning strike; from a fishing cabin on uncertain stilts, to a haunted New Orleans mansion. She was at home anywhere she set down her hat and took off her boots.

In pursuit of a little comfort, Pip did that now, placing the items carefully by her couch and then removing his coat. This certainly was not the place to discard more than that, even with a bolt on her door. What if there was a fire in the night? One should always be prepared for disaster. Something else her childhood had taught her.

Her ankle throbbed and looked swollen. No surprise after the way she'd wrenched it. If she kept it up for the night, it should feel better by morning.

She'd asked the landlord whether there might be any chance of finding a messenger to take a note to Darkest Fathoms— Pip didn't want her little sister worried by her absence too— but he had assured her nobody would travel now until morning, when daylight and the calming of the wind should improve conditions. Poor Merrythought would fret that she'd been abandoned by both sisters! This was a wretched turn of events, but the weather was out of her control. As were several other things lately.

Oh, Serenity, where have you gone?

Damon Deverell said he would have tanned her

hide. The thought made Pip smile, imagining her indignant elder sister, with skirts tossed up, receiving a hard spanking for the first time in her life. Serenity was never the daughter in trouble, never punished, so a spanking would come as a great surprise to her. Pip had often pondered, with no little amazement and envy, her elder sister's ability to remain unsullied and clear of any suspicion. Nobody could be that well behaved all the time.

She remembered how her elder sister used to hold her breath if she could not get what she wanted. The little girl would turn blue in the face, until Delphine, who looked after them, picked her up and set her bare behind on the nearest cold surface. Then, of course, she caught her breath in a startled gulp and got her color back. But that was an example of Serenity's determination to get her own way, which, although better hidden these days, was just as forceful as her sister's.

Could it be true that she'd run off with a male companion, a secret beau of whom they all knew nothing?

But who was this other man, if he existed? Serenity had never shown any particular interest in one beau, even at home, preferring instead to keep several in a circle around her, all admiring from a careful distance. She wanted as many as possible at hand, to catch her if she tripped. Serenity's greatest fear was finding herself alone one day, old and abandoned, with no man to cosset her vanity. She'd admitted as much to Pip one evening, after yet another dreary ball when they sat up late, both unable to sleep— Serenity because of her sore feet from so much dancing, and Pip because she'd enjoyed one too many glasses of punch and her mind was busy scheming of ways to take over the world.

Since their arrival in England, no particular gentleman had stood out among Serenity's admirers. In fact, the competition had been so dull that she was obliged to accept a Mortmain and had done so quite cheerfully under the guidance of Aunt Du Bois.

One must do one's duty. This is what I'm meant for.

Perhaps, after the excitement and champagne of her engagement announcement wore off, Serenity had opened her eyes, seen The Honorable Edwyn Mortmain for what he really was, and realized the consequences of her decision. When she heard the wedding arrangements being made all around her, Serenity must have felt penned in, and with Aunt Du Bois gone soon after they arrived here, there was nobody left to keep whispering assurances and encouragement in her ear. Nobody to tell her what a wonderful thing she was doing for the family and how proud their father would be.

It must have been a shock— like one of those bare-bottomed contacts with a cold surface.

But to run away without saying anything to her sisters, without boasting about a secret lover? Not even to Merrythought, who, unlike Pip, would always provide a sympathetic, kindly ear?

A sudden doubt crept into her mind as she recalled her younger sister's countenance when Serenity was first discovered gone yesterday. There was something not quite right about it— as if she acted surprised rather than felt it. Hmm. At the time, Pip had merely assumed her little sister was still half-asleep when she dashed into her room to tell her the news and show Serenity's note. But now she thought again.

Merry had not appeared overly concerned about their sister's fate, even when the next morning dawned and Serenity failed to reappear. The girl had been a little anxious and fidgety, perhaps, but that was all. She might simply have been fearful of facing Pip, because she knew more than she could tell. Already laid low with a bad cold, Merry was limp and damp-eyed even before their sister disappeared; a convenient circumstance that helped her hide away in bed and complain of weariness if she were questioned.

Pip sneezed. Oh no! She could not become sick too. Not now.

Below her, the noise of the Whalebone Tavern rumbled away, shaking the floorboards. Was Damon Deverell still down there, getting steadily drunker and grumpier? Would he find some hussy to warm his bed tonight? She'd seen a few women glancing his way, their admiration everything but discreet.

But he had given *her* all his attention at dinner. He liked teasing her, apparently, and not many men, other than her father, ever dared. Pity he was such an arrogant devil.

And he chased after a married woman.

There was no doubt in her mind that the woman he chased after was Lady Elizabeth Stanbury. He didn't have to tell her the name. Pip had two good eyes in her head.

Foolish fellow was so intent on solving other folk's problems that he neglected his own.

Her gaze drifted left and rediscovered the black lump by the door where she'd left his coat. He must have forgotten he gave it to her.

She got up and fetched it from the back of a chair, once again inhaling the masculine scents and hugging the heavy warmth of the coat.

Oh, there was something inside the lining of his coat. A square lump. A book?

In the dim candlelight she fumbled for an opening and soon discovered a small pocket. Within that pocket he had wedged a little, leather-bound book. It was much weathered and worn, a ledger of some sort, lists of numbers and items purchased. Household accounts, records of coin spent on tailor's services, rent, candles, visits to the farrier and the blacksmith, books, ink, coal... Not terribly interesting. But the old paper lining inside the front cover was torn. Tucked inside that was a folded, yellowed scrap.

It was wrong to poke her nose into his business, she told herself. She ought to put the book back where she found it, go to sleep and have the landlord return the coat to him in the morning. She supposed she'd have to give it back. It didn't belong to her anymore than he did.

Unfortunately she was not very tired and the more her mind speculated upon the possible contents of that hidden scrap, the more awake and restless she became. Finally she tugged the paper out, unfolded it with care and held it up to the lantern. The ink was faded slightly, the handwriting very neat and studious— as if long labored over.

Items Reqwired to Sayle Arownd the Worlde
Damon Deverell, Nine yeres aged, hys lyste.

I. Nonesuch

II. Compasse

III. Goode dogges (two)
IV. Mrs. Blewett's pye (plentye as wille keepe)
V. Sorwde (sharpe)
VI. Fishing nette (welle mended)
VII. Oyle Clothe Hatte for rayne
VIII. Coin
IX. Grogg Barrells
X. Sundry spare womyns for poiposes of barter wythe natives.

Clearly an expedition of some length and daring had been planned all those years ago.

She laughed out loud. How funny that he had kept this list tucked away. A reminder of something undone, a childhood desire for adventure unfulfilled.

But her laughter petered out as she imagined the little boy who once penned this list. He must have bent over a writing desk, diligently pausing every so often to dip his nib in the inkwell, his tongue squeezed out between his teeth as he applied his attention to the paper.

Carefully she refolded the scrap and slipped it back where she had found it, feeling a little wicked. She shouldn't laugh at something that was not meant for her eyes. Or for anybody's, but his— *Damon Deverell, nine yeres aged.*

With such proud flourish he'd written his name, as if he anticipated great things in store for his future. As she'd always done for herself.

Oh, she should not have eaten so fast and so greedily, for now she had indigestion— a terrible pang in her chest and she could think of nothing else that might have caused it.

She jumped guiltily at the sudden rap of knuckles

against her door.

"Miss Piper, you have my coat."

"Oh. Yes. Er...just a moment." In haste she pushed the little book back inside the lining pocket where she'd found it, dashed to the door and slid back the bolt. "I was almost asleep." Why she felt the urge to lie was anybody's guess. But she threw in a yawn for good measure.

He didn't look convinced. Slowly he reached for the coat. "You seem very flustered. You're breathing heavily."

"As I said, I was almost asleep when you woke me, just beginning to dream." Was it possible, she thought in alarm, that her bosom had finally learned how to heave? No. It was just another sneeze.

He took a step back from the resulting spray and winced. "Dreaming of something pleasant, I hope."

"What?"

He looked beyond her to the small, narrow couch and the flickering lantern, to the boots set neatly, side by side on the floor, and the hat placed carefully on the table. "I heard you laughing."

"I have a tendency to laugh at the least appropriate moments. My aunt was driven spare by it."

"Humph." He moved forward again, taking another glance around the small room. "Doesn't look very comfortable."

"I'll manage. I'm adaptable."

"Mine has more room. You'd be much more comfortable there."

"Do you mean to offer an exchange?"

He looked confused for a moment. "Yes. That's what I meant, of course. It is my—"

"Your job," she finished for him with a sigh. "I know."

But he remained there, now leaning against her doorframe. "Don't think to leave without me in the morning. You need me."

"What for?"

"Guidance. Wisdom." Now he tipped the other way, until his shoulder abruptly contacted again with the door frame. "Protection."

His eyes caught hers and she couldn't blink. Couldn't look away. But there was a fogginess there tonight. "Here's your coat." She thrust it at him. "That's what you came for, isn't it?"

He leaned down to her, his breath warm, tickling the side of her face. "Leave all your problems to me. I'll fix them."

"Well, that's ...very obliging of you. But now I suggest you go to bed." She choked out a soft laugh. "You cannot do much for me until you sober up. You, sir, are inebriated."

"I'm not—" He swayed again. "*H*inebriated."

She'd seen men drunk before, but she'd never seen one who looked even more somber while under the influence. "I beg to differ, Master Grumbles. I wouldn't breathe near naked flame if I were you."

Suddenly he put his hand on her cheek, tipping her face up toward his. "Why are you so...damned...damnably...difficult?"

"I was born this way."

"Me. Me too."

His lips hovered far too close and they were very fine lips. Uniquely beautiful for a man. Oh, she wished she'd never laid eyes on those lips, for now she knew she would compare them with those of any other man she met.

"For all our differences," he muttered, "we are well matched, you and I." Then he laughed huskily at the oxymoron. "How can it be possible?"

"It can't," she whispered, placing her hand gently to his chest. "So put it out of your very sensible mind." The lord knew she was trying hard to do the same.

Pip was usually very decided about men the moment she met them, but her thoughts on this one had veered wildly back and forth, worse than an outhouse door in a hurricane. In that moment she wanted him unbearably, to kiss him, put her arms around him. But it was all wrong. He was there chasing another woman and she had a missing sister to find. He liked things predictable, orderly, and her life was anything but.

Be sensible, Pip. Don't let him know what you're thinking, or else he'll know where to find all your weak spots.

In the sober light of day, he would not want to remember this, even if she could never forget the thump of his heart under her palm. So strong, hard, powerful. Savage as that of a wild animal.

"I am not...not tied up in knots," he said suddenly. "You're wrong in your assessment, Miss Piper."

"Oh?"

"What I am...is undone."

Pip knew that if she was not firm now she would soon drown in his eyes gladly, readily, and to the devil with tomorrow. "What you are is drunk," she said, keeping her voice as steady as possible. "I hope you find your lady friend tomorrow. And that you get what you want in the end."

His eyes darkened. "My lady friend."

At last her fingers found the strength to give him a firm push back into the narrow corridor. "Good night, Deverell." With that she shut her door and bolted it.

Her heart twisted painfully and her skin tingled with a strange, keen awareness of everything that currently touched it— the crepe fabric of her gown, a lose strand of hair against her neck, the top of her stockings under her petticoat. Every tiny part of her was vividly alive in a way it never had been before.

And he caused it all by simply touching her face.

Of course, she still felt the imprint of his hands from months ago, where they had gripped her somewhere else. Possessed her. Marked her as his own. He didn't seem to fear that she would break or bruise easily.

"Nonesuch," came the whisper through her door. "Don't think to leave me in the morning."

"Go away, Master Grumbles," she whispered back.

There was a thud against the door, as if he'd fallen against it. "Don't leave without me in the morning. You... need me."

"What for?" she asked again, as before, amused.

"Your aunt should never have brought you to Yorkshire without me, without even conferring with counsel. What do we know about these Mortmains? Now see what happened. Your sister's gone off, and you're wandering around in the snow chasing after men. More men I know nothing about. I'm the one who'll answer for it when you get yourself in trouble."

She leaned against the door and whispered back, "I relieve you of the responsibility."

"Your aunt thought *she* knew what was best for you. Now I see where you get it from!"

"Go to your room." And then she lied, because it seemed to be the only way to be rid of him. "We'll discuss this in the morning."

Eventually she heard Damon muttering to himself as he stumbled back to his own room, bouncing against the walls from side to side. Then a door slammed. Tomorrow he would wake with a sore head and forget all this.

Confer with counsel, indeed!

Now all she could hear— apart from her own heart beating— was someone singing a cheerful tune in the tavern below, accompanied by a fiddle.

Pip took a deep breath and waited there, leaning against her door, until the foolish giddiness that careened through her body finally calmed to softly bubbling murmur.

She'd never imagined, until she met that man, how she might be tempted.

But what exactly was a "Nonesuch"? He had called her by that name too.

And why, pray tell, did she feel tears in her eyes?

Her gaze swept the small room as if she might find all these answers written on the walls. And then she spied that little book again. It must have fallen from his pocket when she gave him the coat. In her anxious haste, Pip had not pushed it far enough inside the lining pocket.

Well, she could not return the book to him now. It would be exceedingly unwise to go to his door. For both their sakes. Better let him sleep it off.

She ran her fingers over the worn leather cover of the little book and brought it to her nose. Yes, it smelled like his coat, like him.

Pip returned to her narrow couch and sat there, clutching his book to her breast and wondering about Nonesuch.

Then her gaze wandered to the plate on the small table beside her.

Ooh, bakewell tart...

Chapter Nineteen

"Thank goodness you're back!" Merrythought sat up in her giant, worm-holed, four-poster bed looking very limp and damp-eyed. "I thought you had both left me here. I even imagined," she lowered her voice to a hoarse whisper, "that you had both been imprisoned in the attic by Mortmains. That they had some dire plan for me."

Pip hurried across the room, pulling off her gloves to feel her sister's forehead. "Nonsense. You've been reading novels again. What have I told you about that?" Two books on the bedside table— one of them entitled "The Vampyre"— confirmed her suspicions, as did the candles, now extinguished, but burned down almost to the holders.

"I didn't dare snuff them," her sister confessed with eyes like saucers, "until daylight crept through the curtains."

"At least you had Junior to protect you." Pip paused to fuss the big hairy mutt sprawled on the bed with the patient. "I knew you'd be safe as long as he was here with you."

"Yes. He has turned out to be a very good dog, even though he scared me a little when you first took him in. Now I'm glad you did, despite our aunt's protests. I don't even mind when he takes up all the room on the bed. I'd rather that than be alone. In case the Boggart comes out."

"The Boggart?"

"Old Lord Mortmain told me a story about the Boggart. It's a mischievous spirit that lives in the chimneys and comes down them to play tricks sometimes on the residents of the house. Especially, Lord Mortmain said, on young ladies. The Boggart likes to torment young ladies and sometimes steals their pins and slippers, or ties knots in their bed sheets, or grabs their ankles when they step out of bed."

"Merry, you really must learn not to believe everything people tell you."

"But it's true. There is a cupboard by the kitchen, and it has a knot hole in the door. If you stick something through the hole, the Boggart will poke it back out again."

"What a pity this Boggart can't return our sister the same way."

Merry quickly tugged her coverlet up under her chin and sank back down as if suffering a sudden relapse. "Ooh my head aches so."

Grumbles Junior lumbered upright to lick Pip's face while she scratched behind his ears and planted a kiss on the end of his wet nose. "At least you look brighter today and you are not nearly so hot, sister. I'm sorry I was gone all night, but I got caught in the snow storm and missed the mail coach. I was stranded at the Whalebone Inn, a place of much jollity and considerable debauchery."

"Oh, Pip! Were you afraid?"

"Not really. I was more concerned about you."

"About our sister too, I suppose."

"Yes." Pip walked around the bed. "I thought a great deal about Serenity last night." She glanced over at the door. "The Mortmains haven't been up to see you, have they?"

"No, of course, it wouldn't be proper, but the maids have been in with trays of food and they are very kind. One of them took Grumbles Junior out for me this morning. And Edwyn sent a message to say he hoped I was feeling better."

In light of what she overheard yesterday— Edwyn being pushed into marriage with one of the other girls if Serenity changed her mind— Pip knew she had better keep her little sister out of his way. Merrythought was far too kindhearted to let The Honorable down if he turned his bloodshot eyes on her as a consolation prize. She might feel sympathy for him, for she had already remarked that she thought him a poor, sad fellow and that she wished she might teach him to dance so that he would be more comfortable in society. As Pip had said to her father, Merrythought could not have been better named, but that goodness made her susceptible to the slightest tug upon her heartstrings.

Pip took a second look at the books by her sister's bed. Perhaps she should take them away to prevent Merrythought's imagination turning to romance. Novels, like fairytales, were notorious for leading young girl's astray.

"I do hope Serenity is back before Christmas," said her sister.

"Did she say she might be, when she left?"

"No, she didn't say any—" Merrythought paled. "I did not see her before she left."

"Of course, that's right. You only knew she'd gone when I brought the note in to read it to you." Pip walked back around the bed, tugging the coverlet straight and petting Grumbles Junior, who rolled promptly onto his back, legs in the air, presenting his belly for her attention. "You are quite sure you didn't see Serenity that morning?"

The girl shook her head.

"Hmm. Odd. Grumbles Junior must have slept late that day. He usually wants to go out before seven, and he slept that evening before on your bed, did he not?"

Since Pip rescued the mutt from a London street, he'd taken to sleeping on each girl's bed in turn, not wanting to leave anybody out. Even Serenity had not been able to keep him away when he scratched at her door and, although she still made a fuss, once assured his fleas were cured, she had grandly allowed him the foot of her bed. In fact, as the weather grew colder he became a much beloved bed warmer. One thing none of them much liked, however, was getting up in the winter, while it was still dark out, to let Grumbles Junior out of the house. But he could be depended upon, like clockwork, to whine in one's face at ten minutes to seven in the morning.

"He didn't wake you on that day, Merry?"

"No. I—no."

Pip tapped a finger to her lips. "How strange. You're sure? Not even a paw in the face? A lick of the chin?"

Her sister's lips turned down at the corners.

Pip frowned, tut-tutted and looked very disappointed.

"I was only half awake," the girl blurted, "standing on the cold flagged-stone in the passage, and I...I was not even sure what I saw at first. It was still shadowy with only a very little light from the candle in my hand. I just wanted Grumbles Junior to make haste so that we could go back to bed. I...I looked over and saw a figure in the shadows. It gave me quite a scare, for it might have been a ghost. And

I know you don't believe in ghosts, but I'm sure I've seen a few walking the halls of this house. I've heard tormented wailing, and Lord Mortmain says—"

"*Serenity*, sister. What was she doing when you saw her?"

"She was outside the scullery. She looked over at me and put a finger to her lips, like this." She demonstrated, her gaze darting fearfully from side to side. "I asked her where she was going, and she said I was not to tell anybody that I'd seen her. That she would never forgive me if I woke you and raised the alarm. She said the Boggart would come out if I told. In any case, after the dog had done his business, we went back to bed and huddled under the covers to get warm. I went back to sleep and didn't wake again until you came in with her note."

"But was she dressed to go out?"

Merrythought screwed up her face, as she tried to recall the image in her memory. "Yes. She wore a hooded cloak and had her leather valise. When I looked again, and had rubbed the sleep out of my eyes, she was gone. Oh, don't be angry, Pip! I didn't know whether I should say anything to you. I wasn't sure if I really saw her, or if it was a dream. You might have been cross with me for not waking you, but she would have been cross with me for doing so."

"I would not be cross with you. As if I am ever cross with you!" Pip was pacing at the foot of her sister's bed, hands on her waist. "And was she alone?"

"No. A...a man was with her."

She froze. "A man? What man?"

"I wasn't to say. She'll be soooo angry."

"What man, Merry?"

Her sister licked her lips and sank against the

pillows. "The vicar of Thorford. Mr. Lulworth. There, it is done. I told you. Now the Boggart will get me, for sure."

Pip stared. "It could not have been—you must have seen someone else and thought it was Jonathan. Why...why would he be here?"

"She had her arm in his," Merry chirped plaintively from her pillows. "I was just as surprised to see him there as you would be, Pip. I thought he was in love with *you*. Or you were in love with him, at least. You talked of him so fondly, as you never talk of anybody but our pa."

And that was why Serenity had not told her, she thought, chagrinned.

Jonathan's housekeeper, Mrs. Trotter, had told Pip that her master travelled north. That he wouldn't be back until Sunday service.

Deverell had said, *What other men have gone missing at the same time as your sister? That's a good place to start.*

How blind she'd been! Serenity's comments about the "sad little curate" and her teasing over Pip's visits to the vicarage.

Would they soon receive another letter from their missing sister?

The food here is poor, but the company a vast improvement. I bet you are all sorry I left...

"And now poor Edwyn is left behind," said Merry suddenly. "I do feel sorry for him."

Pip shook her head. "Don't. This is nobody's fault but our sister's. She must be the one to feel sorry and make amends."

"Are you angry with her, because of Mr.

Lulworth?"

"I'm angry because she left us to clean up her mess. Because she did not confide in me. Because she is never punished and I daresay she will escape blame here too."

"But you told her she shouldn't marry Edwyn Mortmain if she didn't love him."

That was true. After all this time and all their arguments, her sister had changed her mind it seemed, and put aside her dour view of marriage being a duty. When push came to shove she must have realized she couldn't marry The Honorable Mortmain.

Whether Jonathan was simply a convenient means of escape from that mistake, Pip couldn't be sure. Serenity's full motive in running away was yet to be discovered.

In the meantime, she had left her sisters stranded with another threat of scandal hanging over their heads.

* * * *

Pip dressed for dinner in a very uneasy mood. With Merrythought still confined to bed, it was solely up to her to entertain the ghoulish Mortmains and she knew already that they didn't like her. She was an unwanted guest in their house and only potentially useful because of her father's money. She was the "mouthy" one. They were probably wishing she could have gone missing, instead of her sister.

And Jonathan. What was his part in all this? Was he merely a convenient man to help her sister travel? Or was there more attachment?

Her mind kept circling back to Serenity's scornful

laughter. "*I do hope you're not traipsing across the moor again to bother that sad little curate... perhaps you are in love.*"

Well, she certainly could not let any of this show on her face at dinner. The Mortmains would be watching her closely.

Edwyn had already given her a chilly "So there you are" when he caught her creeping through the passage in the early hours of the morning. Even when she explained about the snow storm holding her hostage outside Whitby, he spared her nothing more than a very sour look and informed her that there was a fire in the morning room, should she need to warm herself. For the rest of the day she had stayed with her younger sister, grateful for that excuse to keep out of his way, but as dinner approached she must face her hosts again. Alone.

But something else happened that drew their attention away from her. Thankfully.

They had another guest at Darkest Fathoms that evening.

"Damon Deverell," she heard him announce himself, just as she was descending the stairs for dinner. "I was hired by Mr. Prospero Piper to manage his daughters abroad."

Appalled, she took the remaining steps at a quicker pace and exclaimed, "Not to *manage*, sir."

In the process of handing his hat and coat to the Mortmain's butler, he spun around to look at her. "Miss Piper. You cannot be rid of me, you see. Tried to give me the slip this morning, did you not?"

Through her teeth she hissed, "What do you think you're doing here?"

Instead of answer, he turned to address Edwyn, who looked utterly confused. "You must be The

Honorable Edwyn Mortmain, our host."

Oh, for pity's sake, what was he up to? She felt her skin getting hot. But he took her hand, raised it to his lips and kissed her clenched knuckles through her evening glove.

"I do hope I am not intruding?" he said, turning back to Edwyn. "Miss Piper did not tell you I met her yesterday on the moor and we spent the evening together at the Whalebone Inn?"

She gasped. "We did not spend the evening together. We shared a dinner and had separate rooms. Kindly don't make it sound worse than it was."

"Of course," he replied gravely. "I would not want anybody to think otherwise. I have been charged with preserving your reputation, madam, not besmirching it."

"Mr. Deverell is a lawyer with Stempenham and Pitt," she explained reluctantly to her host.

Edwyn moved stiffly in a partial bow. "I welcome you, sir, to Darkest Fathoms."

"What's this?" Old Lord Bedevere Mortmain shuffled forward, leaning on his cane, looking very put out because his dinner had been delayed. "Who is it now? Damnation! Let one guest in and you've got five cluttering up the place, before you know it. I knew it was a mistake to bring a lot of girls here. Girls have followers. Soldiers and whatnot. I told you, Edwyn. But no, you thought you wanted one in the house."

His son made the introductions. "This is Mr. Damon Deverell, a lawyer. Mr. Deverell, my father, the Viscount Mortmain."

"*Lawyer! Lawyer?*" The old fellow's face turned red as a beet. "Kill all the lawyers, like Shakespeare said."

"Well, sir," Damon bowed. "I hope that won't be necessary. Although if it is, I believe Miss Epiphany Piper will gladly do the deed for you."

* * * *

They all looked at her.

"Praemonitus praemunitus," he muttered, watching her lips.

She laughed. "Mr. Deverell and his Latin. I understand he was very fond of his Latin tutor at university. I daresay that is why he was such a good student." Her eyes flared as she tossed him a fiery look, a challenge.

Ah, Bertie Boxall must have told her about their adventurous Latin tutor at Cambridge, who also happened to be the only female tutor at his university— perhaps the only one in Cambridge, a fact which spoke to her daring, audacious spirit.

"Yes. I was immensely fond of her," he replied. "She taught me a great deal for which I will always be thankful." As were the ladies of his intimate acquaintance, he mused.

After they had all stood awkwardly for a moment, the old man finally growled, "Well, let's eat then, before I drop dead on't feet."

Edwyn Mortmain remembered his manners just in time to add, "Do join us for dinner, sir."

As they walked into the dining room, Damon caught her arm and whispered, "You left this morning without me. You promised you would stay."

"I thought you'd forget."

"Oh." He shook his head grimly. "I forget nothing, madam."

* * * *

Damon had spent his day combing Whitby for any sign of Elizabeth, but nobody had seen her. Even worse, nobody had even heard of the lady or of her having relatives in the area. Once he'd put out word that he was looking for her, all he could do, for now, was wait. When he found her they would have much to talk about and get straightened, but with the weather against him he could do nothing more for now.

In the meantime, he could, perhaps, help Miss Piper. Make himself useful to her. Darkest Fathoms was also a convenient place to stay. Near to her, which is where he wanted to be.

Had a job to do, didn't he?

He'd written and posted three letters that day. The first two were for his father and Ransom. All part of the new Damon— making apologies. He was concerned about Ransom. Those injuries had looked very bad and he should have paid more attention before he left London, instead of being absorbed with himself. The more he thought about it, the more worried he became. His third letter, therefore was written to Raven, who would surely know what was going on in her brother's life and, if she did not, she should be apprised of it.

At dinner, Nonesuch continued to look at him as if he'd stepped heavily on her foot. Which he didn't think he had. No, he checked under the table to be sure of it.

"I thought you had some other business to tend in Yorkshire," she said quietly. "I did not expect you to come here to Darkest Fathoms."

"I'm sure I can manage two things at once."

"Then you're the first man I've ever met who can. Apart from my father, of course."

He laughed. "I have been told I am both a shark *and* a merciless charmer. Surely one extra small matter cannot overcome a man with my talents."

"I wouldn't count upon it."

No doubt Bertie Boxall had told her everything in retaliation for Damon sending him away from the Courtenay's ball that evening in May. The idiot would spare nothing in his eagerness to grind Damon into the dirt.

Well, good, then she'd know everything. He had nowhere to go in her opinion but up.

This morning, when he woke with a stinging head, he knew what he must do. He was not in love with Elizabeth and she was not in love with him. That affair was already a regret, and he could not let Miss Piper get away and cause him another. So the path was broken and parts of it lost forever, but that didn't mean he couldn't make a new path. His own this time, not trying to fill anybody else's boots. Not aiming for somebody else's goal. Making himself happy.

As his father had said just before Damon left London, *We are all responsible for our own happiness.*

He could not expect Epiphany to fall in love with him— she was too shrewd, too clever to fall for that supposed "charm" of his, and he didn't know how to conjure it in any case. He suspected she was right and women only told him he was charming when they wanted something from him, like Lady Roper. Or to be mischievous, like Raven.

No, he was simply Damon Deverell, a bastard's bastard who happened to do well in his studies and had a capacity for "fixing" people's problems.

He'd complicated his own life. He wouldn't try to complicate hers too. But he could be Miss Piper's friend. Anything he could do for her, he would do.

She'd probably bewitched him. Couldn't trust these foreign girls. Couldn't trust anybody. Well, if he was to be bewitched, he couldn't think of any more enjoyable way.

* * * *

"How are your sisters, Miss Piper?" Damon asked, turning his head to look at her.

"Merrythought is in bed. With a cold."

"I will have the kitchens make up some of my special pottage for her. With your permission, of course, Lord Mortmain."

The old man sniffed. "Do what you like. The apothecary is a devilish expense and does nowt."

Pip said to Damon, "She will be extremely surprised to find *you* here."

"Perhaps I should pay the invalid a visit after dinner and cheer her spirits."

"*Cheer her spirits?* I didn't think that was part of your duties."

"They were recently expanded." He gave her such a look that Pip burnt her tongue on the soup. "What of Miss Serenity?" he said.

"Girl's gone orf," old Mortmain grumbled. "Left my son with not a word, not a *by your leave*. Shot off like a mowdiwarp down 'ole"

"Good lord." He glanced at Pip, who hastily looked at her bowl. "A mowdiwarp."

Drooping further in his seat, Edwyn remarked dolefully, "The young ladies lost their aunt this summer, Mr. Deverell, as you may know. I daresay Miss Serenity desired some time alone with her grief."

"Pah," his father shouted. "She's had her time to grieve. In my day wenches didn't go orf on their own, feeling sorry for themselves. You should have had her at the altar by now and kept girl too busy to go wandering. But no, you had to be soft and wait till the wench dried her eyes."

"There is an established period of mourning, sir," Edwyn replied.

"Bugger it! Look at you sitting there like a ruddy great earwig. No wonder she ran orf. "

There followed an uncomfortable silence during which even Pip began to feel sympathy for Edwyn.

"What brings you to Yorkshire, lawyer?" the old man bellowed from the end of the table.

"I came this way on business for another client. Quite by chance yesterday I ran into Miss Piper. She and her sisters left London so suddenly this summer and I had no idea where they went. By fortunate circumstance yesterday we met again."

"You didn't come to take the dowry money back again then, eh?" the old man demanded, while his son cringed.

"No."

"Good. I told Edwyn he'd have to take one o' t'others if the elder doesn't come back. We can't return that purse."

"But if you had to take Miss Epiphany here, I'd advise you to ask for more."

Lord Mortmain took him seriously. "Should I? Worth more is she?" He eyed Pip with keen interest.

"You certainly ought to have more for putting up with her. Compensation."

Pip suddenly felt laughter squeezing out of her stomach and up into her throat. It was a relief to have Deverell at her side again, even though she had been determined not to need him. It occurred to her that she'd been foolish— eager to take Jonathan Lulworth's advice but balking when it came to Damon Deverell's. And why?

"She'll cost more to feed," he added. "Cake, especially. Muffins."

The more she tried to hold her laughter back, the worse it built, until soup almost came out of her nose. In the nick of time she turned the sound into a ladylike sneeze, half buried in her napkin.

"I do hope you haven't caught cold too, Miss Epiphany," he said.

"I *have* lost my appetite a little," she managed, her voice muffled by the napkin.

"But you usually have such a healthy appetite. You must indeed be ill."

Edwyn Mortmain watched them from between the tall candles and said somberly, "That young lady went out in a snow storm yesterday against our advice. Perhaps now you are here, Mr. Deverell, you might moderate her rebellious side, for we are quite undone with it and she does not listen to us."

"Girl's a fidget," Old Lord Mortmain exclaimed gruffly, blowing on his soup, "and right stubborn with it."

"She is indeed a man's undoing," Damon replied, smirking. "I must see what I can do about that." He looked at her. "I'll take her to bed."

A strong draft blew through the room and made the candlelight dance wildly, even with the doors and windows shut tight against the cold weather. The old man dropped his spoon with a clang, and Edwyn choked on his wine.

"I mean to say, I'll see to it that she is put to bed at once," Damon corrected, eyes looking surprised, grin faltering. "She must rest and be warm."

Another draft, this one tickling her ankles beneath the table, suggested to Pip that her little sister was right; there really was a troublesome, roguish Boggart in the house. And apparently he'd chosen her as his victim.

Chapter Twenty

"Since I left London without making plans, I needed somewhere to stay," he told her, "and you need my help. This seemed the best idea."

"I didn't ask you for your help, Deverell," she hissed as he carried her along the landing to her room. "Nor am I sick." But when she got up from the table her ankle had given way again quite suddenly. Her usually stout ankles let her down.

"You're burning up, woman. Being out in that snow yesterday!"

"I know you're amusing yourself greatly with this masquerade, but it's completely unnecessary to carry me again." But she didn't say that until they had reached her door, just in case he put her down again.

He nudged open her bedroom door and carried her inside.

"I only told you all about Serenity running off because you forced it out of me," she added. "You used your wicked wiles to interrogate me, and it all came spilling out last night."

"Yes," he wheezed. "It is always such a trial to get you to talk. You never chatter incessantly."

"I don't. Chattering incessantly is something I never do. It suggests no decorum or self-moderation." She paused, noting the little bead of sweat trickling down his brow. "Aren't I heavy?"

"Not as much as you were when wiggling and covered in snow yesterday."

"I can stand on my own feet, you know. It is only a *little* throbbing pain in my ankle. I've had worse. Does it look swollen to you?"

"Am I allowed to look at your ankles?"

"I give you permission, Deverell." She stuck out her foot and waved it in the air.

"No. It doesn't look swollen. It looks...shapely. And troublesome."

"How can an ankle be troublesome?"

"I wouldn't have thought it possible either, until I saw yours."

She laughed. "Oh, put me down then."

But he was intent on showing off. Having arrived at the side of her bed far ahead of the scurrying maid, he now realized he didn't have a spare hand to turn down the sheets and coverlet, so he stood there holding her, trying to look as if he wasn't straining in the least.

"Why have you come here?" she whispered, trying not to rest her head on his wide shoulder.

"I'm at your service, of course. How many times must I tell you that before you believe it?"

What did she want him to say, she thought crossly— that he was in love with her and came here just to put his hands on her again? She was getting as bad as Merrythought and letting her imagination wander into the realms of romantic novels.

By the time the maid, struggling along after them with a bowl of something made to his strict specifications, arrived in the room, his arms had begun to shake and that bead of sweat had trickled slowly all the way down to his cheek. Finally the coverlet was pulled down and he lowered her to the mattress with a grunt of satisfaction.

"Such a lot of fuss," she muttered.

"Nonsense." He bent over to remove her shoes while the maid looked on in mild horror. "You will eat this mixture at once, while it's hot," he commanded briskly.

"Do you have much experience of nursing the sick?"

"Not particularly. But I do know how to look after myself." He pulled up her coverlet. "Like you, I've been doing it for some time." While the maid set the tray across her lap he turned away to stoke up the fire.

"Will that be all, miss?" the maid asked, looking sideways at Damon in the same way as Pip eyed that bowl of lumpy green liquid. "I'll be back later to dress you for bed, shall I?"

"Come back in half an hour," Deverell snapped.

"Yes, thank you," Pip said to the maid, ignoring him. "Please check on my sister and tell her I'll see her in the morning."

Deverell swung around, still holding the poker, "And make some of that same mixture for Miss Merrythought. See that she consumes it."

"*If you please*," Pip added, since he clearly wouldn't, and had already resumed rattling the poker into the fireplace, causing sparks that shot out onto the hearth.

The maid curtseyed and hurried out, but left the door open in a very pointed way, with a scowl at Damon.

"I thought perhaps you were going to suggest that you undress me," Pip remarked coolly. "You're so domineering."

"Somebody has to take charge. I cannot stand a job half done."

She reached around to fluff her pillows. "You haven't found your lady friend then."

"No. Not yet."

"So you thought you'd entertain yourself with me."

He glanced over his shoulder. "Why not? Eat your stew."

She picked up her spoon and poked at it. "Smells foul."

"Nevertheless it will help fight off that cold before it takes proper hold. Remember what your aunt called me, *a necessary evil?*"

"What's in it?"

"Herbs, spices, vegetables. A little red wine. All good things in moderation. Hold your nose and eat." Finally satisfied with the roaring fire, he set the poker on its hook and returned to the bedside, where he tidied some books and wiped dust off the glass lamp chimney. His gaze alighted on her aunt's Chinese silk robe, where it hung over her bed post.

"I suppose you recognize that," she murmured, feeling sad suddenly that she would never see her aunt wafting through a room in that robe again. "She gave it to me, a day or two before she died. I haven't had the courage to wear it." She sighed. "I think Serenity believed it should have come to her. She's been very sour about it, even though Aunt Du Bois gave her all the jewelry."

"Oh, I think of all three of you, you're the most like your aunt." He gave a grim smile. "I couldn't imagine anyone else having the gumption to wear that colorful garment with the same aplomb as she did."

But since thinking of her aunt made her likely to cry, Pip changed the subject. "It's not proper for you to be in here," she said, snuffling into the handkerchief he'd lent her. "Did you not see the poor maid's face? Who knows what the Mortmains are thinking."

"As your hired man, I'm allowed certain privileges. Someone has to look after you."

"You're very lucky my aunt isn't here. She'd chase you out with a knitting needle."

"She could try."

"She chased you away before, didn't she?"

"That was before."

"And it's different now?"

"I am. I am different now."

She didn't know what he meant, but suddenly Pip felt rather tired and weak, so when he sat on the bed, took her spoon and began to feed her the wretched stew, she actually let him do it. For once she didn't mind his take-charge manner.

How far they had come, she mused.

His thoughts apparently mirrored her own. "Now I know you really are sick," he quipped.

* * * *

Damon found a pack of cards on her bedside table and, since they could not agree on a fun game for two people, he entertained her instead with card tricks that his father had taught him. It was a while since he'd performed any, and he'd forgotten how pleasing it was to completely befuddle a young lady with his slight of hand. Elizabeth would never have been so impressed, but then he would never have sought to entertain her in this fashion.

The card tricks made him think of his father and their quarrel. He was sorry. He was sorry about a lot of things tonight. This was no time for self-pity, however. Damon had a new path to build.

"It is a strange coincidence, isn't it?" he said. "About our fathers. All those years ago. And then you and I, running into each other."

"I suppose two clumsy, stubborn, independent people might collide once in a while. When you think about it," she paused to sneeze, "it has just as much chance of happening as not. That's life for you. All the planning in the world means nothing when fate steps in."

Shuffling the cards, he said nothing.

"What's a Nonesuch?" she asked suddenly. "You called me one yesterday."

His heart bounced up into his throat.

"When you were suffering the effects of too much of the good inn-keeper's best wine," she added, eyes shining deviously from the shadowy depths of her pillows.

"I don't recall."

She stared, lips pressed together, brows curved in two fallen question marks. "You told me you remember everything."

"I cannot think what you thought you heard," he assured her firmly. "Nonsensical? I might well have called you that."

"No. I'm quite sure it was Nonesuch."

He shrugged and concentrated on shuffling the cards, because he was not ready to tell her that story yet. Perhaps he never would. "Tomorrow, if you're well enough, you can show me Serenity's room."

"Why?"

"You want to know where she's gone, don't you? Five minutes in her room and I can tell you not only where she went, but with whom."

She pursed her lips, a sultry gleam in her eye.

"Do you want to wager?" he demanded.

"I thought you didn't gamble."

"Ten shillings says I can tell you everything within...three minutes of entering your sister's room."

"Fine. Ten shillings, Mr. Know-All. I'm too worn out to argue with you."

"Splendid." He paused. "If I make it in two minutes or less, you have to promise me that amiable mute you once dangled tantalizingly before me."

"Now you're just being foolish."

"I'm never foolish."

Her eyelids drooped as she settled deeper into her pillows, and he thought how pleasant it truly was to sit quietly with her for once.

Before too long, however, the maid returned and Edwyn Mortmain came to show him to another guest room that had been prepared in a far wing of the house.

"Had we been expecting another guest, the bed would be better aired, Mr. Deverell. Nobody has used this room in years, but there is a fire lit. I hope you will not be too uncomfortable."

"Worry not about me," he assured his host. "I am grateful for any bed tonight."

"You've traveled many days?"

"Almost a full week."

Mortmain shook his head. "To travel in winter is always a trial, but I only go so far as London once every few years, in the spring, when a visit to my great aunt can no longer be avoided."

"And this time you had the good fortune to meet Miss Piper while you were there."

"Yes." A thin, fretful sigh, more agitated than thankful. He tried a wilted smile that couldn't quite lift the corners of his eyes, only his lips— and that a tentative procedure which seemed almost afraid of itself. Although he'd begun to walk back down the passage, he stopped and turned back. "It is a change for us here at Darkest Fathoms to have any guests. My brother...Roland...died many years ago. Now there is no other family left. Just my father and I, and, of course, my great aunt in London." He sighed. "She won't come farther north than Biggleswade. Says the cold bothers her joints."

"I see. Well, I come from a large family myself. Sometimes I think to be left alone would be pleasant."

"Is that so?" He nodded slowly. "The grass is always greener, as they say..."

He realized the fellow must be lonely living in that ruin with nobody but his father, and echoes in the walls, for company.

"Well, good evening, Mr. Deverell." Mortmain finally lurched away into the darkness with his solitary candle.

Left alone in the room Damon paced restlessly for some time before he finally laid his head down and slept. He dreamed that night of a child running along wet sand and himself chasing it, never quite catching up, until, at last, he did.

She turned, laughing, hair blowing in her face. And it was Nonesuch.

* * * *

For two days Pip was laid low with her cold and a twisted ankle, so there was no chance of her showing him her sister's room. Deverell spent hours at her bedside, entertaining her with cards, chess and readings from the newspaper. He also insisted upon twice daily dosings of his green stew, which were likewise administered, under his orders, to her sister.

"Are you not wasting your time here with us?" Pip said to him one morning. "What about your lady friend?"

"I'm afraid I'm stuck here in the snow," he replied nonchalantly as he opened the newspaper and casually put one booted foot up on her bed. "So you must tolerate me a while longer."

"God help us."

"Isn't God responsible for the weather? Not much use asking for His help then. Since He keeps throwing you and I together for His own devious sport, He clearly has a perverse sense of humor."

It was not too objectionable to have his company to protect her from mournful Mortmains, so she said nothing more— not even about his uncouth boot heel on her bed cover— and let him read to her an article about fishing. Possibly the dullest article ever, but somehow he made it interesting.

Damon Deverell made everything interesting. He could probably get her excited about cricket, she thought wryly.

He passed along bulletins about her sister's improving health and amused her with comical imitations of the Mortmain conversation at breakfast— which she was, of course, missing. He even took Grumbles Junior out to release some energy in the snow.

A useful sort of person to have about the place. He had his faults, but then nobody was perfect, as she had often observed.

Pip stood at her chamber window, wrapped in a

blanket, and watched him chase the dog about, tossing snowballs and landing on his backside more than a few times.

The sky outside her window brightened, and the snow began to clear.

There had still been no word from Serenity, but now she knew her sister was with Jonathan Lulworth she couldn't be concerned. If her sister must run away with anybody, she supposed Jonathan was the best man possible. Why should Pip be the only sister to have recognized his worth? It hurt, however, that neither had told her. They had let her go on visiting him on the moor, chatting away, making a nuisance of herself. All that time, that summer and autumn, Pip had imagined she was his most eagerly awaited visitor, when, in all likelihood he'd been waiting for her to leave.

She thought Jonathan was her friend— had even wondered, once or twice, whether she was in love with him. Whether she might like him to kiss her the way the Dangerous Mr. Damon Deverell once did. And Serenity had encouraged her in these thoughts, teasing her about the vicar and her fondness for his company.

Mrs. Trotter, the world's surliest housekeeper, had tried to warn her off, but Pip, being stubborn, had refused to listen. It was very hard to find oneself so abysmally misled. By one's own self.

Jonathan would never have removed her shoes to make her comfortable, or sat on her bed and fed her stew. He was much too proper. And probably afraid of her.

Which was why she listened to Jonathan's advice, she realized now; he never disagreed with her, but told her what she wanted to hear. Damon Deverell, on the other hand, told her what she needed to hear, not what she wanted. That was why she was so reluctant to accept his help when it was offered.

Pip smiled as she watched that fearless, sarcastic young lawyer fall hard on his behind again in the snow.

He was quite despicable, but thank goodness he'd found her again.

How long would she have him at her side? How long could he stay?

She dare not ask.

And over he went again. Ouch, that one had to hurt.

* * * *

"Perhaps you'd like to take a ride out today, Mr. Deverell?" Mortmain caught up with him in the passage. "Now that the lanes are passable, I can show you something of the countryside. I confess, being forced indoors by the weather these past few days has made me desperate to get out again, and the horses need exercise. The lane that stretches around the bay is mostly cleared. Naturally, closer to the coast we have more temperate weather than they suffer on the moors."

Damon agreed at once to go riding, for he too felt the frustration of being imprisoned by the snow. Amongst other things.

As they rode out that day Damon found his host glad of new company. The farther they traveled from the house, the more friendly and less formal the conversation became. When Damon asked if they had society nearby, Mortmain explained that he and his father had led solitary lives for some twenty years.

"When both my mother and brother died, it left us with quite a hole in our lives," he told Damon, "and we've never quite managed to fill it. I must say, having the Miss Pipers as our guests has certainly made a change and livened things up." He laughed nervously, and Damon guessed it was a sound not often heard. The poor chap needed practice. "I have great hopes that, after the marriage, my wife will settle in here and...well, I suppose she will decorate the place and shake out the dust. The house is already much more cheerful than it used to be."

Christ, thought Damon, *they must have been bloody grim before*. "So you have very little society here? I wondered if there were other local families with which you dine."

"No. You and the Miss Pipers are our first guests since my mother passed away. We are not...accustomed to lively society...well, I daresay you have seen how we live at Darkest Fathoms. It is very difficult to get my father in a temper to withstand the invasion of guests. He rather lost the will to entertain when my mother passed away. Indeed, some days he refuses to let the curtains and shutters be opened, let alone to think of inviting strangers in. He...grieves for her still."

"Yes, I see."

"But once I have a wife, it is my dearest hope that we might let the sun in more often." Again the sad attempt at a smile.

"Miss Serenity will return soon, I'm sure," Damon said, a perfunctory conciliation.

"Yes, yes. I expect so." But there was just as much enthusiasm in that reply as there had been in the assurance offered before it.

They rode on for a while in silence, both looking out over the bleak, churning sea. "Your father's marriage was a love match then, it seems, Mortmain."

"Indeed. They were fortunate." The fellow turned his head and looked at Damon. "You will be as fortunate too, it seems."

"Me?"

"With Miss Epiphany. I saw the way you looked at her and she at you."

He took a deep breath. "What? I didn't— was it so obvious?"

"Unmistakable. I envy you."

Damon tried to get his thoughts straight. "You think she...Epiphany...has feelings for me?"

"Did you doubt it, sir, when she let you carry her to bed? Her ankle did not bother her all day. Until you came."

"Is that so?" He was amused. Amazed. So many things.

"Miss Serenity never looks at me that way." A few more lines scored Mortmain's already pained visage. "Of course, I have so little to offer a young lady such as she. She is lively, and I am not. Can such a marriage be happy?"

Damon looked out over the grey sea and took a deep breath of salty air. It reminded him of his home on the Cornish coast and he thought suddenly of how he would like Epiphany to see it one day. But...."Miss Epiphany Piper has no desire to marry. She is dead set against it and values her independence greatly. Besides," he rubbed his thigh with one hand, "I have complications now in my life that I could not ask her to take on."

"But Miss Epiphany seems a brave young lady. I cannot think there is much that would leave her daunted."

Smiling slightly, he turned his horse along the path.If Epiphany had grown fond of him and was willing to put aside her sword, he would have to tell her everything about Elizabeth, of course. There was nothing else for it. And Edwyn was right; she was brave. To the point of recklessness.

After a few more minutes of silent riding, he said, "I thought I had friends nearby, and had hoped to call upon them, but I've been unable to find the family. The Grosvenors. They had a daughter, Elizabeth, who would be a little older than you perhaps. She married a Stanbury some years ago and moved south. You do not know them?"

"Grosvenors?" The other man considered the name and shook his head. "There is no family of that name hereabouts. Mortmains have been here in Whitby for centuries, and I can name all the aristocratic families in the county— it is important to keep record of these things, even though we do not socialize. You must be mistaken, I think. But I will ask my father. He would know for sure."

Damon nodded. After a while he said, "I've been fortunate that nobody is ever in haste for me to marry." It was the one expectation his father had never had for him.

"Really? How very pleasant that must be."

Chapter Twenty-One

They were playing chess in her room when the noise of a new arrival alerted Grumbles Junior from his sprawl at the foot of her bed. The dog leapt down, barking savagely and running to the doorway, where it sat, ears pricked.

"My dear Pip, Lord Mortmain tells me you are stricken and lying ill abed. I should have been sent for!" Bertie Boxall strode into the room and stopped dead at once, faced by Grumbles Junior, ready to attack, and the sight of *Master* Grumbles sitting by her bed with his feet up on it.

"What the devil—?"

"Bertie," she exclaimed. "What are you doing here?"

Damon did not put his feet down immediately, although she'd seen him tense at the first word out of the other man's mouth. He moved his bishop first, and only then did he look over at the door, where the dog held Bertie at bay, growling impressively.

"Grumbles Junior, be quiet!" she shouted. "Friend not foe!"

Of course, he did not listen to her. Damon put two fingers in his mouth and whistled, whereupon the dog lurched from side to side once more, and then returned to the bed where it sat beside Damon's chair, still watching Bertie intently.

"Deverell? May I ask, what you are about? Sitting in my fiancée's bedroom in this casual manner? I ought to call you out, sir."

"Your *fiancée*?" His hard gaze flew to Pip's face.

She shook her head, irritated. "Don't be silly,

Bertie. We're not engaged as you well know."

He walked forward into the room, until Grumbles Junior gave a low growl. Damon patted the dog's head and whispered a "Good boy."

Bertie looked rather pale and worn, she thought. "Why have you come all this way? In this weather?"

"I heard that your aunt had died, and I thought I ought to pay you a visit since, as my godmother pointed out, it's been sometime since you wrote." He pouted, glaring at Damon. "Now I see why."

"Mr. Deverell is merely looking after us, on my father's instructions."

"As if I'd believe *that* for a moment. The only person he looks after is himself."

Damon finally put his feet down and stood. "What's your business here, Boxall?"

"To visit Pip, about whom I have been greatly concerned and clearly not without cause."

"*Pip?*" Damon's hands went to his hips. "Do you refer to Miss Piper?"

"And here I find her in bed and you, planted at her side most improperly, lounging like the filthy reprobate you are and, no doubt, taking every advantage of a young lady in need of guidance."

"I'll lounge where I please and if Miss Piper wishes me to go, she'd tell me. I have no fear of her being shy to express a feeling in that regard."

"What do you know about her? You're just a scoundrel looking to seduce her. If you haven't already."

"That's none of your business, is it, Boxall?"

"Oh, but it is. Pip and I had an understanding, before she left London."

"Did you indeed? With *Pip?*"

"It was not quite an engagement, but an understanding that one might occur in the near future."

"I know something that's more likely to occur in the near future." Damon made his hands into fists and took a step toward Bertie.

"Excuse me." Pip got out of bed, having heard enough. "Kindly don't talk about me as if I'm not here. Firstly, I am not a young lady in need of guidance. Secondly, there was never an understanding of the sort, Bertie. You and I parted company as friends. Thirdly, Mr. Deverell, you can put your male bravado back in your breeches. There will be no brawling here today. If there were—" She grandly wrapped her aunt's Chinese silk robe around herself. "—you can be sure, *I'd* start it."

They both looked at her. Grumbles Junior got up and trotted over to her side.

"Now I suggest you shake hands," she added primly. "Because I won't have two foolish men in my company, sulking like little boys. I like you both so you may as well be friends."

Damon gave her a look that suggested she'd just kneed him in an unfortunate place. "Friends?"

"That's right."

Bertie gripped his hat in both hands and exclaimed defiantly, "I don't care to be told what to do."

"Really?" She laughed. "But you all expect me to put up with it." She walked past them both to the door, her dog following closely. "I'm going to find some cake."

"Wait a minute," Damon called after her. "Ring the bell for it."

"No. I fancy some exercise. And from now on there's nobody to tell me what to do. Now, when I come back, I shall expect to find peace declared in this room. Not my room in pieces." With that she swept out, feeling as if she had just conjured the spirit of Queenie Du Bois.

And what a wonderful feeling it was.

* * * *

Damon was too hot to sit. He and Bertie faced each other in utter silence as the sound of her merry whistling faded down the corridor.

Finally Bertie said, "I suggest you leave her alone. Or perhaps she'd like to know about Lady Stanbury."

He rubbed his tight chest through his shirt. "She knows about Elizabeth already, so good luck with that." Apparently word was out. After months of carefully keeping the affair secret, it was all for nothing. Now Elizabeth would need his protection from her husband more than ever.

"You can have any woman, Deverell. Why are you here chasing her? You don't need the money."

He grunted, "Believe it or not there's more to life than money."

"Not to me there isn't." The sallow young man took a flask from inside his coat and swigged from it. "I have debts to pay."

"Perhaps you shouldn't live beyond your means."

"I don't listen to you telling me what to do any more than I'd listen to *her.*"

"Well, go on sinking into that hole then. Soon you'll be too deep for anybody to get you out."

"She can. She's worth a fortune. They all are, those Piper sisters. But you know that, of course."

Damon watched him carefully for a moment, flexing his fingers. They'd begun to feel cramped in those fists he hadn't been able to let go of. "I think she's made it clear what she thinks of marriage and of you as a husband."

Boxall took another swig and burped. "Doesn't matter. I'll sue her for breach of promise. She thinks we're not engaged, but I think we are. She certainly let me act as if I was." He grinned nastily. "Allowed me certain liberties."

"I don't believe you."

"Oh, come on. She's American. They do things differently there. She's very casual, very free and easy. You've heard the rumors. And now," he waved his flask toward her bed, "here you sit as if it's entirely proper to be in her room. That's surely evidence enough of her...lack of morals and discipline. And virtue."

Damon walked slowly to where the other man and watched him take another gulp from his flask. "Miss Piper was never engaged to you and never would be. She has too much self-respect."

"Her word against mine."

"Oh." He smiled slowly and raised both hands to straighten the collar of Boxall's coat. "You might think that now. But you'll change your mind."

"No, I won't, old chap. I need that money, and I'm going to get it one way or another."

"Well, that's awkward."

"For you perhaps. Better luck next time."

Abruptly, Damon lifted the other man by his collar and half dragged him to the nearest chair, dropping him hard into it. Boxall lost his grip on the flask, but when he reached for it, Damon grabbed him and pushed him back into the chair. "You're not going to waste another minute of her time. You're going to pick up your sorry behind out of this chair, go back downstairs and walk out of this house, never to return." He spoke slowly and quietly, but only inches from Boxall's pale, sweaty face. "You're going to get back into whatever grubby vehicle you used to come here, and go back to your poor, delusional godmother, and tell her you've decided you're not ready to marry. Certainly not to marry Miss Piper."

"Why," the other choked out, "would I do any of that?"

"Because I want you gone from here," he replied, his tone sad and somber, "and since I'm a Deverell, I get what I want."

"You bastard. I'm not going anywhere. You can't intimidate me. If you lay a finger on me, she'll know and she won't like it. Go on. Hit me. Let her see you for the brute you are."

Damon thought about for a long, painful moment and then he tightened his grip on Boxall's throat and leaned closer still. "I'm not going to hurt you. This time."

He felt the other man trying to swallow.

"I'm going to do you an enormous favor, for which you will be forever in my debt."

Boxall tried to speak but couldn't do more than rasp out a high cry of dismay.

"I'm going to give you some money to go away, your lordship. Rather than beat you to a pulp here and now, I'm going to make it easy for you. I'll put some money in your pocket and I'll let you go. Back in London I'll arrange for your debts to be paid. At least, some of them. And in return, you'll never mention an engagement to Miss Piper ever again. Nor will you ever call her *Pip*." He finally released his hold on the other man and straightened up. "I trust those terms are agreeable."

He had some money saved—a considerable amount, although a man always needed more. For Miss Piper to be rid of this leech, he would gladly spend it, even if he was left a pauper. He'd find a way to make more.

Bertie jumped to his feet and reached for the flask, fumbling and coughing. "You Deverells...think you can get anything you want."

"Yes. Odd that, isn't it? I don't know where we acquired the idea."

"The Hell that your father came from. and right where you're going."

He smirked. "Quite probably."

* * * *

As Pip came out of the kitchen with a plate of treacle tart— a new discovery for which she had developed an acute fondness— she saw the two men walking across the hall to the front door.

Much to her relief, they were arm in arm.

"Lord Boxall! Are you leaving already?" she exclaimed, going after them.

"Er. Yes." He looked at her sheepishly. "It was only a brief visit. My godmother can't spare me too long. And with Christmas..." His voice tailed off as Damon placed an arm around his shoulders.

"Have a safe and swift journey back, your lordship."

Bertie stumbled out, almost dropping his hat.

"Are you sure you cannot stay to dine?" Pip

cried. "After coming all this way? Have some treacle tart, at least."

But he didn't seem to hear her. Having walked part way across the yard, he suddenly looked back and shouted, "By the way, Deverell, you're lucky Stanbury mistook your brother for you. Nearly killed him, by all accounts. But I don't suppose you care. You're a family of animals, as my godmother says. Not a human feeling among you." With that he turned and literally vaulted into his carriage, the door opened in the nick of time by his startled groom.

Pip looked up at the man beside her. Standing in his shirt sleeves, hands on his hips, Damon was frowning hard at the carriage as it turned speedily and took off up the lane, whip cracking and wheels rattling. "What was that about, pray tell?"

He turned away and walked back into the hall.

"Damon Deverell, you will answer me." She marched after him. "What did you do to Bertie Boxall. You made him leave! I told you to make peace. I—"

He swiped the slice of treacle tart from her plate and shoved it, whole, into his own mouth.

She stared as he chewed slowly, his eyes gleaming with menace. "How— dare you? That was mine and the very last slice to be had. I insist you tell me what happened. Why can't the two of you be friends? I left implicit instructions before I left that room and not half an hour later you're escorting the poor boy out."

With one last swallow, he emptied his mouth, wiped his hand across his sticky lips and said, "That was your slice, was it? And the last one?"

She frowned. "Yes, it was. I was looking forward to eating it."

He leaned down to her and said, "Then you know how it feels. And that's why I got rid of him."

Pip had nothing to say to that. Clutching her empty plate, she watched him walk away, stooping as he passed through the low, medieval arches that were clearly not constructed for men of his size and intolerable arrogance.

* * * *

He wrote another letter at once to Ransom, wanting to know if Stanbury had anything to do with the beating he'd suffered shortly before Damon left London. But fearing his brother would never tell him, he also wrote to Lady Roper, who had her ear to the ground in more than a few unsavory places to catch what she called, "Whispers in certain neighborhoods". He would find out, whether his brother told him or not. And then he'd pay a visit to Stanbury.

It was typical of his damn brother to say nothing, of course, just let him leave London like that, utterly in the dark about the cause of that gruesome damage.

* * * *

Pip soon felt much improved, remarkably so. She thought it likely to have much to do with her aunt's silk robe, but also with not wanting more of Damon Deverell's mystical stew spooned down her throat.

"See?" he said proudly. "It is a miracle cure."

"You should patent it."

"I should, shouldn't I?"

He'd been out riding early that day. Fresh, cold air clung to him as he moved around her room restlessly, top boots kicking up the worn threads of the rug and leaving wet prints across the floor boards.

"But you feel better?"

"I do. And so, apparently, does Merry."

"Good. Good."

She sat in a chair by the fire, a blanket around her shoulders, watching Damon proceed in distracted circles around her room, Grumbles Junior padding after him. Occasionally the dog stopped to look back at Pip, but then resumed his trot behind the restless man. In the past she would have shouted at them both to stop pacing and for Damon to tell her whatever was on his mind, but she was trying to be calm, patient. Trying not to think about him removing her shoes that first night when he put her to bed. Not to think of how he had taken care of her. Not to think of how he'd chased Bertie Boxall out of the house. Poor Bertie, he had looked terrified.

"When Lord Boxall left, he mentioned something about your brother and Stanbury."

"Hmm."

"Something about nearly killing him?" She hoped it was a misunderstanding of some sort. That she'd misheard perhaps.

He turned in the window and scratched his brow with one finger. Looking at those hands only reminded her again of how it had felt to have them touch her feet and ankles when he put her to bed.

She wriggled her toes, which were currently tucked up beneath her. "Please tell me," she exclaimed. "I hate secrets."

At last he stopped pacing and scraped fingers though his hair from temple to crown. "Miss Piper, there is something I must," he stopped breathed heavily, and then continued, "tell you."

Pip waited, forcing herself to be still and

attentive, although every nerve in her body was ready to leap out of that chair.

He walked to the fire and stood with his back to the flames, feet apart, hands behind him. "Lady Elizabeth Stanbury is the woman I followed here, the woman for whom I search...she is with child."

Chapter Twenty-Two

Whatever happened he would put this mess in order, but he needed her to know why he had chased after Elizabeth. The more he began to let himself feel for Miss Piper, the more necessary it became that she understand him.

"I'm certain she has no lingering attachment to me, or she would not have fled, but I must do what I can. For the child."

She was watching him steadily, her hands clasping the blanket she wore around her shoulders. "You're telling me that this is your child?"

"Yes. I believe so."

"I see." Her eyes had dimmed a little. Her fingers toyed with the blanket fringe.

"My brother told me that she travelled in this direction. He met with her before she left London. I had planned to accept my responsibility, but she seems to have other ideas."

"Lady Elizabeth Stanbury," she murmured, not much above a whisper.

"Yes." He took a deep breath and released some of the tension in his shoulders, bouncing once on his heels. "I wanted you to know."

Her eyes narrowed. "Why?"

Ah.

"Because you hate secrets and...I thought... I don't want any between us either. Now that we're no longer sworn enemies." Somehow he managed a bit of a smile, although it snapped back too quickly. *Don't get ahead of yourself. All you have is Mortmain's suspicions about her feelings for you, and what does he know about women?* Friendship must suffice. If that was all he could have with her. As long as he had this woman, somehow, in his life, he would try to be content. How could he ask for more now?

"What do you intend to do then? Once you find her?"

"First I must know what she intends, since she has not properly discussed it with me. Then I will make sure she understands that I mean to provide for my child."

Not moving from her chair, she studied him and wrapped her fingers ever tighter in the blanket fringe. "I am glad you told me," she said finally, her expression sober, her tone sincere. "You may depend upon my discretion, of course. I know I'm a chatterbox, but I am capable of keeping secrets that are entrusted to me."

"Unless somebody feeds you," he teased softly.

"Yes." But she didn't smile.

A tap at the door interrupted this conversation and her younger sister immediately ran in, not waiting for an answer. Upon seeing Damon she froze mid-step, her mouth open.

"Gracious, you must be better, Merry!" Epiphany got up out of her chair.

"What's he doing here?" the girl exclaimed, scandalized. "And in your room!"

"The Dangerous Mr. Deverell is merely doing his job and looking after us, now that Aunt Du Bois has gone."

"Has he come to fetch Serenity back? Or is there to be a lawsuit?"

"That remains to be seen. It might be best if he packs us all off on the first ship back to America."

Damon bowed. "Miss Merrythought Piper, I am very pleased to see your health improved."

"Well, they kept forcing me to eat some horrid green stuff and I can't bear it anymore, so I thought I'd better get up today."

Epiphany smiled again at last. "There!" she said to Damon. "You really must patent your elixir at once."

* * * *

She went to the window at the very top of the tower ruin and looked out over the grey sea. Speckles of white dotted the surface, as waves clashed and curled against a colorless winter sky. There were no fishing boats to be seen today, although sometimes when she came up here, there were three or four balancing precariously on the tossing waves.

This was where she liked to come with her thoughts, for the fresh sea air blowing through the narrow, unglazed window, helped clear out her mind so that she could concentrate. It was not a comfortable place, certainly not somewhere anybody else would chose for their reverie, so she felt safe here, not likely to be disturbed.

A few abandoned birds' nests huddled under the rafters and wind whistled through holes in the roof of the tower, howling a sad dirge. Good thing she was not a naturally maudlin person, she mused, or she might throw herself bodily out of that tower. She wouldn't be at all surprised if Lord Mortmain had a gruesome tale about one of his ascendants doing something that dreadful and desperate. It was the right sort of place for it.

Out there, across the sea, sat Europe. They were

on the wrong side of the country to face America when looking out over water and it made her feel even farther away, but she liked to think that if she concentrated hard enough she might get a message to her father.

What advice would he give her today in response to this latest dilemma?

The salty wind whistled through her hair and slapped her cheeks. He would tell her to stop feeling sorry for herself, of course. Pipers didn't give up. If they came to a mountain, they went around it or over it. Simple.

But her mountain was the largest she'd ever found in front of her and she didn't know how to master it. She didn't want to be in love, but she was. It was too late to save herself from it and now what?

Damon Deverell was hardly a monk, and she'd known that from the beginning. He was also not the first man in the world to father a child out of wedlock, and she shouldn't have been as surprised as she was when he told her. It was admirable that he wanted to accept responsibility for the child. Some men in his situation would run the other way.

He certainly didn't have to tell her anything about it, but he did.

She looked down at the little book in her hand— his book with the old list tucked inside the paper lining. The list belonging to Damon Deverell, nine yeres aged.

So far she hadn't been able to give it back to him. There were opportunities aplenty since he arrived at Darkest Fathoms, but she wanted to keep it as long as she could. It pleased her to have this insight into the real Damon— the little boy in search of adventure,

yet still a careful planner even at such a young age.
Then to look through the other pages and see how
that same prudent nature continued into his adult life,
keeping a strict budget for his expenses, marking the
figures in neat columns.

Now a child would become another item in the
expense column. And Elizabeth? He thought she had
"no lingering attachment" to him. But what were *his*
feelings? Had he chased her all this way only for the
child? Men seldom spoke of their emotions and he
would find it harder than most, having those big feet
and so much stubborn pride in his way.

She was concerned for him.

But was that all she felt?

Despite the wild breeze fluttering through the
tower and whistling against the old stone, Pip felt a
glowing warmth in her heart.

The first time she met him she'd wanted to brush
the mud flecks off his face and the fallen lock of hair
from his brow.

How was it possible for this great, tall man to
seem so in need of ... something.

A kindness? Love?

And whatever made her think that she could
provide it? Surely she was not the first woman to
imagine herself capable of that daunting task.

She wished her father were there to advise her.
Or Jonathan Lulworth. Or Aunt Du Bois. Even
Serenity would put her in her place with a scornful
laugh, reminding her that she was a fool
who knew nothing of men.

But there was nobody to shout at her, or cajole,
or roll their eyes.

All these years she'd longed for true

independence with not a soul guarding or guiding her.

Now she had that freedom and it was not at all what she expected.

Life was unpredictable and finite. She should simply tighten her corset laces, like Queenie Du Bois, throw on her splendid Chinese robe and get on with it.

"What are you doing up here? Trying to catch another cold, woman?"

* * * *

She turned, a mere silhouette at first with the light through the narrow window behind her.

"I came up here to be alone and think," she said curtly.

Damon moved closer to see her face. "Sounds dangerous to me."

"It is dangerous to you." She gave him an arch look.

"You're plotting what to do to me."

"It seems you can do plenty to yourself without my help."

"Yes. I made a mistake."

"Did you? It doesn't seem fair to call a child a mistake."

"I made a mistake with Elizabeth," he clarified carefully, taking her hand in his. "The child is innocent. She and I weren't. That was where we erred. We never loved each other. It was pride, vanity, lust. All the sins. Well, most of them." He raised her cool, gloveless hand to his lips and kissed it softly. "It began before I met you. It was over that summer, and then she came back. Just once. I should have known better."

320

"Yes. You should." Biting her lip, she looked out through the window, wind blowing her hair in all directions. But she let him keep her hand. It was a fledgling bird of hope. "You owe nothing to me, however," she said softly. "Why should you apologize to me? What you did with Elizabeth is not my affair. Ours was a strange acquaintance from the beginning, and when I left London neither of us could know that we would ever meet again. Life is capricious and often chaotic; I've known that from childhood."

She was too understanding, he thought. Any moment now she might swing her hand back and give him that infamous right hook. *Trust nobody.*

"You shouldn't have kissed me though," she added solemnly. "That wasn't fair."

"No. I shouldn't have. I should have finished one thing before I began another. Now I pay the consequences."

"It was wretched."

"Yes it—" He frowned. "The fact that I kissed you, or the kiss itself?"

"Both."

The word hung in the air, fluttering against the harsh wind like a fragile butterfly. She was trembling in the cold, but too stubborn to admit it.

So he tugged her into his arms there and then, needing to shelter her from the raw bite of the wind, wanting to soothe whatever part of her was hurting. He held the loose, wildly blowing hair out of her face and, when she looked up at him with tears in her eyes, he kissed her again, not caring that he shouldn't. Needing her too much to hold back and be a gentleman.

Not that he'd ever pretended to be one.

Her mouth softened, lips parting slowly under his, the tip of her tongue rising to meet his. He felt the same need in her, a heated desire, richer and fuller than anything he'd ever experienced.

But suddenly he realized she had something in her other hand, hiding it behind her back. As he deepened the kiss, he slid his free hand around her waist and tackled her for the book.

She broke away. "Give that back!"

"Just a minute, Miss Piper! This is my book. Where the devil—?"

She took a step away, resting her shoulder to the curved stone wall, looking sulky, but beautifully ravished by the wind and his kiss. Damnable woman couldn't possibly say *that* kiss was wretched, he thought proudly.

"It fell out of your coat," she admitted, breathless. "At the inn."

"Why didn't you give it back to me?"

"Because I wanted to read it. I was amused."

Damon hadn't even realized it was missing. "You were amused?"

"To see how much care you took over every part of your life. Even down to planning a journey around the world when you were nine."

"Ah." He put the book away inside his coat. "That's why you asked me about Nonesuch."

She was silent.

"She was a childhood friend," he said.

"And her name was Nonesuch? Odd name."

"She was an odd girl," he replied wryly. "I suppose she would never have been my friend otherwise."

"What happened to her?"

322

"I...we went our separate ways as we grew up. It was," he shrugged, adding on a halting breath, "necessary."

"How sad. Perhaps if you kept her friendship, things would be different and you'd be happier."

He laughed suddenly and ran a hand down over his face. "I think I am. Now that I have her back again."

"You do?"

Damon approached her slowly, while she stood against the wall looking puzzled. "Well. that's if she still wants to be my friend."

"Where is she then?"

"Here."

"You're not making much sense, Deverell."

After a pause, watching her lips, longing for another taste, he said, "She was my creation, entirely in my head. Until you came along."

Her eyes widened. "*You* had an imaginary friend?"

"And if you tell anybody... I'll have to punish you severely. I have a reputation to maintain."

It took a while. He had wanted to say that he would never forgive her if she told his secret. But he couldn't say it. He would forgive her anything, he realized, horrified. Her gaze explored his face, searching, perhaps, for truth. Answers to questions neither dared ask.

"You reminded me of her from the first moment," he added. "So, if you can see fit to overlook my many sins, perhaps we can—"

She'd lifted both hands to his face. "Be friends?"

His heart ached. "It's a start," he said, closing his eyes and leaning over her. "Come back to me,

Nonesuch. I've missed you."

* * * *

Pip had a feeling she'd never left him. That might explain the familiarity from that first sight, first word, first argument. He had never felt like a stranger to her.

"Friends. I would like that. If we still can. Of course, you're not a little boy anymore. That might make things...challenging."

"And you're no longer invisible to everybody else. Not merely living in my head anymore. Challenging is hardly the word for it."

She reached up and slipped her fingers through his hair, which she had wanted to do for a long time. "Thank goodness I'm not still living in your head. That would be a scary place to live forever. Worse than Darkest Fathoms."

Oh, what was she doing? Befriending a man who, for some reason, needed her. She wasn't used to being needed. Usually she was in the wrong place at the wrong time, an inconvenience, something that had to be put somewhere or managed somehow.

He said friendship was "a start".

But he might decide he was bored of her again one day soon, and leave her, just as he'd abandoned his imaginary friend before. Someone prettier might come along and catch his eye. Anything more important, more interesting.

A simple, uncomplicated friend might not care who he looked at with those wolf-like eyes. And there, of course, was the rub, because Pip knew she *would* care. She wouldn't be able to help herself.

For now though, friends. She would try her best

to be just that for him and not to encourage any other ideas.

This kissing business, for instance, would have to stop.

"Now it's tidy again," she said firmly, as if that was why she'd touched his hair. But as she backed away he took a step forward.

"Shall I do yours for you now?" he asked, eyeing the wind-torn tumble of hair over her shoulder, his wicked fingers flexing in readiness.

"No. Thank you. I can manage. I always do."

He sniffed, hesitated, his gaze lingering over her hair and then her lips, before he finally put his hands behind his back.

This time, when she heard him grinding his teeth, Pip decided to be safe and say nothing whatsoever about it. Instead she exclaimed cheerfully, "Let's go down. We should dress for dinner."

"First, show me Serenity's room."

"Why?"

"I want to look around it. Remember our wager? Now you're feeling better, no more reason to put it off. I want my ten shillings, Nonesuch. You owe me."

Chapter Twenty-Three

"An outsider can often see clearer than one blinded by familiarity," he told her. "One look around your sister's belongings will tell me more about her true self than you would."

"Aren't you clever?"

"I can't help it. I was born with the ability to read character from just a few possessions."

"Do all Deverells show off like you?"

"Yes. People hate us because we're so insufferable. Open the door."

When she did, he walked in ahead of her, hands behind his back, head raised as if to sniff the air. It was fusty for the room had been shut up, undisturbed, according to Epiphany, since the young woman left. He felt a whisper of excitement for he did love games and puzzles— something he'd forgotten about until he ran into Nonesuch again.

His father had a party trick— he could hold an object in his hands for only a moment and then tell its history, everything about it and much about the person to whom it belonged. But it wasn't magic. Damon, with his quick, inquiring mind had long since figured out how he did it— astute observation and an understanding of human nature that did not pass judgment, but simply saw what was and accepted it. Faults and all.

He looked around Serenity Piper's room now, taking it all in. There were two windows, but the curtains of only one had been opened. So she had looked for something in particular, or saw something that stopped her opening the others.

Damon looked out. Like a roughly stitched quilt, the moor stretched into the horizon, under a grey, bubbling sky of discontent. Somewhere out there was where he'd run into Nonesuch in the snow. One her way back from visiting her darling vicar.

He swiveled around and looked at the bedside table. It was empty but for an oil lamp. But the space beside that lamp had been cleared for something that was no longer there.

"Did your sister have a bible, like the one in your room?"

"Yes. Why?" Epiphany's eyes went at once to the empty bedside. "Our Aunt Abellard gave us bibles with our initials inside as parting gifts."

Damon strode to the dresser and mirror next, opened the top drawer and found several pairs of white silk evening gloves neatly folded, beside a velvet jewelry case. Apparently she had not expected to attend any social events.

"I think she would say it is not proper for you to pry through her drawers, Deverell."

Inside the jewelry case there was a faded mark on the velvet cushion and a pin hole. "But she took one piece of jewelry." He showed her. "A sprig of something."

"Yes. A forget-me-not brooch that belonged to our mother, who wore it... on her...on her wedding day." She snatched the case from his hands, closed it and set it back in the drawer.

"Hmph. And that was not significant in your eyes?"

"It was a favorite of Serenity's. I read nothing particular into her choice."

"Perhaps you have been deliberately blind."

She shut the drawer swiftly, narrowly missing his fingertips.

"You said your vicar—Jonathan— was not at home when you called?" he pressed.

"That's right. His housekeeper said he'd gone north and would return for Sunday service. Tomorrow."

Damon nodded. "Well then, you should know by this time tomorrow."

"What is that supposed to mean?"

"I did tell you to think of who else was missing, did I not?" He pointed toward the window, taking a guess that Thorford church lay in that direction.

Her face tightened.

He shrugged as if he was sorry, which he wasn't. "It took me less than two minutes to figure it out."

She stared at him, saying nothing.

"I suppose you're going to weep now over this vicar of yours. Tsk, tsk. You thought he loved you, and all the time he had eyes only for your sister." He put out his hand, palm up. "Ten shillings, if you please, madam. I hope you have better mysteries for me than this one."

"I'm not going to pay you ten shillings."

"That was our wager."

"I never agreed to it."

"Yes, you did." He scowled, pacing toward her.

"No, I didn't."

"You said: *Fine. Ten shillings, Mr. Know-All. I'm too worn out to argue with you.* And then I said: *If I make it in two minutes or less, you have to promise me that amiable mute you once dangled tantalizingly before me.*"

She gasped. "Your memory for words spoken simply amazes me."

"I'm a lawyer. It's important to remember what everybody says. That's how you catch them out in a lie. So what is it to be? Ten shillings or an amiable mute?"

"Everybody lies?"

"Of course. Trust nobody. My father gave me that advice many years ago."

"Then you shouldn't have trusted me to pay you." She blinked, all innocence and then scoffed, "And I already knew who my sister was with. I didn't need you to tell me."

Eyes narrowed, he studied her. "You knew?"

"I simply gave you the pleasure of amusing yourself and showing off again. It's what you do best."

"Oh, no it isn't. There are a great many things I do very well indeed. But if you come here, Nonesuch, I'll show you what I do best."

Laughing, she ran from him and he gave chase, the floorboards shaking under his feet.

She flew around a corner and directly into Edwyn Mortmain, almost knocking him off his feet.

"Miss Piper! Do have a care!"

Damon skidded to a halt behind her and caught her around the waist to steady himself. "So sorry, Mortmain."

The other man looked crestfallen. "Oh. Yes. Never mind." He stepped aside. "Carry on, please. Don't mind me. You young people should have your fun."

But they watched him walk on around the corner, his head bent, hands hanging at his sides.

"That poor fellow," Damon murmured, catching his breath.

She looked askance. "You and Merry should start a club."

"And people call *me* heartless."

"In fact, I do feel sympathy for him. My sister should never have said she would marry a man she couldn't love. But he wouldn't have been any happier if she did marry him. He's had a reprieve, but I can hardly tell him that, can I?'

They walked to her room, their demeanor and their pace decidedly more respectable, as befitted two adults rather than two naughty children.

* * * *

"I can't wear that," she exclaimed as he held up a buttercup yellow gown from her wardrobe. "I'm still in mourning, remember?"

"I think that's gone on long enough," he replied briskly. "I may not have known your aunt very well, but she was a colorful soul and I very much doubt she would have wanted her nieces hiding their figures in black for months of misery."

She pursed her lips and looked again at the gown, as he tossed it onto her bed. "Mourning doesn't just come to an end because you declare that it ought. These things have rules."

"Since when have you cared about rules and etiquette?"

"But yellow is so...bright. I should wear grey first. Half-mourning."

"I thought Pipers didn't do anything by halves."

"Ugh! That wretched memory of yours. What else have I ever said?"

He strode to the window and drew the drapes to keep out the chill. "Let's see. One of my personal favorites. *I find men to be wholly disadvantageous—obstructive to my contentment, destructive to my equanimity and, ultimately, adversaries to my success in life.*"

"True. Still true."

"And this one. *You're a dreadfully smug, officious Englishman and I'm a willful, independent-minded American. Oil and water have a more convivial relationship. Two brick walls have nothing to do, except stand against each other.*"

"Congratulations, I have just discovered the most annoying thing about you, Deverell."

"Now get dressed for dinner, Nonesuch. I'm tired of seeing you in grim black. This house needs some cheer. And wear it for me, your dear friend." He strode up to her, put his finger under her chin and lifted it. "We are friends now, aren't we?"

"Somehow I feel as if I haven't any choice. You do have a habit of deciding things for a lady, as I have observed before." But there was a sadness in her face, he thought. A sudden chink in her armor. That moment of running along the corridor had brought a flush of pink to her face and unsettled the knot of hair at her nape, curling strands caressing her cheeks. His own pulse was still raised. Couldn't remember the last time he ran like that. Together they had run back in time, leaving their troubles behind for just that brief moment.

"Good," he managed on a slippery breath. "Then wear the yellow and stop arguing for once."

She swiped his finger away and examined the gown he'd selected for her. "This color is Merrythought's favorite."

"Because it reminds her of spring chickens?"

"No. Because she informs me that yellow is the color of bruising and decomposition."

He arched an eyebrow.

"Yes." She sighed, hands on her waist. "Merry used to be the sweetest of little sisters. I have no idea what happened to her either."

"Blame it on the English climate perhaps?"

"Or novels and horror stories. She's overly fond of them. But then, I was told once, by a woman in Boston, that I also read too many books— all the wrong sort. I should have concentrated on etiquette and how to please a husband. Instead I favored history, business and science."

"This is not a surprise to me."

She smiled tentatively. "As for Serenity and what has become of her. I am utterly lost. I feel as if my sisters are strangers to me sometimes. So much has changed since we came here."

"Wear the yellow," he urged again. "For me."

Her lips straightened, her lashes swept down and up again, that warm violet color very deep and lush this evening. "If I wear yellow it will be because *I* want to. Not because of you."

Damon cleared his throat. "Yes. Because you want to."

"I am a woman of my own mind."

"You are a woman of your own mind."

Her eyes narrowed as she looked up at him. "I do what I want to do."

"You do what you want to do," he repeated.

"This is not a romance. We're merely friends."

"I could not have said it better myself."

"So there."

He gave a little bow. "So there." But as he walked to the door, leaving her to dress, he couldn't resist adding, "Wear the yellow, Nonesuch. Because you know you'll be beautiful in it and I shan't be able to take my eyes off you. I'm no terribly proper, well-behaved vicar. But you know that, of course. Far be it from me to tell you anything." And then he left quickly rather than see her horrified expression, or have anything thrown at his head.

She wore the yellow.

"Pip!" her sister cried. "You are out of mourning already?"

"It has been several months, Merry, and I believe our aunt would not want us to mourn so long. She was always a great proponent of living life to the fullest, as Mr. Deverell reminded me."

"Oh." And Merry looked from her sister to Damon. "Then I shall wear my blue tomorrow."

"Yes, I think you might."

"Thank goodness for that!" old Lord Mortmain bellowed down the table at dinner. "That child doesn't need to be in black so long."

"I'm eighteen, your lordship," Merry exclaimed, sounding shocked. "I'm not a child.""Eighteen, eh? But you're a little thing. Need a bit more flesh on your bones."

"Father," Edwyn interjected, "that is not the sort of thing one says to a lady."

"And what do you know about it? Whatever you say to ladies it doesn't seem to please any."

Epiphany broke the ensuing heavy silence by asking the old man about something called a "Boggart", a story he had apparently told her little sister. Immediately the fellow's demeanor changed to almost jolly, as he related the tale of an impish demon living in his chimney and sneaking about the house to wreck havoc. Miss Merrythought eagerly joined in to help him tell the story, adding all the pieces he forgot in his recital and, probably, adding some of her own invention. The discussion then turned to ghost stories and murder mysteries of a bloodthirsty bent. Lord Mortmain was soon preoccupied teasing his youngest guest and so forgot to berate his son further, much to Edwyn's apparent relief.

Once he was recovered enough to speak again, he said, "Father, Mr. Deverell asked me recently about other noble families in the county. Do you know of any Grosvenors hereabouts?"

"Grosvenor?" the old man barked. "Not in this county. I'd know if there were any."

Damon was puzzled. His brother had distinctly told him that Elizabeth fled north to Whitby in Yorkshire, to stay with her relatives. Her maiden name, he knew, was Grosvenor. But nobody here had heard of Elizabeth Grosvenor, or Lady Elizabeth Stanbury.

Nonesuch leaned closer and whispered behind her napkin, "Have you ascertained yet that your lover lied when she told you she came here? Tsk, tsk, I could have told you that within less than two minutes. I hope you have better mysteries than that to entertain *me*."

Damon frowned and she gave him an arch look. Of course she could not stand his earlier victory. How did one manage such a difficult, battle-prepared woman? A reflection of oneself, but in petticoats.

His education had not readied him for Miss Piper, although his Latin tutor had done her best. Her lessons were only useful once he got a woman into bed.

"An outsider can often see clearer than one

blinded by familiarity," she added smugly, firing his previous words back at him with effortless skill, and then turning away at once to chide her sister, "Merry, do stop feeding Grumbles Junior from the table."

Could it be that he'd been sent on a wild-goose chase? Ransom must have known he'd take off after her at once. Did he deliberately send Damon in the wrong direction, while pretending the information was forced out of him under duress?

Damon cursed under his breath as he considered this long journey he'd undertaken on a fool's errand. He should have known not to trust his brother's word, but he had been too blind with rage and when his father told him *not* to go after Elizabeth it only spurred him on even more. Stupid.

However, he thought, glancing at Nonesuch, he couldn't remain angry for long, could he? His journey had reunited him with an old friend. Something precious that once was lost.

A friend. Yes. Once again he promised himself that friendship would suffice. It must. He had this business with Elizabeth and his child to sort out before anything else might happen.

After dinner they played whist, with Damon and Epiphany as one team and Edwyn and Merrythought as the other.

"You must sit with me and help, sir," the young girl said to old Mortmain, urging that his chair be placed beside her. "I have only played once before and very badly. I need all the help I can get."

"I'm sure you'd do better without me, young lady."

"Certainly not! Please do sit here, your lordship. I tend to make silly decisions and give away all my best cards if I have nobody sensible at my side."

Edwyn, apparently, wasn't deemed "sensible", but he didn't seem to care. He was evidently glad to have his father's attention diverted from his faults, and occasionally he glanced at the youngest Miss Piper with shy gratitude.

As they went up to bed that evening, Epiphany said she knew now why he had wanted her to wear the yellow dress.

"You're trying to brighten this house up for Edwyn, aren't you? Mr. Deverell, I believe you have a soft heart after all, under that stern exterior. And you don't only do nice things for people when they pay you."

"That is not at all the case, Miss Piper. I wanted you to wear the yellow so that, with the candlelight behind you, I could see the outline of your figure. I'm a Deverell, remember?"

She arched an eyebrow. "I think you've seen enough ladies' figures. Do not get any ideas about mine. And you most certainly could not see through this material."

He merely smiled. Slowly. "Anything you say, Nonesuch." And he left her at her door, her expression exceedingly uncertain.

A letter arrived for him that evening, sent post haste from Lady Roper. It confirmed for Damon that his brother's injuries were believed to have been caused by thugs hired by Lord Stanbury. It was not well known, but the rumor had begun to circulate in the seedier part of town from which he hired his "assistants". Stanbury would not, naturally, do the deed with his own fine hands. But Ransom life, Lady Roper's letter assured him, was out of danger. He would heal, largely due to the efforts of a young lady who had been staying at his house and causing quite a scandal.

As if they didn't have enough of those.

* * * *

Merrythought came to her room that evening as she was undressing for bed.

"Are you in love with Damon Deverell?" she demanded.

"Good heavens! Why would you say that?" Pip quickly turned her back so that her sister could help unbutton her gown. And so that she could also hide her expression.

"I suppose you will try to deny it. You're so stubborn."

"I am nothing of the sort."

"Oh, yes, you are. And I thought you ought to know that I heard him tell Lord Boxall to leave you alone. I heard him promise to pay off that dreadful man's debts. He did it for you, even though you're always so mean to him."

Pip turned, eyeing her sister cautiously. "When did you hear this? You were *supposed* to be sick in bed."

"I heard men's voices raised and I was curious."

"Merrythought Piper, it is rude to eavesdrop!"

"Nevertheless informative."

"You have become a sly child with a dark imagination."

The girl patted her cheek. "I'm not a child, Pip. How many times must I remind you all that I am eighteen?" With that she walked out, leaving Pip to struggle alone with the rest of her disrobing.

She sank to the bed and stared at her candelabra. Damon Deverell had offered Boxall money to go away. Did he have that much at his disposal, or had he ruined himself for her sake? Men could be very proud about the state of their finances— although some, like Bertie, were shameless.

Pip shook her head at her own stupidity. She should have known what he'd done to make Boxall run off so quickly.

Chapter Twenty-Four

They traveled to Thorford church the next day in the barouche box, Lord Mortmain permitting its use this time, since the horses were not merely being inconvenienced for Epiphany. When a Mortmain attended church he must do so in style— even if it was a somewhat tattered state of grandeur with ripped seats and chipped paintwork.

"I didn't think Deverells attended church," Merrythought exclaimed as Damon joined them for the journey. "Aunt Du Bois said they're too wicked."

Pip smiled and whispered back, "Hopefully the church roof won't fall in then."

She looked out of the carriage window, watching the wild moors fly by, thinking of how she had taken this road last week and, by chance, encountered Damon Deverell again. She'd been so pleased to see him, all feverish excitement. Every morning now, when she went to breakfast at Darkest Fathoms, she felt that same shiver of pleasure when she saw him seated at the table, or serving himself from the chafing dishes on the sideboard. But he could not remain in her life forever. They travelled in separate directions.

Perhaps that was what made his presence feel so valuable to her now.

He was seated across from her today, his back to the horses, his face grim, arms folded. She knew he came with them to the church, anticipating trouble, ready to be "of service" again. It would certainly be awkward when Serenity reappeared and, if she chose to do so today, the sermon should be enlivened greatly. For once Pip herself was not the center of the quake, but she must feel its tremors.

What would she find to say to Serenity, when she saw her again? It felt as if a lifetime had passed while she was gone. Pip had, after all, discovered what "love" meant during her sister's absence. That it was simple and complex at the same time. That it hurt and thrilled all at once. That she could not control it and had no cure for it, no witty remark to keep it at bay.

Her pulse hammered away at twice its usual pace, and Damon looked at her quizzically several times, as if he could hear the sound.

In her heart that day she was anxious to see her sister safe, but she was also angry at the furtive manner in which this had all come about— Jonathan and Serenity, creeping away before dawn, like fugitives. She was also concerned for Edwyn and his father, who were the only two in their party still utterly in the dark about what they might encounter today.

Somehow Merrythought held her tongue during the carriage ride and said nothing about their sister and the vicar of Thorford, but never had Pip spent such a nerve-wracking hour.

It was a cold day, the air brisk and biting. There was still snow in places, hunchbacked drifts sweeping across the hills and valleys, but it was nowhere near as bleak as it had been on the day she took the mail coach to seek Jonathan's advice.

She looked for that black crow again, but he was nowhere in sight today. Really she wouldn't be surprised if Damon Deverell could transform himself from a man to a bird and back again if he wanted. He was extraordinary and full of surprises. The oddest man she'd ever known. And now her friend. She certainly needed one.

Somehow, without offending him, she would have to find a moment to ask him about that money he'd given to Bertie Boxall. It was not like her to worry about offending anybody, she thought glumly, but she had finally learned circumspection, so it seemed.

"That must be Mr. Lulworth," Damon murmured as they walked toward the church. "I thought you said he was handsome."

"No. I said he was kind. Your incredible memory has failed you."

"I'm sure you said handsome." He frowned.

"Perhaps that's just what you thought you heard."

Jonathan stood by the arched door, greeting parishioners as they entered. When he saw Pip and the Mortmains, he went as white as his robe, but then straightened his shoulders, as if he made up his mind to be brave.

He had better be, she mused, to take her sister on and keep her content.

But there was no sign of Serenity. As the Mortmains took to their pew, Jonathan came down the aisle and whispered in Pip's ear. When she got up again, Damon put his hand on her arm, but she shook her head. She would do this alone.

* * * *

Her sister was in the vestry, wearing a new, fur-trimmed coat in deep, rich maroon.

"I sold mama's brooch," she said. "I needed a new coat and hat. Do you like it?"

Pip stared at her sister's flushed cheeks and bright eyes. "You sold her wedding brooch?"

"After I'd worn it for my wedding day." Serenity twirled the hem of her splendid coat. "Our mama would have wanted me to make use of it. I could have taken the other jewelry, but I left it for you and Merry."

"That's good of you." She swallowed hard, determined not to raise her voice. "You left other things for us too."

Serenity looked blank. "I couldn't take all my clothes when I left, of course. But you can send them to me now. If there is some little thing you or Merry would like to keep—"

"I referred to the mess of a broken engagement. The Mortmains could sue us for breach of promise, you know."

"Well, that lawyer can take care of it, can't he? He's supposed to be good, and he might as well do something for the fee father paid him."

Her sister's carelessness took her breath away for a moment.

Then Serenity added, "Why shouldn't I cause a scandal for once? You're the one always having fun, not caring. Now it's my turn. I was tired of doing my duty and when Aunt Du Bois died, I realized...we don't have forever. I didn't want to be entombed in that place. Buried alive. I couldn't...I couldn't bear it."

"But all those lectures you gave me about marriage and survival—"

"I meant them. And then I met Jonathan. I suppose you thought you were the only one clever enough for him. Better educated, and informed, and oh, so witty. You have always thought yourself superior, smarter. The girl who knows everything."

"I certainly didn't know about you and Jonathan. You hid it well."

"Yes." Serenity was smug. "Jonathan said we should tell you, but I knew you would never be able to keep it to yourself. You would have told Aunt Du Bois."

"Then it began when our aunt was still alive? In the summer?"

"Of course. I knew him as long you did, Pip. At first I simply wondered what you liked about his company so much. Curious and bored, I took to visiting him without you, and I soon learned to appreciate his goodness. Did you think you were the only one of us who would? Then our aunt died and Jonathan comforted me. I began to realize that I couldn't marry Edwyn Mortmain. It would have been suicide for me, a slow death."

"I wish you had told me then."

"What good would that have done? Given us something else to fight over? Something else to quarrel about? We have never lacked for any of that, you and I. Odd, isn't it," she put her head on one side, "that we should both have fallen in love with the same man after all?"

Pip sat in a large carved chair, with cold blue light from the narrow window falling on her face. She took a deep breath of damp air and ancient stone. "I wasn't in love with Jonathan."

Serenity laughed softly. "Say that now if you must, to save face."

"I can assure you it's true. I know it now because I know what love feels like. I didn't know it before."

Serenity sniffed, tucking her hands into the fur

muff that matched her hat and the trim of her coat. "Then you're not angry?"

"I'm angry only that you left us that way. It was wrong of you not to be open and tell Edwyn Mortmain. To finish one thing before you began another."

"I couldn't face it. How on earth could I have told him? You must tell him for me. You won't mind what you say. You never do."

For a moment Pip could only sit and stare at her sister, trying to think how to break this news to Edwyn and his father. Finally she said, "So you *are* married?" Better get that clarified, she thought. It couldn't be undone if it was contract signed, vows exchanged.

"Yes. We went to Gretna Green. It was splendidly romantic. Like one of Merrythought's novels."

She shook her head, still trying to imagine Serenity as a vicar's wife. In Thorford, no less, this wild place, so far away from ballrooms and cotillions. It was typical of Serenity that her first thought as a married woman had been her need for a new coat. A fancy, fashionable garment that would look out of place in her new husband's parish. How long would this thrill of doing something unexpected, of knitting her husband's socks and pottering about that small vicarage, last for her? Not long.

Serenity had given up on the idea of having a little coronet printed on her stationary, but it was not the only thing she had given up for Jonathan Lulworth.

"Then I must congratulate you." Pip stood and kissed her on both cool cheeks. "At least you married for love, after all, and as your sister I am happy for you."

What else could she say?

Love conquers all or, as they say in Latin: *Amor Vincit Omnia*.

* * * *

Together, Damon and Pip broke the news to Edwyn after they had returned to the house. Serenity had not shown her face in church that day, but had hidden away in the vestry in her new coat, waiting for her husband to wave off the last of his congregation. Slowly, of course, Jonathan would have to introduce his wife to the parishioners and hope for acceptance. If his housekeeper did not let the news out before he could do so. Serenity would have to manage that dilemma herself.

Edwyn had, it seemed, resigned himself to the idea of Serenity not coming back.

"I confess," he uttered gloomily, "that there will be considerable humiliation involved in my former fiancée marrying the local vicar instead. I must see them every time I attend church service, and my father will never let me forget how I failed."

Lord Mortmain threatened to burn Thorford church to the ground. "'Ow is my son to show his face about the county?" he roared. "I know it ain't much of a face, but he still needs to air it once in a while. Folk are going to laugh at my son, and I won't have it."

Damon suggested there could be a settlement and Pip, agreeing it would be for the best, asked him to undertake the negotiations on her father's behalf.

"I trust you to do what is right," she told him.

With Merry's help she packed their sister's remaining things and took them to the vicarage, where they were invited in for tea. A stilted conversation concluded with Merry exclaiming that she thought Serenity looked plump and ought to let her seams out before the stitches snapped.

"What did I say?" she complained as Merry hurried her out to the carriage.

"I think you just brought our sister back to earth. Back to the messy, unromantic reality of marriage. And imminent motherhood."

* * * *

"It is good of you to stay and help settle this matter," said Edwyn. "Surely you have other demands upon your time with Christmas fast upon us."

But Damon had no desire to spend Christmas anywhere else. Now that he knew Ransom was out of danger, family visits could wait, and he had written to Tobias Stempenham to let him know he was earning his fee from their client Prospero Piper. If there should be an issue taken with the sudden way he'd left London, he would deal with that on his return, but once he explained, in person, about the breach of promise, he felt certain his employers would understand. In Yorkshire he could fix the matter with the minimum of fuss and maximum of discretion, far less chance of any gossip getting into the London papers.

But after Christmas he must return to London and his usual routine. He had business to tend there, and life must go on. If only he could persuade Pip to go with him, but then what? Before he made such a major swerve in his road, he must plan. Couldn't simply fly by the seat of his breeches, not after so many years of orderly planning. If one wanted a thing to be done correctly, it had to be done with care and attention to detail.

She and her sister spent an entire day decorating Darkest Fathoms with chains of paper Christmas decorations, pine boughs and holly. Although Lord Mortmain complained of the mess, a few glasses of port and a song from Merrythought, on the newly mended and tuned pianoforte, soon put him in a better mood.

"We have not had music here in a great many years," he said, eyes watering above the port glass. "Too many."

Christmas came, and Damon surprised Pip with a leather-bound ledger, similar to his own, with columns for income and expenditures. Solemnly he explained about keeping her accounts in it, how to bring some organization to her life.

"We agreed not to exchange gifts," she protested. "And I have nothing to—"

"I know you like to be independent," he murmured, cutting across her sentence because he wouldn't have wanted her to give him anything. If she did, he would have been utterly undone and probably not gone back to London when he must. Plans to make. Lists to draw up. Expenses... "I know you like your independence," he repeated, "and this will help you in that endeavor. An independent woman should know where her every penny is at all times. Trust no one else to keep record of it."

He felt that he had done as much as he could to protect her. As much as she would allow him to do.

She looked up at him with those incredible eyes

and he wanted to kiss her, but there were too many people looking on, too much, for now, to be sorted. So he said, "Merry Christmas, Miss Piper."

"I think you ought to call me Pip. Since we're friends now. Very good friends."

It was ridiculous, but he felt as if she'd just given him the greatest gift he'd ever received.

"Damon," she said suddenly, "did you offer Bertie Boxall money to leave me alone?"

He scowled. "How—? Why would you think—?"

"You should not have done that. It wasn't necessary."

With one hand he scratched his cheek. "It was to me."

"You must have bankrupted yourself," she exclaimed, her eyes warm with concern. "I will repay you, of course."

"You most certainly shall not."

"Indeed I shall."

And thus they were off on another argument, although it mostly proceeded in whispers and ended when she looked down at the ledger in her hands and, apparently, remembered that he'd bought it for her. Then all she could say was that he was "impossible".

They didn't mention the money again, but he knew she hadn't forgotten it and that she would, at some point, attempt to make recompense. He wouldn't accept it, of course, but she was stubborn and proud enough to keep trying.

* * * *

A letter arrived at Darkest Fathoms, addressed to Damon.

Your brother was so kind as to send me your current address. He seemed to think I might want to apologize to you, or some such nonsense. But I write now only to reiterate what I said to him, and what he was supposed to communicate to you on my behalf, last month in London.

You have no further part to play in my life, and you will have no role in the life of this child. I must ask you to stay away, for the sake of all, especially the child. He will be raised a Stanbury, the heir to a vast estate. As I'm sure you can appreciate, he will want for nothing. Your presence could only cause him trouble.

Before I left for Kent, I entrusted this message to your brother, expecting that he would know of some way to convey it with more gentleness than I. However, it seems he could not steel himself to find the necessary words when he last saw you, and, instead, sent you off to Yorkshire. Of all places.

E.

So Ransom had sent him north, knowing full well that Elizabeth was not there and never would be.

But had he known who *would* be there instead? Of course. Ransom knew everything.

At the end of her letter, she had scribbled an addendum.

Please be assured that his lordship and I are reunited and happier than ever. He is resolved to raise the child as his own, since he has no other heir. I suggest you hold your peace, and spare further bloodshed, since his lordship believes that suitable retribution has already been served against the responsible party. Let the matter rest and we can all go on as we were meant to be.

Now he fully understood Boxall's last rushed comment to him before he left. Stanbury had ordered the beating that Ransom received, because he had identified the wrong Deverell as his wife's former lover.

And Ransom would not tell him that. He simply took the blows for his younger brother and then, even in that savage physical pain he must have suffered, still had the foresight to send him in the direction of the woman he truly loved.

Well, Elizabeth might think him a coward who would let his brother answer for his sins, but that was not the case. Damon would stand face to face with Stanbury and let him know what a giant mistake he had made by harming his brother.

When he returned to London he must go directly to Ransom and repay him somehow for all that he'd done. But how could such a thing be resolved? How could such a debt ever be paid.

And all these years he'd thought his brother merely tolerated his existence.

Chapter Twenty-Five

"I have business to tend in London," he said to her. "Perhaps you...and your sister, of course, will return soon?"

Pip couldn't tell him about the letter she'd received from her father that day, calling them home. What would he do if she told him she was leaving? Something foolish, something impractical? Something mad. But he had much still to sort out regarding Lady Elizabeth's child, complications, his own family's troubles. She could not expect him to drop all of that and spend another moment worrying about her. He had protected her for long enough.

All those things he'd done for them. For her. Sooner or later he had to set them aside, know that he'd done his job well, and let them go.

So she told him they would return to London in the spring.

"I shall find a house for you," he said at once. "Perhaps the house in Belgravia will still be vacant again. Or would you prefer something smaller for just yourself and your sister? I'll write to your father and see—"

"Oh, we can discuss all that later."

He looked at her somberly. "Yes, of course." He kissed her hand.

"Until we meet again," she said softly, "as they say."

"Indeed. Now, you will write and let me know when you are coming? I'll need time to plan."

"Yes," she laughed lightly in a manner of which

Serenity would be proud. "Of course. Now go. For pity's sake, stop worrying about us. We are not your only clients."

She waved him off and then took Grumbles Junior back inside. Now it was time to break the news to Merrythought.

* * * *

"Pa wants us to go home. He seems to think his venture has been a little disappointing and he calls us home, Merry. He will arrange passage for us on the next ship from Southampton in April."

Merry put down her pen. "So soon? I thought we had until September, at least."

"I think pa has missed us and now, with Serenity eloping... and Aunt Du Bois gone, he doesn't want us here alone."

"But we're not alone," the girl exclaimed. "We have friends here now. The Mortmains and Mr. Deverell."

It surprised Pip to hear that her sister thought of the Mortmains as friends. But when she considered further she realized that Merrythought spent a great deal of time entertaining the old man, making him laugh. Even Edwyn had been seen to smile on occasion, when her sister told one of her stories— as fanciful as any their father liked to tell. But slightly more gory.

"The Mortmains want us to stay," the girl blurted. "I know they do. So does the Boggart."

"Well, we can't stay here. That's just...nonsensical. Now, we have a few months to prepare for the journey. We'll buy some new clothes in London on our way down to Southampton." She paused as Merry stirred her spoon violently through her hot chocolate making an unearthly clatter that went right through her head. "And stop making that noise. You're doing it deliberately."

Merrythought gave her an arch look, spoon poised in mid air. "Now you sound just like Serenity."

"I most certainly do not."

"Yes, you do. She used to say that same thing to you, sister *dear*."

Pip bristled with irritation, while Merry resumed her stirring and hummed under her breath. Another thing that *she* used to do to annoy their elder sister.

"Any moment now you'll tell me I ought to listen to you, pay you all due respect because you're the eldest now," the cheeky girl added.

Still feeling brittle from her goodbye with Damon, Pip got up and hurried out of the room. She had not cried in years, and she refused to do so now.

* * * *

The Boggart immediately began making its presence known like never before. Plates were thrown, Pip's ribbons went missing and her stockings were found draped over the front gates, limned with frost in the early morning light. Strange noises were heard in the chimneys and a great amount of soot blew down Pip's bedroom flue one afternoon, spattering everything she had laid out to pack with a fine layer of the Boggart's disdain.

"I'm sure you are welcome to stay," Edwyn assured her anxiously, just stopping short of wringing his hands. "Indeed, we shall be lost when you are gone again. My father has grown accustomed to the company of Miss Merrythought. As—as have I."

"That is kind of you, sir, but we really cannot stay. My father expects us home. The *Boggart*," and she looked at her sister, who smugly looked the other way, "will just have to go back in his hole with no young ladies here to tease anymore."

"That's not how it works," Merry assured her primly. "It doesn't just go away because you say it will. It's like love. It doesn't go away just because you try to deny its existence." And with her head high, the wretched chit walked off with Grumbles Junior. "I'm taking the dog out. Don't wait up for me."

Pip launched after her, tugging her back by the hood of her cloak. "Oh, no, you're not going off on the moor like Serenity, young lady. We'll have some discipline around here, thank you very much!"

"What are you going to do, sister dear? Lock me in my room?"

"If I must! You're working my—" She stopped, horrified, her hand loosening its grip on the hood.

"Last nerve?" Merry finished for her.

What else was there to say?

* * * *

He had expected to meet with George Stanbury, but his message was answered instead by Elizabeth who arrived in his office on a cool March morning, heavily wrapped in a thick cloak, her face paler than ever, her mouth set in a determined line of displeasure.

"Did I not advise you to leave this matter alone?" she demanded, as soon as the door was closed and they were alone. "Yet you return to London and the first thing you do is try to arrange a meeting with his lordship."

"I can't let him get away with what he did to Ransom. My brother might be willing to let it go, but I'm not. I bear grudges and I don't stand for anybody I love being hurt." Six months ago he would have struggled to confess that he loved his brother, even to himself. Ransom was damnably difficult, but yes, Damon loved him. Not that he'd ever say so to the man himself. Good god, no.

"Grudges? His lordship is willing to raise your cuckoo as his own. Don't you think he's the one entitled to hold a grudge?"

"I don't want him to raise my child. I would have raised him. Or her."

"Out of the question. This is *my* child."

The frustration built, but he kept his face calm. He would have offered her the chair to sit, but she quickly assured him that she wasn't staying. She had only gone there today because she intercepted his message— or so she claimed—and wanted to deal with it quickly. Damon felt sure Stanbury had received the message himself and sent his wife to meet with him because he was too afraid. A conversation in daylight in a law office? No, George Stanbury preferred to deal with his problems in dark alleys, with the help of hired thugs.

So Damon sat at his desk in his own chair and looked at his neatly arranged pens. "Since you are here, Elizabeth, perhaps I might ask... if...there might be some chance in the future...for me to be known to the boy. Not as his true father, of course, but just to meet. I know you think now that there is nothing I can do for him, but in a few years it might be otherwise. And I should like to know him."

"I don't think that would be a very good idea, do

you?"

"If I thought ill of the notion, I would not have suggested it, Elizabeth. I have the child's best interests at heart."

"Then leave him and us alone. Do you think, in your wildest dreams, that he would want anything from a Deverell? To know you? What for? Why? What good can it possibly do? The farther you stay away from him the better." She walked up to his desk. "I know how you work, how you intimidate people into getting what you want, but you don't intimidate me. I want the best for my child and that is not you, whatever you think of yourself." She drew back and placed both hands briefly on her rounded belly. "So don't think to scaring me into letting you into any part of this child's life. If I am upset, something could happen to the child. Now, or later."

He shook his head. "I knew you could be a cold-hearted bitch, Elizabeth. I just never realized that was the real you. I thought there was something else that you hid from the world to protect it."

"Something else?" she snapped. "Such as?"

Slowly he raised his eyes to her hard, cold face. "A human being."

"Well, now there is one inside of me. Isn't there?"

He sniffed and began to rearrange his pens. "Let's hope it's human. You know what they say about my family. Will George still want to claim it as his own then?"

Elizabeth stood for a moment more and then turned sharply, her coat sweeping the floor. "Don't come near me or the child, you bastard."

"Thank you, Lady Stanbury. You'll see your own

way out? I'm rather busy."

Tom stepped aside just as she flung open the door. "Get out of my way," she stormed out, slamming the front door and making the glass in his window rattle.

"Another lady dispatched, sir?" the clerk inquired, coming into the office with a package.

"Yes. Not before time. Although—" He was sorry for the child. Whatever she and Stanbury threatened, he would find a way to see it, do what he could for the boy. Or girl. He'd find a way.

"This came for you by messenger, sir." Tom handed him the package. "Oh, and Mr. Stempenham was supposed to take those steamer tickets over to the Clarendon Hotel in Bond Street, but he's been held up at home. Some young man gone to ask for one of those girls in marriage at last. He says can you take them over to the Clarendon and see to it that the young ladies have everything they need for their trip home."

He was studying the package, barely listening. "Steamer tickets?"

"Yes, sir, that American chap sent for his daughters to go home and asked us to make the arrangements."

He leapt to his feet. "*What?*"

Tom scratched his head. "Aye, those American sisters are going home."

* * * *

In a fury he took a Hansom cab to Bond Street.

She'd promised to write and let him know when she was coming back to London. Now, she expected to slip away without seeing him again? *She* was bloody impossible and yet the woman had the audacity to call him that!

Suddenly Damon realized he still had the package in his hands. As the Hansom bumped over cobbles, he tore at the paper impatiently, muttering under his breath about stubborn women and Americans and all the muffins he'd given her.

As the paper and string fell to the floor of the cab, he found a square leather box inside. He opened it, just as the sun came out from behind a cloud and a bright yellow ray shone down, revealing a rich gleam of gold, nestled sensuously inside dark red velvet.

It was a compass on a chain, like a pocket watch. Inside the lid were two words engraved.

From Nonesuch.

And on a small card beneath the compass, "*For all the adventures you planned to have one day. It's never too late.*"

* * * *

She was pinning her hat in place, trying her best to act as if this was a day the same as any other.

Of course, the wretched sun had to come out today, didn't it? Just as she was preparing to leave and go home. She'd wanted a miserable drizzle so that she could feel some relief at leaving. But no, even Mother Nature plotted against her. On a day like this, with birds singing and a blue sky overhead, she forgot all the things she hated about London.

The maid tapped at the door of her suite. "Miss Piper, a messenger is here for you."

Ah good. That would be Mr. Stempenham with

the tickets.

Pip checked the angle of her hat in the mirror and then the time on her watch. Ten minutes and she'd be off to catch the train to Southampton. Her trunks were already below. She was the only thing that remained in the suite.

She walked to the door and opened it. "Good morning, Mr.—"

Damon Deverell.

Before she could speak another word, he walked her into the suite, closed her door, grabbed her around the waist and kissed her, completely knocking her carefully arranged hat asunder.

And continued kissing her for a full five minutes, until she finally managed to untangle herself.

"I left strict instructions that Mr. Stempenham himself was to deliver the tickets," she gasped out. "I was most clear about it."

"Mr. Stempenham is indisposed, so you're stuck with me."

She knew her face was pink and there was nothing she could do about it. He looked more handsome than ever. His face was less stern, less saddened, she realized. "How—how have you been?" Surely that was the polite thing to say.

"Well, I was perfectly happy until I found out that you meant to sneak out of the country and never see me again. Approximately half an hour ago."

"Yes. I know. I—"

"You're not in love with me then."

She stared, felt herself sinking slightly until she lost her balance completely and toppled onto the Grecian couch. "In love? Why would you ask that? We're friends. It's been decided."

"I changed my mind." Damon sat beside her and showed her his compass. "You remember the items on my list," he said, grinning.

Pip nodded. "There's not much I could do about the other things on it. Although I suppose I could have tried to find those sundry spare women for trading with natives."

"I don't need them. I only need Nonesuch. She was, of course, the first item on my list."

She looked down. "Yes. I noticed that."

He reached for her hand and closed his fingers around it. "I love you."

Her heart was dancing, but she felt very still and shockingly calm. "I—are you sure?" she said steadily.

"More sure than I have ever been about anything in my life."

In less than five minutes she had to be in the foyer of the hotel. There was no time. No time to make a sensible decision. Oh, now she felt panic. That sudden moment of calm must have been the eye of the storm.

"What happened...with Elizabeth and the...your child?"

"I will do anything I can for him, or her, but the Stanburys are determined to keep the child away from me. In the future I hope to change that, but," he sighed, "I can't plan for everything the way I once thought I could. I have to live the life that's in front of me now. With the woman who has my heart and had it from the first sight. If she cares to have me. *However* she cares to take me. Wherever she can fit me in."

He was giving over a great deal of control to her hands, she realized in amazement.

"I would...I would like to have you," she managed in a voice that sounded most unlike her. "Oh, you know what I mean." Composing herself as best she could, she added, "I'm sure I can find somewhere to put you."

Chuckling warmly, Damon leaned over and kissed her. "Where's Merrythought?"

She sighed, clasping his hand tighter. "I'm afraid she wanted to stay with the Mortmains at Darkest Fathoms. She became such an unbearable little wretch that I told her she'd better write to father herself. So she did. I think the Mortmains are happy to have her there. They seemed cheerful. For Mortmains."

Laughing, Damon reached with his spare hand into his coat and brought out the steamship tickets in their envelope. "Well, then, Pip," he said, "looks like you have a spare ticket."

Pip Piper could scarce believe her ears, and they were usually so dependable. At that moment they were shamefully damp. "As it happens, I do need someone to escort me home. It wouldn't be entirely proper for a young lady to travel alone."

He swung both arms around her now and tugged her into his lap. "How long do we have before we have to leave?" he demanded huskily, trying to untie the buttons at her throat.

"For pity's sake, Deverell, have some restraint! We have to go now. If you're serious about coming with me." She hesitated then, laying her hand over his. "Are you sure you can leave everything behind like that?"

He grinned slowly and his entire face looked suddenly boyish. Mischievous. "I'm not leaving anything behind. I'm taking everything I need with me." And he stood, carrying her in his arms.

"Are you sure you can do this? Can *we* do this?"

"I'm a Deverell, and you're a Piper. Together we can do anything."

Damon Deverell, so the rumors went, carried Miss Epiphany Piper all the way out of the Clarendon Hotel that day and into the hired carriage which was taking her to the train station and then to Southampton. And then he leapt up behind her, urging the driver to make haste, before he tugged the window blind down, shutting out the shocked eyes of witnesses in the street.

* * * *

"I can't believe you're doing this, Deverell," she whispered, snuggling against his lovely warm coat. "I never thought you'd ever do anything without carefully planning first."

"Oh, we'll have plenty of time to discuss our plans later. On the boat. In our berth."

Uh oh. She'd quite forgotten that she and her sister were meant to be sharing a berth. And a bed.

"Don't worry," he assured her with all solemnity, "I'll be on my best behavior. Entirely no frivolity. This is merely business."

"Hmm. Doing what you do best?"

He chuckled. "Yes. Every night."

She looked at him. "Not every night surely?"

"What else would you and I do together? I can think of nothing else."

"You really are the very limit, Damon."

"And that, Pip, is why you love me."

She put her hands on her face and held it still to kiss him as the carriage raced hectically along. "Yes," she said, "I do love you. Like you said, from the first moment I've loved you."

"When I found you under my feet?"

"I think, even before then. Is that possible? I've always felt as if I've known you forever."

Damon said nothing to that, but held her close and kissed her until there was nothing left in the world, but for the two of them.

Epilogue
New Orleans 1854

She stormed into the office, pulling something sticky out of her hair and subsequently pulling it all loose from the pins that scattered to the floor around her. "That's the last time I let that man spend an entire afternoon, unsupervised, with The Terrible Two. They create more havoc than a herd of buffalo."

"Hmm." Damon got up from his desk to give her a kiss. "I'm not sure which is worse than the other. Your father or our daughters. And I hope, for all our sakes," he placed a hand on her belly, "that the next one is a boy."

"Why? A third girl would be just as wonderful. With my brains and your looks."

He laughed. "Thank goodness you finally agreed to marry me and make our arrangement more permanent, since you insist on having all these children."

"What else could I do? I had to make an honest man of you, didn't I? Couldn't have folk looking at you as if you were a kept man. Now, get back to work." She smacked him smartly on the rump, and while he returned to his desk she went to her own, directly opposite his.

She turned on her gas lamp and looked over at her husband, who was already reading again, deeply absorbed in his work as he had been before she came in. A warm, blissful sense of pride and satisfaction swept through her from head to toe when she looked at that beautiful man and knew that he was hers.

Pip kept two framed daguerreotypes on her desk: one an informal picture of Serenity and Jonathan

Lulworth with their twins; the other a more formal engagement portrait showing Merrythought with her fiancé Edwyn, Viscount Mortmain. How far away they were, and yet they were both still in her heart, so how much closer could they truly be? One day, she and Damon would take their family back for a visit, but for now they were busy managing Old Smokey Piper's Bourbon since her father had "semi-retired" to play in the grass with his grandchildren. Of course, he was not really retired at all, far too restless to be leisurely all day, but he was learning to trust more and more duties to his daughter and her husband.

"A damn lawyer, Pip?" Prospero had exclaimed in outrage when she introduced him to the man who brought her home. "I always knew you'd be the one to put me in my grave. Now you bring to me this feller — of any you might have had—and tell me you want to marry him!"

"I'm afraid, pa, I'll have to marry him now and you'll have to let me. We don't want any more unsavory rumors now, do we? Besides, he's quite lovely—as the British say— once you get to know him."

It didn't happen right away, but slowly her father came to appreciate Damon's work ethic, his fearless honesty and his ability to get any job done without fuss.

"You know, Pip," he'd said to her recently, "that feller you married ain't so bad. We just have to loosen him up some. He takes life far too seriously. Him being a Deverell and all, I thought he might be wilder."

And she had laughed at that, because Damon was by no means tame. He just hid it better than other folk in his family, and she had discovered that for herself the moment he had her on the steamer ship from Southampton.

Sitting back in her chair, Pip stretched both arms over her head, swung her legs up and set her heels on her desk with a bang.

Damon looked up and smiled, shaking his head. "Stop looking at my ankles."

"I wouldn't dream of it, my darling."

"They're puffy and swollen."

"They're as beautiful today as they were the first time I laid eyes upon them. More so, in fact. I have never beheld such shapely ankles, troublesome for a man trying to concentrate."

Good answer, she mused. Her husband always knew the right thing to say. But of course he did, he was a lawyer. It was *almost* what he did best. Even when he said the wrong thing, she knew now, it was deliberate.

"In fact, I would say those ankles were my undoing, Mrs. Deverell. I was quite tightly knotted until you came along with your ankles and undid me."

Which is, of course, what *she* did best.

COMING SOON

The Peculiar Folly of Long Legged Meg

Also from Jayne Fresina and TEP:

Souls Dryft

The Taming of the Tudor Male Series

Seducing the Beast

Once A Rogue

The Savage and the Stiff Upper Lip

The Deverells

True Story

Storm

Chasing Raven

Ransom Redeemed

Damon Undone

Jayne Fresina

Ladies Most Unlikely

The Trouble with His Lordship's Trousers

The Danger in Desperate Bonnets

A Private Collection

Last Rake Standing

Damon Undone

ABOUT THE AUTHOR

Jayne Fresina sprouted up in England, the youngest in a family of four daughters. Entertained by her father's colorful tales of growing up in the countryside, and surrounded by opinionated sisters - all with far more exciting lives than hers - she's always had inspiration for her beleaguered heroes and unstoppable heroines.

Website at:
jaynefresinaromanceauthor.blogspot.com

Twisted E Publishing, Inc.
www.twistederoticapublishing.com

44822942R00222

Made in the USA
Middletown, DE
17 June 2017